PRAISE F

"Drew Huff roars out of the gate with this strong debut, a radical reinvention of the road novel with shades of Katherine Dunn's *Geek Love* and Joe Hill's *Horns*."

—Duncan Ralston, author of *Woom* and *Ghostland*

"*Free Burn* is a high-octane horror novel that's as full of heart as it is disturbing. It gripped me from the first page and broke me over and over again. This book is everything."

—Steph Nelson, author of *The Vein* and *The Threshing Floor*

"If you imagine a William S. Burroughs fever dream while *Edward Scissorhands* plays in the background, you'll have a vague idea of what lives in the pages of *Free Burn*. Drew Huff's explosive debut spins the legend of Bonnie and Clyde into a story that explores the depths of trauma with unapologetic weirdness. A manic, propulsive tale of blood, sweat, and… other bodily fluids."

—Brennan LaFaro, author of *Noose*

"Jaw-dropping in its uniqueness, stunning in its prose, and captivating in tone, concept, and approach; *Free Burn* is a perfect example of why I am a reader. Drew Huff is one author that other authors NEED to be reading. Stories like this are why I love to read; authors like Drew Huff endlessly inspire me to write. Read *Free Burn*. Read Drew Huff. She will be a force in the fiction world, soon."

—Candace Nola, author of *Desperate Wishes*

BOOKS BY DREW HUFF

Free Burn

Landlocked in Foreign Skin

The Divine Flesh

FREE
BURN

CONTENT WARNINGS

Death, murder, arson, sexual assault, graphic sex and violence, foul language, explicit images, racism, suicide, torture.

This book is intended for adult audiences only. Reader discretion is strongly advised.

Copyright © 2024 Drew Huff

This book was originally published in 2024 by Dark Matter INK. This edition of the book was first published March 4, 2025 by Dark Matter INK.

This book is a work of fiction. Any reference to historical events, real people, or real places are used fictitiously. Other names, characters, places, and events are products of the author's or artist's imagination, and any resemblance toactual events or places or persons, living or dead, is entirely coincidental.

All rights reserved. No part of this book may be reproduced or used in any manner without the prior written permission of the copyright owner, except for the use of brief quotations in a book review.

Edited by Jonothan Pickering
Proofread by Maddy Leary
Book Design and Layout by Rob Carroll
Cover Art by Olly Jeavons
Cover Design by Rob Carroll

ISBN 978-1-958598-94-8 (paperback)
ISBN 978-1-958598-95-5 (eBook)

darkmatter-ink.com

FREE BURN

A DEVILISH HORROR NOVEL BY
DREW HUFF

DARK
MATTER
INK

To Dad

PART 1: MORE HUMAN THAN HUMAN

ONE

I WAS PRETTY sure I'd had sex with Mallory Worner, which would've been great, really—*Who finally got laid? Pincer-monster me, folks!*—but I was also pretty sure we'd killed someone last night.

The headache woke me. A headache like an ice pick up my nose. A throat dry enough to burn. Some rank chemical taste in my mouth. I was spooning her on my sofa, her dark frizz of hair smushed into my face, her smell—cigarettes, artificial jasmine, sweat—thick in my nose, her freckled body blazing fever-hot in my arms, tight against me. Both of us nude from the waist down. I'd already popped a boner.

My Hands were caked in dried blood.

Not hands. The Hands. My pincers.

I held one up, wrapped in its usual cocoon of cotton bandages. Dried blood encrusted the cloth. I flexed a Hand. Flakes of the stuff rained down on Mallory, getting caught in her hair. I brushed them off her.

I lifted my head. Just enough to see her face.

Splatters of dried blood adorned her freckled collarbone and neck and face. Bruises laced around her neck, like someone had tried to—

My stomach twisted.

"Babe?" I asked.

She made a sleepy sound.

Early sunlight stabbed through window blinds, throwing bars of orange across everything. Made my eyes water from the brightness. Half-drunk bottles of generic vodka and Fireball littered my coffee table, along with a ceramic bong, a pile of DVDs, and a velvet ring box. Congealed booze stained the living room carpet. It reeked like weed and cherry Robitussin.

Why am I this hungover? We didn't drink that much last night.

"Mallory?"

She grunted. "Yeah, Triple-Six?"

"Why are we covered in blood?"

"Because we got too drunk to shower," she said.

She nudged her weight into me. I didn't move. Well, one part did, but Jesus, could you blame me?

"Wanna shower now? Together?" Mallory said.

Her hand spidered down my chest. Went lower. She hooked a finger around me, around the base of it. "Want me to take care of this?"

Light struck a vodka bottle on the table. It illuminated the lines drawn onto the glass with a fine-tipped Sharpie. A line for every milliliter. It'd tasted…salty. Not right. But she'd brought it over. We drank. We smoked. Then…we went somewhere. She'd dragged me out the door. Blood. There was blood, yeah, bleeding, and a man slumping to the ground and—

What the fuck did we do last night, Mallory?

One of the DVDs lay open. The title read, *Mallory Worner, Born Evil?*

Oh God.

It was stupid. All that stuff was fifteen years ago. She was twenty-two years old now. It wasn't like she chose to kill people—

—*Turn his head for me, Triple-Six*, she'd murmured, in the half-dim of the lone halogen lamp outside the bedroom window, booze and strawberry nicotine gum cloying her breath, me inside her, *so velvety so warm*, thrusting, groping with a Hand for something, as Mallory said, *Turn his head so I can see it*, and then greasy hair met my Hand, grabbing, tilting something limp *(something dead)* close enough to see—

Blueing.

Oh God. We killed Blueing.

It'd started with that shitty DVD.

Last night—

"COULD YOU DO it permanently?" Mallory had asked.

"Do what?"

"Paralyze someone with the Hands. If you touched them enough. Would it be permanent?"

We were baked to oblivion on my couch, smoking up the last of Ma's stash. I still wore the funeral suit. My Hands hung out, bandaged up, white against black, and I didn't know what to do with my hair, so that frizzed out, too. Three-day-old stubble and hair like a homeless crackhead. Just the look for a twenty-two-year-old freakshow. Weren't you supposed to lose your mother when you turned fifty? Her—the house, it was my house—the house was silent. No Ma. None of her Jordanian soap operas jabbered from the TV. No her, spitting bits of Arabic at me from the couch, saying, *You think that's dusted? This is how good you cook?* And always, *You leave me, I'll die.* Well, Ma, I never left you. You still died.

"Don't ask," I said.

"How many mice did you kill when they ran those experiments?" Mallory asked.

"Thanks for the reminder, babe."

I stared out the window. Red buttes crumbled just outside, dwarfing two saguaros. Fruit rotted on the sand below them. Mallory's trailer looked like a toy miniature from here. A single dirt road stretched beyond the horizon. We lived deep in some empty part of Texas. Roy Pike had dragged Ma and I here when I was about three months old. Ma still hadn't given me a name by then. She never did. I was Project 0666. Even on my birth certificate.

Off a nameless road in Texas, there's a gravel turnoff. Maybe you drive down it for a joke, maybe you're curious, but after fifteen minutes or so of flat brown nothing, you'd probably turn back. If you went down it long enough, you'd see a microscopic town—ten houses, all of them painted in the pastel sugary colors of Jordan almonds, a gas station, a playground sinking into a pit of pebbles—but you wouldn't drive another thirty minutes. Nobody does. Except Roy Pike and his bevy of lab assistants.

If you drive further along the road, it ends in a dirt clearing. There's a two-bedroom shack here, its sun-bleached paint peeling off in strips, and a gray trailer without a vehicle. There are no vehicles here, except when Roy Pike visits. He always carries a gun. No internet. No cable, no city water or sewer connections. No phones, except a landline that only calls Roy Pike. No escape.

Mallory Worner and I rotted away side-by-side in this isolated pocket of desert-hell.

Me, I understood. The Hands. Roy Pike had never needed to explicitly say, *Son, you can't live in society if you can paralyze folks by touching them.* But Mallory?

The jury was still out on whether Mallory counted as a serial killer.

They threw her here when she was seven years old. Right before the State of Texas fried her mother in the electric chair. Mallory's primary skill set had included corpse disposal, brewing trailer park GHB, and luring victims to serial killer mom. You could've put a tiny picture of either lady—Mallory or serial killer mom—on a box of Little Debbies, and nobody would've batted an eye. Both were covered in freckles.

A fist-sized burn scar marred Mallory's right cheekbone. She stood a whopping five foot zero, compact and intense. A massive tangle of dirt-brown curls fell to her waist. Her eyes flattened into lifeless black dots when she got pissed.

A hard edge crept into Mallory's voice. "Doesn't feel good to get asked stuff like that, right?"

"If you don't like the Saran Wrap, you can just say so."

"I love the Saran Wrap. I'd like a Handful of Saran Wrap in me later."

"I can't just—c'mon. Ma died. There's gotta be like, a twenty-four-hour celibate period after that. I'm gonna go soft inside you anyway. Like always."

She scrubbed her hands.

"Don't pretend you're sad if you're not. I wasn't when mine died," she said.

"Yeah? Well, my Ma didn't murder thirty goddamn people."

Mallory's face went taut. Mask-like.

"Could you kill someone? If you touched them long enough?"

I tensed. *Oh God is she having another blank spell?* I scanned her wrists for necrotic spots. None. Okay. Okay, the sedatives were locked in the kitchen, twelve steps away. It'd be fine. Everything was always fine. Prepped syringes were good to go.

"Does it feel good? To use the Hands?" Mallory asked.

No drawl. Her voice still sounds the same.

"Tell me, man. Does. It. Feel. Good?"

My throat felt bone-dry. "I—I don't—"

Mallory stormed over to my DVD cabinet, clutching a bottle of booze. Her knuckles gleamed white. Flies buzzed against window glass. A blood-red sun grazed the horizon.

She tore open the cabinet. Scooped out DVDs.

I faked a laugh. "My porn stash? Really?"

She dug behind the bootleg copies of *Hot Succubi Babes XXX* and its sordid sequels.

"Roy Pike called earlier," I said. "I asked if you could move here and ditch Blueing. He said he didn't want us 'havin' sex like rabbits' so, uh, I kind of thought of a way around that. Um, don't open the little box that's in there."

"Quit distracting me. I know you've stashed it in here—ah!"

Mallory hurled a DVD onto the carpet, picked it up, and thrust it right in my face, shaking. An old close up shot of Mallory—she couldn't have been more than four years old in the picture—took up the DVD cover, rendered in grainy black and white. They'd Photoshopped her eyes red. In dripping-blood font, the title read, *Mallory Worner, Born Evil?*

"Why did you buy this, Triple-Six?" She asked.

Because I had to take a lighter from you last week. Because you almost burned down my house. Maybe I had a death wish. I didn't know. I'd found the DVD in a pawn shop, on my once-a-year expedition to civilization, and Roy Pike had let me get it. Along with the other thing. The thing in the velvet ring box. The thing I'd pawned my best set of kitchen knives for, the thing I'd been trying *really hard* to not think about, and then Ma's pancreatic cancer finally killed her, so I'd stashed the thing in the black ring box behind the DVDs, where Mallory wouldn't look.

Except now she was looking there. Mallory continued rummaging through my DVDs. She found the ring box. Didn't open it. She tossed it over her shoulder like an empty beer can.

She stormed up to me. "That the only one?"

"I—I didn't mean to be weird about your childhood—"

"Why the fuck did you buy one of those shitty DVDs about it?"

"I just thought—your mom—"

"Lorraine," Mallory said, jaw working. "Was not my mom. She was a fucking monster. She had me. She used me. There's a reason I don't talk about that shit."

I swallowed. Hard. "I'm worried about you. You keep having these psycho spells, and I don't—Jesus, Mallory, I thought there'd be some key to the insanity, in your childhood or something."

Mallory glanced at the ring box. Her shoulders relaxed.

"Okay," she said.

"Okay?"

"I believe you. It's something you'd do. Like all those vitamins you put in my food, whenever I come over—"

"What?"

"Dude. I was drugging people when I was five. I know you do it. Triple-Six. Let me make something very clear," Mallory said, slithering closer to me on the couch. "You are *never ever* going to pull one over on me. Okay?"

My face burned. "Okay."

"Can we not bullshit each other, man?"

"Yeah, Mallory."

Ma used to get real dramatic and refuse to eat, so I got good at…I sort of laced her food with these powdered vitamins, and then I kind of started doing that with Mallory, because Mallory would happily live on Kraft Singles, beer, and cigarettes if I didn't cook for her, and that was totally fine. She basically lived here. When you loved someone, you cared for them.

"So. We getting drunk or not?" she said.

Sunset cast the living room in shades of red, like a seedy bar lit by neon. The outline of her nipples poked through her tank top, good nipples, soft boobs. Her lips glistened. Pink. Swollen. Warmth buzzed through me and down in an oh so good rush. Felt everything down there. Cotton, rubbing. *Jesus, what's wrong with you? Ma died this morning, you managed to hurt Mallory's feelings—no easy feat there, champ—and you still wanna get laid?*

Mallory threw the DVD onto the coffee table. "You watch it?"

"No."

She'd brought over a bottle of booze. It'd been chilling in the fridge for the last few hours. Now, she sauntered back to the fridge and yanked out every last bottle of booze, lining them up on the counter in front of me. Our current booze situation was grim. We were down to vodka, Robitussin mixer optional. I squinted at the bottle she'd brought. Little lines had been drawn at precise intervals over the glass. Mallory just kept staring into the open fridge. Maybe there was a prize inside I didn't know about. Maybe Ma's head was in there or something.

Hey, babe—are we losing it? Are we both losing it together? You want me to stare into the open fridge with you until we both lose our fucking minds? I'm cool with that. I am now A-OK with that. I shouldn't be.

"Uh, so Roy Pike said he wanted to talk tomorrow morning," I said. "Something about his higher-up wanting me out? He was pissed. Made it sound like he wanted to put a bullet in my skull. But Ma's dead. I—I might have a way to stay together."

Mallory slammed the fridge. "They'll never let either of us out. Unless we're in body bags."

Roy Pike had called earlier. He ran my life. To date, he'd thrown me into sixteen solitary confinement stays, sometimes in other places, but mostly in the reinforced basement cell below my house. I called it Bubblegum Hell. He made me eat nothing but Communion wafers for six months when I was fourteen. Lots of other fun things. He was a crucial part of my education. If he wasn't calling me a raghead, a camel jockey, or a dirty foreigner kid, I might've forgotten what ethnicity I was.

I was very brown. Probably Middle Eastern brown, if I had my ethnic slurs right.

"You see the little box, on the carpet?" I said. "You want to open it? I was thinking, we could, uh, live together. You could move in. Blueing's gotta get off that court-appointed gravy train sometime."

"I already asked. They'll never let it happen."

"Look, I know it's been a while since we really tried to leave—"

"Escape," she said. "Use the right word."

I yanked up my shirt. A bullet scar gleamed sickly pink on my stomach, close to the navel. Fun fact: I could heal from a bullet wound in, like, three days. So many fun facts around here.

"Sorry for not wanting a redo of my twentieth birthday dinner," I said.

"Would've worked if you'd used the Hands like we'd planned. Took me months to cook up that ANFO. We had the explosion. Got to the car. I told you to use the Hands on whoever came while I was hot-wiring it. They came. You didn't."

Great pep talk, as usual. Mallory bustled around the kitchen, staging shot glasses along the stained Formica.

"This place is gonna kill you soon," she said, shaking her head. "The last time they pulled you out of solitary—"

"So they turned the lights off for a month. Big deal."

She pounded the booze on the counter. "You were a *skeleton*. They didn't feed you, didn't give you water—you should've died."

"Sorry to disappoint."

I plucked the jewelry box off the carpet and held it in my Hand, stroking the velvet. *Die? Not me, babe. My brain went kaput around hour four.* Because of the number of times I'd been subjected to Roy Pike's tender mercies, I knew *exactly* how my brain liked to break. It broke happy, not scary. I'd start hallucinating chicken strips and fried pickles and strippers. Sometimes the strippers had, like horns, and succubus stuff going on. All those reruns of *Hot Succubi Babes XXX* had leached into my subconscious.

Mallory poured shots. "You want popcorn or not?"

"What?"

"You're not off the hook. You wanted to watch the true-crime junk. So, we're gonna watch it. And I'm gonna tell you every last detail that they left out."

Maybe part of me had been curious. Raised by Lorraine Worner, the Barbecue Butcher? The Texan pyromaniac serial killer? What was that like?

"I, uh, wanted to show you something. It doesn't have to mean anything, but legally, I think Roy will have to let us live together, and that'll get you away from Blueing. I pawned some stuff when I went on my birthday outing, so don't worry about—"

"Show me tomorrow."

Something twisted in my gut. *Heartwarming start to this whole proposal thing, champ. Great sign.*

Mallory slid the disc into the DVD player, cords standing out on her neck.

She froze. "Said I wouldn't do this tonight. God—what's wrong with me?"

"Mallory?"

She turned. Sunset haloed her hair in blood-red light.

I approached.

She presented me with the bottle, tilting her head. "Wanna get out of here?"

I blinked. "Yeah, but what does that have to—"

"Do you want to get out of here or not?"

"God, yes."

The Hands pulsed. Hungrily.

She smiled, exposing her canines. "Then, let's get wasted for the movie."

Seemed counterintuitive, but hey, what did I know about escaping the clutches of a quasi-kidnapper, or whatever Roy Pike and his lab assistants were? It wasn't like we lived, gee, *sixty-nine miles away from the nearest town* or anything.

Mallory swigged off the bottle. Then she smirked, licked her lips, and deliberately swallowed, making solid eye contact the entire time. *Those lips.* Was I about to successfully get laid? As in, finish through without losing my nerve? Was I a terrible person for caring? Probably.

She pressed the bottle into my Hand. My thoughts blurred. I chugged—and gagged. Salty. Way too salty. Like bilge water and vodka. But hey, any port in a storm. So I forced it down, and almost immediately started wobbling. What was this, Russian boat-stripper? I'd been pickling my liver since the age of fourteen, and Mallory's booze made black spots dance around the edge of my vision.

"Jesus, Mallory."

"C'mere," she said, and got the movie going.

She lured me onto the couch as the credits rolled, slipping the suit coat off, unbuttoning the shirt. Warm body against mine. I shivered. Oh, yeah. I got the edge of her tank top and awkwardly fumbled with it for a few seconds before she took over. Me and my goddamn pincers.

Her lips on mine, darting wet tongue. Tasting her artificial-strawberry nicotine gum.

Maybe we can actually make this work. Ma's finally dead. Maybe...being trapped here won't be so bad.

I'd made a deal, but I didn't know it yet.

TWO

LAST NIGHT GETS dim here.

Half-recalled memory fragments from the credits on. Thoughts sort of slid out of my skull. My inhibitions? Zero. Ability to hold a train of thought? None. And that was peachy, because when Mallory Worner began to spit out fun facts about *her* life—well. It got bad.

It was the verbal equivalent of dry heaving bile. She talked in godawful spurts, half-slurring them out.

"…Tripoli Hospital Fire? Yeah, that was a fucking nightmare. I can't believe they're saying—dude! I was five. She held a gun to my knee and said either I'd overdose on Benadryl or have no kneecap. I was getting in that hospital one way or the other…

"…We got Charleston Chews before burning warehouses. Strawberry flavor…

"…These actors are terrible. It didn't happen like that. She bashed his skull in before she hauled him into the van…"

"…She never wanted a kid. But. She'd killed a sixteen-year-old boy. Then she saw how much everyone flipped out about that. Compared to drifters. Plus, women with children get away with a lot more…

"…It didn't look like that. It was a red notebook from Family Dollar. Not some leather-bound book of evil. We couldn't even afford real milk, man…

"But you never—we never talked about this stuff, Mallory. We don't talk about my Hands. We don't talk about *her*…

"…Lorraine told me not to get annoying, because she'd kill me. She meant it. I knew in my gut that if I stopped being useful, she would. Her temper got that bad. Especially when she drank…

"…We both hooked a lot.

"...You ever done meth, man? I still crave it. The last time she smoked some with me was...when she killed that Marine. Oh God. Oh God. Him..."

Half-sobbing, "He tried to save me, he tried to escape so I blew his head off with the shotgun and I didn't want to but I did because I knew whatever she'd do to him would be worse. Oh God. I had to get that off my chest.

"...She knew Blueing before they caught her...nobody believed me when I told them. He wasn't some idiot groupie. Not the way they show him. Dude, he's killed people..."

I wanted to hurl. I wanted to help, but I didn't know how.

"She's been dead for twelve years and I still see her sometimes."

"Babe?"

MIDWAY THROUGH, SHE grabbed my Hand, cupped it around her boob, and kept repeating, *Tell me I'm good. Tell me. Tell me I'm a good person.* I slurred something. She blinked and started jerking me off desperately as I sat there, numb and drugged. She repeated, *You like this, right? Tell me I'm good. Don't leave me. Tell me—*

All I could do was sit and think blankly, *Am I normal yet?*

My Hands tingled. Faintly pulsed.

Eventually, at some point, she calmed down.

ANGER. HEAT. NO wonder Mallory had issues. I clutched her to me. She shook.

"Getting mad?"

I made a garbled sound.

"Good. I need you angry. I'm gonna tell you about Blueing, and you're gonna drink four more milliliters of this," she said, tapping the bottle. "Then we're going somewhere."

Huh?

"Roy Pike never said I couldn't use *you* to do it."

DRINKING. SALTY. BURNING. Trying to stand. Failing.

"C'mon. Get up," she slurred.

She hoisted me by the arms. Half-dragged me to the door.

She unwrapped the Hands, fumbling. She took another swallow of booze. "I don't…don't wanna remember this. But I do," she slurred.

GRAY PAINT FLAKED off the trailer door. *Click.* She unlatched it. Called out. *Pulse. Pulse. Pulse.* The Hands throbbed.

BLUEING WAS STRANGLING her, grubby fingers dug knuckle-deep into her neck and grunting, she batted at him, freckled face reddening and reddening as she wheezed and red warmth trickled down my arms, but he kept choking, oh God, she was purple now, oh fuck, what did I do? I sucked in humid, dank air, legs burning to run away but *no—Rip. Tear. Protect—*but I wasn't a monster, I couldn't, I couldn't—

Black shark's eyes met mine. *Help me,* she mouthed.

HE BLED ON the ground, paralyzed, red raw smile gashed across his throat, spasming. Broken glass gleamed in her hand. Blood everywhere. She smiled.

A KEENING, INHUMAN shriek.

Eardrums vibrated. She loomed over the body on the floor, in the half-light and—

Thud. Thud. Thud. Thud-thud-thud-thud.

Wet sounds. Squishy sounds. Blood. Saliva filled my mouth. Red flew up and splattered across her cheekbone. *Pulse. Pulse. Pulse.*

Mallory, I slurred, and I slurred something else, something important. But she ignored me.

Thud. Thud. Crunch.

DRAGGING SOMETHING. HEAVY. Sand scraped my raw Hands. *Wait, they're unwrapped?*

BACK AT MY house. Stumbling around. Every step ached. My arms felt stiff. My bandages half-flopped off the Hands. We slid onto the couch. She bundled an afghan around me. When had I put the suit on again? Shit. The movie...the menu played across the TV...was it over? My brain hurt. She picked up the battered velvet ring box. She opened it.

The ring glinted. Cubic zirconia bits sparkled on a hair-thin gold band. She looked so sad.

"Are you okay?" I slurred.

Everything spun. Her face remained. I focused on it. I tried to hold her, the way I'd done a million times before.

"I can't get on one knee, I'm too drunk. I'm sorry. Will you marry me?" I slurred.

"I did all that in front of you. And you still—"

I always did, Mallory.

Her pupils dilated.

"You wanna have sex?"

"Fuck yeah, babe."

GRINDING. HEAT, BUILDING in an *oh so good* rush. The taste of strawberry and spit, wet and sweet. Her hand frenzied down there. Nipples hardened. I hardened, too. Straddled her. Yes. I moved. She fumbled, unzipped my fly, and I slid everything off.

Her.

Soft. Fever-warm and velvety. Like a half-dream, it slipped in and out on me. Slipping. Slick. *So good.* And she bucked her hips, ground them into me, laughing, as I drifted in and out, in and out like the tide, salty wet—*I can still taste it taste her*—edge of passing out. *Need you.* Twined my arms around her torso. Boobs, *So soft so good so warm please,* and pulsing heat, hot heat, red heat her and me oh God yes, her mouth over mine, soft moving slick. Slick. All of her, slick—*fuck she's wet does she really want me*—oh God the Hands is she looking at them at me—

(!!!!)

Exhaustion. Fake strawberry smell, her body on mine...

I sank into ocean-deep blackness, not all at once, but in broken pieces, like a doomed ship.

THREE

MORNING.

So, I was pretty sure we'd killed Blueing.

"Let's shower," Mallory said. "Did we have sex last night? I feel tingly. Pretty sure we did."

Neither of us looked at the ring box resting on the coffee table. Mallory proceeded to feel herself, channeling all the sexiness of a prostate exam. *Schlorp.*

I couldn't breathe. Was she going to go femme fatale on me? Give me a morning-after breakfast of rat poison? Drown me in the shower? *She's gonna seduce me again. Seduce me to my goddamn grave.*

Mallory coughed up a wad of butter-yellow phlegm and hawked it into a shot glass.

"I need to pee before I get a UTI," she rasped.

Apparently, some days are like that. Kill a guy with your semi-boyfriend, bang afterwards, you know. Normal people stuff.

"Try to stay calm," she said. "I think Roy's still got six cameras scattered around this house. Forgot where he put the mikes. Hey, was my childhood entertaining enough for you?"

"Mallory—"

"Was it good for you, too?"

She got up and walked to the bathroom. I staggered over to the kitchen to make breakfast.

The bathroom shower hissed. Mallory kept her shampoo right next to mine. She liked it if I made pancakes, but not with milk. The only time she'd ever drink milk was if I reconstituted powder. *Okay, babe. You can't get pancakes from scratch if you kill a fucking guy. Sorry, I don't make the rules*. I grabbed a bowl and Bisquick. A giggle chittered out of me. I mixed pancake batter.

The Hands itched. They felt swollen and inflamed on top of everything else, like I'd turned into the Tin Man overnight. Ma was dead, I might've killed someone, and now my Hands felt like going haywire? What, were they infected? Was it stress? Everyone always told me it was ectrodactyly. Some mutant variation gone awry. But c'mon. Ectrodactyly doesn't turn you into a paralyzing freak of goddamn nature. There's variation, and then there's…whatever I got stuck with.

Instead of four fingers and a thumb, I've got two fat fused fingers. Imagine a normal hand, laid out, fingers together, nice and relaxed. Take that hand and jam a skin-colored sock over it. Tuck in the thumb. Split it down the middle evenly, going deep into where the webbing should be, but don't add any fingernails yet. We haven't gotten that far. Congratulations, you've got my hands.

But you still don't have the Hands. Remember what I said about the fingernails? About midway down each of the "fingers," my dark skin begins to harden, morphing into something keratin-esque, and bleaching dull white. Until we reach my fingertips. They end in sharp points. Like talons. Lobster claws. Spurs. Skin merging into bone.

But I don't need to break the skin to paralyze you.

I ignored my itching Hands. I dumped artificial-pancake glop into a heated griddle and ripped open the fridge for real food. I wasn't raised eating sweet stuff for breakfast. Ma and I were too brown for that.

I snuck a few spoonfuls of raw hamburger. Felt *good*. I liked meat raw. It made my throat tingle, warmed my stomach—but tell Mallory? Or anyone? Hell, no.

Half a roasted lamb's head sat on a bed of rice. Mallory probably wouldn't have poisoned that. Mostly because I had a bottle of Heinz and some mustard and a jar of mayo and a bottle of rose water that could've been poisoned way more easily than the lamb's head. Those poor innocent condiments were just asking for some drops of dissolved strychnine or arsenic. You'd have to dump a lot of suspicious-looking powder on the lamb's head to poison it…or dissolve some strychnine or cyanide in a spray bottle and spritz the entire surface, and then you couldn't guarantee a deadly dose on the first try. I mean, c'mon. Mallory was smarter than that. More efficient. What a smart girlfriend I had. What a great relationship I had.

Well! As far as I was concerned, Bisquick was already poison. I grabbed a fork. Dropped it. Grabbed it again, Hands shaking. It was fine. Totally fine. Everything was peachy keen here. Probably just a fever dream, right?

"I didn't do it," I said to the drywall. "But if you saw anything, don't snitch."

Another giggle welled up in my chest. *Don't snitch*. I ate bits of meat off the lamb's face, chewing the cheek meat. Salty, fatty, delicious lamb.

Mallory bounded out of the bathroom, wrapped in a towel. Water droplets beaded her curls. "You're pale, Triple-Six. Something wrong?"

"What did we do last night, Mallory?"

"We watched a shitty movie."

"And?"

"Does it matter?"

I flipped the pancakes.

"Maybe not. I guess some nights are like that. You get drunk, burn the toast, and, gosh, I don't know—*wake up with half a memory, covered in bruises*. Average bender. Who really needs details?"

"Speaking of," she said.

I threw the pancakes on a paper plate. Mallory waltzed through the living room, collecting every bottle. Including the ones with boat-stripper booze. Then she scooted past me to the sink and poured everything down the drain.

"That's a waste," I said.

"How much do you trust me?" Mallory asked.

I started the coffeepot. "What did we do last night?"

"Let me handle the food. You look like you're about to faint."

Hey, babe, I almost said. *Did we kill Blueing or not?*

But it died somewhere en route.

"Don't go into your bedroom," she said.

"What?"

"Just don't, man."

I sat down at the dining table, scratching my bandaged Hands. I watched her bustle around. No rat poison or broken glass in sight. She fried eggs. Made coffee. Black. As the itch worsened on my Hands, I finally snapped and started unearthing them.

"Free admission to the freakshow," I said.

"Do I ever stare?"

"Lot of firsts around here, Mallory."

"God—will you just spit it out? Whatever the fuck you're building up to?"

She picked up a plate in each hand and walked over. "Don't grope under the couch cushion, either."

Is it Xanax time yet? When Mallory had her psycho episodes, her eyes went blank. Or she'd get this weird Texas accent. Or kill random animals. Set things on fire. I'd force-feed her a sedative cocktail to limit the casualties, so maybe we both sucked at being normal people.

I glanced at Mallory as I unwrapped the Hands. Her eyes weren't dead. Yet.

I got to the final layer of bandages. A cool breeze whispered against the fabric, easing the itch.

Hey, champ—ever think you might just be freaking out?

I ripped off the last of the bandages.

Mallory hissed. She froze, stock-still, and stared at the Hands. *You never reacted—*

I glanced at my Hands.

A brand-new network of vivid red veins pulsed on them. Like rivers of slime mold. Between them, blister pink skin flared and itched. My breath hitched in my chest.

Freak.

"Triple-Six?"

My mouth worked, but nothing came out. These new Fun Veins weren't random—they emerged from the bony tips of my Hands, branching down the rest like a demon's fishnet stocking, ending around my wrists. They faded back into the skin. Everything itched. Did I mention that? The Hands now felt like balls of living mosquito bites chained to my arms. Scratch these new nightmares? God no.

Something warm clamped down on my shoulder and squeezed.

"That's abnormal," Mallory said, in the dry, matter-of-fact tone of a biologist explaining sex.

"Gee, you *think?*"

"They don't look bad. Eat now, worry later."

She plopped down right next to me and ate, cutting her eggs into precise squares.

"Did we kill Blueing last night?" I asked.

She leaned in. Her voice hardened. "This place is going to kill you. It's going to kill me. So, I said it wouldn't. I need your help."

"So he's—he's—"

"Dead. Dragged him to your room. Sorry, man."

Something made the Hands shake. Maybe it was me.

Edward Sal Blueing had been a grungy Australian dude who'd liked to call me a "little demonspawn shite." Dusty hair, dusty skin, all topped with a sweat-soaked Stetson hat. Two thick tattooed lines encircled his neck, like blue chokers. When I was twelve he'd seen me looking at Mallory. He'd leered, grabbed her ass like she was a possession, and he—

Don't think about it, don't think about it, you can't get angry.

—Kissed her on the lips and even then it'd made my stomach hurt, made the Hands throb, made me want to—*rip tear kill*—say something, but he was her court-appointed guardian—*Lorraine gave him custody of me before they fried her,* she'd said once—so what did I know, and he'd smirked at me after, and Mallory just went blank and silent.

We thought we'd be free once Mallory turned eighteen. Then Roy Pike chained Blueing to her via the legal system, citing mental instability. Mallory Worner couldn't live in society. Mallory Worner was a danger to herself and others.

Blueing's killed people, Triple-Six. They never caught him.

I shoveled eggs into my mouth, trying to numb my brain before it showed me Blueing's maggoty corpse—

—Turn his head, Triple-Six, she'd said, skin on mine, pulling away as I stood, *Turn his head for me. Like that—*

"Did—did we—did we fuck in the same room *as his body, Mallory?*"

"Speaking of. Things are getting time-sensitive…it's July."

"What the hell does that mean?"

"Flies. Decay."

Nope. Not hearing this. I couldn't even look at my own Hands right now. Now I'd helped kill—done something—and Mallory wanted me to handle a dead body? Why did she have to be like this? Why couldn't we just be together and be happy? I loved her. Why couldn't she love me?

You know why, champ! The Hands! If you ever forget, just look down when you're jerking one off.

Mallory glanced out the window.

"Shit. Roy Pike's here," she said.

Sure enough, Roy Pike was strolling up to my shack, clipboard under his arm.

FOUR

I CRAMMED MY Hands under the table—then remembered my less-than-stellar attire. A black suit blazer, reeking of weed. Nothing else. I'd gotten laid—did normal people wear clothes during that?

I jumped up and bolted to the couch, yanking on my pants. I ripped the middle couch cushion off—

An oil-black gun gleamed in the crevice. A .22.

I froze.

No time. A gun in the couch? Great. Peachy. I hurled my bong in, by the gun. Bong water spilled out. Great. Add some more stains to the old under-cushion region of the couch. Stains that weren't jizz. Think of it as variety. A couple of hair ties gathered lint alongside the bong and gun. I nabbed one. Replaced couch cushion. Covered the bong. Covered the gun.

Everything's fine, champ. Keep saying it! Mallory got a gun. Good for her. Everything was normal. We didn't bang in the same room as a dead body. We weren't incredibly screwed-up, unlovable freaks.

All's normal here!

No shirt in sight. I buttoned the blazer. It actually made me look seedier. Me? Shirtless? A terrible experience for everyone involved. Ungodly amounts of hair sprouted everywhere, and I wasn't stocky enough to make the thick mat of hair look macho. I was built like a gender-swapped Olive Oyl. No less than three inches of wrist and ankle poked out of everything I'd ever worn. The perks of being six foot four.

I ran into the kitchen, turned the oven on. On with the oven mitts. They were elbow length, concealing the veined Hands. Okay, okay, this could work. I was so excited to get a surprise visit from Roy Pike that I just had to whip him up a snack. It was a feasible lie. He'd make so many shitty comments and jibes about my *damn Arab food* that he wouldn't notice how anxious I was. I dumped a whole package of frozen kibbeh balls onto a baking sheet and threw it into the oven.

Mallory hadn't moved. She sipped her coffee, still wearing zilch but a towel.

Roy Pike sidled up to the door, work boots clomping on concrete. He was a bitter, rawboned geezer with a hairpiece like a taxidermied rat and a white handlebar mustache. His age-spotted hide flaked off in long strips like rattlesnake skin. He wouldn't have been handsome young, either. He was built too lean for it. Leather work gloves always covered his hands, even if he wore a suit. But no suit for him today. Sweat stains spread underneath the arms of a gray T-shirt, emblazoned with *If y'all see me, I'll be in Aruba!*

Mallory reddened. "Oh my God. Not that quote. She said it right before they fried her in the chair—"

"Jesus. They put a quote from a serial killer on a goddamn T-shirt?"

"People like morbid shit, man. But Roy and I have things to settle. He's just trying to get under my skin."

Bruises purpled around her neck. A flyspeck of blood remained on her cheek.

She loosened her towel. "Well. Two can play that game."

Tap-tap-tap-tap! Machine-gun rapid knocking at the door.

I didn't move. I lurked by the oven, chewing the inside of my cheek.

"Can you get that?" I asked.

Mallory grunted a yes, got up, and pulled open the door.

"Miss Worner," Roy Pike said. "Is Project 0666 here?"

"Uh, yeah. I'm here," I called from the kitchen.

Roy Pike squinted at me over Mallory's shoulder. "We need to talk, son."

"Nice shirt, Mr. Pike," Mallory said. "Did you watch her execution, too? Blueing had it on tape."

Roy scowled. "Move, Miss Worner."

"Maybe I won't, Mr. Pike. Are you here to harass my friend?"

"Woodshed burned up last week. Ain't that a real shame, Miss Worner?"

Mallory had a shark's grin. "The investigation established it was an accident, Mr. Pike. Dew drops reflecting the sunlight."

"Came across a lighter in the dust nearby," he said.

"Everybody smokes."

"You smoke, dear?"

"Everybody smokes," she said.

One of her hands scrubbed at the other.

"Come in, Roy," I said.

Mallory hesitated, but she moved aside to let him in. She shot me one of her brief Worner glares: a deadening of the eyes, a flattening, the slightest twitch of her eyebrows. A microsecond's glare. Then her face smoothed back into its mask. Roy Pike sidled over to the wooden dining room table, rapping his clipboard. He didn't sit down. He was waiting for me to come over. I didn't.

"Think you oughta wash that rat's nest on your head, son?"

Asshole.

I plastered on a smile. "How can I help you, Roy? I'm cooking some snacks. Are you hungry?"

"Anyone ever come for you?" Roy Pike asked.

"What?"

Come for me? Like, in a sexual way? I eyed Mallory.

"Simple question, Project 0666. Has anyone ever shown up here, askin' for you? Talking to you?"

Roy's upper lip lifted a little. "They might've looked…non-human."

"Uh, no."

"Ever talked to the Devil? Or someone resemblin' him?"

"I'm not crazy," I snapped. "Just because I hallucinated some stuff in solitary doesn't mean—"

Doesn't mean I'm crazy like Ma.

Roy exhaled. "You should've died in that cell. Don't it seem a little odd? You survivin' thirty days without food or water?"

I shrugged. The fridge hummed. The A/C whined.

"Miss Worner," Roy Pike said, not looking at her. "Tell him 'bout all these bottles. Tell him about Edward Sal Blueing."

Mallory remained expressionless.

"I don't understand," she said.

"You understood your mother just fine. How old were you, Miss Worner? The first time you drugged someone. Four? Five? When did Lorraine teach you?"

One of Mallory's arms wrapped around her torso and hugged it.

"You wouldn't have drugged Project 0666 with a low dose of something, dragged him to Blueing, and had him do your dirty work? It's rather convenient that you were just outta range of the cameras, Miss Worner. You know when we switch their locations."

No response.

"We want to live together," I said.

Roy Pike put his head in his hands and sighed. The smell of cooking kibbeh—cumin and beef—filled the air.

"We're stuck here, right? So let Mallory move in. She practically lives here already. We can get married, if you want us to be married before we live together. We bang and everything—"

"Why are you standing over in the kitchen like that, Project 0666?"

"Because he can," Mallory said. "It's his house."

Roy Pike wouldn't look her in the eye. He studied the dining room table. "Miss Worner, were you raised in a barn?"

"You know *exactly* how I was raised. You knew *exactly* what went on. Have a good day, Mr. Pike," she said softly.

I strode over to Roy Pike. I had six inches on him, easy.

"Yeah. Have a good one, Roy."

He didn't flinch. Didn't budge. He crossed his arms. "What's Blueing goin' to think about Miss Worner movin' out, son?"

Nausea prickled my guts. *Blueing. He knows. He knows what we did.*

"Reckon he's doin' good enough?"

"Good—yeah, he's healthy as ever. Totally," I said.

"Shake on it, son."

I put my right Hand out, but he shook his head. "Show me your Hands."

"Why?"

It was exactly the wrong thing to say. After years of placidly showing him the Hands, now I was refusing, and worse, for no good reason. Project 0666 did not argue. Project 0666 took everything with a smile and made snack platters, as if possessed by a Stepford Wife.

He ripped the oven mitt off before I could react. Recoiled like he'd seen a cottonmouth underfoot.

Shit.

His gaze rested on the ugly net of veins over the Hands. His cement-gray eyes widened, then narrowed.

I cheerfully asked, "So, can Mallory move in or not? My Ma's dead. Everyone dies. Everything's dying. Everything's mutating or fucking dying around here."

"He had a bad night, Mr. Pike. I spent most of it on suicide watch. His mother died two days ago. Whatever else you think of us, can't this wait a few more days?" Mallory said.

"Where'd you hide Blueing's body, Miss Worner?"

"What'd you do with the underwear I showed you when I was twelve? The ones with Blueing's cum all over them? You knew what he was doing. I told you. Over and over."

What?

Felt like I'd gulped down a package of corroded batteries. There was a metallic taste in my mouth.

"Miss Worner. If I'd 'ave put a bullet between Edward Sal Blueing's eyes, he would've come back worse. I'm surprised he ain't come back already. I made a very simple bargain with you, after the first time you poisoned him. Think you tried acetaminophen, that time."

"What do you mean, 'come back worse'?" I asked.

Roy leaned closer to Mallory. "Simple bargain. I wrote it, and you—bein' an eight-year-old murderer at that time—signed it with a red crayon. Would you like to see the photocopy of said document?"

"I didn't break our bargain," she said.

"I fulfilled my end. I kept you out of the juvenile mental institutions and corrections facilities, and I gave you the freedom to avoid the gore-slingin' gawkers they call true-crime journalists. Didn't I? Gave you three square meals, education, and medical care. All I asked was that you not kill Edward Sal Blueing."

"I didn't. Technically."

Roy, what the hell?

"You kidnapped me," Mallory said. "Stuck me here to rot. What'd Triple-Six ever do to deserve getting stranded with me?"

Roy Pike gathered his three BIC pens and the clipboard, with slow methodical rhythm. Flakes of eczema fluttered off his age-spotted arms. His leather work gloves bulged in weird spots. The back of his hand. Tips of certain fingers.

"Neither of you are fit to live in society, Miss Worner. Pardon me for reducin' the casualties where I can."

I cleared my throat. "Hey, what do you mean, 'Blueing's gonna come back worse'? You're screwing with us, right? What's going on?"

Roy stared at the dingy carpet and went for the door. He opened it. Stepped out.

"I truly do care 'bout you, Miss Worner."

"Oh," she said, shoulders tightening. "I've always known. Exactly how much you *care*."

He slammed the door as he left. Windows rattled.

"I—"

"Body's rotting on your carpet. Can't leave it to fester."

She hadn't said the last thing. Nope. Vomit wasn't tickling the back of my mouth.

"Blueing?"

"Yeah. C'mon. We need to dismember his corpse."

"Dismember?"

"Cut it into pieces."

"Oh."

Pain snaked along my left wrist. *Pulse.* Another baby vein birthed to life. Mallory ripped the cushion off the rust-orange couch and removed the gun. Her boobs jiggled under the towel as she moved. She trudged over to our pile of crumpled clothes, picked out my dirty T-shirt, and wiped the gun with it.

"Do me a favor, man."

"Yeah?" I asked.

Her eyes hardened. Something in them died. Went flat.

"Catch."

Her aim was impeccable.

The gun sailed straight towards my face.

I caught it with my bare Hands. Cold metal chilled my skin.

"Mallory?"

She yanked on last night's denim cutoffs, added her bra and tank top.

"You keep that meat cleaver sharp?"

"We are *not using* my goddamn meat cleaver to—"

But she was already digging it out of the kitchen drawer. It glinted in the sunlight. I clutched the gun at my side like unexploded ordnance. Waiting. My Hands pulsed, burning with a sweet, wretched fervor. Like someone had injected the palms with a mix of heroin, sugar, and sulfuric acid. Sweat trickled down my nose. I tasted salt.

"Let's go," she said.

My balls shriveled into my intestines and decided to live there.

I followed her down the hallway. Half-dried blood muddied the carpet. A trail of wettish droplets. *Oh, God. It's—something really happened.*

Faint drone. Hum through the door. Not mechanical. Organic.

Flies.

"What did I tell you about July?" Mallory said.

She opened my bedroom door.

Putrid air rushed out, humid and hot, like a parody of something tropical.

FIVE

ONCE, I'D RETURNED from the concrete cell in the basement—a month-long vacation from Hell. The meat had been left in the fridge, and Ma had just let it rot and rot because she was throwing some temper tantrum—so. I was fourteen years old. August stretched ahead. I'd cracked the fridge open for a soda, wanting to celebrate the sheer luxury of existing in a location that didn't smell like bleach twenty-four seven.

It roiled out.

The ungodly, rotted death-stench of month-old meat. Mold carpeted the fridge interior, covered all in fuzzy splotches of green and white and gray. Blackish, dried fluid puddled at the fridge bottom.

I slammed the door and threw up. Ma threw a fit. They lugged in a new fridge.

But I never forgot that smell.

Mallory Worner opened my bedroom door.

I smelled it. Death-stench. For a split second, I was fourteen again in August, cracking that rank fridge open. I dry-heaved. Tasted stomach acid and coffee. Clusters of flies prowled around the doorframe, feasting. Like a Cracker Jack box. *Oh, there's a prize inside, all right.*

"Just a body, Triple-Six. It can't hurt you."

We entered. The drone worsened. Drowned out the thud-thudding of my heart. Fat hungry flies tickled my skin, crawling. Crawling on my face. They'd crawled on his rotting flesh and now, gee whiz, they felt like sharing the love and pathogens so now they crawled on mine, okay, oh God oh God. A strangled sound burst out of me. I swatted at them. Clawed. Got relief for a microsecond. Then another wave of flies landed. Gnawing.

Mallory fumbled for the light switch. *Flick.*

A dirty incandescent bulb flickered once. Amber light threw long shadows over the joint. Flies flurried up. Faint blood sprayed on a far wall, along with a small, deep hole that didn't go all the way through. Bullet hole. Okay. Okay. Stare at the wall. Not so bad.

She nudged me. "Well?"

They do a lot with drywall these days. Interesting texture. Ancient tack marks marred the surface. Gypsum crumbled out of the bullet hole, like white powdered sugar. *Or bone meal, champ.*

Bone.

I laughed. It hurt. The Hands burned. *Pulse. Pulse. Pulse.*

"Look at it, man."

"Look at what?"

"Triple-Six."

Another laugh burst out of me.

Blueing's corpse lay dead center on the gray carpet.

He hadn't died from the gunshot.

Blueing was already stiffening, his neck taut. Wet, dark stain between his legs. *His chest twitched*—I blinked hard. It hadn't. But I kept thinking it would, that as the seconds slipped by, he'd breathe. *Not dead. Not dead*, my brain screamed. *Nope.* A wound yawned open on the back of his neck like a red rictus grin. White vertebrae gleamed out of the flesh. Cleanly cut tendons and ligaments curled out of the sides. But the raw patch of skin on it was worse. Raw as meat market sirloin, inset with tiny blisters.

Exactly shaped like one of my Handprints.

Flies chorused.

I clasped the Hands together. Shakes rode up my arms. Heat rose to my face. Wait. Suddenly, all of this made perfect sense. A sick kind of sense. I'd never checked out of my last solitary confinement stay. Yeah. I was nuts. I was sitting on concrete, in pitch-blackness, tripping into nightmares. Thanks, brain.

I closed my eyes. Squeezed. Opened.

Dead Blueing still festered on my bedroom floor.

"I'll cut his head off. Hold it for me," Mallory said.

Turn his head, Triple-Six. Like that.

I didn't move. Sweat pooled under my armpits. Summer heat broiled the room. Mallory crossed her arms, shoulders tense.

"I tried every other option," she said. "You know he's killed people? Used to brag about it when he drank? I know you remember."

"Oh, yeah. Killing people. Wouldn't ever do *that!*"

She white-knuckled the meat cleaver. "Keep your shit together."

Spitting image of her. You ever hate the mirror?

I'd only ever seen a few pictures of Lorraine Worner. They didn't exactly keep an album of friendly family memories. Just the ones that got published in the papers. Her holding baby Mallory—face blurred out—with a smile like something dredged from a sink drain. Another one of her in a prison jumpsuit, mid-stride, maybe on the way to court. Then the famous one. Her sitting in the electric chair, primly, as if it'd turned into a throne. The State of Texas pulled the switch.

Mallory Worner eyed me coolly, turned, and grabbed the corpse's hair. Tilted its head back. Rested the meat cleaver on the base of its neck. *Lots of meat to go through. Yum-yum.*

"Not even wearing gloves?" I asked.

She grunted. Pressed the knife in.

I stared at the drywall. I kept swallowing. *Schhhlllorrp—keen. Crunch.*

The things I did for my semi-girlfriend.

"Triple-Six, I need you to hold the head while I get his arms. C'mere."

Oh fuck no.

Blood coated Mallory's hands and forearms. Her fingers meshed in Blueing's hair. She held the head out like a sack of trash, gore dribbling from the neck. Pattering to the carpet. Flies dotted its skin. Its eyes half-opened, already dull and dry.

"Can't hold this all day, man."

Nothing but a silent roar in my skull for a solid minute. Mallory huffed, sweat filthy in her dirt-colored snarl of curls, sweat oiling her Little Debbie knock-off nose and freckles. *Hey, babe—is there a book on corpses? One of those little Golden Books? Baby's First Body Disposal?*

She thrust the severed head at me. "*Triple-Six.* Here."

Mallory jiggled the severed head. Bumped it into my chest. The nose hit my ribs.

"Jesus Christ, I'll take it!"

I snatched it up by the hair. God, it was heavy. How much did heads weigh? *At least you're always A-HEAD of everything!* Ha-ha, hilarious, I was holding the severed, mutilated head of—*oh boy his chest is caved in*—a guy I'd seen alive two days ago, ha-ha, *hilarious,* right?

I giggled.

Something *thumped* outside. Like a coffin lid. Nowhere to run. No place to run, except out into fifty zillion miles of desert. Desert that would fry the skin from your bones for the coyotes and vultures to chew. What would Roy Pike do, if he found the body? Kill me? Kill Mallory? Nobody would ever find us.

The corpse's—*his, Blueing's*—hair, rank and rasping my Hands. *Pulse.*

Pulse. Pulse. I gulped down lungfuls of stagnant, rot-filled air, foul like a Southern attic in midsummer, brimming with decaying mice and palmetto bugs.

"Gotta do his arms next," Mallory said.

"Don't make me look."

"Then don't."

"Why?" I asked, "Why are you like this? It's sick. Don't you know—"

"I only do what I know how," she said.

Apparently, all I knew was carting cadaver pieces. Because I did it. Wrapped them up in torn bedsheets. The pile of bits in the corner grew. Flies rioted over the white cotton bundles. She cleaved the cadaver. Yum-yum. She put Blueing's head to the side. Which meant my bedspread. Blood and spinal fluid seeped through the blue duvet.

"Don't wrap it, Triple-Six."

Turn his head, Triple-Six. I want him to watch.

"Oh?"

"We'll bury that first. Shovel's in the shed?"

"Where the hell else would it be?"

"Let's start burying," she said, licking blood off her lips, "C'mere."

I came. She smiled up at me, wiping her mouth on her sleeve. Lips parted. Warm hand spidered around my torso. Pressed me closer.

Then she sighed. "Can you trust me?"

No.

"Yeah."

"Burying time. Hold his head. Still have the gun?"

I nodded.

"Good," she said, and her smile grew sad.

She released me. I held Blueing's head by the mutilated neck. The .22 glittered in my waistband.

July wasn't hot. It was Hell incarnate. The second we ventured outside, every breath stung. Overhead, noon sun glared down, too bright. Dry static prickled the hairs on my arms. A bitter breeze cooked the moisture out of my skin. Dry heaves started.

His skin feels like plastic over an overripe peach.

This time I threw up. Half-digested bits of lamb and stomach acid slopped onto the red dust.

"C'mon, Triple-Six."

We rounded the corner of my house.

And Roy Pike, sitting at a folding table, under a makeshift umbrella, with a bottle of Gatorade and a copy of *The Road,* promptly put his book down and reached for his hip holster.

"Roy!" Mallory cried, "Oh, Roy! He has a gun! Help! He cut off Blueing's head!"

She batted her fucking eyelashes.

"I—"

I got tased twice in my chest before I could say a complete word.

I blacked out. Thank God.

SIX

THE BANDAGES WERE wrapped up to my elbows now. The itching got worse.

But I had my usual cell to mutate in, and it was a solid three stars on my five-star scale. One star for lights, one star for the cot. Peachy. If they kept me in the dark? Automatic zero stars. I mean, c'mon. You can't rate a solitary confinement cell if you can't judge the decor.

Bubblegum Hell lacked windows. Icy fluorescent lights—so charming—stayed on twenty-four seven. Deduct one star. Bubblegum Hell measured exactly twelve paces by twelve paces. It wouldn't have been home without a floor drain, so there was one smack-dab in the middle of the sealed cement floor. Bubblegum-pink paint glossed over the cinder block walls in an unbroken, slimy skin, except for the three chips in the paint above the steel sink. A biological pink.

There were two cots in Bubblegum Hell this time. Both could've fit under my thumbnail. Better than sleeping on tile. Add a star. I had one scratchy wool blanket and the finest industrial sheets, complete with mystery red stains. The steel door had a slot for food trays.

Said food tray had come in five times so far. Cafeteria food. Breakfast stuff twice. So maybe a few days…but it could've been two hours or two weeks. They'd done things before—feed Project 0666 nothing but breakfast food for a month and never dim the lights, watch his perception of time unravel—but did it matter? They weren't about to slap a bus ticket to Dallas in my Hand. Or Mallory's.

No hallucinations yet.

Maybe because I wasn't alone in Bubblegum Hell this time.

There were two cots in this cell.

"Hey, babe," I said at one point. "I'd ask if it's your first time in a cell, but

I think we both know that it isn't. Fun fun fact—I scratched a heart into the paint behind the toilet in here when I was fifteen. I carved our initials."

Mallory snapped, "Your fucking point?"

"See, now I know you're real. You'd be nicer if I was hallucinating."

She was changing into a fresh set of beige prison scrubs, so I had my back turned to give her a tiny bit of privacy.

"Think about the implications of this living arrangement," she said. "Roy Pike didn't call the authorities. He didn't take us to a jail, or a mental facility, like I thought he would. Doesn't even have the resources to put us in separate cells. He might if he'd had time to prepare, but not something immediate. Think about what that means."

"What, that he's an actual kidnapper? He's just some random asshole that decided to keep us captive in the middle of the desert and run experiments on me?"

"Nobody official would put us in the same cell."

"Why?"

"We—"

"We're both involved in a killing. We're different genders. We've got a long history. So many things. Sometimes I forget how naive you are."

"Why did you do it?"

She didn't respond. She finished changing, and then pivoted back around to face her cot, like one of those wooden figurines in old cuckoo clocks, those mechanical dolls on their tracks. She puppeteered herself into a lying position atop the cot. Was she trying to sleep, or pretending to? You never knew, with Mallory Worner.

She and I occupied separate ends of the cell. We'd moved our cots to opposing walls. She kept tapping her nails against the wall. Clusters of staccato taps, pauses, and more tapping. Drove me nuts.

"Can you not?" I asked her.

She stared at me for a solid thirty seconds, then resumed tapping.

Clink! tap-tap-tap-tap.
Clink! tap-tap-tap-tap.
Clink! tap-tap-tap-tap.

I SLEPT. A lot. Veins laced up my arms. I'd snap awake, feeling imaginary electrodes clamped onto my Hands, tingling, about to *hurt*. Nausea. But hey—it wasn't dark. Thank God. Anything but that. I didn't think. When a thought floated up—*Mallory tried to frame you for Blueing's murder. Nobody's ever actually loved you. Your Hands are mutating. Remember your*

Fun Teeth?—I'd bang on the steel door a few times and beg the attendant outside—some hulking Mexican dude in a lab coat—for sedatives. Without fail, he'd slip them through the tray slot.

Sleep.

A WITCHING HOUR. Blinking awake. Pink walls, lurid fleshy pink, seen through bleary, half-gummed eyes. Dried spit crusted around my mouth.

They're going to pull the footage and show him, repeated in my brain, and sick cold sweat broke out.

Something was *in me.* Something *not me.*

Something small and hard and warm was dwelling in my guts. It branched, threading into limbs, and made my body stand. I had nothing to do with it. Couldn't move. Couldn't speak. My body shambled to the steel sink. Pulled off my shirt. Stuffed the sink drain. Had to see. Something. My Hand turned the faucet. Water filled the basin.

The bodies are burning I can smell them.

Where did you hide the bodies you little freak? Where did she hide the bodies where did she hide them why can't you remember?

My Hand turned the faucet off.

Safe. Safe here. Safe.

Something craned my head over the still water and there I was, reflected in the surface, slack-faced as a Xanax-fueled zombie. Mouth half open, drool beading at the corner. Half-lidded eyes. But my eyes weren't right in the reflection, they weren't green, they weren't the same eyes I'd gotten from Ma, they were—

Black.

Mallory Worner's eyes.

I could practically smell her, she was *there,* in me. My body walked back to my cot. Lay down. Thoughts hazed into other dreams. When I slipped into a better one I was holding her, skin to skin, our breathing synchronized. It happened a few more times, the thing piloting my body, dragging me to the sink, muttering, *safe here,* in nebulous half-thoughts.

A THICK FILE folder sat at the foot of my cot when I woke. *Road Train Killer,* read the typed label on the front. I didn't open it.

Mallory smiled at me during "breakfast."

My stomach dropped.

It wasn't Mallory's actual smile. Every tooth showed. Her gaze flattened into twin black dots, dead as a Morse code printout. Her grip tightened around her plastic spork. Syrup-coated fruit salad drooled off the spork and plopped back onto the tray.

I'm stuck in here with her.

"C'mere," she rasped, "I'm thirsty."

I tossed my juice box at her. "Here."

She licked her lips. Fluorescent light made her burn scar and hair look greasy. She set her tray on the floor and stalked over to me.

I raised my voice. "Hey! Hey, Sedative Guy, there's something wrong!"

Clatters from outside. Metal clangs.

"You know what I want," Mallory said, and sprang.

She managed to stab the back of my bandaged Hand before Sedative Guy burst in and dragged her off me. Spork tines punctured through the cloth. Pinpricks of blood bloomed.

Cursing, she snarled, whipped around, and sank her teeth into his throat. Dug in. He hissed. Seized her shoulders. Tore.

"Jesus Christ!"

Skin came. Peeled off. A fist-sized scrap of bloodless skin dangled from between Mallory's lips. She chewed a few times. Spat it out.

Sedative Guy threw her over his shoulder and drew a hypodermic from his pocket in one smooth motion. Good form. He jabbed her in the thigh. He rubbed a hand over his skinned throat. It wasn't bleeding. No muscle or tendons showed. A smooth, dolphin-gray hide shone beneath the dude's outer "skin," dotted with pores.

Mallory slumped.

Sedative Guy nodded at me. "Want a jab of the good shit, too?"

"Uh—"

"Nah, nah, never mind. I shouldn't give you more than I already am. They tell you anything? They didn't, did they? Pike's being Pike, and precious Pike's throwing another temper tantrum…look, you gotta lay off the sedatives, yeah? And this crazy chick? You gotta stop fucking her," he said, gesturing to his torn throat.

Sedative Guy's rubbery lips barely moved when he spoke. The corners of his mouth held them taut. I kept thinking he'd smile, and then they'd split apart vertically, like if you bent a tube of hamburger in half.

"She's not crazy. She's traumatized," I said.

Sedative Guy rumbled a laugh. "Same difference. Anyway, you gotta stop having sex, stop with the drugs and the booze. Stop all this soap-opera shit, dude. Just staves off the inevitable."

"Staves off what? What the fuck is happening to me?" I asked.

He gingerly carried Mallory out. "You just gotta trust the process."

He wore a twine bracelet on his left wrist. Cowrie shells beaded it. He'd shaved, but black stubble grained the entire lower half of his narrow face. He wasn't built normally. I felt like an asshole for thinking it, but he wasn't. Sedative Guy looked like a cobbled-together golem. Thick trunk of a body, rope-thin wrists and ankles and neck. Imagine four twigs duct-taped to a barrel. There wasn't an ounce of fat anywhere on him either, so it wasn't some kind of thyroid issue like Cushing's or any of that.

He moves like he's wearing a shitty Halloween costume that doesn't fit right.

"Where are you taking her? Please. Don't take her away. Don't hurt her. She has these crazy episodes, but she'll be fine."

"They'll be here in two minutes," he said, and left me alone in Bubblegum Hell.

SEVEN

THE DOOR CREAKED open. Roy Pike and some youngish brown-haired dude entered, both of them wearing tan suits. Both men carried clipboards and pens.

"Project 0666," Roy said. "This is Lamiel. We'd like to ask you a few questions—"

"Where's Mallory? What did you do with her? Is she okay?"

Roy Pike rattled out a cough. His eyes were bloodshot. He looked about ten pounds scrawnier than when I'd seen him last, and his cheekbones strained through his frog-thin skin. Clumps of snowy hair clawed from beneath his silver hairpiece, which lay askew. Something white dotted his left pant leg. On the inner thigh. White and crusted. *Is that—*

No, it's toothpaste or something, no fucking way is that what I think it is. That's not dried jizz.

"She's handcuffed and sleepin' on the couch upstairs," Roy said. "Don't need her overhearin'."

Lamiel wielded a neon-orange gel pen. "Make him unwrap the bandages, Roy."

"Son—"

"Aye-aye, cap'n," I said, picking bandages off my Hands. "So. Is his name really Lamiel, or was that one at the bottom of the fake-name list?"

Roy went stiff. He shot a glance at Lamiel, but Lamiel ignored him.

"I can git it to stop. Like what happened with his teeth, a coupla years ago. The acid trials hurt his, uh, hands there—"

"Roy, dear. Haven't you gone through this phase long enough?"

Lamiel had a breathy, soft drawl. Bits of Pepto-Bismol-pink lipstick flaked off his lips. They were full lips. The lush mouth of a hedonist. The dude didn't seem a hundred percent hetero, which was cool by me, but was this, like, Roy Pike's boyfriend or something?

I displayed my bare Hands. "So?"

"Well, that's certainly a failure," he said.

Been a failure my whole life, buddy.

Roy Pike fiddled with his work gloves. "I can—"

"You can't. Shall we find this child something useful to do?"

"What do you mean, *useful?*"

Both of them ignored me.

Roy coughed. "Please—"

"No. I've indulged you long enough," Lamiel said.

Poor Roy. Couldn't Project 0666 be a good little abomination of nature and cut the veins out?

"You want me to be useful?" I asked.

"I'd like to see what, exactly, your morality is," Lamiel said.

"Morality? I jerk off like five times a day, man. When I'm not being starved for funsies."

He smiled. "Did you ever have the idea to defend Miss Worner? Given your…unique abilities, Project 0666?"

"Maybe I thought about drugging him. Maybe my Hands went nuts around the guy."

He patted my shoulder. "You can tell me anything, you know."

The ancient A/C unit droned. I leaned my head against the sweating cinder block wall of Bubblegum Hell. I closed my eyes.

"I had dreams about him."

From when he hurt me.

"He wasn't unattractive. Bisexuality is really very common—"

"I dreamed about ripping his fucking throat out. With my teeth. Not the ones in front. You know I grew an extra row of teeth behind my first? When I was fifteen? They're sharp."

"Did it hurt?"

My Fun Teeth. Product of a stint in solitary.

"I wish," I said.

"What do you want, Project 0666?"

"Excuse me?"

"What do you *want?* More than anything? Money? To protect others? To dominate them?"

"I want my Hands gone."

He laughed. "But why?"

"Gee, they're paralyzing monstrosities that hurt anything I touch. Totally great to bring on a date. Great conversation piece."

"Is it *love*?"

I snorted. "Nobody's ever gonna love a freakshow like me."

"Even Mallory Worner?"

I didn't respond. I didn't think.

"Did you kill Edward Sal Blueing?"

A cold feeling congealed in my gut.

"I—"

"Perhaps I'll rephrase the question. *Why did you kill Edward Sal Blueing?*"

It just went downhill from there.

"YOU DIDN'T GET angry at Blueing? Not even once?" Roy asked.

"I mean, I knew the guy was a piece of shit," I said.

"Were you aware of the abuse, Project 0666?"

I clutched the Hands together in my lap. Hard. "Not—not all of it."

Sedative Guy had lugged in some folding chairs. Roy Pike slumped in his, but Lamiel sat on the edge of his, jotting down stuff in a leather-bound book. Disturbingly pale leather. A few moles spackled the cover's corners.

Lamiel's voice remained steady. "Did you ever feel that Edward Sal Blueing deserved to die for abusing Mallory Worner?"

Absolutely.

"No," I croaked.

Veins burst from how tight I clasped the Hands, trying to hide the shakes. Wet blood soaked through my bandages. Lamiel stared at them. Pursed his lips.

Roy sat up in his chair. "Didn't hear that, Project 0666. Why don't I repeat the question again? *Did you ever feel that Edward Sal Blueing deserved to die for abusing Mallory Worner?*"

"No. I'm not like that," I said.

Sweat beaded on my forehead. *Monster.*

"Were you aware the abuse was physical and verbal, Project 0666?"

"Yeah."

Turn his head, Triple-Six. I want him to watch.

"Were you aware that the abuse was sexual?"

Everything spun. My ears rang.

"Mallory Worner was sexually abused by Edward Sal Blueing from the age of seven, up until the day he died," Lamiel said. "It…was extensive, from what we've seen of the evidence."

Sexual. She'd said he hurt her. She'd said—where the hell had I been?

"Mallory needed your help to kill Blueing, didn't she?" Roy said.

I swallowed.

Roy Pike leaned closer to me. "She's petite. Mallory Worner had enough. She ran to you, the only other person she could use, and you paralyzed him. Then she shot him in the stomach and slashed his neck open with a piece of broken glass. We found that glass, Project 0666. In the top shelf of Blueing's refrigerator."

Sweat beaded on the back of my neck. "So? Wasn't he some fanboy of Lorraine's? Maybe she came back from the dead and killed him."

"You implyin' he deserved it?"

"Why didn't you do anything to get him away from Mallory? Why'd you let him stay?" I asked.

"Did you like defendin' Mallory Worner? Protecting her?"

"I—shit, I don't know. Why are you—"

"Your mother died the day before."

"Yeah."

"You enjoy watchin' Edward Sal Blueing get his just desserts?"

My voice broke. "No. I can't remember any of it. Swear to God. We drank something…"

"Of course you can't remember," Lamiel said. "She roofied you."

"*What?*"

Roofied? Like, *date-raped? By Mallory?* They had to be screwing with me.

"We conducted a drug screenin' shortly after we placed you back in here," Roy said. "You tested positive for alcohol, marijuana, and GHB. Mallory Worner drugged you with a low dose before the incident."

"She wouldn't do something like that," I said.

Roy Pike stared right at me. "She drugged someone in a similar manner at the age of four. You know anythin' about the Worner case? At her mother's bidding, Mallory Worner personally helped dismember, burn, and bury no less than thirty victims."

"A four-year-old! Jesus Christ, are you listening to yourself? Mallory didn't even like bringing up Lorraine, let alone—"

"When we examined the pieces of Blueing's body, his genitalia had been mutilated," Lamiel said. "Beyond recognition. Stomped on, repeatedly. The imprints match a pair of Miss Worner's shoes."

I wiped my face with a shaking Hand. *Roofied. Framed. You think she didn't know what was what when she dragged you over to his corpse and started cutting? Oh, Mallory knew.*

"Project 0666?" Lamiel said. "Would you like to move out of here?"

"What about Mallory?"

"Perhaps I could arrange something—"

"*No*," Roy said.

Roy Pike and I stared each other down. His jaw worked.

Well, that was about as helpful as a mariachi band at a funeral.

"Fine," I said. "Tell me about the Road Train Killer."

"I don't got time for this."

"Why do you want to know?" Lamiel asked.

I lied. "Read something about it. Think Mallory or Blueing mentioned the name, I don't know. I'm bored."

Don't look at the bed. Don't look at the file.

"He was only a *suspect* in that case, son. Don't be gettin' any ideas."

"Blueing?" I asked.

"In the Road Train Killer case," Roy said. "In case you were wonderin', a road train's the Australian term for a semitruck with multiple connected cargo trailers...they don't do 'em in America, but they have to when you're shippin' through the Outback."

He wheezed a little. "Road Train Killer was a truck driver, see? Was active in the late eighties, early nineties. There were eight victims found, probably more. He or she was a serial killer. Liked to carve eyes out and mutilate the victim's faces before death. Then the killings suddenly stopped. They never caught the Road Train Killer—"

"Roy, quit being melodramatic. It was Blueing. They know. He's already signed on to that afterlife program the Hell Wardens like to trot out."

Lamiel sighed. He bustled out of Bubblegum Hell. "Clean up your experiment, dear. You're getting too old for this."

Roy Pike didn't follow. He pointed at my Hands.

"I can make your life a hell of a lot worse, son. Make that stop."

The Hands were more like the Forearms, now. Unearthly veins streaked up my arms, some of them that godawful red, and some of them buried under my skin. From the elbows down, I was a dead ringer for any poster of the circulatory system. Other than that, peachy keen. Between the veins, my skin looked normal, sort of olive.

"Why do you care so much?" I asked.

Roy struggled to his feet. His upper lip curled. Dentures glittered.

"I can make Miss Worner's life a livin' hell, too. See you in six hours. I expect to see less of them veins."

"Roy, are you okay? You don't seem like you're doing well. Have you tried talking about whatever's going on?"

"I don't have long."

I edged closer to him. "Lamiel's not too thrilled about any of this, is he? That's why you waited for him to leave. I'll give you two choices. You can stop this Guantanamo Bay bullshit and tell me why I'm really here, or I'll find an excuse to tell Lamiel how gung ho you are about continuing your little experiments. Because it's about the veins, isn't it? It's never been about Blueing."

I snatched off his leather work glove.

"It's always been about this," I said.

A small spur of bone jutted from his wrist. Like someone had uprooted one of his canine teeth and replanted it just below his palm. Grime crusted the base, where skin and spur melded. Smaller spurs dotted his knuckles, all of them enamel-glossy, some of them thin as slivers.

His other arm snapped towards me—

White-hot pain slammed through my jaw. Taste of blood. Something hard and small came loose. I spat. A blood-slimed tooth clinked to the cement.

Roy Pike turned on his heel and left, fist still streaked with my blood and spit.

I'D BEEN MEDITATING since Roy left. Or trying to. Kept falling asleep and into weird dreams. *Less veins, less veins, make it stop,* but I kept scratching at the cinder block with a Hand, feeling—in the half-asleep delirium of dreams—something soft and fleshy tear open, feeling something mucus-slicked in my Hand, clawing red slits into the wall. I'd snap awake. No slits. The veins continued growing.

I studied the Road Train Killer file.

Mentally, I danced around the situation. I detailed every component of my fine industrial lunch—limp garlic toast, canned pineapple, a carton of skim milk, and a paper boat of spaghetti that boasted ketchup-slurry in lieu of sauce—more chemicals than a refinery chemist's wet dream.

Blueing had been a serial killer. I didn't know what to do with that. I read about the Road Train Killer. About Edward Sal Blueing.

My industrial lunch cooled on the tray, untouched.

I got halfway through. Glanced at it. Ketchup stench filled the air. In my guts, my heartbeat raced. A quivery sort of feeling. *Dismembered.* So many words. Liquefying garlic toast. *Raped after death repeatedly.* Two red cherries gaped in the pineapple fruit salad. *Massive internal hemorrhage.* Red. Like his ripped-open neck.

I bolted to the toilet and dry-heaved. Nothing came up.

The pictures were worse.

I put the papers face-down on the blanket. Didn't need to see them again, even out of the corner of my eye.

They brought back Mallory, still sleeping, and plopped her on her cot. I wanted to kiss her, touch her, tell everything was going to be okay. She'd

been right. Blueing was a monster. Blueing would never, ever, hurt her again. But I didn't. The Hands. They started itching again.
They burned invisibly.

EIGHT

"YOU GOT AN hour left, Project 0666," Roy Pike said, wheeling in a TV on a cart.

Dust clotted the crevices of the television. A VCR player whirred below. Roy pointed the remote at the screen like a sniper preparing his shot. He inhaled.

My swollen mouth throbbed. "What's this?"

"An instructional film, son. Watch."

Mallory Worner lay on her cot, atop the blankets. She rolled over to face Roy Pike and me. She didn't move after that. Didn't speak. There was nothing human about her face, nothing living behind the expressionless black eyes. No emotion contaminated them as she watched us. Watched the footage.

The screen flickered to life.

Shitty CCTV footage played. Shoppers rolled through a trash-strewn grocery store. Even far away, I could make out the blackened gum mottling the rotting linoleum. Midday. A weekend. Families chugged beers in plain sight. Could almost smell the sweat and heavy summer heat, the sunscreen, the oily summer customers lazing through the few aisles in view. Plastic pool toys rowed the shelves. Turquoise pool noodles jutted from a cluttered display.

Lorraine Worner came into view, dominated by her dirty crown of curls. Rhinestones glinted on her jeans and black tank top. She perused the boxes of inflatable flamingos and beach balls and water wings. Someone had opened one of the boxes and inflated a hot-pink beach ball. It lay smack-dab in the middle of the aisle, next to its ripped-open box. Lorraine kicked it as she passed by. It flew out of frame. Her back twitched. Stiff. Each step jerked ever so slightly. She stalked back and forth a few times, finally beckoning to the display. A child slithered out from between the pool noodles. *Mallory.* Mallory was a shrunken-down version of Lorraine.

The audio was garbled. A tinny rendition of "All I Wanna Do" obliterated the smaller noises.

All I wanna do, is have some fun…and I got a feelin', I'm not the only one…
All I wanna do…

Subtitles appeared on the screen.

Lorraine: *You gonna fuck this up for me, kid?*

M. Worner: *Naw, ma'am.*

Lorraine jabbed a finger down the aisle, and yanked Mallory close, as if disciplining her.

Lorraine: *The guy in the red shirt. I'll be waitin' in the van. Fifteen minutes. Do it in ten, and I'll git you a hit of smoky candy, if he's got enough in his wallet for a few grams. Start bawlin'.*

Mallory nodded. Both stalked off-camera. A few minutes passed. Shoppers flowed down the aisle.

"She looks like she's five," I said. "Does she even understand what she's doing?"

Roy Pike was removing a box of razor blades and a box cutter from his jeans pocket. He lined them atop my cot, along with a roll of bandages and two Oxycontin.

Mallory skipped down the aisle, tugging a construction worker by the hand. Splatters of dried concrete covered his vest and red T-shirt.

M. Worner: *I don't know where Mommy is! She was right here…I think…I think she said she might go smoke outside.*

Her face was beet-red from crying. She shook.

M. Worner: *I don't wanna go alone. I'm scared. I feel shivery and sick.*

Another subtitle. *M. Worner was suffering from drug withdrawal at the time of this footage.*

They went off-camera. Roy Pike turned the TV off.

"His name was Jesus Gonzalez. He was thirty-two years old. Family man. Had three kids of his own and a wife. His charred head was found in a field outside of Candleton. Never did find the rest of him. Lorraine, you see, had a habit of keepin' most of the burned remains for her own amusement."

He raised his voice. "You think we should see your interview tape, Miss Worner?"

Mallory had been silently watching us the entire time. She lay perfectly still on her cot, face expressionless. Sweat darkened beneath the arms of her beige scrub shirt.

"I asked you a question, Miss Worner," Roy Pike said.

No response.

"Your sense of smell can trigger some mighty vivid memories. If you ain't into watchin' the interview, I could bring over some human limbs and gasoline, burn 'em up in here to trigger those good ol' memories—"

"*What?*" I asked.

My chest hitched. Burned human flesh. Oh God. What was Roy Pike doing? How crazy was this asshole? Was he—was he going to kill me, or Mallory, if I pushed him the wrong way? I had to calm him down. Get some more time. Anything.

"Make your mutations stop. I'll be back in an hour."

"Roy, this is crazy. You've tried to make me normal for twenty-two years, and none of it worked. Not the injections, not the electrodes, not the solitary confinement or starvation or battery acid."

"Maybe you're right, son. Maybe I should just kill you both and be done with it."

He said it like someone debating what they wanted for dinner. Maybe maqluba. Maybe heat up some kibbeh balls, instead. Blood drained from my face in a dizzy rush. He meant it. He could do it. Nobody would ever look for Mallory's corpse, or for mine. *Pulse-pulse-pulse.* My Hands tingled.

"I'll tell Lamiel."

"Lamiel's the one who *wants* y'all dead. The hell you think he meant by 'clean up your experiment'?"

Atop the gray cot blanket, the razor blades glinted.

"You…want me to use those?" I asked. "Want me to slice open my Hands? Remove them? Remove the veins? I'll do anything. Just don't…"

Roy Pike said nothing.

I gritted my teeth. "Okay. Give me six hours. I'll hack every one of those veins out of my Hands. But you're gonna take Mallory upstairs so she doesn't have to see it. Deal?"

"Five hours," he said slowly.

"Fine, I'll take it. Deal. Now go take her away."

Roy Pike left.

Sedative Guy came in. He held a paper cup of pills and a set of handcuffs. He hunched over Mallory. His back blocked her from view. I heard the blankets shifting. She'd sat up. He offered the pills to Mallory and said something I couldn't quite make out.

"I said *no*," Mallory said, voice raised.

"C'mon, gatito. C'mon, lil' kitten. Take your pills. They don't want you upstairs unless you're sedated."

"Babe, just let them sedate you," I said.

"Don't cut your Hands open, Triple-Six. It won't work. Don't you remember? The last time you—"

She hissed. "You're hard. You're hard as a rock."
"Huh?"
"Not you. *Him*."
Sedative Guy?
Sedative Guy shifted a little. "They let me watch the footage, earlier. Was that really how quick it was, with Lorraine? I've seen a ton of those docuseries on her, and I—"
"A fucking true-crime junkie," Mallory said, then snorted. "You're one of *those*. I must be dead. I must've died. I'm in Hell and all of this is a punishment."
"Don't make me shove these pills down your throat, gatito," Sedative Guy said, reaching for her.
"Don't put anything in my mouth unless you want to lose it."
A pants zipper unzipped. Sedative Guy's.
Is he—am I just sitting here, watching this asshole do this?
"Hey. Maybe I can give her the pills," I said.
They ignored me. Pills rattled. There was a swallowing sound.
"Wrists out, Worner," Sedative Guy said.
Handcuffs ratcheted shut. Sedative Guy stood back from Mallory. The handcuffs gleamed around her wrists.
"I had to dry swallow those pills," Mallory said. "Let me get some water from the sink. I'm thirsty. I have to pee."
"C'mon. I'll let you use the bathroom upstairs. You can take a shower. I wouldn't mind seeing that."
Mallory nodded. She tapped on the wall as Sedative Guy escorted her out of Bubblegum Hell. She shot me a Worner glare as the door clanked shut.
Yeah, babe, I'm a failure. I get it. Okay?
I examined the sharp stuff on my bed. I dry-swallowed an Oxy. Tried not to think about Sedative Guy watching Mallory shower. Her shampoo. How could she wash her hair, all handcuffed like that? How could she even move or think, all doped up on sedatives, lumbering around in the shower?
My nose burned. Tears blurred everything.
Why can't I fix you and make you not-crazy, Mallory?
I picked up a razor blade. I sliced open the bandages over my Hands.
I have to do this. I can do this.
But none of this made sense. That was what kept getting me. There wasn't a lab here. They hadn't run any tests on my mutating Hands. The only guy—besides Lamiel and Roy Pike—was Sedative Guy, who seemed to act as a guard and med dispenser. An orderly? Something was fucky with that dude, too. That skin under his skin...was I going to turn out like that? Was there another skin inside my old one?

I tickled a razor blade along the edge of a vein. Carve 'em out. I should've asked for some needles and catgut to stitch myself up. I'd done that before. That was why Ma never cooked. She wasn't allowed around knives. Not after what she did when I was seven. I still had the scar on my left elbow.

I pressed the razor blade in—

Something tightened around my neck. Cold metal tickled. A warm body pressed into me from behind, a man's, the smell of him—tobacco, rancid sweat—too familiar. *Blueing.*

I froze.

Oh God that's a knife.

"Hullo, luv," said Edward Sal Blueing, his hot breath worming into my ear.

Was I hallucinating? No…no, this was too raw.

Blueing pressed the knife in harder. "You're gonna do a little somethin' for me, luv."

"You—you're dead," I heard myself say.

"Oh, I'm dead alright."

Wet warmth. More pressure against my throat. Thick smell of blood.

"'Cause ya fuckin' killed me and desecrated my body, you murderin' little *shit*," Blueing seethed, "You and her. All cozy like peas in a pod, shaggin' each other next to my corpse."

"I'm sorry. I was high. I didn't know!"

He dug the knife in deeper.

NINE

"YOU LIKE THE file I left for ya?" Blueing asked.
Blueing might come back as something worse...guess what, champ?
"You left that file?" I wheezed.
"Bleed, lil' nipper. Bleed."
Shit, shit, shit. What do I do? Sedative Guy's upstairs with Mallory. Nobody's going to hear me if I scream. The last time Blueing was this close to me nobody heard me either oh God nobody heard me nobody.
I elbowed him, but barely. He chuckled.
"Remember last time I said that? Little nipper. I called you that 'cause—"
"Shut up!" I snarled.
Nobody heard me, nobody heard me, he's hurting me, he's stroking my hair as he makes me do it, it tastes wrong, he's calling me little nipper, he's hurting me, make it stop, make IT STOP, I DON'T WANT TO DO IT!
"—Oh, oh, are you ashamed of that?" Blueing said.
His free hand wriggled into my waistband. Into the band of my underwear. He cupped my balls in his hand. Warm. His palm was feverish and callused.
I used to dream about ripping your throat out with my teeth, Blueing.
I liked those dreams.
"You're the one who should ashamed, you fucking—"
Pedophile. Rapist. But you can't call him that, because then that makes it real, champ, and anyway, you were twelve, and anyway, it only happened once, and he was drunk off his ass, and he thought it was funny to make you, y'know, do it, and he had his hand in your hair, and wasn't it fucking hilarious, mate, ha-ha, real funny, making the scrawny raghead kid suck him off?
Blueing squeezed.

White-hot pain skewered up my groin. I thrashed. It hurt no matter what, so I thrashed, twisted. The knife clattered to the floor. His grip slipped. I whirled. Punched. It hit him square in the soft gut. He doubled over. I lunged for his arm—

"Wait. Wait," he said, coughing. "You don't have to do that."

The Hands. They're unwrapped. He doesn't want me to touch his bare skin.

I kicked the knife away. It skittered under Mallory's cot, rasping the cement as it did.

"Get the fuck out of here, Blueing," I said.

"I can't. I need somethin'."

I kicked his knees out from under him. He fell ass-first on the concrete floor. He didn't flinch. Didn't get up. Blueing didn't have a scratch on him. His sandy hair grayed at his temples. Tobacco stained his ruined teeth. A blue neck tattoo strangled his throat like a choker—two blue lines and a padlock. He hadn't had that when he was alive.

"Do I need to say it again?" I asked calmly.

"Nah, mate. Mate, really, I was just kiddin' around about the lil' nipper stuff—"

"You needed something?"

"Your blood," he said. "After I killed you. Two birds, one stone."

Was this fine rendition of Blueing just another solitary confinement hallucination? *No. Those actually make sense, most of the time. And they're always happy.* If he was a figment of my imagination, why would a dead Blueing be scared of the Hands?

"Reckon I'll just talk for a bit," he said. "Hell's real. I made a deal with 'em so they wouldn't fry me when I died. I'm sort of a bounty hunter. When people need someone gone, they use us—put a ritual target on a guy, we touch 'em, and bam. Instant death, easy does it. Hell's janitors."

Blueing wasn't getting punished for being the Road Train Killer? Ever? *Pulse. Pulse. Pulse.* Hot anger rose up my throat.

"Good for you. Now get the fuck out," I said.

"All right, all right, I will. Just give me some of your blood, mate. Then I'll go."

"So you can kill me in some elaborate, long-distance way with my blood?"

"Got bigger fish to fry than you, mate. You're just a side thing. Really."

"You're lying."

"No, really. Let me talk."

The rage seemed gone. If it'd ever been real to begin with. Blueing's emotions never lasted long. He had vague states of action and inaction, caused by vital external stimuli like whether or not he had enough Miller Lites in the fridge.

"I've got, uh, this coworker. The bossman wants me to catch the bitch skivvin'. Need your blood to power a ritual. Don't know any other demonspawn that'd help me."

"You're all in Hell, trapped into eternal slavery?" I asked.

"Bloody grim way to put it. We get summoned. Beck and call. Some idiot on Earth performs the right ritual, says the right words, and ding. You're ritually bound to a target. The bond's sort of an anchor to Earth. Normally, you can't touch anything besides the target, lots of bloody safeguards, all that."

He shook his head. "Better than being scrubbed."

"Scrubbed?"

"Non-existence. Destroyed. Or," he said, and laughed, "you get the same bloody thing everyone else gets. Sand the ego off. Send it back to Earth for another go 'round. I reckon she's more scared of that."

Had he done that to Mallory? Or those fine folks he'd killed in the eighties? Threatened them with a knife when he—*Rip. Tear. Kill!*—when he hurt them—*when he fucking raped her?* Copper rang through my mouth. Bubblegum Hell blurred into a pink haze, edged in red. *Pulse. Pulse. Pulse.*

"What d'ya want, mate?"

Her to love me.

I forced out a laugh, to hide how psycho I felt. "Open the door of this reinforced basement prison cell below my house. Get me out of here. Take away my monster pincers. Y'know, just the wants of your average twenty-something dude."

His blood would taste like gold trickling down my throat.

Veins exploded on my arms and Hands, daubing my skin in oily red fluid. Didn't smell like blood. Smelled like digging up an ant's nest and inhaling the chemical insect musk.

"What if I could? Or I knew someone who could?"

He's lying. Haven't you seen literally any movie ever about this shit? Don't deal with the Devil! And Blueing? This goddamn guy? Is he even human now?

But Mallory and I had to get out of Bubblegum Hell, ASAP. Had to escape. Roy Pike was getting crazier by the second. If I didn't get us out of here, he'd probably kill us. My options weren't great. My craziest hypothetical plans prior to this point had involved trying to seduce Lamiel. Now, Blueing could apparently open the door. I could carry Mallory until I found a car, if she was too sedated to walk. Maybe she'd kill some people along the way once she woke up, y'know, just to spice things up. Maybe she'd have a psycho episode. Or maybe, just maybe, there'd be a moment during our escape when I'd have some convoluted excuse to rip my shirt off in front of her, and there'd be abs underneath it or something instead of hairy scrawny me, and she'd say, *You're my* hero. *You're so brave and badass and amazing, Triple-Six. I love you,* and I'd reach for her—

But the Hands. She'd never ever love me while I had them. That was a fact of life.

"You can get rid of my Hands?"

"I might know a guy. Maybe."

Get rid of the Hands? I'd do anything.

"It's a deal," I said.

Blueing flickered out of existence like a ghost.

I touched my throat. My Hand came back bloody. I got the knife out from under the cot and tucked it into my waistband. Just when I thought I'd hallucinated the entire thing, Blueing appeared. He white-knuckled the grimy handle of a tackle box.

He set it down. "Follow my instructions. To the letter."

"Instructions? You said you just needed my blood."

"Your blood and your cooperation. You want out of that cell or not?"

"You're telling me that Hell and magic exist. I'll go along, sure. So go open the door."

"Not till after we're through."

He cracked open the tackle box. White candles and a salt canister filled it, along with a disturbing number of paring knives. A poison-blue fishing lure peeked out. Blueing fumbled in his pocket. Fished out a sandwich baggie with a single hair in it. A curly, long, dirt-brown hair. Like Mallory's. Like her mother's in the CCTV video.

Oh, no.

"Is that—"

Blueing grinned like a demon calculating exactly how much interest you owed on your soul. "We're summoning Lorraine Worner. Good old Lori. The Hell Wardens caught her crawling back from Earth when she was supposed to be down under. Dunno how she got an anchor point, but the bitch managed it."

His mouth twisted as he said the last bit, twitching into a half-smile. An asymmetric expression. He was lying about something.

"You know Lorraine Worner?"

He rumbled a low chuckle. "Know her? I knew Lori before they fried her."

She even has a nickname. Isn't this stellar, champ? You're finally meeting your potential mother-in-law! All I had to do was summon an undead serial killer from Hell. Okay. Peachy. Blueing began counting out candles and beckoned me over.

"One more thing," he said. "Don't ask her for a damn autograph. You might get it."

He lifted his shirt. Across his belly, in white scar tissue, gleamed a curlicue *Lorraine*.

My voice died on the way up, tried to reanimate, and failed.

"Good to know," I managed.

THE RITUAL.

The fluorescent lights in Bubblegum Hell flickered. Dimmed. A fly died in midair and fell to the cracked concrete. Blueing poured salt in a circle on the floor, about the diameter of a dinner table. I clutched a filleting knife. Pressed it to my shaking palm. He motioned for me to cut. I froze. This was *insane*. Summon a dead serial killer? Blueing motioned again, irritably.

The veins streaked up to my elbows now. Hard, bony plates crept further and further up the Hands, like the bastard lovechild of a crab and a crocodile. Nothing helped them anymore. They tingled, electrified by the power building in the cell. *Monster. Freak.*

I sliced open the soft part of my palm. Blood oozed.

Blueing nodded. "Draw the circle."

I finger-painted a circle outside of the salt, as he began to chant words in a guttural language. They ran together in a gargling string. Salt stung my cut.

The second I closed the circle, it glowed—a low, red light like a neon bar sign. Blueing cracked open a pamphlet, not missing a beat, and drew symbols on the floor around the circle. Right on the floor, with a Sharpie. The world's oddest graffiti. He mimicked finger-painting the symbols, so I did. A few were even recognizable. A dollar sign, a padlock without a key, handcuffs, kitchen matches with little fires on their ends, but most were stuff straight out of a fifteenth century alchemy textbook. I tried to make them neat as possible while finger-painting in blood. Eat your heart out, preschoolers.

Power, rising from the ground like dry heat.

Blueing threw the hair into the circle after I finished. Red light bathed the cell, glistening off the stainless-steel sink and toilet like blood. Goosebumps prickled along my arms. The temperature chilled in the cell, except for the Hands, which only felt hotter. My breath fogged. I shivered, wobbling where I stood.

Still Blueing chanted.

A whiff of sharp cigarette smoke. In the center of the circle, a ball of faint red light gathered. Around the edges, glowing symbols breathed. Was that real fire on the match doodles? I wiped my bloody palm on my pant leg, barely noticing the sting. Everything grew thick and hazy, charged like lightning coiling itself into a bottle.

The circle attracted the Hands, and I followed, letting the magnetic pull drag me in.

He finally stopped. "Throw in a hair. Quick, now. And a right dab of blood."

"Why do you need my hair?"

"Just *fucking do it*," Blueing snarled, "before the bloody thing blows."

A ripple shook the air, unstable. Like a missed heartbeat. No time to argue. I ripped a few hairs from my scalp. Tossed them into the circle. The second they hit the air over the edge, some invisible, static force sucked them into the center. Blood pooled in my palm again. I flicked a gob of it in. Right on the money.

A whining hum. Cold air cut right through my thin cotton scrubs. Spilled fruit syrup on my dinner tray froze.

Power.

Something invisible squeezed my throat for a split second, then released. Symbols burned white hot around the circle. Kerosene and gasoline smells, acrid. *Snap!* Lights exploded overhead. Bits of glass rained down onto the floor, glittering—

A blinding flash.

Then nothing but half-gone light, Blueing, me, and a woman standing in the middle of a smoking, charred circle on the floor.

Lorraine Worner.

Her eyes were flatter in person. Somehow.

She growled, "Eddie, why the fuck am I here?"

Then she saw me.

And *smiled*.

PART 2:
LIVING DEAD GIRL

TEN

"**HOWDY, BABY WARDEN,**" she said.

Baby Warden?

Lorraine Worner.

She was Mallory gone to seed—rougher skin, the beginnings of smoker's wrinkles polluting her lips, and a million rhinestone bangles dangling from her wrists. Cheap costume stuff. On her right cheekbone bulged a burn scar identical to Mallory's. A flimsy black camisole and bejeweled jeans clung to her. Curly tufts of bang fell across her leathery forehead. Dirt-brown curls matted, snarled, and snaked down to her waist. She had Mallory's button nose, those cutesy facial features, her freckles, a dimple on her left cheek… but this was demonic Little Debbie, long crazed and black-eyed.

She reeked of cigarette smoke, moldy carpet, and gasoline.

And she made Edward Sal Blueing look about as deadly as a tranquilized dingo.

I hovered at the edge of the circle, Hands clasped together. Her empty gaze slithered over me, top to bottom. Her upper lip curled. Something squirmed in my guts.

She called me Baby Warden. Like she knew me.

I'd summoned an undead serial killer from Hell about half a second ago, and I couldn't exactly take it back now.

"I—"

"You summon me or not? Ain't got all day, honey," Lorraine said, teeth bared.

Her voice was a nasally drawl. The product of decades of smoke inhalation. Cigarettes. Speed. Firecrackers. House fires. Victims, burned alive and smoldering.

She whirled to face Blueing. "Eddie. What's this?"

"Dunno, luv. Looks like ya might be busy," Blueing said, smirking.

"You didn't. You *wouldn't*."

"Nothing you can't handle, Lori."

"Now I gotta kill my Baby Warden? You fuckin' kidding me?"

The shit-eating grin slid off Blueing's face.

Why the hell were these fine folks calling me *Baby Warden*? A band around my neck prickled. Okay, the work meeting from Hell was underway. What next? Surprise, surprise. Blueing hadn't gotten to that part.

"Blueing, I did what you told me to. Now pay up," I said.

"Pay up? Eddie, what'd you tell Baby Warden here?"

Lorraine sidled up to Blueing, her hands stuck in her pockets with the thumbs jutting out. He gulped. Stumbled back a step.

"Just to summon you," Blueing said. "The little bastard doesn't know—"

"That he just called a hit on himself?" Lorraine said.

"*What?*"

A sick feeling bloomed in my stomach. The blood. My blood. My hair had been thrown into the mix, too. Still smoking, the symbols on the floor resembled a demon's doodled margins.

"Real low, Eddie. Makin' me kill my Baby Warden…who put you up to it? One of the Hell Wardens? Mr. Beelzebub?"

Blueing's lips twitched into an attempt at a smile. "They know, Lori."

Know what? What's a Hell Warden?

"Who told 'em, Eddie?"

"Don't shoot the bloody messenger. You chose to slip out, luv. Not me."

"Fuckin' traitor. After all these years?"

Okay, great. Blueing had screwed me over to screw Lorraine over. Was this some kind of a sting? Entrapment? Poor Lorraine. Could an undead serial killer get a break around here?

"Just so we're clear—I'm the target she has to kill?" I said.

"Mmm-hm, Baby Warden."

"You touch me, and I drop dead? Just like that?"

"Yup."

"Holy shit."

Blueing stood between Lorraine and I, steps scuffing in the ash.

"You murdered me," he said quietly.

The jovial, easy persona slid off Blueing, and he simply stood there, staring at me with cold hatred. "You and Mallory fucking Worner. Thought I would let that go? Nah, mate. Lori'll play with you till you're dead, and if you think she can't hurt you without touching you, you should ask the last three idiots who summoned her. Ate their vocal cords, didn't ya, luv?"

"Mm-hmm, Eddie."

"Have fun with him, Lori. I'm headin' upstairs to rape your little ankle biter till she bleeds. Then I'll slit her throat and fuck her corpse a few times till it cools."

(Rip! Tear! Kill KILL HIM!)

The Hands throbbed. Pulsed.

Oh God. Oh my God. Mallory. He means it.

Lorraine snorted. "Think I'd let you kill my spawn? After she sent *me* to the chair? Eddie. You're a failure. Only good thing you could ever do was hold a ball of hair in your fuckin' mouth 'fore they fried me. And you almost screwed that up."

"I did it for *you!*"

She spat on the ground. "You wanted to feel special. Nothin' more."

Dead in one touch. Sweat pooled in the small of my back, beaded on my upper lip. *If she kills you, Mallory's drugged and defenseless.*

"Well, Baby Warden," Lorraine said, turning to me. "You heard the score. I can kill you. You wanna keep bein' a Baby Warden?"

I froze. I tried to say something. It died in my throat. *Pulse. Pulse.*

She shoved Blueing aside. He glowered at her. She ignored it. She stepped closer to me. I towered over her, but still felt like she stared down at me through her nose.

"What'd you git out of it, anyways?"

"What are you—"

"Bein' coy, Baby Warden?" she said, reaching. "Fine. How long's it gonna be 'fore they send you back to haunt me?"

You wanna let her kill you, at least Roy won't get to. Would it really be *that* bad to just cash in my chips a little early? Take some initiative in my life? I'd never be normal while I lived. Nobody would ever love a freak like me, especially not now. Maybe it was time to give up for good. But Mallory. Nobody was left to defend Mallory Worner. Blueing would…would do something to her—

He's going to rape her! He's going to kill her! Blueing could do it, and he wanted to, I knew it in my gut.

"You could always be somethin' else, kid," Lorraine said. "Be my Honeydoll…"

Lorraine shifted her weight onto the balls of her feet, grinning.

"W-were the movies accurate?" I asked.

"Tryin' to flatter me?"

"I'm wondering if the Barbecue Butcher wants to play. Tell me about yourself. I mean, c'mon, Lorraine. You're toying with me now."

Pulse. Pulse. Pulse.

"Mm-hmm. Wanna bargain, Baby Warden? Offer me some kinda deal? Override the ritual target? Save your scrawny hide?"

She reached up. Her bangles grazed the edge of my scrubs. Her fingertips groped, inches away from my neck.

"A bargain?" I asked.

"Bless your heart, honey. How fuckin' blunt do I gotta be? I'm all but gift-wrappin' you an opportunity."

Her tongue flitted out. Flicked the center of her lower lip. Retreated. My Hands shook. My arms shook. Her lips gleamed with spit.

Edward Sal Blueing flickered out of existence. Just gone. Had he gone upstairs? Had he gone back to Hell? Was he real? *Yeah, he's real, you know he's real, he's gone upstairs and he's going to hurt—*

I had to bargain. *Now.*

"Let's make a deal, Lorraine," I said.

"Sell me on it."

"What's a Honeydoll?"

"Tell you when I got the needle for it. Sell me on this bargain, Baby Warden."

I backed up further, going over the edge of ash. *Sell her on it.* How happy would the Barbecue Butcher be if everything she got to kill just died with one touch? Not very.

"Here's my offer. It's been, what, how many years since you really burned someone?"

"Twelve years and eight months," she said.

"Want the opportunity to do it again?"

Another step closer. Her eyes gleamed like decade-used motor oil. Emotion drained from her face, rendering it into a pocked female mask. Her right hand flicked at her side, as if she held an invisible lighter. My back hit the cinder block wall.

"Take a lotta trouble to override the ritual," she breathed.

"I can bleed again."

"I know, Baby Warden. But do you wanna?"

"Yes," I said.

She blinked. Forty-year-old nipples stiffened underneath her camisole, standing out against the flimsy fabric. I gagged, once, but turned it into a fake-cough.

"You chokin'?"

Don't look down. Do not look at the undead pyromaniac lady's rack.

Clatters sounded down the hall, outside the walls. She didn't bat an eye. I stared straight into those flat, black peepers.

"Let's negate the insta-death, Lorraine. If I can evade or fight you off for a full twenty-four hours—outside this cell—you let me live, we go our merry ways. But if you kill me, you can gut me however you like. I mean, c'mon. You want some dumb instant heart attack to drop me? You're the Barbecue Butcher. Why don't you act like it?"

A dim pulse in the air. The Hands warmed.

"Try a week," she said.

"Three days, seventy-two hours. Take it or leave it," I said, sweat trickling down my back.

"I can do whatever I want or need to kill you? No limits? Anythin' at all, Baby Warden?"

"Yeah, sure."

Then Lorraine leaned in close, grinning like a clean, bright junkyard icebox with something dead caught behind the door.

"You want them Hands off, kid? We can swing that into the bargain."

Yes! Terrible idea, probably. But what other shot did I have? I had to get upstairs before Blueing hurt Mallory.

"If I win, you'll take away the Hands and let me live?"

She kept beaming. Beauty pageant teeth, but after decades of chain-smoking.

"Sure, honey. Sure thing."

More clanging from outside. Lorraine knelt down and scooped up a handful of the salt left on the floor. She plucked a cigarette and matches from her pocket. Struck one across her thumbnail. A flame quivered.

"I'll be immune to the soul toxin shit those puppies can dish out, then," Lorraine said. "Part of the bargain. We'll seal it so. Now bleed."

Soul toxin?

She stuck her cigarette between her teeth. She lit it, shaking the match out. Smoke curled up towards me. I wriggled my cut palm, reopening the wound. Blood pooled in my Hand. She beckoned. Maybe all of this was a trick. Maybe not. Didn't have time to think. Was Blueing on the stairs? Touching Mallory? *Hurting Mallory?* I reached out.

Pulse. Pulse. Pulse.

Lorraine dumped her handful of salt in my bloody palm.

"Three days," she said.

I nodded.

"None of your fuckin' coworkers git to interfere."

"I don't have a job," I said.

"Then you don't *know* you got a job. But I'm talkin' about the Hell Wardens...you wouldn't want freaky monster-things like them runnin' around on Earth, would you?"

"Demons? God no. I don't want Hell Wardens here."

"No interference from 'em?"

"None, Lorraine."

Demonic guards? Talk about villains. Why bring more abominations to stop this one? The Hell Wardens sounded like trouble. I had enough trouble here.

She stirred the pool with the lit end of her cigarette, muttering, "A callin' card for me. We gotta have that. You do something, it summons me to your location. It's just official stuff."

"What?"

The cigarette didn't sizzle. Lorraine glanced up at me.

"How 'bout igniting a fire, kid? If you ignite a fire, it'll summon me. Nobody does that anymore—unless you're livin' in the Stone Age. See how nice I am? Ain't nothing to worry about."

"Okay, yeah," I said. "It fits."

She extracted her cigarette out of the blood. It glowed red at the tip. Not orange. Blood-red. Exhaustion slammed me. When had I gotten so drained? I eyed my cot. I slumped against the wall.

"We got a deal, Project 0666?" Lorraine Worner asked.

I'd never told her my name.

I swallowed. "Yeah, we've got a deal."

Lorraine stubbed out the cigarette on my neck. Burning, white-hot pain seared through the skin. Little yelps came out from between my teeth. She wrenched my hair and twisted it back. She giggled.

"Ain't had a cigarette burned out on you before?" she said. "What a fuckin' pussy."

Crack! A gunshot. Just outside. Footsteps, running closer. *Shit. Roy Pike? Great timing, champ! Just tell Sedative Guy about your intro to magic. Get some tasty Thorazine to brighten these humble days in Bubblegum Hell.*

The cell door unlatched with a soft click. It swung out an inch.

"Doesn't start until I'm outside the cell."

"Just waitin' Baby Warden."

Waiting? For what?

Bang-bang-bang-SLAM! Someone yanked the cell door open.

Mallory Worner stood, blood dribbling down her arms, eyes wheeling.

"Triple-Six! Run!" Mallory screamed.

Lorraine shook her head. Eau de Lorraine wafted off her hair.

"I taught her better'n this," she said, then vanished just like Blueing had.

ELEVEN

MALLORY WORNER LOOKED very awake as she sprinted up to me. Her hands were free, the handcuffs gone. Fresh blood was smeared over her lips and chin.

"Triple-Six, *c'mon*!"

Her blood-slimed hands seized the front of my scrubs and tugged. *Where's Lorraine?*

Footsteps boomed down the stairs.

"You're not—"

"Slipped the pills down my shirt. Guy didn't see. Thanks for trying to drug me, asshole. Dude. I've been tapping Morse code at you this entire time," she panted. "Remember? When we were kids and we used the flashlights?"

Clomp. Clomp. Clomp.

The cell door hung wide open.

Then Sedative Guy filled the doorway, hypodermic in hand. His rubbery lips trembled. His pupils were dilated. His skin glistened with sweat. A .45 jutted from one of the pockets of his lab coat.

"Worner, calm down," he said, holding up his other hand, palm out.

His index finger was gone. There was nothing but a ragged stump above his first knuckle. Blood oozed from the stump, pattering to the cement. Quarter-sized droplets dotted the ground.

Mallory bared her teeth. Blood glazed them.

He lunged at her.

Pulse. Pulse. Pulse.

A dizzy rush. Time slowed as Sedative Guy reached, mutilated hand groping, *his knuckles are so hairy*, within the bitten-off finger something glittered, as if his bones were aluminum toys so easy to—*rip. tear. kill*—to crunch, and sugar-sweet energy snapped through my Hands, *so good they feel so good,* pulsing, pulsing, pulsing, like arousal.

I grabbed his wrist.

One Mississippi. He faltered, arm muscles slackening. *Two Mississippi.* His body twitched, face spasming as his knees gave out. *Three Mississippi.* I caught the back of his head in the crook of my elbow. Lowered his limp body to the concrete.

I released.

A fever-hot body grazed my back. I whipped around.

Lorraine darted away, something held between her fingers. She vanished. Blinked into existence behind Mallory. She snapped her arm around Mallory's waist. Dragged her close. Jabbed the hypo into Mallory's neck, thumb working the plunger down—

I grabbed Lorraine's arm.

Nothing happened.

Half the clear liquid in the hypo was in Mallory. Mallory thrashed, clawing at Lorraine's wrist, gouging scratches into her flesh. I yanked as Mallory bucked. Lorraine spun, hissing. I knocked her hand off the hypo. Mallory tore it out. Threw it to the ground. I stomped.

Crunch.

Glass shards shredded my hospital grippy socks and feet.

"It—it hurts. Oh Jesus," Sedative Guy moaned.

Oh God is he paralyzed for life what the fuck did you just do? Monster. Freak.

The lab mice. I'd held those lab mice for sixty seconds, and they stopped moving after zero point seven seconds, which was what they said would happen, okay, fine, but half the mice died after thirty seconds, in my Hands, my Hands, limp small bodies in my six-year-old Hands and twelve of the mice eventually moved and went back to normal, but the other forty-eight never moved again so Dr. Hitch had euthanized them after I left—

"Baby Warden," Lorraine said, halfway up the stairs.

Mallory staggered past her, clutching the rail in a death-grip. "Gotta... gotta hotwire the...hotwire the car..."

Lorraine slapped her. Hard. It jerked Mallory's head to the side. But Mallory just gripped the stair rail and continued staggering onward. How sedated was she? Her left cheek was already swelling. Blood welled out of her mouth, dribbled down her chin in one stream. She fumbled through the upstairs door.

"Thanks for lettin' me touch stuff. I love a good bargain," Lorraine said.

"W-what?"

"You said 'anything,' honey. Anything I needed or wanted to do in order to kill you. I ain't bound to only you anymore, which means I ain't gonna phase through everythin' else like a ghost."

"I—"

Lorraine could interact with the world. Set fires. Hold knives.

Keep Mallory away from her. Find Roy Pike's keys. Get out of here! You can't help Sedative Guy now. Focus!

I went up a few steps. "Blueing held stuff. Why couldn't you?"

She opened the upstairs door, its blue paint sticky in the July heat.

"Can tell you never been to jail, Baby. Prison politics. Eddie's bein' a good snitch to the guards, so they gave him a lil' more slack on the leash."

She chuckled. "Not me. Never me."

Sedative Guy had a gun. I needed something besides the knife in my waistband. Was it worth it to lose sight of Mallory for a few seconds to go back for the gun? Or see if he had a radio? A taser? Car keys?

I turned my back on Lorraine and ran back downstairs.

Sedative Guy didn't say anything as I went through his pockets. The cigarette burn on my neck throbbed.

"I'm sorry," I said. "Do you have a radio? Is there someone I can call for help?"

His mouth worked, but nothing came out. A scarlet Handprint wrapped around his wrist. His breathing seemed normal. I took his gun. The .45 felt ice-cold in my Hand. I tucked it alongside the bowie knife. I rifled through empty, capped syringes and vials of sedative. I swiped a few.

"Triple-Six! HELP ME!"

Mallory.

My guts wrenched like I'd chugged liquid nitrogen.

She screamed again. *"Triple-Six! She's hurting me!"*

I sprinted upstairs.

I hurtled through the doorway, over the saffron-yellow carpeting, up through the hallway, a faint smell of smoke thickening as I ran closer, *okay, okay,* each step too slow, then out into the dining area, ashtrays smoldering on the table. Ma's door was closed, smoke curling out from under it. I ran past it and hit the kitchen.

Wasn't Mallory drugged, like, five seconds ago?

Nighttime. 00:06, glowed the oven clock. The kitchen light wasn't on. Dirty yellow paint lacquered the cabinets. Every knife had been lined across the rose-colored Formica counters. Light from the open fridge washed over Lorraine, leaving half her face in shadow. She held my chef's knife at her side.

"W-where's Mallory?"

She grinned, burn scar wriggling. She opened her maw. She said, in a perfect imitation of Mallory Worner's voice, "Triple-Six! You found me, man!"

What.

"You know we got the same fuckin' vocal cords, right? She's the same size as me. Just pitches her voice lower so she don't sound like me. My spawn, honey."

A smile twitched at the corners of her mouth. She'd left the fridge door hanging open. Chilled air swirled out. She stalked closer. Blue tattooed lines circled the base of her neck. At the center, a tattooed padlock the size of my thumbnail rested in the divot between her collarbones. The tattoo was identical to Blueing's.

"Mallory ever try to kill you?" Lorraine said.

Freckles dotted her leathery arms, along with dozens of small, round scars. Shaped exactly like the burn on my neck. Cigarette burn scars. Her rhinestone bangles concealed most of them.

"So what if she goes a little nuts?" I said.

She'd have her blank episodes, do crazy shit, and sometimes I got hurt before I forced the sedatives down her throat. So what? Mallory needed help—I mean, what was I supposed to *do*? Fight back? Yeah, sure, I'll hit my fun-sized semi-girlfriend. The one who hid corpses. Totally. Great idea.

Lorraine's nose wrinkled. "You really never figured it out? The hell's the matter with you?"

I backed up. Smacked into the cupboards behind me. Lorraine white-knuckled the knife. She groped for the hem of my shirt and lifted it. Lifted the knife to my chest. The edge tickled. Little black hairs curled over the blade.

"Baby Warden, we got some accountin' to do."

I grabbed her wrist, clenched on it—

Nothing.

Warm skin throbbed under mine. Skin like a sun-warmed crocodile's. She didn't blink. She pressed the knife in. Red-hot pain burned in a thin line. I tried to scream, but a strangled, choking noise came out instead. *Punch her. You have a free Hand, just fucking punch her!* But she looked just like Mallory. So tiny. Five-foot-nothing, maybe a hundred pounds soaking wet. Black spots formed around the edge of my vision.

"Y'all remember flayin' me in Hell?"

"I—"

"Fuckin' demonspawn."

Smoke stung. I coughed. There was a fire somewhere in the house.

"Where's Mallory?"

"I'm surprised you liked screwin' her, Baby Warden," Lorraine said, and licked her lips. "Ain't she a lil' loose down there?"

Pulse. Pulse. Pulse.

I spat.

Lorraine Worner startled back. My gob of spit shone on her cheek, dribbled down. She stared up at me, burn scar on her cheek crinkling, lips pulling away from her teeth, dead-eyed. She wiped my spit off her face with her free hand.

"Huh," she said.

She struck. Grabbed my balls in her free hand. Squeezed. Stabbing pain sheared straight up, a spike of nausea with it. *Oh God oh God don't rip them off.*

"Wanna snack, Honeydoll?"

Her, squeezing. For a split second, I saw everything from the outside—me, shirtless and gasping, six foot four, wiry, dark-skinned, wild homeless-looking mass of black hair poofed out, stubble pocking my chin, bloodshot green eyes bulging out, and of course, the Hands. The monster pincers veined up to my goddamn elbows. Looming over this tiny lady like the villain from a B-movie, like a monster.

She released. She forced the knife deeper. Wet heat trickled down my chest. Blood. *Punch her. Claw her eyes out!* But I couldn't move.

The front door burst open, banging against the wall.

Roy Pike stormed in.

Sweat gleamed on his scalp. He carried a giant Styrofoam cooler, piled to the brim with dead white rats, and a revolver was holstered on his hip.

TWELVE

ROY PIKE DROPPED the cooler. Albino-furred dead rats slopped out, bodies squishy and limp. They scattered across the kitchen linoleum. Light from the fridge spilled over them, blanking out their open, pink eyes.

"Worner," he said.

Lorraine whipped around to face him, knife in hand. She released me. I jumped away from her, snatched up a handful of napkins and pressed them to her handiwork. Bleeding out wasn't on my to-do list.

Lorraine strutted up to Roy. "This here's my business. Ain't a thing you can do about it."

"Get back in your cell, Project 0666. Before you git worse."

He didn't look at me as he spoke.

"Roy," I said. "This isn't Mallory. She'll hurt you—"

"Better dead than changed."

His eyes were too bright. His gaze burned like an inquisitor charring heretics at the stake.

"You git on your knees and pray. Now."

I backed away from him. Blood soaked through the napkins I held to my chest. Lorraine brought the bloody knife to her lips and licked my blood off the blade. *Honeydoll,* she mouthed at me. Yum-yum, y'all.

Roy leaned heavily on his left leg. Blood had soaked through the jeans of his right leg, but the denim itself wasn't cut or damaged. He drew a revolver from a hip holster, something out of a cowboy special.

I edged towards the living room. Had to find Mallory.

"Roy—"

"I can handle *it*," he said, pointing his revolver at Lorraine Worner.

It? Jesus, what's this guy on? The lady was a nightmare, but an *it*? How far was the word *it* from the word *raghead*? Not as far as people thought.

"You never did git over the fact you took so long to catch me," Lorraine said. "Ever think how many folks might be alive if you'd've figured my case out 'fore Mallory flat-out told you, Mr. FBI-man?"

Lorraine locked into place, focused purely on Roy. Roy pointed his revolver at her, his breathing ragged. Two junkyard cats about to fight over the filet mignon scraps.

I bolted for Ma's room.

I clamped a hand over the cut on my ribs, gasping for breath. Blood dribbled down and trailed on the carpet. Sweat formed on my belly. I grabbed the doorknob. It almost burned my skin. I tore open the door.

A wall of black smoke billowed out, suffocating and oven hot. Eyes stung. Throat and nose shriveled up. I blinked away tears and barreled in, keeping my head low to the ground. Fire covered the far wall, consuming the carpet as it spread. A plastic bottle melted. Ma's hair oil. Acrid stench of burning plastic and artificial rose and smoke. I hacked. House fire. Smoke went up, you went down. Beneath the haze, a small body laid on Ma's bed. *Mallory.*

Went to scoop her up. Froze. My Hands weren't covered.

Each breath made me dizzier. No time. I ripped my shirt off and wrapped it around a Hand. Snatched a pillowcase. Wrapped the other. Grabbed Mallory's shoulders. I dragged her off the bed. Her feet *clomped* to the floor. Limp. Her head lolled. I tried to support it as I half-walked, half-ran out into the living room.

I sucked in fresh air. Just a few more steps to the front door, and it was cracked open. Just had to get us outside before the fire spread.

"Project 0666," Roy Pike said.

Zing! Needle-sharp pain. Taser hooks stabbed into my chest—

(!!!!!)

Spasming, spasming, frying against the carpet, rug burn, spasming, a godawful screaming sound—*is that me? That's me.*

Cold air caressed my right Hand. The pillowcase wrapping had fallen off. Roy Pike's finger curled around the trigger again—

I lunged up and grabbed his arm, *one Mississippi*, his hand went slack around the taser and it fell, *two Mississippi*, his mouth spasmed, his face went blank, Roy Pike was collapsing, *three Mississippi*, and as his eyes swiveled to meet mine, he hit the carpet. Back-first.

Oh, look, champ! You DID get a convoluted excuse to rip your shirt off. See how that went? No abs. Just taser hooks and misery. Too bad, so sad. Tough titty said the kitty.

I swallowed the second Oxy I'd been saving. Warm fuzzy numbness swept through me.

I ripped the taser hooks out of my chest. Left the taser. I fished through Roy's pockets. Found a set of truck keys. Success.

"Baby Warden," Lorraine called, from the kitchen.

Fire spread out from Ma's room. It leapt to the rust-colored, crusty couch I'd woken up on with Mallory Worner. Flames licked the oak coffee table. My bong shattered. DVDs vanished into the blaze. *Mallory Worner, Born Evil?* Joined the rest.

Lorraine stood in the dark kitchen, scrawling something on a scrap of paper. "Maybe we should set on down and chat. This is good clean fun, but I want my Honeydoll, and I'm already gettin' bored."

"What's a Honeydoll?"

She grinned like a person who'd won a million bucks off a two-dollar scratch ticket.

"Oh, you'll find out," she said.

Fantastic. More cryptic answers from the undead serial killer. I grabbed Mallory and dragged her outside.

THIRTEEN

MA HAD DIED. It only seemed fair that our house should die, too. Flames leapt from her bedroom window, clawing at the night sky. The Milky Way gauzed overhead in an endless glittering river. No moon marred its expanse. Stars jeweled throughout it like funeral gauze. Cracked concrete steps led down to the gravel driveway. Clots of sage grass waved in a rippling sea. The lone halogen streetlight jutted out from its concrete block like a buoy. It threw down industrial light. Roy Pike's rust-spotted truck lurked beneath it.

"Babe? You doing okay?"

Mallory made a cute little sleepy sound. Blood was still smeared over her mouth from when she'd bitten off Sedative Guy's finger.

I clicked the key fob. The truck made a promising noise and lit up. So far, so good. I drew the .45 from my waistband. Bats chittered at saguaros. Gravel poked through my socks as I walked and somewhere in the dark, a coyote bayed—a haunting call.

Goosebumps prickled along my arms. I unlocked the truck and heaved Mallory in, situating her as best I could. Hopefully she'd sleep. I retained the key.

You can't leave them to burn.

But the fire. Lorraine, for God's sake. Go *towards* the serial killer that wanted to fricassee me? I was still bleeding. Each breath stung my raw throat as I sucked in cool night air.

Okay, Sedative Guy, but Roy Pike? That asshole?

A memory. Him, growling, *Eat it again, raghead.* Eat it again, raghead. The vomit. My vomit. My purple-streaked vomit. Him, standing over fourteen-year-old me, making me eat it.

Still. I couldn't leave him to burn. Nobody deserved that. Everyone had people they loved, even that guy.

I steeled myself, then ran back into the burning house.

Fire kissed the edge of the hallway. A wall of heat, something like an oven turned to high. No time to look for Lorraine. Roy Pike was lying on the carpet, flames licking at his legs. Sedative Guy. Get him out before the fire blocked off the basement. I plunged into the hall, lungs stinging from the heat and smoke, past my old room—*there's a window inside, use it if the fire blocks off the hallway*—and hit the blue basement door, ran down the stairs, fire roaring in my ears.

Sedative Guy didn't make a peep as I lugged him up the stairs. His finger-stump wasn't bleeding anymore. It'd scabbed up. That wasn't normal. Wasn't right. My arms ached. Each step felt like slogging through wet concrete.

The hallway.

Fire raged outside, almost engulfing the entrance. Not enough time to drag him out through the front door and return for Roy Pike. Had to get Roy, *now*.

Sweat boiled and ran down my body. My room. The window. I staggered over to the door and nudged it open. Dumped Sedative Guy.

"Sorry."

I ran through the gap between the fire and wall, thinking, *Just ignore it, just ignore it, it's not there, champ*, tucking my head down. Baby flames danced across the dry hem of Roy Pike's jeans. I slapped them out. Got his bony shoulders. His chest rose and fell. Still breathing. *Okay*. I dragged him back into the hallway, away from the fire.

"Mm-hmm," Lorraine said.

She stood in the middle of the inferno, in the living room, waist-high in flames. She rested her hands on her hips.

"Don't need to run, honey. You're demonspawn. C'mere," she purred.

Demonspawn?

"I'm a freakshow experiment, okay?"

"That what they told you?" Lorraine asked.

"They—Roy Pike—said they injected my Ma with stuff. Holy water. What's demonspawn?"

"Only injection your mama got was from the demon that banged her, Baby Warden."

Oh, God no. This wasn't happening. This Jerry Springer skit from Hell *was not happening*.

She opened her arms. "You adapt. You're adaptin' right now. So c'mere. Sit in the fire awhile with me, and you might like it. I need you to be fireproof."

"I—"

I don't have time for this.

I ducked back into my room, dumped Roy Pike, and tore open the window over my bed. All the covers and sheets had gone. The carpet had been shampooed. I could smell it even through the smoke.

Clean air swirled in. I heaved Sedative Guy onto the bed. Slipped out the window. Dragged him through, dumped him on the sand, left him face up. I clambered back inside. Grabbed Roy.

Mallory's voice echoed down the hall. "Triple-Six?"

I got Roy onto the bed.

Closer, just outside the door. "Triple-Six, I need you. Please, don't go."

Something hot tightened inside my chest.

In the near-dark, with only the outside glow of the fire for illumination, she entered my room. Couldn't see her face. Just her cigarette ember, and the reflection of it in her eyes.

"Stay here with me," she said.

"You're not real. You're her. Shut up."

"Triple-Six," she murmured, "I love you."

No.

"I love you, Triple-Six."

Why the hell were my eyes tearing up? Why did it feel like someone had squeezed my guts and released? *I love you, Triple-Six.*

I jumped out the window and dragged Roy Pike out, just as the fire reached my bedroom door. Lorraine padded over to the window. In the frame, firelight rendered her into a black silhouette.

Lorraine called, "Got a ride? Nice little car you can drive away with? Well, kid. I ain't gonna stop you. Go on."

I tensed.

She took a drag off her cigarette. "Be seein' you."

It wasn't a hard choice, to run back to the truck. Mallory was fine. She was sleeping on the passenger side. I could see her. She hadn't said she loved me. That was her psychotic undead serial killer mother, who just so happened to be screwing with me and who could also vanish and reappear at will. So many fun facts here.

Another fun fact.

I didn't know how to drive.

Blue light flickered in the corner of my eye. The Hands suddenly pulsed. Heated.

Blue fire appeared over the road in a thin wall. Cold blue, like fire from a blowtorch or Bunsen burner.

Eldritch fire. Great. Add it to the list. It'd burn me all the same. Heat baked off.

Fire grew. Lorraine could pop up any minute, full of fun facts about my heritage. Or Roy Pike, with his cooler of dead rats and ability to call a person an *it* to their face.

All it takes is one *it* to transform a living, breathing human being into something else. A doll. A monster. A thing you can break or discard. You don't love a *thing*. Go sleep at night, Roy Pike. You didn't really hurt Project 0666—he's a *dirty Arab!* He's an *it!* He's a *doll!*

Honeydoll.

I shivered.

I unlocked the miserable car and hopped into the driver's seat.

Bit-O-Honey wrappers littered the floorboards. It reeked like cinnamon Altoids and tobacco. A half-empty jug of SunnyD festered in the cup holder.

Time for an impromptu driving lesson.

I stabbed the key into the ignition and turned it. The engine sparked. The truck sputtered to life, sounding about as healthy as a chain-smoker with stage IV lung cancer. Okay, then. I grabbed the steering wheel, worn mirror-smooth from age. Put the car into drive. Tapped the gas. It lurched.

Bang-bang-bang. Bang!

A godawful knocking came from under the hood. Even through the car's shell, heat broiled.

Bang! Bang! Bang!

It got louder. Angrier, somehow.

Demonspawn freak.

I floored the gas. The truck jolted forward, almost colliding with the light pole. I slammed the brakes. Cranked the wheel in the direction of the blue fire. The unnaturally blue fire. The smokeless fire.

Roy Pike and Sedative Guy wouldn't be paralyzed forever. Three Mississippis of the Hands on an adult human being equaled about twelve hours of paralysis, and I knew that because I'd grazed my favorite lab assistant with the Hands when I was fourteen. Dr. Judith Hitch. She'd died last summer. Heart attack.

Bang! Bang! Tap-tap-tap.

I hit the gas again. The truck didn't go. A grinding sound came out. I gave it more gas, the engine squalled, and the truck finally oozed forward at like five miles per hour. Wouldn't go faster. Was it sabotage? Shit, what was I supposed to *do*? I couldn't outrun Lorraine or Roy on foot, especially carrying Mallory, even if we got through the fire. I had to make this work, but Jesus, was there a car bomb or something? Had he put a lock or something in the—

It's a stick shift, Triple-Six.

It's a stick shift, Triple-Six, Mallory had said, one summer when we were fifteen. She'd been trying to show me a diagram of an engine. The memory of her voice continued, almost audible, as I struggled with the truck.

Dude, you've gotta hit the clutch and shift into different gears, or you're gonna fuck up the engine. That's how it works.

"I wish you were awake, babe," I said.

Clutch. Where was the clutch? A baby pedal rested to the left of the gas and brake pedals. I stomped down on it and cranked the gear-stick-thing into the number *two*.

Click.

The grinding sound stopped. I hit the gas, got off the baby pedal, and the truck went faster. I gave it more gas. The wall of blue fire loomed closer. Hotter. *Hotter and hotter until it fries you alive!*

The truck made funny struggling noises at forty miles per hour. Okay. Another gear? I hit the clutch, shifted up, and tapped the gas. The truck went faster. Holy shit. Had I mastered driving? Was I actually doing this? Hell yeah! My heartbeat pounded in my eardrums. I ground the gas pedal into the floorboard. Fire arced, clawing up and up towards the sky, spreading across the sand, closer and closer and bigger, the heat growing—

The engine whined. Blue all around for a split second, rubber burning—

Speeding away, through dusty road, into the cold night. Nothing but black and headlight beams. Bumps. My burning house shrank in the rear-view mirror.

It collapsed in on itself with a *whomph* and a flurry of sparks.

Bye, home. Wish I could say I'll miss you.

I let out the breath I'd been holding and guided the car down the gravel road. The gas meter was three-quarters full.

Bang! BANG! Bang!

Maybe it was just a normal truck thing. What did I know?

I was driving an actual vehicle. Mallory and I had finally escaped. If the dashboard clock was accurate, I only had to survive Lorraine for seventy-one more hours. Then I'd be free of the Hands forever. They couldn't keep me from living a normal life outside. *Maybe Mallory'll love you then.* How bad was Lorraine Worner, really? I mean, the lady didn't seem like the brightest bulb. All she did was threaten me. I'd seen scarier shit from the horror flicks Ma used to watch. What, was she going to blow cigarette smoke in my face and try to seduce me again? Please. I grinned.

Bang. Bang. Bang. BOOM!

Nope. I flicked on the radio, determined to drown out the knocking. Lynyrd Skynyrd played while I rummaged through Roy's glove box for food.

It cut off.

Roy Pike's voice rumbled out of the car radio. *"Don't even bother tryin' to run. I can find you, son. Wherever you are."*
The music kicked back up.
Suddenly, I wasn't hungry.
BOOM! Bang! Bang! Grrr…
Now it sort of sounded like the engine was *snarling* at me. Did the car hate me that much?
The engine stalled. The truck jolted to a stop.

FOURTEEN

BANG-BANG—

The hood flew open.

A blackened hand clawed around the hood's edge. A dainty hand. It slammed the truck hood shut. Headlights illuminated the figure.

Something resembling Lorraine Worner stood in front of the truck.

An eyeless burned corpse in the shape of a woman. Empty sockets. No eyes. A scorched optic nerve trailed out of a socket, down her cheek, like a black tendril. Charred patches of skin flaked off, illuminated in the high beams of the truck. A black patch of skin dotted each temple, perfectly round. An electrode's imprint. She'd had an electrode on each one of her temples. Most of her hair was burned off. A few untouched curls dangled from her pallid scalp. Blackened lips crackled open like a well-burned hot dog.

I dry-heaved.

"Fuckin' moron kid," she said, and chuckled. "Lettin' me pick my poison. Don't even know how a car engine works. Ever hear about somethin' called *internal combustion?*"

Her calling card. Her goddamn calling card. Start a fire, and presto, Lori's there. I swallowed. Anything with an engine would summon her. Cars, boats, anything.

How could I have been so stupid?

Lorraine leapt onto the hood, crawling up towards me. She rapped on the windshield. Thrust her eyeless charred face up to the glass.

"Reckon I can drive for both of us, Baby Warden. C'mere and talk."

Static buzzed. The windshield seemed about as thick as Saran Wrap. I turned the key. Got a dry *click*. The gearshift. Wouldn't start. I jerked it to park.

Lorraine shook her head. "Whatcha fixin' to do, Baby? It'll summon me even closer to you when that engine catches, now that I know where you are."

"Oh, so there's some awareness involved in this? That's how this works?" I said, voice raised so she could hear me.

Her upper lip twitched venomously. "Don't git too smart on me."

I turned the key. I eased one foot on the gas as I did.

Chuffa-chuffa-BOOM!

The engine smoothed out. A sudden blast of Eau de Lorraine wafted through the truck cab, almost thick enough to run a butter knife through. My nose demanded to go on shore leave. Heat swirled to my right. Lorraine. I fixed my gaze on the road ahead.

Drive, just drive, and then maybe open the door and hurl her out when you get enough speed. Don't look. She wants you to look at her.

Five miles per hour. I cranked the truck up to second. Added more gas. Gravel crunched as the truck picked up speed.

Something fever-hot clamped around my wrist. Bits of blackened skin crackled off and fluttered to the floorboards.

Twenty miles per hour.

Her fingers tightened. I lunged, grabbed the gearshift with my other Hand. Stomped the clutch. Jerked the gear stick to third.

Mallory made a rattling gargling sound. Lorraine had her forearm braced across Mallory's throat, pinning her to the seat. With her other hand, she clutched onto my right wrist.

Shit.

Forty miles per hour.

I wrenched out of her grip. She startled. I got a Handful of her curls, twisted. She hissed, clawed at my face. Streaks of heat burned down my cheeks. *Her nails.* An ash-gray fingernail flew off. Landed on my scrub shirt. I wrenched the truck door handle, kicked it open, and threw Fun Corpse Lorraine out into the night.

She latched onto the side mirror. Leered. Her feet found the footstep outside the truck.

Faster.

Fifty miles per hour. The truck whined. I shifted into fourth.

Lorraine breathed on the window glass, fogging it up. She traced a heart.

She's only holding onto the mirror with one hand right now.

I swerved to the left. Hard. The truck door swung open, knocking into her. She wobbled but got both hands tight around the side mirror. She snarled, spat. Yellowish spit oozed down the windshield. I slammed the driver's door shut. *Thunk!*

Sixty miles per hour.

The knife wasn't in my waistband anymore. It glinted at her shoulder, tucked into her bra strap.

Fun Fact: Her bra made it through twenty gazillion volts.

I swerved right. Mallory smacked into the passenger window. Lorraine hit the driver's side. Her hand slipped. She groped along the front of the truck, white knuckling the side mirror with one fist—

Snap!

The side mirror broke off.

Lorraine grasped a windshield wiper. It held for a split second. She grinned, teeth gleaming. Then the wiper—white from decades of sun-bleaching—snapped off. The base remained, now perpendicular to the windshield. It pointed to the sky.

Lorraine fell off the side of the truck.

I shifted down to third, second, first, then cranked the gearshift into R. Reverse.

She's already dead. She's already in her Fun Corpse form, man. It doesn't count.

I reversed. Something solid collided with the back of the truck. Then it wasn't there. The tires rolled over something like a log—

Lorraine shrieked.

Then the log-thing—*Lorraine, you ran over Lorraine, but she's dead, you hear me, she's dead!*—was gone. She'd probably vanished. Wait. If she could disappear and reappear at will, why wasn't she just appearing inside the truck cab right now, ready to shank me? Why the hell was she doing... whatever this stuff was, with the heart on the window glass?

The grease from her finger still limned the heart.

Lorraine appeared in the middle of the road. I cranked to first, ready to run her over again. But she dropped to her knees and dove under the truck, knife in hand. What was she—

Pop!

Air hissed. The truck shuddered to the ground. She'd stabbed one of the front tires. Lorraine stood, coming out near the driver window. She reached for the window. For me. Her eyeless gaze drifted down, maybe to her charred arm.

She stiffened. She touched her face, probing around her empty eye sockets.

"So that's why you're green 'round the gills," Lorraine said.

A thumbnail-sized chunk of burned flesh peeled off. She continued feeling her eye sockets, as if this just happened on a causal basis, just your everyday transformation into an electrified corpse, no biggie. Oh, and I couldn't start a car without summoning her to my exact location. Can't forget that.

She leaned in, face expressionless. "They were supposed to shave me bald. The current fries you quicker."

Jesus Christ.

Napkins stuck to the cut on my ribs. It stung. There had to be a gas station or something up the road. Somewhere to hide out. Get a better ride.

A scrap of notebook paper rested on the center seat. I plucked it up.

Something wasn't right here. Something felt wrong. Baby Warden. Honeydoll. She acted like I knew her. I had a target on my back, a mysterious piece of paper, multiple injuries, mutating Hands, a flat tire, and a nickname I already hated. Baby Warden.

I floored it. I didn't look back.

FIFTEEN

I'D EITHER FOUND the world's most cryptic poem, or the shopping list of an incubus, and neither option sounded peachy.

Blood. Sweat. Cum. Tears? Spit?

I blinked at the scrawled words on the Post-it note. "What the hell, Lori?"

As I drove into civilization, I pulled out vials of sedatives and read the labels, trying to calculate how long Mallory would be unconscious.

Midazolam.

All of these vials were either midazolam or lorazepam. Which fit. Those were both injectable sedatives, fast-acting, with short durations—and I'd seen the proof in the goddamn pudding, believe me—but what I didn't see was Haldol. Haloperidol, to be precise. It was a strong antipsychotic, and if Mallory had been biting fingers off in any standard psych ward, they would've used Haldol first. Midazolam and lorazepam were pre-surgery, normie sedatives.

Which means what, champ?

They weren't treating Mallory Worner as if she had a mental illness. Or they weren't equipped enough to have Haldol. She'd gotten half the syringe.

Mallory was awake and staring out the passenger window after twenty minutes. She tapped against the glass.

Clink! tap-tap-tap-tap.

"Remember?"

"You okay?"

Her little drawl crept in. "The flashlights. We talked with 'em at night, when we couldn't be together. Morse code."

Long. Short-short-short-short.

Six.

She'd been tapping out the number six, in Morse code, three times. *666.* Triple sixes.

I eased the truck down a freeway, going about forty miles an hour, and pulled off at the first rural-looking exit. Which meant the exit sign that only had one gas station, as opposed to three gas stations, two fast-food joints, and a hotel, all sandwiched onto the sign and sun-bleached. The dashboard clock read 2:12 a.m. I parked behind the solo gas station, a bleak-looking oversized shack with wood shingles and hornets' nests thrumming under the eaves. An ad for Pepsi engulfed half of the neon-lit sign overhanging the roof. *Clyde's Gas N' Go, 24 HR Service and COFFEE!* it exclaimed, in Creamsicle-orange lettering.

"Good location, Triple-Six," Mallory said, drawing her .22 from her scrub pocket. "Hopefully there's only one cashier. An inexperienced one. That makes it easier."

"Whoa."

She clapped my shoulder. "This is exactly what I wanted, the entire time. We got past the desert. We're in town. Now we get some money and a new set of wheels. You go find a nice, sweet normal girl, and have a ton of babies with her. Do me proud, man. Get that white picket fence life."

"Mallory, I don't want anyone else."

"You've never had anyone else."

"Okay, sure, but—"

"Don't argue. We still need funds and a different car. Odds are good that Roy Pike's put tracking devices in this one."

Considering that all of our previous escape attempts revolved around trying to get a vehicle, I concurred. Mallory said she'd go inside the gas station to scope things out. She told me to drive the truck up front and wait. I did.

Minutes passed. I got antsy. Sure, we needed to go Grand Theft Auto, but I couldn't "start a fire," which included starting any kind of engine, unless I wanted to summon an undead serial killer from Hell to my exact location. To kill me. But two could play at the exact wording game. If someone *else* started a car engine for me, would it still count?

Ads covered the gas station windows. I couldn't see inside. Why was she taking so long?

Time to find out. But I hadn't exactly taken an intro-to-armed-robbery class. I didn't have anything to cover my face with. I put the driver's mirror down. Time for a new question—how threatening did I look, on a scale of one to ten?

I flicked the overhead light on.

My eyes were so bloodshot you could barely tell they were green. A manic, unsettling gaze. Dark circles surrounded them. I possessed the hooked nose of an Iranian goatherd, along with sharp features, and my face was even sharper now, skull-gaunt like a wraith. Bruises darkened my right cheekbone. Blood crusted down my nose and split-open lip. Black stubble carpeted everything south of my ears. My hair puffed out in a crazed mass around my head.

All in all, a solid nine on the threatening scale. One point deducted for lack of muscle. I possessed the fine muscle tone of a toothpick on a juice cleanse. I glanced down at the Hands. Yep, still pincers. Veined up to my elbows. I looked like a cross between a schizophrenic homeless guy that'd been in a bar fight, and a terrorist that forgot his bomb vest and turban on the Greyhound.

Enough stalling. Enough self-pity.

I clenched my jaw and scooped up the .45. As I exited, I hurled the truck keys into the darkness as hard as I could. Let Roy trawl for them.

I waltzed up to the front door of *Clyde's Gas N' Go,* gun in Hand.

Bells jangled over the door when I entered. A whoosh of frigid air rushed out and cut through the muggy night. It smelled like fried grease and sugar. The shelves were full to bursting with an eye-bleedingly bright array of chips, Twinkies, candy bars, you name it, packaged in Technicolor splendor, crammed in dinky aisles. Everything else was colorless, from the walls to the gray-smudged tile on the floor. Racks of raunchy pens and lighters leered by the register.

Mallory Worner held the cashier at gunpoint.

She didn't move a muscle when I came in. Her face was expressionless, her posture steady. She kept her .22 aimed at the cashier's chest. The guy had his hands up. Sweat beaded on his forehead.

My throat caught.

Holy shit.

"Empty the register. Cash on the counter."

"Babe?"

She stiffened. Turned her head an inch towards me. "You weren't supposed to see this."

"What do you mean?"

"Go wait outside. I'll give you the keys, then you go live a happy life somewhere far, far away from me. My life's fucked, man. Yours isn't. God—you're covered in blood. Who cut you?" Mallory asked.

Dear old Lori. Your mom.

"You're not gonna believe me if I tell you," I said.

"Uh," the cashier said. "Look, I got kids—"

"Would've covered my face if I had something," Mallory said. "I don't want to kill you. Get faster with the cash."

The cashier was a giant black dude with dyed red hair like Betadine.

"You have the Hands. How did *anyone* hurt you up close? You're so sheltered you can't throw a punch?"

"Can't be too sheltered, babe. You roofied me pretty fucking well when we killed Blueing."

"Oh, shit," the cashier said, hand frozen in mid-grab.

"Don't distract me right now," Mallory said.

She turned back to the cashier. "You. I know you pressed the panic button two minutes ago. The cops are going to show up in about five. Right? Is that everything in the drawer?"

"Ask him for his keys," I said.

"He's literally standing in front of you."

"It feels weird. I'm not a criminal."

"Oh my God," Mallory said. "Fine. You got keys?"

The cashier shook his head. "I lose that car, I lose this job. My probation officer—"

Mallory cocked the hammer back. *Click.*

"Sounds like you've got keys, man. Put them on the counter."

He did so.

Well, there went my first attempt at carjacking. And when had Mallory learned to rob gas stations? Was that in one of Lorraine's picture books or something? *Baby's First Armed Robbery?*

I figured I'd already fucked up my life this much, so might as well go full throttle. I couldn't just stand here like a jackass while she robbed this gas station. *Ah, what stellar logic have we on display?* "Well, my girlfriend jumped off the bridge, so I said I would, too." *Dude, what are you doing? Seriously, what are you DOING?*

I stepped closer to Mallory and drew my gun.

"What are you doing?" Mallory said.

"Helping," I said.

I trained my .45 on the cashier, forcing my Hands to not shake. One pincer-half curled around the handle, the other half fished for the trigger. I could totally do this. Definitely.

Mallory groaned. "Just take the keys and go."

"I'm not leaving you to rot."

"You don't even know how to fire a gun," she said. "Give it to me."

The cashier gulped. "I got a family. Really, I got pictures in my wallet."

"I can't drive, Mallory," I said.

She breathed out, coal-black eyes narrowing. "Don't use that name. You never use names, doing this."

"Someone's trying to kill me," I said.

"Tell me who. I'll kill them first."

She walked up to the counter and reached towards the pile of cash. The cashier loomed over the counter, dead-still except for his mouth. His tongue twitched out and kept licking his lips.

An uncomfortable feeling prickled in my gut.

Pulse. Pulse. The cashier. A split-second decision flashed over his face. Mallory scooped up the cash, gun clutched in her other hand, finger looped around the trigger guard—

He grabbed her wrist.

CRACK! My Hand spasmed around the trigger. The gun fired into the cigarette display behind him. He let go. Hit the floor, lightning quick. The gunshot blasted into my ear, deafening it. Half-torn packets of cigarettes and chew cans flew out. Clattered to the tile. Streams of cinnamon whiskey gushed from cracked bottles.

What the fuck is wrong with me? I swallowed. Stinging smoke streamed out from the gun's muzzle.

"See. Look what happens," Mallory said. "My boyfriend's got a hot trigger finger."

Oh, I'm your boyfriend now? How convenient.

My right ear buzzed. The cashier eased himself up using the countertop, panting. He stared at my free Hand for a solid second. Like he'd gotten a sneak-peek at the freakshow.

"They're, uh, fucked up prosthetic hands," I said. "We got them as a joke. They're not my real hands. Don't look at them. And before you ask, yeah. I can jack off just fine."

He shook his head. Stared past me.

"What are you—"

Hot fingers dug into the back of my neck. Eau de Lori mingled with the sulfur gun smoke in the air.

"They call it gun*fire*, honey," Lorraine Worner rasped.

Her hands spidered around my throat.

Shit.

I couldn't fire a gun. Couldn't even start an engine.

"Mallory—"

Lorraine squeezed.

SIXTEEN

I THRASHED. THE cashier had seen Lorraine. Why the hell wasn't Mallory helping me?

Lorraine throttled tighter, digging her nails into my skin. I tried desperately to breathe. Couldn't. *Pulse. Pulse. Pulse.* The Hands itched and ached to touch.

I twisted. Physics finally took my side. She'd had to stand on her tiptoes to throttle me.

I threw her off me. She thunked onto the linoleum. I sucked air into my lungs.

"*Mallory! Get the keys and run!*"

Mallory didn't so much as blink. She stuffed cash into her scrub pockets. The cashier's eyes bulged like ping-pong balls.

Jesus, was she deaf?

Lorraine scrabbled up, thankfully not in her Fun Charred Corpse form. Her bangles jingled. She grunted. Beelined for me.

I sprinted for the counter. Mallory ignored us. Poor Lorraine. This had to be the world's shittiest family reunion.

"Mallory!"

Her head whipped towards me, crazed curls bouncing.

"Stop it," she snarled.

Stop it? *Stop it?*

I dove behind the counter, shoving the cashier dude aside. I jammed my gun into my waistband.

Lorraine hit the counter. Inches away from Mallory.

Mallory spat. "This isn't funny. Stop making fun of me."

"What?"

Lorraine vaulted over the counter. I jumped back. Smacked into the cigarette display. *C'mon, Lori! Take a smoke break! Leave me alone!* Fireball fumes drenched the air in booze. Lori snatched a red BIC lighter off the stand.

"Did I ever treat you like a freak?" Mallory said, methodically grabbing cash. "When you talked about all the shit you saw in solitary?"

"Ain't that sweet, kid? My own fuckin' spawn, pretendin' I don't exist."

"Like you give a shit," I said.

"Git down. On the ground."

I nodded to the cashier. *Run.* He booked it over the counter, and Mallory didn't shoot at him.

Lorraine kicked my shin. Pain. It buckled. *Splish.* Spilled booze drenched my clothes and skin. She flicked the lighter on. Stepped over me. I scrambled, but there was nowhere to go.

"Mallory. *Help me.*"

"She's not real, man. Quit it."

Fire danced. Oh God. Oh shit. The alcohol. It'd catch. Cotton. It'd sear my skin and fry and hurt and Mallory was gonna just watch it happen because she thought—

Lorraine grinned. Lowered the lighter.

"Bye, kid."

Because she thinks she's hallucinating, dipshit!

"The cashier," I said. "C'mon! *He saw her!*"

The flame licked across the puddle. Flew to my clothing. Heat roiled up. *Stop drop roll.* I knocked Lorraine away and hit the ground—*no it's covered in fire*—smashed into the cigarette display, smothering into it. Pain. Heat. Burning hair.

"Lorraine?" Mallory said.

Her voice snagged on something as it came out. Strangled. Her skin gleamed bone-white under the fluorescents. Freckles stood out like ink.

I extinguished Flambé Me. Some arm hair was singed off, but no major burns. My skin felt like a typical sunburn.

Lorraine, hands resting on her hips, nodding, snatched up a menthol cigarette and lit it.

"Mm-hmm. You're gonna be a delicious lil' Honeydoll by the time I'm through rebuildin' you. Fireproof at a fuckin' minimum."

Mallory aimed the gun at Lorraine. "You're not real. You can't be real."

"Go ahead, honey. Pull the trigger. It ain't gonna do much."

"They fried you in the chair."

Lorraine bit through the cigarette. It fell to the ground and sponged up booze. Ash flakes materialized on her skin. Her eyes flickered, but remained. Poor Lorraine. Could a psychotic undead serial killer from Hell get a break around here?

"You liked watchin' me fry?" Lorraine said softly. "I know you got it on tape. We've been havin' so much fun these past few years. Thought I wasn't real? That help you sleep at night?"

Silence.

"I'm better'n anythin' your fuckin' brain could cook up, *Mallory*."

Mallory swallowed.

The cashier had disappeared.

Police sirens bayed faintly in the distance.

Lorraine hawked a loogie onto the floor. Lurid food wrappers practically glowed. Keys glinted on the counter. I stood.

"We need to get out of here. I can't drive," I said.

"You drove to get us here," Mallory snapped.

"I can't start a—fuck, Mallory, I can't drive! Come on!"

Lorraine's gaze flitted to the keys. I slammed my Hand over them.

"Go ahead. Make him drive," she said.

Scorch marks stained the display. No more booze puddle on the floor. The fire ate it all. But a *drip-drip* plinked down from the display. Lorraine moistened her lips. Fingered the BIC lighter.

Mallory tugged on my shirt. "Oh my God. Now she's gonna—"

Lorraine idly thrust her left hand into her cutoffs. And not into her pocket. She reached for another cigarette with her right hand.

"Uh, is she—"

"Arsonists like to jerk off at the scene of the crime."

Those sirens were getting louder.

We ran.

Lorraine didn't follow.

As we sprinted through the entryway, into the night, I clicked the key fob. A yellow Kia *click-clicked!* in the space near the door. Besides Roy's truck, no other cars littered the lot. I slapped the keys into Mallory's hand. We jumped in. The pristine Kia smelled like fake lime and coconut. Mallory started the car. Blue and red lights neared.

"Never wanted you involved in any of this," Mallory said, and sighed.

WE AMBLED DOWN the freeway. No faster. Mallory muttered something about it being a dead giveaway.

Here we were. Hunted by multiple people. To date:

Folks, we've got one fine roster tonight! Tenacious packs of hunters are gathering from miles 'round to find the Living Dead Girl and her fuck-up of a boyfriend, the Pincered Freakshow!

The police. *Folks, we know they might seem pedestrian—insert canned laughter—but don't underestimate their ability to cut off resources and escape routes. The Living Dead Girl's got some tricks up her sleeve, but does Pincered Freakshow? No!*

Edward Sal Blueing. *Folks, he might not even show up, but we think he's a contender still! If he is, then hoo boy, are they in trouble.*

Roy Pike, who can apparently do magic. Mr. Wizard, but evil and depressed and neurotic. *Folks, Roy Pike always gets his man. He's psychotic enough to do it, and he's too old to give a shit. Who knows what other stuff he can do?*

Lorraine the Immane, aka the undead serial killer from Hell. *Hoo boy, folks, have they got themselves a predicament! You thought your mother-in-law was bad, check this pyromaniac demon-lady out!*

So quit. Sit down, curl up, and wait. For her or Roy…does it really matter which one? I rolled down the window. Night air suffocated.

The only injection your Mama got was from the demon that banged her.

My Hands itched and pulsed. How far would it go? What was gonna happen to me? If I couldn't get my shit together, would I actually turn into…like some kind of *real* demon? Something, maybe a moth, tickled my right Hand. Something tangible. I balled my fist to grab it, but it wasn't there, and I clutched empty air.

I finally said it.

"What'd Lorraine mean?"

"About?"

"When she said you'd been having fun these 'past few years.'"

"She says a lot of shit. I just ignore it."

"What?"

"I've been seeing Lorraine since I was ten."

"Since the day they executed her. July sixteenth."

Blood. Sweat. Cum. Tears? Spit?

Her shoulders tensed. "How'd you know?"

There wasn't any sane way to say it. I'd just been set on fire by an undead serial killer. By my potential mother-in-law from Hell, actually, and had the pleasure of watching her jerk off pre-arson.

I sighed.

"Because Lorraine's trying to kill me."

SEVENTEEN

MALLORY DROVE. I talked.

The more I caught her up to speed, the more lifeless she got.

I'd asked her, once, when we were both fourteen, both hip-deep in a fifth of Smirnoff. *You ever think she...* I'd trailed off. *Which she?* Mallory asked, but oh we knew which one. I didn't have to say her name. *Mallory, did you ever think that maybe she loved you? In her own way?* And Mallory went salt-white and still. She looked like that soap-corpse someone dredged in Lake Sapon—Dr. Hitch had a whole lecture on saponification, complete with fun pictures—not quite like something dead. Like something that'd never been alive, period.

Lorraine gave me this, she'd said, pointing to the burn scar on her cheek. *So I'd look more like her. Because that kept her from killing me. When she lost her temper. Don't ever fucking ask me again, man.*

Blank-eyed, gone, zombie-pale. Living Dead Girl.

Mallory looked like that now.

"Uh," I finally said. "What do you, uh, think? About all this?"

"What'd Roy Pike bribe you with?" Mallory murmured.

"Huh?"

"You know exactly what I'm fucking talking about."

She turned her head to study me. Dissect me.

"This is an experiment, right? You all think it's funny. God—I should've known. I didn't escape desert-hell. I wonder who they got to play Lorraine. Good acting."

"What?"

She narrowed her eyes. "Hm. Maybe you aren't in on it. You're a terrible liar. Too many tells. You're a jittery person, man."

"What the hell, Mallory? I don't get—"

"You're so naive," Mallory said, and jerked her head back to the road. "Lorraine's not back from the dead. She's not some fucking ghost. All of this is an experiment. Think about it. You and I both managed to escape from desert-hell at last? That easily?"

"It didn't seem that secure, I guess."

"Exactly."

"But you said you'd been seeing her for years."

"Could've been an actor. They've fucked enough with us. Could see them doing that."

"What a great actress, able to claw her way out from under a goddamn engine block. Makes total sense."

"What if it had a compartment hidden somewhere?"

The car's dashboard clock read *3:48 a.m.* Lonely highway lights flickered in via the windows. Nobody followed us.

"Why? Seriously, why would Roy Pike waste this much time and energy on us? He hates me. Roy's last scrap of professionalism gets used up on you."

"Either it's so high up that it's not official—we're talking government-level shit—or Roy Pike's been running his own private experiment. He worked for the FBI. He was an expert on serial killers. He caught Lorraine. This has to be some government experiment."

"They had to put us in the same cell, Mallory."

"Lorraine's not…back," Mallory said. "Because she can't be."

"I've spent the last few hours wondering if I needed a straitjacket, you know, in between dodging her."

"You've hallucinated before. What if it's both?"

The endless pit of solitary. No time. No point of reference. Nothing. Until the lights flicked on, the fun started—something hot welled up in my chest and made my voice crack.

"I'm not—I'm not a lunatic. Okay?"

"Never said you were."

Mallory bit her lip, still for a second. Then she reached over and rested her warm hand on my pillowcase-swaddled shoulder.

"Don't. The Hands. They're getting worse. I can't stop it."

"It's okay," she said.

She wiggled her fingers. "See? I'm fine."

Amber lights shone like flares in the night. The car engine droned on. I touched the window, and it felt lukewarm. The heat dissipated after sundown in desert-hell.

I wasn't crazy, right? Definitely not. Normal people hallucinated elaborate strip clubs, too. *Turn it into an ad. It'll go over great, just peachy. Vivid* hallucinations are ALL YOURS, ladies and gents! Call this toll-free number, go directly to an unlit cell for thirty days!

Yeah.

"I don't think Lorraine's a hallucination," I said.

"Because?"

"One, she's awful. I've never—look, if my brain decided to go kaput outside of solitary, it'd be fun. Or neutral. Two, it's never happened outside of solitary, *period*. I'm not like—"

"I know," Mallory said.

I sighed. *Not like Ma.* She heard voices if it got really bad, but she never saw stuff. She'd just threaten to slit her wrists if I got more than three hundred feet away. Sometimes she'd spice it up, threaten to eat a bottle of sleeping pills or chug the Drano. I tie a mean tourniquet. Been tying them since I was six.

"Hallucinations aren't like the movies," I said. "You see, like, one thing, and half the time, it's related to some outside experience. If I had a stomachache, maybe I'd start seeing a glowing knife stabbing me. That sort of thing. And sometimes, you kind of understand it's not real."

Mallory stiffened.

"You okay?" I asked.

"Fine, man."

"Mallory...I think this is real. Not an experiment. We need to start talking about Lorraine."

"Shut up," she said.

Her eyes were going blank again.

Shit.

"Maybe we should pull over. Get some sleep," I said.

"What happened to the fever dream bar you told me about? Sounded pretty elaborate to me. You're crazy enough to hallucinate that."

Pulse. Pulse. Pulse. I took a deep breath. She was lashing out, no big deal.

"I'm sorry. Okay?"

"It's one or the other. Either you're so crazy you hallucinated it—"

"Mallory."

"Or," she said quietly, "you're such a fucking loser that your wet dreams turned real."

She jerked the car wheel.

Blank episode.

The highway shoulder screamed. *Get her.*

I went to grab her arm. Flinched back. Shit. The Hands weren't wrapped.

"Mallory!"

"Stop it," she whispered. "*Stop it.*"

The car bumped, groaned, vibrated from the gravel. Off-road. It dropped. My stomach flipped over. *Just MOVE HER!*

I rammed her with my shoulder. Her hands slackened. The car wheel slipped around. She grunted, went to grab the wheel again. I beat her to it. White-knuckled the goddamn thing. Vibrations from the off-road jellied my arm sockets, chattered my teeth. Back onto the road. Move the wheel.

I forced it over. Mallory was pinned against the side window. She shook. At least she didn't try for the wheel again.

"You wanna die, too? Thought that was just a me thing," I choked out. "Okay, babe. I'll drive. Let's stop for Benadryl."

Loser. Freak. Monster. No wonder she wants to kill you both.

"No matches for you, babe," I said, voice oddly pitched.

Stuff burned up a lot around Mallory. Something to do with the sunlight refracting through dew drops. Apparently. We didn't have dew in desert-hell. I'd find Mallory, matches stuffed in her pockets, too many lighters, glassy-eyed. So what if I babysat Mallory? She had more issues than National Geographic, and one gnarly aim with a knife. I'd slip her a benzo and make up white lies after she returned to normal.

But this one?

My fault. *Monster.*

"I-I'm sorry. I'm so sorry," I said.

She wouldn't hear me.

I said it again. Again. My eyes got blurry, but I didn't take my Hands off the wheel to wipe them. I said it again.

Nothing.

I nudged her foot off the pedal. It clomped onto the floorboard. The car slowed. Nobody behind us. Good. I eased the wheel over, pulled off onto the highway's edge. Turned off the car. Mallory's head rested on the window glass. Her breath fogged it. I hit the door locks. I found ACE bandages in the glovebox, along with hand weights. I wrapped up the Hands without looking at them, clear up past my elbows. Mallory's eyes gaped open at nothing. Her jaw was slightly slack.

I said it again.

Nothing.

I gently touched her arm. No response. There wouldn't be one. Some small black patch rotted on her arm. About the size of a grape, soft to the touch. Sometimes those took a day to disappear. At least it was just the one. At least there weren't any blisters this time.

I cranked the seat back as far as it could go, reclined it. She slumped. I caught her by the shoulders before she hit her head. It lolled. I could hear her slow breaths.

"Mallory, we're going to sleep for a few hours. Okay?"

I sort of bundled her up and held her, half balled up, head resting on her chest, hair scrunched underneath my chin. Jasmine shampoo. Cigarette smoke. Every now and again, she'd blink. Her pulse rate was normal. Technically. *None of this is normal.*

If she came out of it, I'd feel her shift. If she tried to escape and start an arson career or kill—do something dumb to herself—I'd feel it. Exposed cutting scars peeked out from her shirt sleeve. Her arm fell out of her lap. I lifted it. Corpse-limp. I placed it back. Long lengthwise scars—one apiece—marred her forearms. She'd had them the day I met her. She didn't talk about it.

I said it again.

Eventually, her eyes closed. Mine too.

Lorraine. What the fuck did you do to her?

"Goodnight," I said. "Love you."

But Mallory only breathed, in and out, like the life support machine for an intubated coma victim.

A SOFT GRUNT. It woke me. She reanimated. Her sharp elbow dug into my ribs.

"What—what happened?" Mallory asked.

Still dark. *4:30 a.m.*, according to the dashboard.

"You fell asleep at the wheel," I said.

"Whatever you say."

She clapped a hand to her forehead. "Oh. God. Did you park us on the edge of the freeway?"

"Where else?"

"Cops, man. This is a stolen car."

"Guess I missed that part of Carjacking 101," I said. "And why the hell are you so worried about the cops, anyway, if this is all some loony experiment?"

"Scoot over. I'll drive."

Great. I scooted. *Hey, babe. Maybe get better at the whole "ram the car into an overpass" schtick. I'd hate to be something besides red mush on this fine Texas asphalt.*

But she seemed lucid enough. I nodded. She fired up the car and eased it back onto the freeway.

"So...where are we going?" I asked.

"Testing the limits, seeing sights," she said. "Let's see how much Roy Pike put into this theater set."

"Mallory—"

"It really does smell like actual Texas, he got that part right," she said, wrinkling her button nose.

I sighed. A car whizzed past occasionally. Flat, darkened land surrounded us, deadened by night. Through the far gloom, blackened lit shapes twitched up in mechanical motions. Oil derricks, probably. Every mile or so, a gold streetlight blinkered through the darkness.

Blood. Sweat. Cum. Tears? Spit? The paper still sat scrunched up in my pocket.

A car crept up from behind. Something moving in the dark. A flicker above it? I thought I'd seen something over it. Churning in the night sky. No stars.

Engine roar grew louder. Light from a streetlight grew. We were about to pass another. And one mint-green car winked in the rearview mirror. Vintage, maybe from the fifties, if those *Outer Limits* episodes were accurate.

Around it swarmed a plague of glowing fireflies.

Like a cloud of locusts, ready to devour anything in their path.

This, too?

"Mallory," I said, fighting to keep my voice calm. "You see what's behind us?"

"A car."

"No, it's—"

"Keep your cool. Don't panic."

The light receded. Mallory glanced back. The fireflies weren't as visible now. Just an occasional flitting glow. Like sparks from flame. No sound. The FireMobile followed behind us, not close, but not far. I squinted and could kind of make out the flying lightning bugs above it. Fireflies roiled in their vortex. Poor little guys. Somebody needed to get an entomologist on speed-dial.

Mallory smiled. She patted the inside of my thigh. *Oh, yeah.* She peeled off her beige scrub top. Underneath, she wore a low-cut tank top. White.

She wasn't wearing a bra.

Jesus fucking wept! Her boobs jiggled every time the car went over a bump. There were a lot of bumps. Thank you, Texas Department of Transportation. Warmth pooled in my belly. There was a head calling the shots, and it sure wasn't the one up top.

"Excess jizz causes panic attacks," she said, still grinning, crooked teeth visible.

"Sounds medically accurate to me," I said.

Maybe the FireMobile would be gone. I checked. Nope. My hallucinations didn't last this long, either. Except the bar one.

"Let's pull over. Get some condoms. Cigarettes."

I opened my mouth to say yes.

Lorraine's going to KILL YOU, dipshit! Sure, go and get sucked off by Mallory. Those veins haven't reached your dick yet. Maybe Lori'll wait to stab you until you're mid-jizz. All it'd take was one mistake. One accidental flick of a lighter, and presto, Lorraine would appear. Besides me...Lorraine didn't exactly seem happy to run into Mallory.

I sighed. "Where are we really going, babe?"

I tried not to stare at her rack. That tank top clinging to it. I had a FireMobile in tow, an undead serial killer on the hunt for me, two rapidly worsening Hands, and Mallory thought I was one screw loose from going postal. Fantastic.

"A biker bar. For starters."

"What?"

EIGHTEEN

"**YOU NEED A** shirt," Mallory said. "Wait in the car."

We were parked outside a Walmart, next to a rusted-out camper and a rustier steel drum. Drunks hooted in the parking lot. She'd tied her hair back, kept the scrub top off, let her boobs take center stage. I waited. She came out with goodies. I threw on a T-shirt emblazoned with *Blue Lobster*.

"Really, babe?"

"Found one for me, too," she said. "Classy shit."

She held up a T-shirt that said *Roast 'em, honey!* In dripping-blood font, above a cartoon BIC lighter and cartoon Lori bangles. Then she put it on.

Something curdled in my stomach. *Pulse. Pulse. Pulse.*

"She killed, like, thirty people, right?" I asked.

A hard edge to her voice. "Not counting the arson casualties. They had two other shirts like it. Might as well wear it. I'm Mallory Worner. What else would I wear?"

Veins itched up my arms. Tingled. Reached midway between elbow and shoulder, digging deeper and pulsing something like the pleasure-pain of scratching a mosquito bite until it bled. *Pulse. Pulse.* Unstoppable. *Monster.*

"Got condoms. Wanna bang?"

I stared at my creeping, creature-feature veins. I pushed on one. *Disgusting freak.*

"Don't—don't touch me," I said.

"Oh," she said, voice small.

Her eyes glistened. She started the car.

We drove on, silent, for about twenty songs on the country station, then Mallory pulled onto an exit ramp. No symbols on the sign, nothing but a faint orange-red glow through foliage. Gravel crunched under the Jeep's tires. Bloody, maraschino cherry-colored light reached for us through the black leaves, strengthening as she drove on.

"Wonder if it's still here," she muttered.

We burst through into a gravel parking lot, right in front of the bar.

A mint-green car was parked by the edge. On the roof crawled a swarm of fireflies. I hissed. *Jesus. It's the goddamn car.*

"What's wrong?" Mallory asked.

"That weird car I told you about. Look."

She shook her head. "People are weird. You don't know the half of it, man. You've never stepped foot outside our place for more than six hours. Unless it was a lab. Or one of Roy's facilities."

"Mallory, the car's *covered in fireflies.*"

She grunted. Parked the car.

"You ever touch money?" Mallory asked.

"No, but—"

"Keep tabs on the car. If it bothers you."

I sat up straight. "I put the groceries and house stuff on a list and some guy in a van dropped them off every Thursday, okay, yeah, but I still cooked. Cleaned. I'm not five."

"But everything's weird to you," Mallory said. "Not your fault. Just how it is."

She slapped a twenty into my Hand and curled my pincer around it.

Isn't it supposed to be paper? It felt greasy, even through the bandages covering my Hands. Why didn't it look like the movies, all nice and uncreased? Why weren't any of the bills lying flat? Galaxies of creases kept them half-curled. How many generations of germs had bred on this humble twenty? Ugh. I could smell the hint of dried sweat on it.

"People actually snort coke with this? Stick it up their nostrils?"

"Germaphobe."

She smirked, but it didn't last long. "Here's my life. Lorraine and I ate a drifter she'd offed. Once. She bashed in his brains a little too hard. Couldn't burn him like usual, wasn't her style. God—she could be so picky."

"*What?*"

Something froze in my gut.

"Don't remember much of the movie, do you?"

No, Mallory, I don't. Big shocker.

Mallory continued, "She only burned them alive. Chained, first. I held her cigarette. After she drenched them in gasoline. So. We didn't have any work for two months. No food. No booze. No cigarettes. Lorraine got antsy, went prowling, hit too hard. Didn't want to waste the meat."

She swallowed. Lips tightened. "I didn't care. I was hungry. She—she tried.

To be nice about it. Mostly because it was less trouble for her if I wasn't spooked. So she roasted and shredded the meat and made sandwiches on Bimbo Bread. If I kept it down for thirty minutes without throwing up, she'd give me half a Raspberry Zinger."

"Jesus, Mallory."

"Can't look at a Raspberry Zinger without wanting to hurl," she said.

Cannibal. My best friend and semi-girlfriend was a cannibal. *But how did it taste, babe?* Some manic giggle threatened to burst out. Lorraine Worner was A-OK with eating people. What a fun fact. Learn a new thing every day.

"I'm sorry."

"You know jack shit about the real world," Mallory said.

"But how—how do I help?"

Did Hallmark have a card for this? In the "Serial Killer Family Member" section, perhaps?

"You can't," she said.

"I'm not talking about the situation."

How do I help you?

"Neither am I," she said.

I put my right Hand over hers. Her breath caught. My heart pounded. *Don't screw this up, please.* But I probably would.

So I said the thing I'd slurred on the night we killed Blueing, the thing I hadn't wanted to think about saying to Mallory because she hadn't responded after I'd said it, but then again, she'd been a little preoccupied—blood still splattered on her cheekbone—so hey, maybe she hadn't heard me? I just wanted her to know it. It didn't matter what kind of stuff she'd seen. Or done.

"Mallory, I love you."

She squeezed my Hand. Let it go.

"Then don't."

She shoved open the car door, exited, and slammed it shut. Something numbed. Good. Lump in my throat? Nope. Nada. I followed Mallory. What else would I do?

When they fired the electrodes, in whatever cell or lab they'd housed me in, I learned to visualize pain as static, something off another forbidden channel, something I stuffed into an imaginary Coke bottle. If I visualized it hard enough, I could dull the pain to a prickle. Retreat into yourself. They can do anything they want, to your body, but you're always safe inside your head. So, stuff the pain—the sensation, all of it—into a glass vintage Coke bottle. Heft the bottle in your hand. Is it warm from lying on a wooden porch rail on an August afternoon? What color is that porch rail painted? Peeling bubblegum-pink paint? Is it raw red cedar, too new to even splinter? Or, what if the Coke bottle's cold, because it was never outside at all? Is it frigid, condensation pearling on it from the fridge? Pick something. Make up a story. Then, you insert an imaginary cork. Pretend to dig a hole. Is the shovel rusty? New? Painted? The devil's in the details. Literally. Throw in pain-bottle, bury. See each shovelful of dirt, smell the rich loam, nullify numb it make it disappear.

Now it doesn't hurt. Because it's not there.

If you can't make your own imaginary pain relief, store-bought is fine. I prefer Fireball. Kraken Rum. Grey Goose.

We started for the double doors of the bar. It loomed over us, gargantuan, wooden, surrounded by parked Harleys, and lit by neon. A neon sign curved on the building front, *Asphalt Rose,* and a red neon rose accompanied it. Crowds of leather-clad bikers hung around the entrance, smoking and laughing. They ignored Mallory and I, so we returned the favor and went in. A shock wave of noise—chattering, grunting, boots pounding on the wooden floor, Johnny Cash blaring from a jukebox, glasses clinking, yelling—filled my ears. So many people. Never seen that many people in one sitting. I froze. Dimly lit, loud, candy-colored neon flickering on the wooden walls. Enough to give you a seizure. Pool tables in a far corner. Ashtrays overflowed at each table.

Mallory tugged my arm. "C'mon. Let's sit."

"Yeah, sure. Good idea," I said.

She guided me over to a table and plonked a greasy menu in front of me. The only thing greasier in the joint were the fried pickles. Bits of black varnish flaked off the table. My borrowed shoes stuck in congealed puddles of spilled booze on the floor. There were only two ways out—the door we'd come in and another side exit, behind the pool tables. I had to concentrate to find it. Too crowded. Bikers, elderly couples, and a throng of college students loaded this bar. Ten to one odds it was over max capacity. I shook my head, gnawing on my lip.

On each table, a tealight candle burned.

Something prickled the back of my neck. I turned.

Lamiel stared at me from the bar. Same bland face. Black lipstick. He flaunted a leather jacket. His hands writhed with fireflies.

I flinched. Looked down at my menu again. Tried to control the frantic yammering of my pulse. *Maybe he's just out to drink. Or get laid.* Or maybe, just maybe, if I dug through his jacket, I'd find the keys to a mint-green car and two million fireflies. Roy's boss was here. What a great start to this fine evening.

"Look at the bar. See him?" I asked.

Mallory twisted away a little and rested her head in her hand, hair down. Her gaze darted over to Lamiel. Then it lingered over the booze behind the bar. She looked like a bored chick in dire need of shots.

"Met him in the facility. Something's wrong with him. Kept mentioning the work Lorraine made me do. After Roy left, he asked if I wanted a job. Like—"

"Work?" I said.

Mallory's legs shut. Her arms squeezed her chest. Hard.

"Not the killings," she said. "Like—"

She stared at the flaking table.

"Like getting fucked for money."

"You—you were *seven*—"

"Lorraine didn't give a shit if she had a buyer," Mallory said.

Grayout. Faint ringing in my ears.

"They told me Blueing hurt you," I heard myself say.

"Use the right word, Triple-Six," Mallory said, very softly.

My Hands pulsed. A low, nasty anger that'd sparked during the ride over smoldered in my chest.

She turned back to me, leaned in.

"Understand this. He told me about some brothels looking for hookers. Like it was nothing. I'm going to kill him. I'm going to kill Roy Pike. And then, I'm going to *fucking murder* whoever they got to play Lorraine."

No that's my job rip tear protect—

Wait, what? *Throb. Throb.* What the hell was I thinking? Oh, God, *did I even think it at all?* Didn't feel like me. I couldn't breathe. Fizzy bubbles rose up my spine and crackled in my skull. The Hands. I had to get them off. Before something happened. Again.

Had to win the bargain. Then she'd love me.

Black decayed patches polluted Mallory's forearms.

Living Dead Girl.

The first time I met Mallory Worner, she'd waltzed down the dirt road to desert-hell with Blueing, seven years old and already sporting a black eye. I gave her a brochure I'd made before he yanked her away. Even then, her eyes were old as dry wells. I should've seen it. Should've done something.

"I—I, uh, think we need to leave," I said. "Now."

"Why?"

She leaned closer. "Is it because he's here? Because you're in on this?"

Her nose was an inch from mine.

"Why leave, man?"

"We should hole up somewhere safe until the deal's over. Lorraine—"

"*Enough,*" Mallory said.

She slammed a BIC lighter onto the table.

I gritted my teeth. The candle-flame flickered. Lamiel sipped his old-fashioned and glanced at me. He stood.

Mallory's hand brushed her hip. Brushed the .45 tucked under her scrubs.

"Flick the lighter on," she said.

"You're insane. Bring Lorraine here?"

Lamiel looked once, then vanished into the crowd. I gaped.

"He'll be back," Mallory said.

She tilted her head. "Flick the lighter, Project 0666."

"Screw that."

Get shish-kebabbed by Lorraine? Sorry, babe, no deal there.

"I'm not asking," Mallory said.

"What, you're gonna make me?"

"It won't make Lorraine appear. Unless you're in on this. Or they're following you. They might have the actress ready to jump out. If they do? I'll kill her."

No expression on her face. Dead eyes. Her lip twitched up.

"So do it. Prove you're not. End this."

I stood. "No."

"How many electrodes did they use last time? Sixty?"

Seventy-two.

You don't have to take this. Leave. My Hands tingled. *Pulse. Pulse.*

"Do it," Mallory said, and met my gaze. "Or I scream. Right here. In this bar. I'll cry. Pretend you tried to hurt me."

My stomach dropped.

"I'll scream. Everyone here will believe it. Because I'm a cute white chick with freckles." Her voice was like stone. "And you're a giant Arab dude with pincer hands. To them, you're a monster."

"Shut up," I hissed.

I clamped a Hand over my mouth, horrified. Heat building in my chest. Summon Lorraine here and die, or refuse and get slandered publicly. These Texan bikers would beat the shit out of me, then I'd have a nice holding cell to die in when Lorraine caught up. Death now, or death later.

"Flick the lighter. Five seconds, or I scream like a damsel in distress."

A frustrated shriek built in my throat.

She can't pull this if you zap her with the Hands. No, couldn't do that. I wouldn't. But maybe I could lie. I ripped off the bandages over a Hand and gave Mallory the coldest look I had in me. Sweat beaded on my forehead.

"I-I'll get you with the Hands," I choked out.

She didn't so much as blink.

"Five," she said.

I scooped the lighter up. "Mallory. Don't screw with this. Please."
"Four."
"Mallory—"
"Three."
Now she licked her lips. Readying.
"I'm sorry—"
"Two."
I didn't want to put anyone in danger.
"One."
She inhaled.
I flicked the lighter. A flame sprang to life and danced.
Eau de Lori—gasoline, cigarettes, carpet crusted with black mold—wafted around me. A hodgepodge of cheap sparkle bangles and watches clinked on the table. I turned, heart pounding.

Mallory startled.

Lorraine Worner leaned on our table, both hands placed palm-down, gripping it, and loomed over me. She wasn't in her charred corpse form. Low amber light glittered across her eyelids. Cheap silver eyeshadow caked them. A cigarette smoldered between her teeth. Smoke, unfurling up. Her bangles sparkled. Her eyes darted around the bar like a meth-crazed spider.

She grazed the tips of her fingernails against my cheek. "Baby Warden."

"You," Mallory said softly.

Lorraine winked at me. Whipped around. Stalked off into the crowd without saying so much as howdy.

Mallory shook her head, red flushing her cheeks, breathing ragged.

"Babe, that's not—"

"Don't *fucking* lie to me, Project 0666. You planned this. Didn't you?"

"What?"

"Should've known you'd be with them. I'm going to kill her. Don't be here when I'm done. Just don't."

She raced after Lorraine, gun in hand.

And flicked the safety off the .45.

NINETEEN

THEY WOVE IN and out of the crowd like reef sharks. I scrambled after Mallory. Manipulative bullshit or not, nobody deserved to be attacked by Lorraine fucking Worner. Including me, but I'd gotten myself into that mess.

I tucked my exposed arm in as I searched. Hot, drunken bodies banged into me every five feet or so. Waitresses lugged trays laden with beers. The air thickened into hellishness.

Lorraine, ten feet ahead. Her rhinestone bangles caught the light. Mallory edged closer, red neon bathing her in light like blood. Red glittered off her moist lips. She held the .45 low. They stalked over by the pool table just as a cute bleach blonde lowered a tray of drinks. Lorraine lunged at Mallory. Shoved her at the server. The tray flew out of the server's hands. Drinks exploded on the floor. Alcohol baptized it, spilling in long puddled lines by the cramped exit. Drunks groaned. Booze dripped off of Mallory's face and arms. The server blurted out some apology, but Mallory kept her eyes fixed on Lorraine. Lorraine plonked a spare stool down in front of the exit. Then she saw me. Smirked. Swerved for the front entrance.

"—So, so sorry! Wait, is…is that a *gun*?"

"No. Move," Mallory said, stepping forward.

The cute blonde server blocked her. "What is *wrong* with you?"

Time to use those fabled people skills.

"Babe," I panted, "why don't we get your other shirt out of the car, and wipe some of this off? Leave the toy gun."

Please don't skin me alive, Mallory. Her glare could've melted glass. I lifted my eyebrows so she'd get the hint. She opened her mouth. Then closed it.

She giggled and slurred out, "But the other one's so *boring*."

I blinked. The cute-girl impression was jarring. Blondie turned to me.

Saw my Hands. She recoiled, stepped back but caught herself and pasted on a smile that didn't reach above her nose.

"Let's get you cleaned up, babe," I said.

I winked at the waitress, and she moved aside. Mallory went over to me, smiling. She grabbed my wrist so hard I almost yelped. Glass broke somewhere up front. We ran towards it.

Lorraine emerged from the crowd, weaving back. She hadn't tried to kill me yet, which seemed worse somehow. Alarm bells rang in my brain.

"Mallory. You should go—"

"Follow me again, and I scream," she said.

Mallory bolted before I could respond. Lorraine beelined for a swinging door on the far wall. An acid-green neon sign over it read *Employees Only*. Beer morphed to sticky glue between my non-existent fingers. I wobbled over to the door, Johnny Cash blaring all around. Pans clattered behind it and mixed with the sizzle of frying grease. I shoved my way in.

Everyone, from the Pope to crack addicts stealing from Nana, has two seconds that changed them forever. Not always for the better. You know your two seconds. Everybody's got at least one. Veterans have dozens.

These are the things that breathe under your skull at night.

One Mississippi. Two Mississippi.

An aproned, rickety-built woman hunched over the deep fryer. Strands of sweat-caked gray hair peeked out from a hairnet, the tips of it dyed an acidic green. It almost vibrated against her sallow skin. Crow's-feet obscured her eyes. Moles mottled the aged right half of her face, but not her left. Some union logo keychain dangled from her black jeans pocket—jeans gone almost as gray as her hair, from laundering. *Teamster. That's a teamster logo, with the horse, someone's a trucker, maybe her husband, maybe her.*

Half the kitchen fluorescents were burned out. Raw, sliced meat bled on a cutting board by the grill top. Heat baked off it even from where I stood. The circuit breaker box on the far wall looked old. Knives glinted on a magnetic wall strip. Dead flies dotted the inside of the fluorescent plastic. Striped horseflies droned over the grill.

Lorraine Worner skulked behind the cook. Mallory reached for her, one hand poised.

The cook turned back to the meat. Weird white things were in her ears— *are those earbuds? Where's the cord?*—something rainbow, some teeny-tiny rainbow flag pin glinted on her apron strap. Cook grabbed a handful of meat. Snatched up some, maybe to throw it on the grill.

Lorraine ghosted over to the fryer. Plunged her bare hand into boiling oil. Scooped up a handful, face serene. The cook turned back. Her eyes snapped open. Her lip snarled up, throat worked—

Lorraine flung the deep fryer oil into the woman's face.

She shrieked. Blisters bubbled over her skin. She clawed her hands to her face, staggering. Sizzling filled the air. Smell of cooked meat. Porkish. *Oh god oh fuck.* Pork.

Lorraine yanked a knife off the strip. She pounced. Knocked the cook to the floor—*whump.* Straddled her, knife in hand—

"*Hey!*" Mallory called.

Lorraine tilted the cook's head back and slit open her heaving throat, one smooth motion. The wound gaped. Like Blueing's. Blood bubbled out. The cook, still trying to scream. An odd, choking rasp. Blood spurted out of her neck and melded with the bits of rotten chicken and crumbs ground into the grout of the tile floor. Her hair soaked up blood, mixing the red with the green, *Christmas colors,* except this wasn't Christmas and she was still alive and she couldn't see because the blisters had bulged over most of her eye sockets, she was blisters now, steam rose from her face. A mask of blisters.

Lorraine stood, whirled, ripped a paper towel off, and stepped back to the fryer. Dipped it into the still-hot oil.

I sprinted over to the dying woman on the floor. I cradled her head with my good Hand. Through the maze of blisters, we locked eyes. Hers were blue, dull antique blue, but then they glazed over. Dead.

Mallory raised her .45. "Get on the fucking ground. Who hired you? Who are you?"

Lorraine snarled, "Dumbass kid. I ain't anyone else. I'm *Lorraine fuckin' Worner.*"

"Mallory. Run."

Her jaw worked. She didn't look at me. Her finger wrapped around the trigger. Lorraine twitched—

Boiling oil flew at Mallory's face. She ducked. Stray droplets landed on her cheek. She hissed, jaw working. Her eyes squinched shut.

Lorraine tore the gun out of her hand. Tossed it on the floor. Mallory scrabbled for it, skin blanching more by the second. Pink weals formed on her neck, her freckled skin dirty with fryer oil and sweat. I lunged for the gun—

Warm skin.

I'd touched her hand as we both scrambled for the gun.

Oh, shit!

I flinched away. Accidentally hit Mallory's left leg as I did. Mallory's left arm had already started to spasm. Her left leg went limp. Now Mallory couldn't stand. Or walk. Or run.

Lorraine grabbed her daughter by the throat. "Ain't this nice? I can touch you now. And you got a lil' boyfriend. Want me to bring out the baby pictures?"

"You're not real," Mallory rasped. "Lorraine's dead."

"Oh, I'm dead. Now I ain't real? You thought that was how it worked? Bless your heart."

She threw Mallory down. Spat on her. Lorraine cracked open the microwave. Threw in the knife, a fork, and the oily paper towel. She pressed cook. The microwave hummed to life. Sparks exploded inside, hungry to ignite. Mallory slowly turned over.

"I'm going to kill you," she said.

"Again?" Lorraine said. "Ain't that sweet? Your little boyfriend know you threw me in the fuckin' chair?"

Mallory said nothing.

"He know you killed me? Sold me down the fuckin' river?"

Lorraine pulled off one of her bangles. But—not a bangle. It was a man's watch, attached to a thin rhinestone strap. She waved it in front of Mallory's face.

"Remember hidin' this one?"

Oh God.

Lorraine's "bangles." They were trophies. Rhinestone-dripping, bedazzled trophies. Her arms were covered in them.

"Remember him? Remember how his brains looked after you blew his head off?"

"He wasn't—I had to. You—she was gonna kill him anyway."

"We gotta go through them baby pictures one of these days," Lorraine said, and looked at me. "All three of us."

The gun sat only five feet away. I could slide it over to Mallory, but it wouldn't do much good. Not if boiling oil didn't faze Lorraine. Or waist-high flames. Or getting run over by a truck.

Microwave would explode soon. If we got lucky. The realization hit me. The booze spilled over the floor. Spilled by the exits. Lorraine, standing in front of the circuit box. The lights. The A/C. All the people trapped inside.

Lorraine was orchestrating one of her infamous arsons.

No. This ended here.

"Lorraine," I said. "Kill me. Get this over with. End our bargain. You don't have business with anyone else."

She dumped fryer oil on the ground. "Who the hell told you that? Eddie?"

Mallory crawled for the gun. Crackling sounds came from the sparking microwave. Lorraine continued throwing handfuls of deep fryer oil around, like a kid hurling water balloons. A vacant grin spread over her face. She let out a giggle.

Man, first the gas station, and now this?

She reminded me of Blueing. It was like...she didn't even have real emotions or pain, just this endless cycle of shallow states. Always externally based. There's a fire? Time to fap, time to fuck, time to have fun. There's my only kid, who's apparently the reason I'm dead? Time to snarl out some insults and hurt something. Oh, look, there's some dipshit I can make a bad deal with. Time to bargain, time for fun. Rinse, repeat. There was...*nothing,* really, inside her.

Dude, what do you think "sociopath" means? Mallory had snapped when we were both sixteen, and I asked her what that meant, because Dr. Hitch had called her a sociopath, said she was just a sociopath like her mother, that she was empty inside and would always be.

She says you're like that, I'd said. *How can someone be empty inside? What does that even MEAN?*

That's what a sociopath is. Don't listen to the true-crime bullshit about them, or the therapist hug-boxing about "personality disorders." Sociopaths don't feel things. They're shallow, physical people, because that's the only human thing they can relate to. Physical things. Sex, drugs, rock 'n' roll.

They're not masterminds? I'd said.

Most of them can't look past the next twenty-four hours, man. They have no capacity for impulse control. Can't plan, won't plan...they're an appetite shaped like a human being.

You don't seem like that. They said you just had BPD, that's different.

And she'd looked at me, with those black shark's eyes of hers, and she'd said, *What do you know about me?*

Mallory picked up the gun. She aimed, mouse-quiet.

Lorraine strode over to the circuit breaker box, opened it, and studied me. "Don't bitch. I'm givin' you what you really wanted all along."

What?

Mallory fired.

The bullet phased right through the center of Lorraine Worner's skull and dug into the far wall.

"No," Mallory said. "No, no, no. This can't—"

Lorraine hit the breaker. Everything plunged into darkness.

Distant screams from the bar. A hysterical laugh. Stagnant, greasy air choked me. The microwave crackled. Dim orange light spilled out, cutting into the black.

Lorraine lit a match on her thumbnail.

Mallory wiped her eyes. Too close to the oil about to burst into flame. The Hands itched. Then Mallory's arm went dead and slumped to the floor. She moaned. Gaze unfocused. *Blank episode?* Shit, this too? I ran over to

Mallory and tried to drag her. Her legs sagged like wet lead noodles. Her feet trailed through the cooling puddle of the dead cook's blood. Blood drenched our arms. It daubed Mallory's forearms and hands. She just lay there, practically comatose, as I lugged her. Goosebumps crazed over her skin.

"You okay?"

She didn't respond.

Lorraine threw the match. It landed on the oil-soaked floor. Fire curled, gobbling up the oil, spreading. The burning stench of meat intensified. Blisters exploded as the flames drew closer to the cook's cadaver. Lymph dribbled down her face like candle wax. Blood boiled as it heated. Her hair caught. Fire crowned her head, shriveled the hairnet into nothing. The steel tables, the cutting boards, the fryer vat sat, engulfed in fire. Burning plastic melted. Noxious smoke. I hacked.

Lorraine Worner, eyes closed, head relaxed like she'd taken a trip to Hell's sauna, hair glittering in the firelight, stood unburned in the center of the inferno.

I scooped up Mallory. My arms screamed and shook, but I held on. She didn't complain.

I bolted out into the darkness, into the seething crush of panicked bodies.

WHOOMH! The microwave exploded. The door blew open. Fire clawed out of the doorframe and caught the booze puddled on the floor.

The screams worsened.

TWENTY

PANIC. ACRID, SWEAT-DRENCHED smoke in my nose and mouth. Someone pushed me from behind and I stumbled. Caught myself. *Get the people out! Protect. Protect*, and the word pulsed in time with my Hands. *Protect*.

I wobbled towards the pool table exit. "Mallory? You doing okay?"

She grunted. "L-Lorraine's dead. She's dead. I killed her. I saw the tape."

Okay, that's a no. I shifted her weight in my arms. I coughed.

People clustered around the blocked door, shoving and panting and screaming. Flames licked along the edges of the frame. A thin trickle of cool air blew in. The exit door was cracked open.

Living bodies wedged in the frame and stuck fast. About to broil alive. Guttural yelps came from the blockage of people. Smoke poured out. Soon it'd reek like hair, like charred meat, like tallow. *Like fucking death, Project 0666. That's what a person burning smells like. Never, ever ask me again.*

I'd asked Mallory that one summer.

"Move," I wheezed.

Nobody moved, except to shove. That wouldn't work. Fantastic. I half-shoved my way to the front. Heat built. Had to get out. Pulses throbbed in my Hands, zinging up to my shoulders. Sweat dribbled down my back and face. I tasted salt, copper.

Up front, the neon light was blocked by another crush of bodies.

"Tripoli," Mallory said. "Tripoli Hospital all over again."

One hundred and seven casualties. Mallory had a picture stowed away that some newspaper had taken of the fire. She never showed it to anyone. *Lorraine's in the crowd of rubberneckers, watching her handiwork. She's... rubbing one out as it burns. She's got her hand down her pants, Triple-Six. It's* disgusting. The feds got so busy looking for male suspects that they didn't see it until later. Much later.

Gunshots cracked through the glass door.

Holy shit! Shit!

I dropped. Mallory slipped. Her head tilted up as my chin dipped down. Our faces thumped against each other, bruising my lips. Her teeth clacked. Red lines between her bottom teeth. *Blood. From when she bit off Sedative Guy's finger.*

A man screamed. Someone sobbed, repeating in a manic garble, *The rosebushes. The rosebushes won't get planted.* In the pile of trapped bodies, a brunette woman struggled at the bottom, waving her arms like a drowning child, her acrylic nails kept catching the light, *clear talons,* clear plastic talons and the firelight kept shining through them, amber fingers. The other bodies writhed as one. One mass of flesh. The brunette struggled like a fly in amber. She raked her nails over a twenty-something girl's arm, who was above her in the pile. Gouges bled. The arm hung there, limp and dead, as she clawed at it. Flesh slithered under the plastic talons.

Another gunshot cracked.

Everyone who could move hit the floor. People crouched and lay face-down, faces streaked with tears and snot. In the primitive firelight, in the half-dark, through the smoke, a bearded dude in a yellow neon cowboy hat and matching leather vest looked up from his spot on the floor and patted his hip. Feeling for a holster. His white beard had been braided into two plaits. Red pony beads studded the braids. He drew his gun but didn't aim. He cocked his head. Closed his eyes.

I left Neon Cowboy to it. The people had stopped jockeying for the doors. The pathway was clear. Gunshots or not, I could heal. I readjusted Mallory, straightened up, and strode towards the exit. Had to try and get some of those people out of the body-pile. Who the hell had decided to fire into a crowd of people trying to escape from a burning building? Where were the wounded? No blood yet. I reached the door. Looked down at Mallory. Her pupils dilated and softened. Through the thin fabric of our shirts, her heart pounded against mine.

Focus, dipshit.

I coughed. "I'm gonna have to put you down to help the people trapped in the doorframe—"

"Triple-Six—"

Shards of glass crashed on the floor. I scanned. No blood, no pained cries.

"Okay, there's a table I can—"

"There's another exit. I remember. It's through the employee break room, back between the restrooms. By the front. See?"

"You remember?"

She coughed up a wad of brownish phlegm. "Lorraine. She took us here. Almost burned this place down. But she chose—"

Mallory hacked again. "—But she chose an old oil derrick instead. Could've been a power station. It was the Wirework Place, that was what I named it. She took us here. We used the employee break exit."

"We can't leave these people to burn."

"Course not. We go outside, help from outside. C'mon, man. We can't help if we're dead, too."

"But—"

"You have a better option?" Mallory said.

I'm just remembering the last time you had to show me something, babe. Just kind of wondering if you're having a psycho spell and luring me into a corner. Just a little bit. You want the fire to roast me alive and then you'll nosh on me a bit, just like your mom. You guys could make a box set of cooking videos—The Worner Clan: Human Flesh BBQ! Family Fun!

"C'mon. Get back to reality. We're in a burning fucking building. Get your ass to the break room, *Project 0666*."

It jolted me back. She never, ever called me Project 0666 unless something was *wrong*. She'd only done it four times, ever. I never ever called her Mallory *Worner*.

"Point to it," I said.

She did. The bathroom sign glowed in hot-pink cursive above a little hallway to the left of the front door. I stepped over a few people. Dead or alive. Didn't know. Smoke flooded the top of the hallway. I hunched over. Entered.

Mallory rasped, "It's the middle door. Between the men's and lady's rooms."

Beside us, the hallway gaped. Wooden push doors caught the firelight outside and gleamed, varnish thick as window glass. I groped across the doors.

A warm metal knob met my Hand.

I turned it. It opened.

Darkness. Unlit, except for an *exit* sign beaconing the far wall. So dark, the exit sign practically hung there in the blackness. I staggered through. The break room was empty, the air relatively clean and chilled. I sucked in whooping lungfuls of it. Something fever-warm stroked my cheek in the darkness.

"Babe?"

But she didn't answer.

"Babe, is that you? Or is it—"

Lorraine Worner chuckled. Inches away from my face. Invisible in the darkness. The reek of her swirled around, all cigarettes and gasoline and decay...marred by something sweet-smelling. Fake coconut and pineapple.

"I'm horny, Baby Warden. Might wanna fuck somethin'. Maybe you."

"Because you didn't fuck me hard enough the first time with that bargain bullshit?"

"Ain't my fault you rushed into it."

"I don't have time for this," I said, and started running for the exit.

"I'm hoooorrrny, honey," she hollered, then her voice shifted to Mallory's. "I'm so horny, man. I need you, right here. Right now. C'mere. C'mere, Triple-Six. I love you."

I love you.

Heat rose through my chest.

That's NOT Mallory. That's Lorraine. Get your shit together and save the people!

I bolted through the exit door, shoving it out. Mallory shivered in my arms. The night baptized us, humid and warm as blood. Tinged with smoke.

"Don't move, Project 0666," Roy Pike said.

He'd been waiting outside the door. He stood in front of us, revolver in hand. Blood droplets flecked Roy's mustache, beading the white. Lamiel was nowhere in sight.

Mallory stiffened. "Roy fucking Pike. Of course."

"Miss Worner. Still settin' fires? Still seeing your mother?"

"There are people trapped inside. I have to help them," I said, keeping my voice steady. "Let's focus on that, and if you're still dead set on killing us after, we can have a duel or something. Deal? Did you even call 911? Roy, there are people *wedged in the door frames, burning alive.*"

He snorted. His mustache twitched. "People die all the time, son."

"Was that what you said when Lorraine was out killing people in the nineties and aughts, and a seven-year-old had to solve your own case for you? Huh? Human beings matter. People are *dying in that building, Roy!*"

My voice broke at the end.

Pulse. Pulse. Pulse.

Exterminate the obstacle. Kill it. Move it. Exterminate, put innocent down, run into building, pry victims out—*I need more space, I need to move*—pulsing, pulsing up my arms.

"Listen to how you're sayin' that. As if you ain't. Human."

Energy screamed through my legs. Run. Charge the obstacle. Eliminate obstacle.

"Oh, dear. What are you doing with that gun?" Lamiel said, striding out of the night.

A vortex of fireflies crowned the air above his skull. He blinked at us, as if this whole thing was some dinner party he'd shown up late to. He cut off any escape to the right. Roy shifted, flanking my left. Behind me was the door and the burning down *Asphalt Rose*. Crackling split the night, along with an occasional scream. The screams wavered as if from the bottom of a pit.

The inferno. They're at the bottom, in an inferno, and they're dying.

Roy aimed the revolver at my chest. "Put Miss Worner down, Project 0666. Nice and slow. I know this looks bad, but I'm not killin' you. Not really. You close your eyes, and you'll wake up in bed, back at home."

"No," Mallory said.

She strangled her arm and good leg around me. She had her gun clutched in her good hand. "I'll never let him go."

"Fine, Miss Worner. I'll shoot him now. The bullet will phase right through you, 'cause you're human. He's not. Or should I say, *it's* not. Project 0666 is an it. Nothing more than a perverted fusion of energy and flesh—"

"Roy Alexander Pike," Lamiel snapped, "Enough of that nonsense. Clean up your experiment, and then we're going home."

"Close your eyes, Miss Worner," Roy said.

"No. You can't—"

"Project 0666 is bein' terminated."

"You're gonna shoot someone unarmed?" Mallory asked.

He glanced down for a half-second. "It's only a—"

"You call Triple-Six an *it* again, and I'll rip your tongue out," Mallory said softly. "Trust me. I know how to make it…take a while. What do you think I'll do to you if you shoot him?"

Pulse. Pulse. Pulse.

My pulse drowned out the chaos around me. The gun, my Hands, Roy Pike—nothing else existed. Roy took a step back. Shut one eye. Took aim.

BANG!

The exit door banged open, gunshot-loud, and Lorraine stormed out, hands on her hips.

Roy startled—

I body-slammed the guy. Mallory's weight helped. He grunted. His grip on the revolver loosened. I tore it out of his hand, shoving it into my waistband. Roy kicked out at my shin. I sidestepped, panting.

Roy Pike spread his hands. Blue fire gathered between them. Familiar blue fire.

Without saying a word, Lamiel moved to block my right. Roy blocked my escape to the front. Lorraine the undead serial killer crept closer, the heat of her body tickling my back.

And inside the *Asphalt Rose*, screaming. Burning people. Melting people. Human beings who were dying because of my stupid, idiotic bargain with Lorraine Worner.

I've gotta get out of here I've gotta get out of here I've gotta get out of here—

I mentally repeated it even as everyone closed around me. My arms ached. I couldn't hold Mallory much longer. The pulses running through the Hands quickened, growing sweet yet painful. They heated.

Click-click.

Mallory cocked and aimed her gun at Roy Pike's head.

"Miss Worner," Roy said. "Take my gun from Project 0666. He won't hurt you. Hand it over right quick."

Sirens blared in the night. Getting closer. Someone had called 911. Good. Now it wasn't my problem. Around us, dead grass rustled. A person or two staggered out of the front exit and collapsed. Smoke heated my back, swirling out from the employee break exit. The fire. It'd spread there, too.

I have to get out of here, I have to get out of here, I have to get them out of here, I have to…

Roy's voice softened, "I'll give you your freedom, Mallory. Cash. A new identity. Protection from Lorraine."

I tensed. Because he was right. Mallory could take the magic gun from me, toss it to Roy, and I'd sit and watch her do it.

Her jaw set. "No."

"I see," Roy said.

Lorraine caressed the back of my neck, skin scabrous. Flakes of her sloughed off and fell down my T-shirt. *She's in her Fun Corpse form. She wants to rape me. I'm pretty sure she put it on special for the occasion.*

"C'mere, Honeydoll," Lorraine whispered, "You run back inside with me. Don't let Pike shoot you. We'll have a lotta fun. Put my spawn down and c'mere."

Heat. Wetness. Something wet slicked down the back of my neck, starting at the hairline, teasing down. Her breasts nudged into me. She ground into me, smelling like an ashtray, and of fake coconut and pineapple, and ran her tongue down the back of my neck again.

Bleakly, I realized I was hard.

I've gotta get out of here I've gotta get out of here I've gotta get out of here—

I felt something.

Physical pressure in the Hands. Was I holding something? *What the—* But I held nothing. Nothing I could see…it felt like squeezing invisible, oily fabric.

I almost dropped Mallory. Roy Pike lunged. I slashed the air on pure instinct.

Snagged something. *Good. Familiar.*

Electricity zinged up my arm as I tore. Everything moved slowly.

I tore a blood-red rift into the air.

It glowed faintly crimson, and it *pulsed-pulsed* like a squeezed heart. A slit—no wider than my Hand—dilated out into a dark hole, lined with scarlet light. *Look, Ma, I made neon.*

Had I gone crazy for real? No. No, my hallucinations made more sense than this. At least those titties were from hot succubi, not peeling electrified undead serial killers.

Lorraine hissed. "I ain't goin' back. Never again."

"What?"

Holy shit. Was this *Hell*? Had I opened a *literal portal to Hell*? An icy gush of air blew out of the rift. Not hot at all. Goosebumps broke out on my arms. Where was the fire? The pitchfork-wielding demons? Screams of the damned?

Apparently the damned all had laryngitis.

It reeked like ozone and rain.

"You seeing this, too?" Mallory asked.

Cords stood out on Roy's arms as the blue fire he held intensified.

Mallory pointed. "Triple-Six—"

"I know," I said.

Certain death here, and probable death—or worse—in the literal portal to Hell. What a wealth of options.

Roy huffed. Roy shot three blue fireballs at me. They ripped through the night. I ducked. They sputtered out on the gravel. Lorraine rebounded, her dirt-brown hair streaming behind her, tangled and livid.

I ran into the Hell-rift, with my semi-girlfriend, semi-cannibal in tow.

Lorraine followed close behind.

TWENTY-ONE

TRY LUGGING A pretty girl with a dead leg. Try doing it when you've got scrawny arms streaked with demonic aching veins, pincers for hands, and oh yeah, you've got a cigarette burn a'sizzling on your neck, a slice across your ribs, and a pulped-up face. Your adrenaline's almost burned out. Add one undead serial killer chasing after you, subtract sanity.

Now try doing that with a nail gun going to town against your forehead.

Hell felt bad.

At first.

The second I hurtled into the rift, sharp stabbing pain erupted on my forehead. It dulled as I ran through darkness. Rift squished shut. I heard Mallory's sharp inhale as she tensed. She was in pain, too. Ozone-stench filled every scrap of the blackness. I sprinted through it. Footsteps clunked behind me. Lorraine apparently got over her reservations about Hell.

Energy danced in the air. It pulsed to the same beat as my poor head. The Hands glowed red. Light danced in the freakshow veins, like neon arcing. A ghostly chain spiraled out of the cigarette burn on my throat, emitting scarlet light. It was thin as one of Ma's necklaces. It terminated somewhere behind me. It tugged as I ran.

The ritual bond. It's the bargain, made visible.

Which meant it connected to Lorraine. How could I hide from her now? Could I even run away? Didn't matter. I kept running.

What does she want, anyway? To kill me, rape me, or eat me?

Silence of the Lambs came back to me: *All of the above, but maybe in a different order.*

Then, in the distance, below me: grape-colored light.

No. It can't be.

The pain ebbed down to a tingle. *Pulse. Pulse.* I hotfooted it towards the purple light, it was at the bottom of a hill, glowing in the night. Arms screamed, legs burned. Mallory wiped her nose on my shirt and sniffled. Hot mucus seeped through cotton. Just over the hill. It was always just over a hill.

I'd been here before.

Ran down. Eau de Lorraine wafted closer. She panted behind me. Hit the bottom. Close. I looked forward.

Naamah's Pleasure Palace!

Violet neon tubes curled into a massive sign. In pink, just below, it proclaimed, *No Cover Fee! GIRLS! GIRLS!* A line of dimly lit bodies and hulking forms circled the strip club, laughing, muttering, shifting as I sprinted closer.

Naamah's made great chicken fingers.

A six foot auburn goddess with horns and nipple tape guarded the door. She tsk-tsked over a clipboard. Was this Candy? Or was she Crystal? But this couldn't be the place, not here, not now, because this place wasn't *real*.

Right? It'd always been a fever dream.

I shoved past the line. Got complaints. Returned shoves. Lorraine got knocked back and cursed somewhere behind me.

I yanked the door open. "Sorry!"

Candy *growled*. I ran a step inside before she grabbed my arm, glowing freakazoid veins and all. She yanked me to a halt.

No effect. None.

Skin chilled against mine.

"Hey! Wait out—"

Her too-amber eyes widened.

"Oh, my. Mister Mysterious. You're back again."

"We're at a strip club, man? She has horns? You're seeing this?" Mallory rasping, voice still rough from smoke and crying.

"Yeah," I wheezed.

So who's crazy now, huh?

Candy brushed her pillowy hooker lips against my ear and breathed, "And you finally brought *all of you*."

Lorraine's footsteps crunched. I concentrated every ounce of willpower on not popping another boner, please Jesus have mercy. Not in front of Mallory. Not now. I'd gone soft during the running, and I really, really didn't need another confusion-induced boner right now. Not after Fun Corpse Lorraine. Her spit still cooled on the back of my neck.

"Uh, Candy? I'm in a hurry here," I said.

Candy leaned back, grinding her double D-cups against me as she did. She let go.

"Here for the meeting?"

"Wha—yeah. Yeah, totally."

"I thought you'd be a Hell Warden," she purred, "Big head-honcho. See us more often, will you?"

"Who the fuck is this?" Mallory asked.

"Where's the meeting?" I said.

"Back behind the stage, baby."

"Thanks," I said, and sprinted.

Thump. Thump. Footsteps over glossy granite floor. Violet and hot-pink and acid-yellow reflections glittered. The stage. I turned.

Holy God I'm in heaven.

Oiled women. Boobs. Toned asses. Taut tanned muscles working hard in all the right places. They ground and spun around the poles on the stage, *Jesus,* was that one full-on nude? Yes, oh yes. She pouted at the audience. She was rubbing her wet glistening vulva on the pole, the pink of it just visible, clit peeking out, pink nipples rock hard, pink lips, gleaming ebony hair—black pubic stubble—barefoot onstage. Said stage was a bed of coals. Heat radiated.

Shit. I'm hard.

"You came here. Didn't you?" Mallory said, voice barely audible. "It's—it's all real." Something hot spread through my back. Pain. I stumbled. Turned. Mallory latched her arms around my neck like a barnacle.

Lorraine. She sprang again.

I jumped back. Ran. Had to get back behind the stage. Mallory's weight shifted. I caught her. Lurking things chuffed irritably at their tables. We were blocking the view, so fair enough. I hotfooted it. So did Lorraine. *Wheeze. Wheeze.* Sweat drenched my *Blue Lobster* shirt. My arms were numb.

Behind the stage. A hallway painted black, lit by a single dangling bulb. Black-painted doors, three in a row. One slightly propped open.

A voice like a chain-smoking lumberjack's rasped out, "...Need to know. I won't give out specifics."

"Just bloody tell me."

Blueing.

"Tell me how Lorraine Worner managed to secure that bargain, Blueing. Again," the voice said.

"Said I was sorry, didn't I? I have a bloody plan."

Had to be it. *Sure, go into a meeting from Hell. That worked out great last time.*

Lorraine had almost hit the hallway. No time. *Maybe if you let her kill you, she won't hurt Mallory.*

"Babe?"

Mallory shook her head. Beads of sweat trickled down her nose.

"She said she'd come back and kill me she said she'd come back she said she'd *come back*," she whispered. "She always said she'd come back and I didn't believe her because she was dead and I killed her, I killed her, *I fucking killed her—*"

What else had Lorraine done to Mallory?

Pulse. Pulse. Pulse. Boiling heat rushed through me, savage and sweet.

Time to keep going.

I kicked the door open. Shoved it shut. Whirled around.

Edward Sal Blueing sat at a metal table, facing what could only be described as Satan. Imagine discount-horror-flick Satan, sans goat legs. You know. Vivid red skin, massive horns, a hulking six foot nine dude with more muscle than a coroner's coterie. Slitted yellow eyes. Actual talons. No cape for him, though. Satan wore a rumpled button-up with a metal badge. He had normal fucking hands. How'd I draw the short end of the cosmic stick there?

Blueing and Satan didn't even bother looking at us.

"Possession is hard," Satan said. "Unless you know them, love them, hate them, et cetera."

"But Dunkirk—"

"*Warden* Dunkirk."

The door ghosted open. Lorraine eased her way in. Her gaze flicked over to Blueing and Dunkirk. She froze.

"Fine, mate. Warden Dunkirk," Blueing said. "What about that border-jumper a few decades back? Isn't the bugger still roaming around?"

Dunkirk sipped something out of a mug. Cracked leather restraints littered the metal table. A large window showed a great view of the ladies on stage, but he didn't even glance up.

"Technically, it wasn't possession," he said.

"Something from here's running the show, mate. Sounds like possession to me."

"It wasn't."

"I'd need ingredients to possess some bloke or his corpse, then. What kind?"

Possession?

Mallory dry-heaved.

Lorraine crept closer. Her smell strengthened. Stale cigarette smoke, gasoline, mold—a whiff of fake piña colada sugarcoating it. Air rushed over the back of my neck. Within grabbing distance.

"Hey, Eddie?" I said.

"You! You're—but mate, you're supposed to be *dead*," Blueing said.

I felt Lorraine tense behind me. *Rub it in. Rile her up.*

"What can I say? Lori's about as dumb as you told me."

His eyes flitted to her. He swallowed, hard.

"Bless your heart, Eddie," Lorraine said, voice deadly soft.

Blueing stood. "You can't hurt me now. Don't even try."

Fireworks already. I edged over to the wall. How'd I open the rift-thing last time?

"Ain't you heard?" Lorraine said. "Struck a bargain with my Baby Warden. I git to have fun before it's over. Can touch whatever the hell I wanna, Eddie."

Okay, slash through the air with a Hand. How hard could that be? I tried it. Nothing. Nada.

No way out of Hell.

"Worner. Return immediately—"

"Ain't gonna."

She stalked over to Blueing.

Don't panic. Think, dummy. My stomach churned. Last time, I'd felt something invisible. The Hands had pulsed. I'd been panicked. I'd been mentally screaming, *I've gotta get outta here.*

"You tried to fuck me over, Eddie. I should fuckin' gut you. Lord knows I'm fixin' to."

Blueing balled his fists, but they shook. "Conniving bitch. Pity you didn't go trekking through the Outback in '82."

"Lots to burn there, Eddie."

"Small women were my favorite, luv. Like you. Easy corpses to move 'round. Had it down to a science by then."

I've gotta get outta here I've gotta get outta here get to a motel get to motel—

Dull heat throbbed in the Hands. Exhaustion slammed me. I staggered. Could I even do this again? But then I felt it. Not-silk, tickling in my palm. Slimy. More of a membrane. Like sticking my Hand into a bowl of cut okra.

Ask discount Satan for help? Nope.

"Listen to me, you two-bit fuckin' amateur," Lorraine said. "I got eight folks in my roster before I turned *seventeen*. Without countin' the ones I fried in the sixty-seven fires I'd done. I'd know—had a lil' notebook I wrote all this shit down in. So—"

Blueing opened his mouth to speak, but she cut him off.

"—All I'm sayin', Eddie, is that I got more books written about me than you got murders."

I reached out. Snagged the membrane. Tried to tear it. I couldn't. Like trying to cut through a lead blanket with a butter knife. Dunkirk stared. Sweat beaded. Blackness expanded around the edges of my vision.

"I can't," I said. "Shit. I can't do it."

"Focus. Don't panic," Mallory said.

She pecked my cheek. It tingled where her lips touched.

"Don't look at them. They're not there."

"Help me kill my spawn, and I'll call us square, Eddie—"

"Don't call me that."

Ignore them. Inhale. I forced another inch into the rift. It gaped open a foot. Exhale. Black dots swam in my vision. Good for them. I kept tearing. The momentum built. The rift grew. *Motel. Get to a motel.* Within the rift, halogen light cut through darkness. I shifted my palm, smearing blood over the rift. It sliced open the rest of the way, like a red-hot knife through butter. Easy-peasy. *The blood.* This poor Hand was the one I'd cut in the ritual. Magic blood.

Lorraine's eyes widened, then narrowed. "Ah, shit. Blueing. Mr. Beelzebub. Grab the Baby Warden. Both y'all. Git him. You don't git ahold of him before he enters that, you won't know where he's gone. Unless—"

She ran at us.

I beelined through Door Number Two.

The rift began to heal itself.

Not quickly enough. She clawed her arm through the shrinking hole, got a handful of my shirt. I slapped it. Hard. She chuckled.

"She always comes back," Mallory said dully.

Mallory clubbed Lorraine with the .45, but it phased through her. Like a ghost. No dice. Lorraine got her other arm through. The rift stopped closing. An automatic door situation?

I crumbled to my knees, concrete scraping them. I couldn't open another rift. Not again. If she got through here, we'd be fucked. I picked open the cuts on my chest and palm, blood oozing out. Slathered it on the rift. *Close. Seal. Whatever, just stop existing.*

It started to close again. Lorraine's arm slithered back into Hell—

What would happen if this rift closed on her arm?

I seized her wrist. She yanked back. I held harder. The rift shrank, only an inch away from snapping shut on Lorraine's elbow.

Another tug, more force. "Git off me!"

Half-inch.

"But she's not—"

Mallory reached into the rift. It dilated as she did, exposing a sliver of Lorraine's face. She touched Lorraine's cheek. It remained solid. Mallory ran her thumb over the matching burn scar. Lorraine jerked back and bit Mallory's hand.

Mallory hissed. Blood oozed out, coating Lorraine's teeth and lips in gore. Lorraine released Mallory's hand, leering. I yanked Mallory back.

The edges of the rift licked Lorraine's arm, making a sizzling noise. Her drawl grew distant and pained. "Y'all go *fuck yourselves.*"

I released. Her arm retreated back into the rift, but bits of skin scraped off. The rift skinned it like a handcuff lined with razors. *Oh, Jesus.* Her muscle glistened beneath the scraps of skin and fat that had been carved off. Like a discarded opera glove, a tube of skin slopped to the cement. Blood glazed the interior of the skin, over a layer of cream-colored fat. Yum-yum, y'all. Skinned serial killer arm.

I dry-heaved.

I collapsed. Mallory landed on top of me. Her ribcage bashed into mine. In the lemon-yellow light of some motel sign, I glanced down at the Hands.

"I'm sorry, I never wanted her, or the her inside me to…." Mallory said, right before I passed out.

TWENTY-TWO

SOMETHING PECKED MY poor cheek. I groaned. Twitched. Just what I needed, Lorraine back for Round Two. Then it pecked again, and I opened my eyes.

Mallory was craned over me, poking, her hair tickling my forehead. "Triple-Six. C'mon. Wake up. Please."

Concrete bit into my elbows as I sat up, and a sharp bolt of pain ricocheted in my skull. Everything ached. Still semi-dark out, so it hadn't been long. I'd bit it right in front of a motel. The yellow sign once said, *Solo Motel*, probably in the seventies. Now, it read *So Mote*. Cigarette butts littered the ground. Used needles glinted in the streetlamp light. Jizz stained a discarded red satin thong, pungent even from ten feet away.

"Oh...Jesus, where are we?"

Strain leached into Mallory's voice.

"I can't move my leg. *Please*."

I'd already helped kill Blueing. I'd seen others die. My Hands were steadily mutating. *I was mutating.* Everyone wanted to kill me. I'd managed to break the rules that kept Lorraine from killing her non-targets, and she didn't need to sleep or eat or do anything besides hunt me. I couldn't shoot her. Couldn't call the cops. Couldn't start an engine without summoning her, or fire a gun. And she wanted *something*, something besides killing me, or she would've killed me by now. She wanted *me*. All of me. She wanted to eat me alive.

Rape me, kill me, eat me, burn me. In what order, though?

How much worse could it get? What was the point of even trying?

But Mallory needed my help.

"It's okay," I said. "I've got you."

I sucked in a deep breath. I scooped up Mallory. My arms screamed bloody murder. I ignored them. I shambled towards the motel entrance.

Mallory dug a wad of gas station cash out of her pocket and counted.

"We're good. For now," she said.

"Here? You'll catch AIDS off the curtains."

Her face grew grim. "You got a credit card? Any nicer motel won't give us a room without one. They like names. IDs. Anonymity's more important right now."

Blood oozed out of the bite mark on Mallory's hand. She pressed her T-shirt against it.

"I need to patch you up," I said. "Where do I buy medical stuff?"

"You've got a four-inch slice across your ribs, and you worry about my hand?"

I tried for the door handle, but she got there first. I shoved my foot in the door gap and nudged it open. The Hands itched. I kept them well below Mallory's bare arms.

The clerk—a chubby squib of a geezer wearing a bleach-stained tweed blazer over a tank top—didn't bat an eye when I entered the lobby, wheezing and red-faced. I put Mallory down on a crumbling faux-leather couch and smiled the same grin that usually worked on Roy Pike and his ilk. Vacant enough to not drop when the snide jabs come. But this clerk had the face of a Russian after two rounds in a Siberian gulag, and the cheer to match.

"Hey," I said. "You got any rooms? We just went through town and had some car—"

"Don't care," he said.

Had to respect his honesty. He had a bit of a twang when he spoke, so I figured we were still in Texas. Sweat darkened the front of his wife-beater tank top. Silver chest hairs fluffed out of the neckline.

"Okay, then. Any rooms?" I asked.

He stared past me at Mallory for a long moment.

"By the hour? Or by the day?"

Heat rushed to my face. "The day. It's not like—never mind."

He shrugged, quoted a number. I continued smiling. Thoughts pulsed through the thin veneer of calm—*Blueing. Mallory. What the hell is Blueing up to? Roy's gonna kill you, Lorraine's gonna kill you, Discount Satan saw you and stared, the Hands*—Veins streaked to my shoulders now. Worse and worse. Interesting.

I forked over the cash numbly, smile frozen into place. Got a key in return, with fossilized gum caked onto the brass. Mallory sighed when I picked her up. Flies droned. I walked down the water-spotted hallway, cigarette smoke from decades past reeking, dirty-rose carpet, like a robot. Until we reached room twenty-one. She unlocked it. You couldn't have paid me to put her down on the goddamn floor.

The hallway budded off like an amoeba, creating squalid rooms along it. Dirty-rose carpet covered the floor, full of mystery stains. A king bed sat in the center, mattress sagging. A splintered wooden chair and a recliner in the corner. A cracked mirror hung on the wall. One narrow window. I flicked on the light, and baby roaches skittered away. One colossal cockroach crawled on the wall.

"Look, babe," I said. "They even sent the motel mascot down. Talk about quality service."

She snorted, then her freckled skin reddened. Her eyes went red. Something wet dribbled out of her eyes. She made a funny desperate sound. Another sound.

Wait. Was she *crying*?

Mallory didn't cry. When she was seven, she had vertical scars running down her forearms from a suicide attempt. They were dark pink, gleaming, when she first arrived. She didn't cry. Blueing screamed at her; she didn't blink. Roy Pike came rolling around, making snide Lorraine remarks, and she took it. I came back from a month in solitary, skin and bones, and she went dead-still for a long moment, then hugged me and gave me her stockpiled Peach Rings, scrubbing her hands together. Dr. Hitch called her a borderline sociopath after she found the dead jackrabbit, and Mallory just studied the ground. Mallory rarely yelled. She might kick. She bit me during her psycho episodes.

But Mallory didn't cry.

I went over to the bed and laid her down on it gently.

Mallory was crying.

"Are—are you okay?" I asked.

She stared at the stained wall. "You need to leave. Before she hurts you."

"Been there, done that, bought the goddamn T-shirt," I said, and I stroked her hair with my bandaged Hand. "She doesn't exactly want to send you on a beach vacation. You need help. I'm not going anywhere."

"Wasn't asking," she said.

I groaned. Not this again. I got up and paced, trying to think.

My brain drifted. Something in my chest shook. My teeth chattered. Grayout, punctuated by images of the cook bleeding out. Her eyes. They'd fixed on mine, then…gone. Blank zeros without luster. Blueing, the man with the bleeding throat grin and red-as-sin Handprint. The man I'd helped kill. Frantic, manic energy kept me moving. I passed by the fly-spotted mirror. Me, the monster with veined arms and pincer hands. For a split second, I saw Lorraine Worner, layered over my reflection like colored film.

"You saw Naamah's?" I said. "It was real. All of it's real. I opened a portal into Hell. Mallory, I don't think I'm human. I don't know. Fuck me. I made a deal with Lorraine and now she's going to kill me."

"Should've believed you," she said.

"I really went there. That place."

And hungry dark eternity in a soundproofed cell, I remembered the acidic clawing of my stomach before it died and I curled up into a ball on the hard floor, cold concrete floor freezing my cheek, praying, *Get me out of here please.* Thirst. Dizziness like a clamped vise around my head, too-thick tongue swelling in my mouth as I swallowed on reflex but nothing in the swallow, no spit—all gone—the cracks on my lips growing. Stickers with cords trailing down, warmed by my body heat, and in the blackness—no smell in particular no sounds mostly—occasional spurts of electric pain. Bad at first. Then I craved the tingle, lusted for *some fucking reality* in the concrete void without time, slamming my elbows into the wall, slamming *anything* into the wall for the sensation, *I've gotta get out of here,* I'd mentally chant, chant in different voices even—maybe God hated mine so try another one, try something—but it always ended the same way. Wait for the pretty lights, Project 0666. Lie and wait and dream. Hadn't I felt something in the Hands then? Shuffling in the darkness. Then the rich scent of rain and ozone.

I always ended up at *Naamah's Pleasure Palace* sooner or later.

The strippers cooed over me but didn't give me any lap dances. Some beleaguered succubus worked the deep fryer. Time felt slippery. I'd help cook. They fed me. I survived. Chicken fingers, greasy and salty and topped with blood-colored ketchup and one time I actually drank something—*blood, champ, let's call it for what it is*—red and metal-smelling and corn-syrup sweet and learned that was some kind of nutrient shake the girls liked, they could even drink it on stage because if it dribbled down it looked like blood—*c'mon, it was blood plus whatever else*—but anyways, they *always* said, *Bring all of you next time, baby,* and I'd say, *I'm here. Right?* And one time I got something besides a laugh in response. *You're separated, baby. You're wandering. Is someone watching your body?*

Nobody is, I'd said.

The people in white coats were. Roy fucking Pike was. I'd fantasize about *ripping* and *tearing* with the Hands, and wouldn't his skin tear like oily silk, a smooth gliding rip, just one little rip and he'd die and I'd be free.

I thought up shit that'd make Lorraine Worner proud.

Me at fifteen, probably day twenty in solitary—lights off, electrodes, no food or water—thought, *I need teeth. More teeth,* and delirious, I saw Roy Pike's towering lean figure in front of me, he'd slapped Ma the other day and said she was mentally unfit and yeah, the unwashed dishes fermented in the sink, mouse shit reeked it all reeked whenever I came back and sucked down the stench of dead roaches piled in our unused oven, live ones roosting in the month-old Fritos, Ma's unwashed hair—but he'd *slapped* Ma, and he left before the *pulse-pulse* of my Hands started. Roy fucking Pike, wrinkled and age-spotted, forcing me to sit at the dining room table and eat Communion wafers, chug blessed wine until I threw up, by then Mallory had grabbed a knife from my kitchen and stood there turning it in her hands, and our eyes had met right before the pre-vomit drool filled my mouth, and I'd thought—*Babe, that's my job. I need teeth. Better teeth*—and *splat,* I'd thrown up right on the table and Roy fucking Pike picked half-digested purplish Communion wafer out of his white hair, leaned in towards me and said, *Eat it again, raghead,* and he didn't stop until I ate every scrap of my own vomit. So I saw him in that cell, visible in the dark like an apparition. I remembered.

And I thought—at age fifteen—*Lean down, fake-Roy. C'mere. Get closer to me, get closer to the* dirty raghead kid *and lean down to spit in my face. Do it,* and the hallucination actually did and—

I ripped his throat out with my teeth, tasting hot blood, thinking, *But I don't have good teeth I need better teeth need better teeth*—and the skin came off like butter like roasted chicken skin slipping off, chew chew swallow—*hungry, I'm so fucking hungry*—then fake-Roy spasmed on the floor before he dissipated into the darkness and a sharp brutal surge pulsed through me and I liked it.

I liked it.

I need better teeth.

Pain, stabbing my gums like a needle. *Need better teeth.* I fell asleep as I kept thinking it. Woke up, still in the pitch-dark. Something warm tingled behind my teeth. Felt good. Oh yeah. They let me out ten days later. By then, the *good* feeling had died off, replaced by an ache deep in the roots of my teeth. A molar was loose. All of them loosened. Didn't matter. My fancy new teeth—crocodile-esque—had already grown behind the first row. I'd gone home, pretending none of it happened. Nope. Roy Pike was fine. I didn't get angry. Only monsters got angry. I wasn't a monster. Right? *Right?* Wiggled my loosening dull teeth with my tongue. Bolted to the toilet and threw up. Hyperventilated, chanting, *Nope nope nope I'm good I don't need new teeth after all, nope, nope, make it stop, MAKE IT STOP!*

BACK IN THE motel room.

The lamp on the bedside table threw out urine-colored light. A tomato stain dirtied the dust-clotted lampshade. Mallory's leg was still paralyzed.

"...You win. Go ahead and take me," Mallory muttered, staring at the wall.

I took off my shirt like some archaeologist about to unearth a cursed tomb. Veins carpeted my arms. They branched and streaked up past my shoulders in poisoned maraschino cherry splendor and ate past my armpits. Row two still sat behind my teeth. The hard parts of the Hands were contaminating further up. Like real lobster claws.

"Make it stop," I whispered.

"Triple-Six?" Mallory asked.

The shaking in my chest worsened. Now my arms quivered. I paced. Dull heat rose. What the hell was wrong with me?

Mallory held up her arm. "Wait."

I curled up in the chair, sank halfway in, and kept on shaking. Oh God. I was a monster. Demonspawn. Maybe I deserved to die. I had Roy's fancy revolver. If worst came to worst, I could always ask him to put a quick bullet through my skull. He'd probably videotape it for funsies.

"Triple-Six."

Mallory looked at me from the bed, without judgment. I wanted to kiss her. If I kissed her, she'd grope her tongue across the sharp back row of my teeth without flinching, same as any of the rest of me. She called them my Fun Teeth.

"Seriously. Leave while you can," she said, and her tone softened. "I care about you enough to not pull you into my bullshit. I poisoned them, you know. When I was four. Do I sound like a good person?"

"Mallory, *I love you.*"

She turned her head to the wall.

"Maybe we can just hide here until my bargain's up with Lorraine," I said. "We don't need to fight her. I'll keep you safe."

But was I really going to let Lorraine waltz off into the sunset, killing innocent people? What about my worsening Hands? Those weren't getting better.

"I lured people to her," Mallory said. "Pretended to be a lost kid. Then she killed them. I helped her cut up and bury whatever was left after she burned them alive. Part of the reason I got put in desert-hell...too many death threats after Lorraine started talking. Victim's families. One of them strangled me during a live interview on TV when I couldn't remember where she hid the rest of the remains. Then you have Lorraine's little cult. God—she has so many fans. People wrote to her in prison when she was alive. She tried to blame me for everything, man. Said I was a sociopath kid. That it was all my idea."

"Holy fuck, I'm sorry. That's...that's...Jesus, Mallory. How could anyone think that a kid would do that?"

"I have nightmares about the lady strangling me. Not about anything

Lorraine did…I barely think about her. But that lady—I'm eight years old, I'm dying under all those studio lights, I'm sweating, and I know that everyone in the audience h-hates me…s-she's shrieking at me, *Where did you hide him? Where's Hunter? You killed my baby boy, you manipulative little cunt! You're a demon wearing a little girl's skin!*"

"Mallory, you were a *child*," I said. "You didn't know anything else. You were just trying to stay alive. You were one of Lorraine's victims, too. Ever think about that?"

She shook her head. "Only I lived."

"Because you killed Lorraine. You stopped a serial killer when you were, like, seven! Mallory. You're a *hero*."

"Know what happened when that lady pounced on me and started throttling me? Huh? Fucking *nothing*. Everyone watched her do it until I blacked out. Wish they would've let her finish the job."

Something cold prickled through my stomach. "Babe?"

Her eyes flattened into black, plastic dots.

Oh God. Is she having another episode?

"Remember the birthday list?" Mallory asked.

"Yeah?"

The week of your birthday, you got to pick one thing to put on the shopping list under "other." Roy Pike approved or disapproved at his leisure.

"Know what I put down for my tenth birthday?"

I didn't say anything. Thumps came from the room next to us. Muffled shouts. The A/C hummed.

"I wanted to watch Lorraine's execution," Mallory said, and she tilted her head. "It was a month away. But they didn't let me go. Nobody under eighteen's allowed. Blueing went. Taped it."

"What?"

Mallory's body jerked once. It slumped onto the bed. Her right hand twitched compulsively, thumb flicking. Her eyes closed. I fished in my pocket for the sedative vials. Found nothing. Nothing in my pockets. *Shit. Where did the sedatives go?* I scanned the room. Anything sharp? Wait. The gun. I jumped and yanked it out of her waistband right before her hand slapped over mine. She grunted.

Eyes opened.

Empty. Flat.

She sat up, eyeing me like I was a nice roasted hot dog skewered on a stick, dripping and ready to eat. An aroused flush pinked her cheekbones, limning the burn scar.

A faint drawl polluted her voice. "Ever thought maybe you should git runnin'?"

"Jesus, Mallory. Stop trying to scare me."

And sure, she got a little Texan drawl when she had her psycho episodes. Which made sense. She'd lived there and around before desert-hell. It didn't mean anything. This was Mallory.

Is it, champ?

I think I knew then. The blank episodes. I knew, in the pit of my stomach, exactly what had crawled around in Mallory's skin for all those years, why Lorraine Worner knew more about me than she should've. Why Lorraine was so obsessed with me—

No.

Like a blank white nothing. Realization.

No, that can't be true.

I ignored it. I jammed it away. I was getting paranoid. This was Mallory Worner, and I loved her.

"I knew who you were, honey," she said. "Known you a long fuckin' time. Anyone ever told you how it feels to git zapped by them Hands you got?"

Pulse. Pulse. Pulse.

"Quit it," I said.

"It's real tingly-like."

She held up her hands. Blisters formed on her wrists. Two small dark patches. They gave off a faint smell like a dead decayed mouse, like—*smells like Blueing's corpse, champ*—wait, there were three patches now. Three necrotic patches of skin. Within her grasp were the sedative vials she'd pickpocketed from me.

She maintained eye contact.

"Hated you for years," she said softly.

I don't care, just don't go batshit on me or kill yourself. I can take it. I can take and take and take it. That's love, right? That's all I know.

She lurked on the bed like some crooked-toothed gargoyle with frizzy hair and tits.

"Think anyone'll ever love a freak like—"

"*Shut up!*"

I shook. I took deep breaths, heart pounding. No matter what Mallory Worner pulled during these spells, if she'd hit me, or tried to set shit on fire, whatever she'd done to me, I always ended up apologizing. Begging. Walking on eggshells because, Jesus, she always seemed one bad day away from killing herself. And I loved her, I did but—why? Why couldn't I just be *honest?*

The girl on the bed smirked. *Mallory* smirked. This was Mallory. Totally.

"Sometimes I fucking hate you, too," I said.

I stormed over to the wood chair. Grabbed it.

"I'm getting more meds, and I'm telling the asshole at the desk to not move the chair. *Stay*," I said, breathing hard.

"You ain't got the balls to coop me up, you fuckin' pussy."

"Watch me," I said.

Oh, God. What the hell was wrong with me? Was I really about to trap my semi-girlfriend in a seedy motel room like—like some kind of predator? *Dude, she's having a mental breakdown! Just keep her safe! Who cares what this looks like?*

She clawed her cheek. Three red scratches oozed over. Blood dribbled down her cheek and ran in the wrinkly flesh over her burn scar.

"You wanna drug me again?"

"D-don't hurt yourself. Please. Please don't hurt yourself, babe."

She shook the sedative vials. "Touch one of these, I gouge an eye out. We're gonna have some real fun."

"Mallory—"

"I ain't her. It's never been her. You know that don't you? Deep down?"

"Don't pull this shit. Please. Stop pretending. Tell me—tell me you love me, babe."

Her voice lost the drawl. "Run while you can."

She was so tiny. So fragile. I laid next to her on the bed and she rolled over to face me, expressionless. Blood soaked into the brown bed cover.

"You ain't gonna drug me...Triple-Six?"

"No. I swear to God I won't. I'm sorry. Don't hurt yourself. I love you. I really do," I babbled.

"Good boy. You can touch me now."

I wrapped my safe arm around her. But it felt...wrong. Like spooning a giant spider. Kind of gross, yeah, okay, but if you played it safe it wouldn't eat you. This was Mallory. She just had funny moments. Right?

Denial's a river in Egypt, champ.

Eventually I drifted into sleep, arm coiled tight around her. Her breathing became sleepy. It wasn't sexy. Thank God. The absolute last thing I needed right now was to accidentally get hard and jab poor Mallory with the boner.

What if this isn't Mallory? What if Lorraine wants you because you've done it before with her, holy shit, holy fucking Jesus, DID YOU FUCK HER? Have you fucked a serial killer?

No.

Maybe Hell was real, maybe demons were real, and maybe I could pull some tricks with spatial distance now, but it was far more likely that Mallory Worner had developed a split personality that resembled Lorraine. Mallory had diagnosed borderline personality disorder and severe PTSD. If anyone would develop an elaborate split personality, it'd be her. Plus, who ever heard of a dead person possessing a living one? Silly Triple-Six, possession was for demons.

But you don't know, do you? Doesn't it make a godawful amount of sense?

No.

I wiped away that line of thinking. It was crazy. I didn't need more crazy. We needed supplies and food and a plan.

We'd gotten maybe thirty minutes, tops, on the side of the road. My adrenal glands were about to go on strike. But I couldn't sleep for long. Mallory was getting worse. We didn't have food or medical supplies. Take her to the store with me? She'd probably scream. A quicker Go Directly to Jail, Do Not Pass Go, Do Not Collect Two-Hundred Dollars than goddamn Monopoly.

So it was up to me. Catnap, wake up, slip out the door while Mallory snored. Baby's First Store Trip. I needed cash.

I slipped my Hand into Mallory's pocket. She stiffened.

"What the fuck are you doing?"

Casual pickpocketing, babe. Totally not going to a store, definitely not leaving you alone.

"I, uh—"

"Spit it out."

"Well, uh, I sort of helped, um, at the bar. And…during the robbery. Yeah. Yeah! Shouldn't I get some of the cash? It works like that. Right?"

"Oh my God," she said. "Just take what you want. You could've asked."

"Sorry."

She sounded more normal. Maybe this wouldn't turn out horribly. My thoughts thickened as I lay there and breathed. Right before I went to sleep, I thought I heard Mallory mutter something.

"You were supposed to scare him."

Huh?

TWENTY-THREE

BABY'S FIRST STORE Trip involved a half-mile trek to Walmart, greasy pillow-case rags crawling with mites wrapped around my arm, me deciding to call Roy Pike, and an impromptu lesson on burner phone etiquette.

"But do I get a case for it?" I asked, holding up a ten-dollar clamshell cell phone.

The poor dude working the electronics section blinked again.

"They don't make cases for those anymore, sir. It's—it's not that kind of phone."

"All I have to do is put the little card in, and it'll work?" I asked.

I'd arrived at 6:00 a.m. It was now 6:20 a.m.

He nodded.

"This your first time dealing drugs?"

"Uh—no," I said. "I'm a very stable member of society. Where's the condom aisle?"

"A12, down on the right."

"Thanks," I said, and trudged over.

I chucked the burner phone, sans case, into my cart. I added a charging cord and the Pay-As-U-Go card. Concrete floor gleamed with fresh polish. Aisles lay abandoned. The few souls shopping took one look at the crazy-haired brown dude with bandaged arms and gave me a wide berth. Fantastic.

Aisle A12. I threw the most normal-looking box of condoms into the cart. Apparently there existed a plethora of different ways to manufacture a plastic sock. Learn something new every day. But she'd gotten a box earlier, so, when in Rome. I'd never worn one before.

When are you going to call Roy, champ?

Magic revolver chilled the skin underneath my waistband.

I hurried through the rest of Walmart, hunting up powdered milk and Nesquik—crush up a Benadryl and watch it disappear—rubbing alcohol, Benadryl, NyQuil, bandages, ACE bandages—for the Hands—gauze, SPAM, Peachie O's gummies, Cup O' Noodles, oranges, a box of plastic forks, a pack of Irish Spring soap, toothpaste, a pack of toothbrushes, and a BIC lighter.

I paid. The cashier didn't bat an eye.

As I walked back to *So Mote*, I cracked open the burner phone. Fully charged. I punched in the digits on the service card, fumbling. Me and my goddamn monster pincers.

What the hell was I going to say to Roy Pike?

Hey, Roy! How's life treating you? Lost your magic wizard gun in a bar fight adjacent to Hell? Maybe it's the probable demon-blood in me, maybe it's Maybelline, or maybe it's all those reruns I watched of Deal or No Deal, but Roy, I've got your gun, and I'm ready to give it back. Stop trying to kill me, Deal or No Deal? Tell me how to defeat an undead serial killer from Hell, Deal or No Deal?

I entered *So Mote*. Decades of cigarette smoke residue browned along the walls like mold. Hopefully nobody had moved the chair I'd jammed under Room 21's doorknob after I'd tiptoed out. If Mallory got out—

Speaking of, Roy. Protect Mallory Worner, Deal or No Deal?

The chair remained as I'd left it. Thank God. I yanked it out from under the knob and stood, fingering the room key. Already the humid air stank like a scalp that hadn't seen a shower in two months.

I set the bags down. I dialed Roy Pike's cell number.

It rang.

And rang.

His terse voice told me to *Leave a message, I'll git back to you.*

I swallowed. "Mr. Pike, uh, it's Project 0666. I've got your gun. I'm more than willing to give it back, but I want something in return. I need to get Lorraine Worner locked back in Hell, but I don't know how...look, Mallory's having a rough time. If you hate me, then do it for her."

Eat it, raghead.

I exhaled. Okay. Olive-branch time. Hating Roy Pike was bad. Getting angry was bad. I teased my tongue over my Fun Teeth.

"Roy, I know I'm probably some kind of abomination, and yeah, maybe I should die. But Lorraine's hurting innocent people—she can physically touch whatever the hell she wants. *Whoever* she wants. I'll trade you your revolver—and I'll keep it in good condition—if you help me put her back in Hell as soon as possible. And—"

My voice broke.

"And if it means you have to…to kill me to end the bargain, I'll let you. Okay? You win. Deal or No Deal?"

I hung up.

Some numbness crawled through my arms and legs. Die. Get a bullet through my brain. Never live a day without the Hands. Something about the sheer fact that I never got to hand Ma anything without her flinching, never got to shake someone's hand without worrying I'd hurt them, never got a day without stares…all I wanted was to hold Mallory's hand and feel her skin on mine. Just once.

On cue, the Hands pulsed. Again. Way to go, life-ruiners. Keep on pulsing. I unlocked the door, crept in, and plonked the bags onto the filthy carpet.

Mallory casually looked up from the pile of money she was counting on the bed. A plastic shopping bag sat on it. A Raspberry Zinger lay atop the bag, cut neatly in half. Right next to a halved Sno Ball.

Faint green rimmed her pale face. Sweat glistened.

"You're back early," she said.

"You got out."

"You forgot the window. We're on the ground floor. Want a Sno-ball? They're her favorite."

She didn't look at me. She bit into the Raspberry Zinger.

She gagged.

"Jesus, Mallory," I said. "Don't eat—"

Her throat worked. "I get dessert first this time around."

"What are you—"

"Did you get condoms?" Mallory asked, and made a face, "I left my birth control back at home. Wanted to get my tubes tied, but Roy Pike didn't approve it."

Wait, what? My chest wound throbbed. Heat from the July sun tried to break in, held back by cheap-o blinds and a window that'd seen too much. That lone cockroach trucked along the baseboard. Probably my long-lost cousin at this point. Down the hall, eighties tunes crackled on the radio.

"Do—do you want to have sex?" I said.

She scrubbed her hands together. "That's dessert, Triple-Six."

It probably said a lot that I wasn't even kind of hard. *Roy, do you ever check your goddamn voicemail?*

Mallory hopped off the bed and rummaged through the spoils of Baby's First Store Trip. She fished out the condoms. Threw them on the bed.

"Babe, we need to make some kind of plan. Tell me about Lorraine."

She moved too quickly. Her voice was too casual.

"We are *not* basing the safety of the known world on your ability to pull out. Could you imagine? Another Lorraine?" She shuddered a little. "Another me?"

"The burner phone's mine," I said numbly.

"Keep it."

Deal or No Deal, Roy?

She pulled out the medical stuff and pointed to the bed. "Go. Don't argue with me. You first."

I didn't. As I laid on the bed, half-asleep, Mallory lifted my shirt up and squinted at my chest wound.

"Not deep. But you'll have a scar."

The smell of rubbing alcohol. Cold liquid. Burning.

"What aren't you telling me, Mallory?"

Split-second pause.

"You won't have to worry about Lorraine," she said. "So relax."

"I made the bargain."

She placed gauze over the scabbing wound and secured it. Mild pressure. Fever-warm hand on my skin.

"Just let me make you happy, man."

She gave a sad little laugh. "I can do that much."

She leaned over and kissed me.

I opened my mouth to talk—

Knock. Knock. Knock.

—And jumped about a foot off the bed. Mallory hissed.

Someone was knocking at the door of Room 21. I heaved myself up. Heart pounding, I tiptoed over to the peephole. Maybe it was room service. Yeah, and maybe I'd win the lottery after getting struck by lightning. I looked out.

Nothing. Just a water-stained hallway with cracks in the plaster.

"Don't open it," Mallory said. "It's a trap."

No shit, Sherlock. I turned back towards the bed and started walking.

Knock. Knock. Knock.

"Oh, come on," I said.

I looked again, and presto, nothing. Nada. But the Hands grew hot, so magic bullshit was afoot. Sighing, I grabbed the doorknob. It chilled my palm. I opened the door.

Blue fire sprang up in a circle, waist-high flames. A circle of fire on the carpet. *Shit.* I lurched back. Fire. Something thumped to the wall. Mallory. Her breaths came in and out, she backed across the carpet, eyes frantic, bluebell fire gleaming off them.

"Fire," she breathed.

Then it vanished. No burning down, no ash or smoke, just gone.

A folded paper sat on the carpet.

Mallory let out a rattling breath.

Hand shaking, I plucked the folded paper up. Unfolded it. Resume paper, cream-colored and thick. Scribbled in jagged letters, the note read:
No Deal. Don't make me come get it.—Roy.

TWENTY-FOUR

NEITHER OF US spoke for a long time. Mallory nudged me. Dead silent, I handed Roy Pike's revolver to her. We stared at it. Carved symbols covered the aged wooden handle, darkened in spots by remnants of sweat. He'd held it often.

And I'd bet his aim was impeccable.

What do you offer a guy after you've offered everything?

Another silence.

"Eat the other Sno Ball. I...can't stare at it anymore," Mallory said.

I ate it.

"Four hundred and fifty dollars left. The register was full," she said.

"It's enough to stay here. Until it's over," I said.

She stepped closer to me. *Pulse. Pulse. Pulse.* I could feel her body heat. Warm. Vital. Alive. Something sweet on her breath.

"C'mere," she said softly. "The shower's good. Start there?"

I pressed into her. Warm. Warm woman. Her boobs squished into my chest. Heat flowed in a smooth soft wave down to my belly, *good* like liquid gold—*like honey*—sweet. Dipped lower. *Throb. Throb.* Hard. Rock-fucking-hard. Her hand creeped under my shirt. Hot skin. Traveled down.

Had to be glowing. Invisible red-hot coal, throbbing.

"I'll just lose it again. You know how this goes, babe," I said.

"No. You won't."

Her flushed freckled skin, pink lips.

"C'mon," she said, and paraded me into the bathroom. "Let me have my fucking dessert."

C'mon.

Oh, yeah.

I DIDN'T LOSE it.

I didn't think, *Oh my God, Oh Christ, she's so tiny, I'm just looming over her like a sea monster! Am I a monster? Why the fuck can't I concentrate? Fuck!*—

Slick soap in the shower, hot water. Irish Spring suds, her dirty tangled hair, our sweat, mingled. Red, uncovered veins beat with my pulse sickeningly. Reached into my non-existent pecs—*don't let her put her mouth on them*—but her mouth kissed down lower. Lower. Water ran in rivulets. Her head was buried in my black pubes, nose tickling my balls—*don't stop*—then her black gaze flicked up and then her pink lips sucked around my dick—*so slick so slick Jesus yes so warm*—sucking, sucking the pleasure, sucking the white-hot throbbing nexus of *yesyesyes*, slow long *oh so good* and the Hands pulsed but everything was pulsing so okay, okay, okay, Oh Oh Oh—

(!!!!!)

Bleach-scent of cum. Her tongue lapped over the dribbling slit, licked her lips. Her eyelids fluttered. *Yum-yum,* she mouthed. Swallowed.

I heard Lorraine's voice in my skull. *Fuckin' swallow it, Mallory.* Shredded man-meat between mushed white Bimbo Bread—almost like skin—*Choke him down and you git the Zinger. Now eat it, kid.*

Post-jizz emptiness. Nausea.

Seriously, what was with that Raspberry Zinger she'd gagged down?

Yum-yum. Yum-yum, Mallory.

Mallory stood. "What's wrong?"

She ground against me, but the Irish Spring smell burned my nose. Too chemical. Too harsh.

I shook my head, tired. *Am I just another person you choke down, babe?*

It wouldn't matter in a few days.

"Let's try the bed. Let's go all the way," she said.

SHE SLICKED A condom on my dick. Used her mouth to do it. Jesus, what a mouth. I wound the usual Saran Wrap around my forearms and Hands.

"You're spoiled," Mallory said, right up against my ear. "Most guys have to use these. I love the tickle when you come in me, but…"

I grinned. "I can pull out. I swear. I've seen it in porn. If I can't trust porn…shit, next thing I know, you'll be telling me some of the boobs aren't silicone and saline."

She snorted. "Oh my God."

Plastic sock over my dick wasn't actually too bad, but I was having fun giving her a hard time over it. Pun intended. *Hey, champ! When are you going to think about Roy Pike?*

"You need an anatomy lesson, Triple-Six."
"Oh?"

I cupped her little face in my Hand and leaned in. Sweet peach gummy ring smell on her breath. Crusted sugar around her lips.

"Hands or tongue?" Mallory whispered.

"Both, babe."

I felt for her. Wetness warmed through the Saran Wrap over my Hand. *She's so horny!* Dark pubes. The hard engorged bead of her clit, hard like a ruby. Soft lips. Both sets. She closed the distance above, mouth lips working and her cooch pulsing, pulsing. *Fuck yes. Yesyesyes.*

"Know what a cervix is?"

The baby-hole up higher in the vag.

"Yeah."

"C'mon, put your Hand in. Feel it."

Slick. Perfect. Her smell. *Flip her over, thrust it in you know she wants it God she's so fucking wet.* Something clenched inside me. *Throb. Throb.* Hard again.

Mallory threw her head back, moaning. Her hips twitched.

Something softer deep in.

"Feel how soft it is, man?"

I exhaled. "Yeah."

"Means I'm fertile," she said, and kissed the tip of my nose. "It wants your cum. So we've got to be careful."

"Careful," I said.

Her voice chilled a little. "You don't want me pregnant with your kid. You just don't."

LYING OVER HER, weight on my forearms. *What if I smother her? Shit, I can't just put all of me on her?*

I was in her halfway and her velvety-soft cooch worked, wanting me, slick muscles—*so go in*—but I couldn't. I balanced over her. Her pupils dilated. Cheeks flushed. Sweat beads jeweled her scalp and curls.

I started. "I—"

Her palms slid up my chest. Her hands curled around my shoulders, squeezed, dragged down, pulling me deeper and deeper into her, *pulse pulse pulse,* so slick so *good*—

She hissed. Flinched her right arm back.

Froze.

"My arm," she said, voice distant. "I—I can't move it."

I went soft inside her. *Oh no. Oh God no, not this. There's a hole or something in the bandages, she didn't just touch the edge and get zapped?*

"You touched the veins. Didn't you?" I said.

"Yeah."

Monster. The Hands were getting worse. Spreading. I swallowed back a wave of bile. *Fucking freak. You hurt her.*

"Shit. I—I'm sorry. Oh God. I didn't know, *I didn't know.*"

Little bubbles of hysteria formed in my chest. The Hands. No matter what I did, they'd hurt people, no matter how careful I was—Hands. What a sick fucking joke. They weren't hands. They were demon pincers, bred to paralyze.

Mallory shushed me. "Just throw on a shirt. It's not that bad, Triple-Six—"

"*Yes it goddamn is!*"

"Take a deep breath. Now."

She sat up, flicked the lamp on, and crossed her arms. Pink skin blushed over her right hand, like a sunburn gone awry. The creamy light cast shadows under her lower lip and nose and boobs, darkened her hair into a frizzled cloud.

I sucked in air, chest shuddering. "Happy?"

She dug my *Blue Lobster* shirt from under the stained pillow and tossed it at my face. Numb, I put it on. Now the monster veins were covered. What an efficient freak of nature I was. The Hands, the Arms, and now the Chest. I tongued my Fun Teeth.

And blinked.

Two of my lower incisors wiggled. A lot. *Loose.*

"Let's keep going," Mallory said. "C'mere."

"You're kidding, right?"

"You'll get blue balls if you don't finish. Bad for you."

"Your fucking arm's shot, Mallory."

"I've got two. It'll only last twelve hours."

She turned the lamp off. She groped for me in the darkness, functional hand darting like a minnow.

"How *horny are you,* babe?" I asked.

She found me. Rubbed.

"C'mere," she murmured. "Let me. Just one last time."

Sweet building heat. Pulsing. *Yes. Screw it.*

Zing!

A text message came in. I cracked open the burner phone. 12:18 p.m.

Dread swelled as I read. *We need to talk. In person. 6PM tonight, go to Huey's BBQ. Sit at the bar.*

I didn't recognize the phone number.

"Don't make me wait, Triple-Six."
I didn't.

THRUST. THRUST. THRUST.

Her, squeezed around me—*so tight so fucking slick*—her under me, hair tickling, breaths coming in sharp pants, thighs strangling around my hips. Straddling. *Deeper. C'mon.* Electric rhythm, tingling, and did everything revolve around down there, the throbbing, throbbing pleasure point of meeting? Yes it did, *thrust thrust,* everything pounding, pulsing, yeah, salted sweat stinging my chest cut, some sound—*me?*—guttural grunt every thrust, her hot skin like melted vanilla ice cream, so pale and freckled, I sucked on her neck—*no vanilla*—her shoulder, sweat-taste and something sweet.

Deeper. Oh, God yes.

Thrust-thrust-thrust—

Pressure. At the tip of my dick. *Something's wrong, it's going to break, get out—*

I jerked myself up but she matched me. Grabbed a handful of my hair. A little moan.

"It's—"

thrustthrustthrustthrust—oh God why the fuck was I trying to stop—thrustthrustthrust—

Silent *pop.* Inside *pop.*

More sensation. *Wait, the condom—*

(!!!!)

Limp. Drained. I relaxed on top of her. Didn't withdraw. She grunted once. Reached her good hand down to her clit and rubbed, rubbed until her breath caught, her cooch tightened around me, hips jerking up once. She slumped back.

I sat up, pulling myself out of her. It had to be fine. Right?

A slimy piece of latex slipped off me. Jizz smell.

Mallory hissed. Tensed.

I pinched it. Soda bubbles numbed my brain. *No.* This was a nightmare. It wasn't real, couldn't be, not pincered-freak me. I held it up. Turned on the lamp.

Our broken condom dripped with my semen.

"Maybe I didn't—"

"Take a look, man."

We both stared at her pink cooch, her with dead eyes and no facial expression. Only it wasn't pink, not all over, because dribbling out of her and sticking to her thighs?

Semen.

Lots of it.

Mine.

"What did I tell you?" Mallory said. "I—"

She jumped off the bed. Bolted to the bathroom. Slammed the door behind her—*BANG!*

Faucets ran.

I got up. Walked over. Knocked on the door.

"Mallory?"

"Go away."

I opened the door.

She had one leg propped up on the edge of the tub. One hand scooping up water, scrubbing herself like a fiend. Mallory's limp arm lolled. Her rinse-water clouded the tub like diluted milk. *Jesus God, that's a lot of jizz.*

"Fuck you," Mallory said, still scrubbing.

"I—I'm sorry. I didn't want it to break."

"I know."

"Look, I don't get how all of this works, Mallory, but—are you, like, pregnant or something?"

Everything spun.

I continued. My words jerked out like shrill Morse code. "I—I m-meant it. What I said earlier. I love you, Mallory. If it's not...if it's just a normal baby, I'll be there. We'll raise it together. No matter what happens."

I tried not to imagine some monstrous black thing gestating in her like a cancer, like a canker—*what else would it be, you freak?* It didn't help. A real baby almost seemed scarier.

She sighed and stopped scrubbing.

"Would you want that? To start a family someday?"

"Uh, I never really—"

"You thought about it before abortion," she said softly. "Adoption. Before any other alternative. It tells me a lot."

Mallory padded over. Her gaze skewered me.

"If you want that, find someone else. You're about to feel bad for yourself, aren't you? It's not you, Triple-Six. I will *never, ever* have kids. Not with you, not with anyone. I can't even—I can't even keep myself stable, man. You want to throw a fucking baby into the mix?"

"No, I just—"

"Just what? Your mother's dead, Roy Pike's gone, everything's gone to shit, and now you need to feel better about yourself, so bam, here's a fucking baby? Let me go squeeze one out? You can't function without someone to coddle. Used to worry that I'd come in one day and find you sucking your Ma's tit. Or vice versa."

I gripped the sink faucet. Veins broke open, oozing. "I should've let Ma kill herself?"

She imitated my voice. "Mallory. *Mallory!* Do you *love me? Oh, Mallory!*"
Fuck you.

"I'm trying to do the right thing. Has to seem pretty goddamn weird to you, *Mallory Worner.*"

"And?"

"You roofied me to kill a guy, dragged me over to his body, and framed me for his murder. A million other things I can't remember. All I ever try to do is love you—and you treat me like dog shit."

"Blueing? I was trying to help you. I did you a favor."

A favor?

I'd never get Blueing's rotting body out of my head. The cadaver pieces, bleeding through the sheets. His dead skin. Her, throwing the .22...and she'd done me a *favor?*

"It needed to be both of us, Triple-Six. Not just because of the bargain I made with Roy Pike. If I wouldn't have implicated you, they would've grabbed just me. Thought they'd take us into town. To a jail. Or a facility. Had a rough plan from there. We were going to die in that fucking desert, man, and you didn't even—I know what your mother did to you. You got blackout drunk. You told me. You cut your Hands apart and I—"

"It's great to hear another reliable story from Mallory Worner," I said, heart hammering in my ears. "The diagnosed borderline. You know how badly you have to fuck up to be diagnosed with borderline personality disorder at age sixteen?"

"Don't bring my BPD into this."

"How fucked up are you, Mallory?"

"*I AM fucked up! How many fucking times do I have to say it!?*"

My eardrums ached. For a long minute, she froze, ankle-deep in milky tub water, staring at me. Her lips pressed together. She stomped out of the tub and shoved past me into the room. She yanked her clothes on.

What the hell could I say?

"I'm leaving," she said hoarsely. "I'm not pregnant. Not yet. There's emergency birth control at the store. I'll get some."

"But Lorraine's out there."

"I told you. I'll handle it."

She took forty dollars out of the money pile. She pressed the rest into my Hand.

"You—you need more than this," I said. "You can't just go. Please. I'm sorry."

She found the white cardboard backing from a package of Sno Balls, held it against the wall, and scribbled something on it. Threw it on the bed.

I stood, dead grayout prickling the edge of my vision, fogging my brain. Mallory's lips brushed mine.

"Thanks for dessert. Take care of yourself."

"You can't—"

"You've got the nicest smile, man. You know that? All eye crinkles. God—you put everything in it. I never told you…"

She half-smiled. It didn't reach her eyes. She opened the door, good hand clutching the knob.

"Don't know where she'll stash me. After I'm gone. But if they find me, tell them to bury me somewhere by the ocean. Don't…" She swallowed. "Don't let them cremate me."

I heard someone say, "Okay."

Maybe it was me.

She closed the door behind her.

She left.

TWENTY-FIVE

I SAT ON the carpet. I'd been sitting on the carpet for an hour.

In the end, what did it matter? Did any of this matter? Were the thoughts and feelings of a monster anything but electrified gray skull-jelly?

I pressed the revolver to my temple. Cold metal burned against my skin.

It was loaded.

I'd checked.

A red trickle of blood ran down my left arm. Already healed. It healed up the second I dug the razor blade in. I couldn't even kill myself right.

I rested my Hand on the trigger. The note I'd left housekeeping—*Sorry for the mess. Keep the cash.*—sat on the bedspread. I could end the bargain here and now. I could send Lorraine Worner back to Hell. She wouldn't be able to hurt Mallory. Or anyone else. Roy Pike wanted it this way. *Maybe they'll let you work at Naamah's.*

Pain, sure. There'd be some.

You think Mallory would want you to blow your brains out, dipshit?

Mallory seemed three-quarters of the way there herself.

The burner phone vibrated. I let it ring. What a funny noise it made. I choked back laughter. Kill myself in a cheap motel room. Because— what? Because I had the mother-in-law from Hell? What was this, Jerry fucking Springer? Was the roach on the wall going to crawl down and reveal himself as my long-lost father?

If you knocked her up... She'd get an abortion anyway. It didn't matter—

If she doesn't. And you did—you want Mallory to have to tell your kid that Daddy killed himself? You want that? Is this all you've got?

But I couldn't—

YOU CAN TELEPORT!

Is this REALLY all you've got?

"No," I said. "You know what? I can solve this."

And if I couldn't? Let Roy Pike take over my suicide plan. He'd probably do a better job at killing me. So I put the gun down. I took the bullets out for good measure and stowed them in my pocket. They glowed faintly blue like anglerfish lanterns.

I got up and tried to open a portal for the fifth time.

"Take me to Mallory Worner."

Pulse. Pulse. Pulse. I slashed the air. No dice. No invisible membrane. A wisp of red smoke curled up from both wrists. I stopped after that. Maybe it was like a refractory period—you opened a portal to Hell, you couldn't do it again for a day.

If I was Lorraine, what would I do next?

Kill people? How did she even kill people? Did she target specific groups, or were pincered Middle Eastern dudes not her thing? I ached for weed. I'd have sold my Hands for a bong rip, or a shot of Fireball, get the creative juices flowing. I'd never read anything about Lorraine. *Mallory Worner, Born Evil?* had been buried at the bottom of the DVD box.

Wait a second.

I found the room phone. Black mold thrived between the keys. I picked it up, heard a noise. I pressed zero. A friendly lady answered. She'd smoked a hundred packs of cigarettes too many. I could smell her over the line.

Yes, sir, you can do that. We don't got streaming services yet. Yeah, use the remote. Lemme know if you got issues with the set. You paid cash? It's fine, oh, bless your heart, you're honest. If it's only the one movie, don't worry 'bout it. Glad to help, sugar.

I fiddled with the motel TV until I found the movies.

Lorraine Worner had four documentaries lurking in the Pay-to-Rent section, and all of them bore the sheer authenticity and seriousness of a can of Easy Cheese. Grainy black and white Lorraine in the chair, *The Barbecue Butcher: Interviews*. Teenage Lorraine, wearing braces with red rubber bands, fire obscuring half the picture, *It Begins Here: The Worner Case*. Of course, we had a Mallory and Lorraine picture, too, a red-filtered shot of both of them, *Pyromaniac, Killer, Parent: The Softer Side of Lorraine Worner*.

I clenched the remote so hard that veins burst. Dripped scarlet onto the bedspread.

The softer side of Lorraine fucking Worner?

Mallory didn't know how to read when they put her in desert-hell. Basic stuff, maybe, signs like *Exit* and *Bathroom* and *Stop*, but no sentences. Seven years old. She could recite the chemical formula for any oil, petroleum, or dollar-store cleaner, or concoct colored flames and bombs out of random crap under the kitchen sink.

But she couldn't read a sentence.

She'd never been to any kind of school. Dr. Hitch had a field day with that, trying to homeschool me while teaching Mallory basic written language.

I'd asked her, *Why can't you read? Do you need glasses or something? Because she didn't want me knowing how. Drop it,* she'd snapped.

I asked again, at seventeen. *Seriously...you knew how to read, right? Right?*

Hard-eyed, she'd said, *Can't escape if you don't know how to read a map. Or write an SOS. We moved around so much...nobody cared.*

Okay, that documentary was out.

I went with *The Sociopath and Her Lighter,* which featured good old Lori against a collaged background of her victims. Lots of victims. Credits rolled across the screen. Relief washed over me. In every horror movie, learning about the bad guy equaled instant success. Lorraine *had* to have some kind of weird weak spot I could exploit. *Maybe it's all those bangles. She can't walk in front of a magnet.* I forced back a hysterical laugh. All her bedazzled death trophies.

I watched. Maybe two reenactments. Corny, dumb melodrama. Lorraine's actress kept scratching at her wig and smearing her fake freckles, which got a snort out of me. Real Lori didn't sashay her hips when she walked.

The rest?

"...After lacing the macaroni with ant and roach poison, Lorraine Worner claimed she watched her father and two brothers perish before setting the house on fire...she was fourteen years old. There was a fourth, unidentified corpse identified in the remains after authorities put out the blaze, which was initially believed to be Lorraine...later, she admitted to luring a classmate behind the house and bludgeoning her to death with a baseball bat. She then placed the body in the house..."

"...From 1984 to 1996, Lorraine Worner murdered twenty people, possibly more. The severed, burned heads were eventually recovered, but the rest of her victims' burned bodily remains were never found..."

"...Property damage is believed to number somewhere in the millions, despite Lorraine's claims that the targets of her arsons 'weren't being used anyways'..."

A ragged mugshot.

"...From June 1996 to May 1998, she served two years in prison for aggravated assault, narrowly avoiding a manslaughter charge. Lorraine claimed that the victim—eighty-year-old Nell Lincoln—had thrown a mug of hot tea at her face. Nell Lincoln had numerous skull fractures and was comatose by the time medical responders arrived at the scene. Lorraine's crowbar was still caked in blood..."

Some silver-haired expert droned, "The Worner case is interesting for two reasons. One, she didn't appear to have a specific race, gender, or any other specifiers when selecting victims—you don't normally see that with these types of crimes. There's always a 'type' they go for. Lorraine was very...opportunistic, let's call it. Two, Mallory Worner. Alright, serial killers have children—look at Ted Bundy, look at BTK—but they don't involve their children in the murders..."

A picture of Lorraine holding a tiny baby wrapped in a towel, face expressionless.

"In June 1999, Mallory Worner was born..."

And then the lady herself started talking. Lorraine, clad in a beige jumpsuit, sat at a steel table. Handcuffs trapped her hands. She tilted her head right at the camera and leered a little.

"...Did you have Mallory in a hospital?"

"You think I could fuckin' afford a ten-grand bill to shit out a baby on some white bed?" she spat. "Naw, I had her in the trailer. She lived."

"Are you aware that Mallory Worner tested positive for methamphetamine and barbiturates at the time of your arrest?"

"That ain't my fault. That crazy fuckin' kid. I told you, she wanted to kill some of them folks, she really did. You ever see her so much as cry?"

So I watched.

A sick twisty feeling unraveled in my gut. I chewed an orange peel. Three teeth wiggled, one barely attached to my gums. I plucked it out, put it on the bedside table. Good little tingle played along my jaw. *More teeth*.

I paused the movie. Checked the burner phone. The caller hadn't left a voicemail, so I sent a text. *Tell me where to find Mallory Worner. Tell me about Hell. Why should I meet you?*

Quick response. *Time can be adjusted. I'll tell you ALL ABOUT HELL, Project 0666. But I'm afraid you'll have to work for what I give you.*

Great, another cryptic text.

I texted, *Who are you?*

A friend with mutual interests. Call me.

I'd already blown an hour watching the documentary, and all I'd learned was that Lorraine had an IQ of 130-something, gave absolutely no fucks at all, and oh, yeah—*how she killed people.*

"...She drove the often-unconscious victim to a secluded location, and bound their hands and feet together, first with zip ties, and..."

An interview. Lorraine put it best. She laughed at the camera, reveling in her fun, fire-fueled memories, "...then I liked to layer the ties, use duct tape before I slapped the chains on, that kinda thing. Wasn't made of money, now was I? The chains were real fancy, real expensive shit. Ain't smart to git corpse-juice all over 'em. So. I'd pick an accelerant. Gasoline. A classic, easy to git. Kerosene, I liked the smell better but not as much as some booze. Booze. Fancy. You can chug it while they fry. Dinner and a fuckin' show. If there was brush or grass, I'd stuff some into their clothes. Dump the accelerant on."

Her voice dropped. "They wriggle right 'bout then. So. I'd light a match. I'd throw it on the thing."

"Where did you bury them, Worner?"

She closed her eyes. "Could almost taste the smoke."

Roy Pike's voice, off-camera. "Did you hear me, Worner? Where did you bury the remains?"

"Sometimes I think I'm still there. In a field. Fire. Smoke. Burning. They're dead, gone, and there I am, alive. I ain't gonna die. Count on it."

She grinned her rictus grin and clammed up. Interview over.

Thirty or so dead people, reduced to ash, dental records, charred bone. Families left with nothing to bury. The youngest—a pudgy sixteen-year-old kid who gave the wrong woman a ride. Nice kid. Great fertilizer for the grass. Lorraine the Immane. Step on up and git yourself a T-shirt. Go on, now. Here we are now. Entertain us, Lori.

Pulse. Pulse. Pulse.

"I'm going to find out where she buried you all," I said softly. "I swear to God."

The lone cockroach wriggled his antennae at me. The motel room hummed with silence. I pulled out the Sno Ball cardboard. Mallory's little note. She'd written a phone number on it. I dialed.

A click. Nothing.

So I called the cryptic texter from earlier.

"Yes, child?" Lamiel said.

"You working with Roy Pike or not?" I snapped.

"You're asking if I want you dead?"

"I made a bargain—"

"Oh, I know," Lamiel said. "So do the Hell Wardens."

Tense energy vibrated through me. The Hands started to go nuts again. Lamiel sighed. "You've been given an assistant. I'll send him over."

"*What?*"

Click.

An assistant? What, was pseudo-Satan Dunkirk about to roll up in DRAG-U-LA?

I gnawed my lip. Two more teeth plopped out and fell to the mangy carpet. I left them. They fit the decor here. Who knew what I'd sprout? I already had my Fun Teeth. What a blast those were. What a fan-fucking-tastic life I led. Who knew what horror currently gestated inside Mallory? Something pincered? Sweat pooled under my arms.

Brrrrriiiinggggg!

The motel phone rang.

Front desk lady again, "Enjoying the movie?"

"I...I guess."

Her voice changed.

"It's one about me, ain't it?" Lorraine Worner said.

Holy shit.

"How—how did you—"

"You gotta tell me which movie. Some of 'em ain't great."

"Where's the front desk guy, Lorraine?"

"Tell me, honey. Which one?"

"*The Sociopath and Her Lighter*," I said.

"That producer was a real fuckin' twit, let me tell you. Had this whole 'child-protector' image thing I'd been pullin' off, and then the fucker ruined it when he brought up all that shit with Mallory. They cut my interviews to ribbons. Blueing still proposed to me, though. Bless his heart. One of my biggest fans."

Wait, Blueing? *Edward Sal Blueing?*

"He—"

"Men were sendin' me marriage proposals left and right, honey."

And Mallory looked just like—

My mouth went dry. He'd been raping Mallory. For years.

Silence.

She snorted. "Did y'all screw his corpse after you killed him?"

"Where's the front desk guy?"

"Git on down here and see. Made you a snack. C'mon and say howdy to Lori. Or I burn this motel to the fuckin' foundation."

I hung up. The window worked. I could escape. But she'd probably blocked off the other exits. The drunks and addicts here wouldn't wake up in time to escape the blaze. Anyone above ground level? Utterly screwed.

Unless I said howdy and ate my snack.

My legs tingled. Numbed. I forced them to move. I tucked the revolver and the .45 into my waistband.

I went.

TWENTY-SIX

I SMELLED THE meat before I saw the brains splattered across the wall.

Old man, sprawled on his back, tweed blazer open. Blood clotted the carpet. The top of his skull was gone. Pinkish jelly globs. Not gray. Glazed, half-open eyes. Mouth slack, fillings glinting at the far back. The reek of shit. Drying wet spot between his legs, mixed with red. His slacks were pulled down and the waistband puddled around his knees. Gray pubic hair, bloody and gray and gore covered—*Fuck am I smelling?*—

He'd been castrated.

Dark blood gelled syrup-thick over the stump of what used to be his penis. Oily roasted meat and salt smell hung in the air.

"Would ya look at that?" Lorraine said. "It's snack time."

She lurked behind the front desk, behind a giant air fryer parked atop it. It chirped. She pressed a button, bangles clinking. Sizzling sounds, muffled by glass.

I saw my Hand reach into my waistband and pull out the .45. I neared the desk. The smell intensified. A silver platter gleamed by the air fryer. Pill bottles on it, staged in pristine rows, some generic, some orange prescription, and one blue behemoth—NyQuil, sludgy-sweet NyQuil. Xanax. Unisom. Midazolam. Haldol.

What the hell is going on here?

My mouth and throat welled. Pre-vomit spit. Dull heaves hitched in my chest.

She tapped the air fryer's glass. "Say howdy."

"Howdy," I heard myself say.

In the air fryer.

I saw.

A can of Lawry's Seasoned Salt lay open on the desk. Fat sizzled and popped along the skin—*skin of what, champ?*—and she'd crusted the salt on the outside, ok, the cut end looked black and scabbed, almost necrotic, and a seam along the meat—*what meat, champ?*—had burst so clear juice oozed out like lymph, like some ungodly hot dog at Hell's 7-Eleven, and something rank, sickly-sweet smelled under the grease-stench, not death but maybe urine or urine and death, which made sense, right, they both went together like French fries and ketchup and oh, look at that, there's tater tots in the tray, too. Burned pubic hair mottled the—*the what, champ?*

Lorraine opened the lid. Shook more Lawry's over the tater tots and the sizzling, roasted, finger-lickin' good—

She'd castrated him and cooked his genitals in the air fryer.

I threw up. Half-digested orange glopped onto the carpet.

"You makin' more room for your snack? Hell, I even brought mac 'n' cheese," she said, and tapped a cardboard container on the desk.

Dried maroon crusted under her fingernails, and on her knuckles.

"What's that on your arm?" She asked, "You try killin' yourself, honey? Reckon it'd do somethin'?"

Footsteps. Someone was coming down the hall. I turned. So did Lorraine. She held a gun.

A girl, wearing Cookie Monster sweatpants and black eyeshadow. Face still chubby. Couldn't have been more than seventeen. Purpled needle tracks lined her bare arms. She rubbed her eyes with the back of her hand, staggering towards the lobby.

Lorraine's hand flicked up.

Sound. White ringing in my left ear.

More brains oozed down the wall. Different wall this time. A faint red spray. The girl spasmed on the floor for a few seconds, bruised arms twitching, a liquid *glog-glog* and then trickling fluid. Spreading blood puddle stained the carpet. Couldn't see her head well. Thank God. Acrid gun smoke tanged the air.

Oh fuck she killed her didn't she?

Something hot strangled my left forearm. Lorraine's hand.

But the .45 was in my right Hand.

I put it to my temple, and I stared at her. She didn't let go.

"Bargain's over, Lorraine," I said. "You win."

"You wanna do this the hard way?" She jerked her head to the dead man. "Go on, then. Die. Maybe you oughta finish slittin' your wrist first."

"Jesus, lady! Just kill me! You set this up, got me where you wanted me, and now you won't kill me? Trouble performing, Lorraine? They make pills for that."

"You really ain't that smart, are you? I should kill you now? Git sucked back on down to Hell forever? Probably never gonna see topside again. Wardens might even annihilate me. Or I stretch it out, git a few more days of fun."

Hey, Lamiel? That help coming anytime soon?

She leaned close to me.

"Or maybe I git longer than that. Maybe I git my Honeydoll along for the ride, too."

I started to squeeze the trigger.

"Baby Warden—you remember the exact wordin' of our lil' bargain?"

"I'm not letting this continue, Lorraine."

"Oh," she breathed, "you can do it. I'll take pictures for Mallory while you're trapped in Hell."

"Trapped?"

"Might even cut your corpse open, take a few beauty shots. Be a real scream for Mallory."

"If I die, you win. Go directly to Hell, do not pass go, do not collect spare organs."

"No," she said, and licked her lips. *"If I kill you.* Not 'Baby Warden offs himself.' Your body's your anchor here—if you kill it, you're gonna be stuck in Hell."

"But you're dead. How are you here?"

"Our bargain's actin' as the anchor. So, you'll be rottin' in Hell, and I'll be livin' it up here until the time limit's done…and also I've gotta give you what I promised, 'cause you'll have won by default. Can't kill you if you've killed yourself already."

She slowly smiled. "What's gonna happen if you win, and I don't pay up? Did you specify any penalties? No. Any time limits to pay what I owe you? No, honey. You didn't. Think on that."

Lorraine had a free pass. Forever. Lorraine would be stuck on Earth, but mostly alive and here for her comeback tour. Because I hadn't exactly given Lori a deadline for the actual fulfillment part of the bargain, had I? *Take away my Hands and give me normal ones.* I hadn't specified a time frame or penalties for delaying the reward, no *you've got two days to pay up after the conclusion of the forty-eight hours if this poor dude wins, or else.* I swallowed. Meat spat in the air fryer. Fluorescent light reflected off the old dead man's glasses.

"Like you'd tell me the truth."

"Don't matter which way you slice it—I'm gonna come out on top."

She released my arm. I lowered the .45.

"So quit nosin' around. You set on down and eat your fuckin' tater tots, and then we're gonna have us a chat, honey."

Thoughts kept trying to enter my brain—goodies like *I'm so fucking screwed* and *oh God there's no way out of this*. I merrily functioned. Castrated dead guy? Ha-ha, talk about spotted dick.

"What, no broiled cock for me?"

Lorraine sighed. She took the lid off the air fryer. "Eat your fuckin' tater tots."

I put one in my mouth. I gagged.

Anger flared in Lorraine's gaze. She pointed to the pill bottles.

"Look at all the familiar friends we got here," she said, too softly. "Choke down some fuckin' NyQuil, too."

"What—"

"Swallow it!"

Shallow breaths. She clenched the Nyquil, knuckles white.

"Fuckin' *swallow it,* you piece of shit. Know how hard it is to escape Hell's prisons? Even for a fuckin' second? An hour? And you—"

She hissed. Twisted the lid off the NyQuil.

"It's part of your snack, honey. Motel's rigged to burn. Drink up. And then you're comin' with me. I wanna drink of somethin' else."

Coming with Lorraine? Serial killer road trip? Drink of what? *Lamiel, c'mon!*

She climbed on the desk and stood, NyQuil clutched like a club. Nose to nose with me.

"Drink. It."

"No."

"Demonspawn monster."

I didn't react.

She tilted her head a little. She reached out. Touched my hair. Stretched one of the coils, let it bounce. Then she wiped her hand on her shorts like she'd touched dog shit.

There's no way out of this bargain. I can't even kill myself to escape her. Oh God.

Lorraine wrinkled her nose. "Anyone ever tell you that you reek like camel shit, and those Arab spices you cook with?"

"Get fucked, Lori."

She sprang. I crumbled. I hit the floor, face up. *Shit.* I scrambled, tried to throw her off. Couldn't. *How? How is she this strong? She's tiny?* She grabbed my throat and pressed her thumbs into my windpipe. Choking. I inhaled. Thin sliver of air whistled in. Not enough. *Pulse. Pulse. Pulse.* Lorraine adjusted her weight. Her thighs wrapped around my chest. Rib cut burned. Eau de Lorraine filled my nose.

She spat. Hot saliva ran down my chin.

She raised the NyQuil bottle over my mouth and brought it down. Hard.

White-hot pain flashed through my teeth and lips and lower face. Tasted blood. Broken teeth—*Not the Fun Teeth, though, champ*—lip split. Low cry came out. *No.* She raised it again. *No, not again not again please—*

Again.

Snap. I screamed. Salty blood bubbled. I thrashed under her. She didn't budge. *How is she this strong? NO not again, not again, please Lorraine don't—*

Again.

Lorraine leaned over me. Some foreign smell underneath Eau de Lorraine and her hairspray, some artificially cloyed, candy-sweet cheap perfume sank into me. Gold glitter freckled below her bloodshot eyes. Silver dust caked around unhealthy red tear ducts. Her curls smothered. Heat. Pain. Pain, throb-throbbing.

Something wet and hot slicked over my pulped mouth. Slurping sound. Lorraine pulled back, tongue and lips dripping blood, her throat working. She leaned down again. Lapping. Her tongue.

Her nipples were rock hard as she slurped up my blood.

She pulled back one last time, something white stuck to her lip. A tooth. Mine. She wiped her mouth with the back of her hand, still holding the blood-coated NyQuil bottle, and the tooth fell off her. I didn't see where it went.

I bucked. She wobbled, snorted, and raised the bottle over my face.

Brought it down.

Again.

Springy sound. Cracking. Pain.

Then the weight lifted. There was a muffled thud. A screech. Someone lifted the back of my shirt and yanked me to my feet. I turned.

Edward Sal Blueing.

"Get moving, luv. Car's outside."

I tried to speak. Broken teeth and spit and blood dribbled out.

"You want my bloody help or not?"

Lorraine was pulling herself up.

"Kid—"

I nodded to Blueing. We bolted out the glass doors, and into a dirt-crusted pickup parked out front. Blueing hit the gas. I shot a look back. Lorraine stared at me through the glass, silent and still.

Everything else shrank into nothing until we hurtled over an unlit highway so dark it was practically solid, sliced through by the truck's headlights. I opened my mouth—*Jesus,* it hurt. Hot pain screamed through my face. More broken teeth. I spat them out.

"Did Lamiel send you?" I croaked.

Edward Sal Blueing looked like death warmed over. Pale skin glistened with sweat. Cuts and scrapes marred his face. His Stetson hat was missing. Another vein birthed to life along my right shoulder. I ran my tongue around my mouth. Felt soft gums, my Fun Teeth and a few molars. *More teeth.* I shivered. Had—had I even thought that?

Blueing cleared his throat. "Mate. We really need to talk."

"No."

"Oh, come off it, lil' nipper—"

"*Fuck you!*"

I coughed. Blood splattered out. Tears formed in my eyes. *I'm alone with another predator now. Oh god. Oh god, don't think about that. It hurts.*

Blueing sighed. "Can you let me talk for a few seconds? It's information you need, from our mutual friends down under."

"What could you tell me that would change any of—any of *this* fucked up shit?" I said hoarsely.

"Lori's been trying to possess someone. Someone close to her, or related," he said. "Everything she's told you is a lie."

TWENTY-SEVEN

"LET ME GUESS," I said. "You need some ingredients for a 'counter spell,' some magic mumbo-jumbo to prevent this from happening, which just so happens to involve my blood. I give it to you. Then I wake up, trapped in my body as you pilot it across the country for Blueing's Electric Boogaloo, Part Two: American Adventure."

"Why possess *you?*" Blueing asked. "When I could sucker anyone else into it, mate?"

"I'm not your fucking 'mate' or buddy or friend, Blueing."

"Someone's touchy."

Citrus car freshener failed to cover the stench of decaying meat. No, not quite meat...sickly-sweet. Familiar. *Your bedroom all over again, champ.*

He gestured to his bruised face. "The Hell Wardens are bloody livid about Lori. They get mad enough at me...they'll destroy me. Permanent annihilation."

"Sounds good to me."

Edward Sal Blueing let out a noise halfway between a growl and a whine. "Where's Mallory, mate?"

Bodily fluids. Possession. I slowly pulled the slip of paper out of my pocket. *Blood. Sweat. Cum. Tears? Spit?* I wanna drink, she'd said.

I swallowed. Tried to forget the broiled cock in the air fryer.

"What's this?" I said, and gave it to Blueing.

His breath caught. "But she—"

"Is this a possession spell or not?"

Blueing's voice dropped to a needy whisper. "Where's Mallory?"

I shook my head.

His hands gripped the wheel.

"We need to find her," he said.

Dried blood caked under his nails. Unbuttoned jeans. Fast-food wrappers covered the floorboards. Canvas tarp wrapped around some lumpy misshapen heap lay on the backseat. Nausea shot through me.

"On holiday for this," Blueing said merrily. "Hell Wardens gave me a safari pass to catch Lori."

"What's in the tarp?"

"Garbage, mate. Used it all up."

I kept my voice from shaking. I did that much. "What's in the fucking tarp, Eddie?"

He shrugged. "Not any girl you knew."

I'm going to kill you.

The Hands pulsed and pulsed. Something like an endorphin rush tingled over my lower face and eased the pain. Pleasant warmth. The ebb and flow of charged blood rebuilding, carrying, recreating—energy like a midsummer sun.

I really need MORE TEETH.

Something inside pulsed, *Yes. Yes! YES!*

Pulse. Pulse.

I stared out the truck window, drugged and warm, for an hour—if the dashboard clock was right—and ignored the canvas-wrapped human lying dead on the backseat. The engine whined underneath tinny radio music.

Alien thoughts sang through my head. *Kill him (it) KILL IT—*

He broke the silence with a guttural laugh. "She's the spitting fucking image of Lorraine, isn't she? Smells like her, too. Don't worry. We'll find her."

The crotch of his jeans bulged. Blueing slid a hand down, slid it inside, his pupils engorging like fed leeches.

"We're gonna find her. Gonna take care of her. Oh yes."

—See the threat see the pulse in its throat, RIP TEAR—

He only gripped the wheel with one hand. I could probably jerk it away. Ram the truck into the nearest solid thing. Blueing and I weren't wearing seat belts. Good. Two birds, one stone. Eliminate the threats to others.

—Look at this thing talk, this killer of innocents ARE YOU LETTING IT BREATHE? WHY? Tear its throat out bathe in the blood (taste good, it tastes so good and salty aren't you thirsty?)—

That included me. And wouldn't it be quick? Quick enough at this speed. Less painful than my other options. Sure, Lorraine would be free—but what the hell else could I do?

—You will have the FINEST TEETH but please wait, take BETTER TEETH for now (loaner teeth, splendid for tearing)—

A sharp jolt shot through my Fun Teeth. It spread through my mouth, roof, cheeks, and descended into my stomach. Esophagus teeth. Was I about to get esophagus teeth? Maybe I deserved the Hands after all—everything I touched turned to shit, with or without them, including the bargain I'd made with an undead serial killer from Hell.

I forced myself to concentrate on my surroundings.

"You got a way to contact her?" Blueing asked.

"A phone number that she probably changed," I said, putting the Hands together. "Lamiel sent you?"

"The lipstick bloke? Yeah."

He took his hand out of his jeans and pawed through the glovebox. *Take the wheel. Two birds. One stone.* I shifted in my seat.

Blueing dug out a tiny burner phone and tossed it to me. "Try calling her. See if she'll tell you where she's at."

"Then what? More mumbo-jumbo?"

"Gotta dump the bloody trash. Need more room back there," he breathed, and his tongue flitted out briefly. "Have to be able to reach everything right quick. Right quick."

The body in the backseat. I wished I knew her name. Everything felt slow and surreal, like trying to run through molasses in a dream.

"What's the plan?" I asked.

"Huh?"

I scratched at an itchy vein. "How are we going to keep Mallory from getting possessed?"

Blueing glanced out the windshield, hand slithering back into his jeans. "You find her. I take care of it. Of her. Lori won't be able to possess her."

The Hands were going berserk—pulsing, itching, all of it. Bone covered them up to the wrists.

—*More bone (keener to stab) would you like more?*—

I picked up the phone and dialed the number on the Sno Ball cardboard. *Please, Mallory.*

Two rings, then a click.

"Yeah?" Mallory said.

Relief. She was alive, thank God, and she could talk.

"Mallory. It's me," I said. "You're in danger."

She laughed, a strangled sound. Like something got stuck in her throat.

"*You.* I can't believe this," she said. "How'd you get this number?"

I'd called the same one she left. Was she losing time again? Didn't matter.

"Seriously, where are you?"

"Outside a gas station with a broken-down car. Spent my money on a blanket and Cup O' Noodles."

"Mallory, that's not safe. What if some weirdo breaks in?"

She sniffled, and her voice grew shaky. "T-there's this guy. He's been right outside my car for the last two hours. He's just *staring* at me. I don't know what to do."

You sure knew what to do with Blueing. But a wave of hot rage wiped out the thought. Some guy was trying to hurt Mallory. Some creep. *Pulse. Pulse.* My Hands shook. Rip—*the stomach open strangle threat's entrails around its neck*—reality apart, find her, then tear the threat apart. Break his arm. Put him out of commission. I glanced down at my lap. I'd already gotten halfway through unwrapping the Hands.

"Lorraine wants to possess you. I need to keep her from doing it. Where are you? I can help. Please."

A long pause. I muted the radio.

Blueing pulled over and muttered under his breath. Electric lights glowed in the distance, amber and too-sterile white.

She told me an address that meant zilch to me, then added. "It's over off the interstate. A crappy little gas station with an orange roof."

Blueing opened the truck doors. He grabbed the canvas-wrapped corpse. It sagged.

"No," I said. "No. You can't just leave her like that."

"Can't have it in the truck."

He dumped the corpse on the ground. Something metallic fell out as he did. Blueing plucked it up as he re-entered the truck, and put it on the dashboard.

Mallory grunted. "How soon can you get here?"

"I don't know," I said.

"I see Lorraine, too. Out the car window. Waving at me."

The temperature dropped twenty degrees. I shivered.

"Listen. Don't open the door, don't talk to her, just hang tight until I show up. Okay?"

"Yeah. Okay, man," she said, then hung up.

A brass name tag sat on the dashboard. *Annie C.* It had a horse sticker on one of the corners.

"Got a knife, Blueing?"

He started the truck. "Gotta drive on for a bit."

I took a deep breath. I delicately put the phone back. Blueing flinched a little when the Hands got close. Good.

"Put her name tag back," I said quietly. "Then her family can identify her. You can do that at a fucking minimum."

But he chuckled, stroked the name tag once, and drove on. We left the poor dead girl on the side of the road, wrapped in a rotting canvas tarp. Nameless. She didn't have a name now. It'd been stolen. Anything could come by and do what it wanted to her.

TWENTY-EIGHT

FIVE MINUTES OF driving went by before I snapped.

"Pull over. I need something sharp."

Blueing snorted. "What for?"

I slowly inched my Hand over, keeping eye contact with his bloodshot gaze the whole time. He squirmed.

"I'm going to get Mallory," I said. "I have to bleed to make that happen. Capice?"

He swallowed visibly. "Sure, mate. No need to get ruffled."

Blueing drove off the road and cut the engine. He scrounged up a pocketknife. The blade seemed decent enough, so I took it. I hopped out of the truck. Warm night air smothered me like a damp washcloth over the nose. Sharp little pains shot up from my gut to the back of my mouth. I held the knife where I'd had it before and pressed in. No dice—the bone had spread over my palms. The blade didn't so much as scratch it. Thanks, Creature-Feature Body.

Wrist, then. I dug in, trying to get a baby cut. It stung. A stream of blood oozed out. I baptized my other Hand in it too, for good measure. Dim lights twinkled ahead. Amber. Orange. Like the roof of the gas station. I let my focus fuzz out.

I'd done this before. I could open a portal again. I had to.

Mallory. I need to go to Mallory Worner's location. Mallory. Jasmine and cigarette smoke, strawberry nicotine gum, her dirty nails, the way her burn scar caught the sunlight—pink and shiny, it glittered, somehow—the way she scrubbed her hands together, her soft, low-pitched voice just veering on husky, and her black death-stare. *Mallory.*

Nothing. Nada. No weird membrane to feel.

I balled my fists. I repeated the address she'd given me under my breath, blood dribbling down to the ground. Okay, the gas station. Visualize it. I could do that much. *We're traveling down the interstate, dead night, and we pull off. The gas station's got an orange roof. Sun-bleached tangerine orange. It's microscopic, some Ma n' Pa place with a Pepsi logo squeezed in on the sign and the cashier's got a Louisiana drawl they tease him about, yeah, the guy outside sells crawfish out of a Styrofoam cooler and—*

The address.

I breathed out. Folds of invisible silk brushed against my Hands. I lashed out. Sliced at the air. It tore open, smooth as melted butter. A glint of orange peeked through. *Yes.*

I jumped through the rift, still trickling blood.

I ONLY GOT to look around for two seconds before Mallory popped out from behind the gas station. She sprinted at me. I tensed. *Shit. Is that Lorraine?* Then I saw her non-leathery skin, and the milliliter of life left in her eyes. Mallory. Rhinestones crusted her black tank top like barnacles, and she wore a jean jacket over it. Thick black liner ringed her eyes. Gaudy silver eyeshadow glittered.

Mallory doesn't wear that much makeup, champ.

She stopped in front of me. Her lips trembled.

"Oh my God. Triple-Six!"

She threw her arms around me. I held her close. She shook a little. An odd, nasally sound burst out of her. She rubbed her hands on the back of my shirt.

"Are you okay?" I asked.

"Yeah."

Her smell. Cigarettes. Hairspray. Something…rotting? Weird.

I lisped when I spoke. "The Hands. Watch out. My mouth's all fucked up. Lorraine. Is she here?"

"She vanished. Like something out of a movie."

"Babe, did she, uh, try to get your fluids?"

"Fluids?"

"Blood. Sweat. Tears, spit, and, uh, cum. Any of that?"

She burrowed her face into my chest. Heat seeped through my shirt. Black decayed patches carpeted her hands.

"No," she murmured.

Out of the corner of my eye, a flash of white. A Styrofoam cooler sat on the sidewalk, with a puddle of water underneath.

"The guy that was bothering you. Where is he?"

We pulled apart. Blood coated her hands. Some of it soaked through the back of my shirt where she'd wiped them.

"He's gone," she said.

A sick feeling crawled in my stomach. I ignored it. Lorraine might be running around. The Hands pulsed, sending sweet pain spilling up my arms. It wasn't safe here. And Mallory really needed a hot meal—

I don't think Mallory's here, champ.

She loved me. What else mattered?

"Babe," I said. "Do you, um, need to get that birth control stuff still? I can take you. I figured out that the Hands can open rifts through reality. I sort of did that to get here. Did Lorraine have a skinned arm?"

Her cheeks burned scarlet. Her eyes darkened.

"Oh, I been thinking a lot lately. 'Bout that."

About something from Rosemary's Baby or the Omen, growing inside you? Courtesy of me, certified demonspawn?

"I didn't get Plan B, Triple-Six," she said.

I swallowed. "I know you don't—you don't want to have a baby. That's okay. I can open a rift to a pharmacy, or something."

I had to force the words out. What the hell was wrong with me? This was the easiest decision I'd made in the past week.

She stripped off her jean jacket. Decay blanketed in streaks up her arms. Pus beaded. She wrapped the fabric around her hand. A weird tingly feeling electrified the inside of my mouth, numbing my split lips. She grabbed my wrist, and gently placed my Hand on her stomach. Warmth. Her heartbeat hammered through the thin tank top.

"I'm not getting Plan B. I know it should be too early to tell, but God, I think I can feel it. I'm pregnant."

Her voice shook. "I-I want to have your baby. And—"

Pregnant.

"What?"

"I want to have your baby. I want—I want to be a family, man. I want all that soppy shit, the wedding and the baby and the Christmases. We can do better than our parents. I know we can, Triple-Six."

She grabbed my jaw and kissed me, thrusting her tongue deep in—*ouch, Jesus*—and one of her hands crept around the back of my neck. It stroked with mechanical rhythm. Addictive saliva. Pitcher plant nectar, too sweet, something rotting—*old meat dead meat*—nope, nope, just happy living girl, with her half-decayed hands smearing something creamy across my skin as she stroked—*oh God her flesh is ROTTING OFF*—but okay, we'd all had bad days, so maybe this was Lorraine—*no it's NOT!*—and maybe all those blank episodes weren't episodes and maybe she'd been possessing Mallory for—*years, holy fuck, does it rot you?*—and maybe it didn't matter because I could just let her love me and believe and pretend and not taste the rot in her mouth.

"I love you," she whispered.

I love you.

Everything I'd ever wanted to hear her say. *I love you*, and I'd seen her stomping on Blueing's balls, seen the red raw blood fly up and splatter on her cheek, and still loved her. Screw Lorraine. Screw her weird mind games. I could still win this bargain. Then there'd be no more freakazoid Hands. I could finally make love to Mallory and not have to worry about hurting her with the Hands. We could have children, and suburban holidays and normal jobs. We could create that. Now we even had a little baby to love. We'd loved each other so much that we'd created a new life from that love; we'd kindled a child.

I could make it work. I could take night classes or online courses. Get a job. Any job. Mallory could stay at home and take care of our children and love them, and maybe that would keep her stable. And if Roy Pike wanted me back in desert-hell…would desert-hell even be that bad, if we had a life there? Ma was dead. She didn't need me to babysit anymore. Mallory loved me. She trusted me enough to get over her whole 'I won't ever have kids,' thing. If I loved her enough, she'd get better. No more sedatives, no more psycho episodes, no more arguments and suicide attempts—from either of us.

Right?

"I love you, too, babe," I said. "I always have."

I opened a rift in a haze of bliss, blood mingling on our hands. Mallory wiped her lips, painting them crimson with it, and we kissed again. Salt and iron and pitcher plant nectar. *And rotting meat.* Warmth, blooming in my belly. Her boobs perked up. Now both of us ground against each other, smeared with gore, exchanging it, only stopping to clamber back through the rift.

PITCH-BLACK NIGHT. GRAVEL grated underneath our shoes. No truck headlights. No running engine, either, but a faint smell of exhaust. The Hands pulsed. Mallory tensed.

"Blueing?" I said.

Crunch. Crunch. Insects buzzed. Raspy, gargling breathing a foot behind me. I whirled around and hit something squishy. It fell to the gravel with a *thump*.

"Augh," Blueing groaned, from the ground, "What the bloody hell's wrong with you? I was trying to piss."

"Funny," I said. "I didn't hear you pissing. Your jeans are zipped up. Almost like you're full of shit."

I'd punched him in the gut, where his skin was covered by his T-shirt.

"Stage fright," Blueing said. "I don't like them little birdies starin' at me."

Sure, Eddie. He was a dark, balled up silhouette on the ground. I walked over and crouched down by him. I needed to make this message stick. Mallory stayed back.

Her voice broke. "I thought we were safe. What's going on?"

"I'll make it safe," I said. "Trust me."

Canvas tarp around the dead girl—around Annie, she had a name—and her name tag still sat lonely on the dashboard. Could've easily been Mallory.

Something burst in the roof of my mouth. Stung.

A taste of blood.

—Kill it kill the threat PROTECT THE INNOCENT—

I reached for him. "Need a hand up, Blueing?"

"Don't touch—"

I seized his bare arm and squeezed it. *One Mississippi.* It spasmed, starting from the wrist, spreading up. *Two Mississippi.* It went limp. I released it. Blueing swung at me with his good arm, uttering panicked whimpers. I sidestepped. He fell again. Mallory snickered.

"Go start the car, *Eddie*," I said. "Do it with one arm. I believe in you. And if you decide to pull something again, you can have a day as a quadriplegic."

I slicked my tongue around my mouth. Sharp new things jutted out. Roof-things.

More Fun Teeth.

Blueing spat as he stood, and stumbled over to the truck. A minute later, it rumbled to life. Headlights lit us up. I yanked open the truck door for Mallory, but she shook her head.

"I wanna sit by you," she said. "Backseat?"

Had I hit some cosmic jackpot? We nestled in the backseat, me wrapping up the Hands, her getting bloodstains all over the seats, and Edward Sal Blueing shooting glances at Mallory in the rearview mirror. His face turned whiter each time.

Now call Lamiel. Make him put the Hell Wardens on!

But Mallory wet her lips until they glistened, slid her left hand down, down, and wrapped it around my dick, loosely holding the shaft, and every thought went mushy. *More. Touch it. Touch me. Love me.* Her callused thumb rested on the tip, right over the slit—wet and probably oozing pearly beads of pre-cum—and rubbed it in crazed circles. Dead gray flesh sloughed off of her hand. She'd dip to an agonizing slowness, stop, then rub-a-dub dub at like two-hundred rpm, smirking at me.

She sat like a man, her legs spread wide, and her free thumb and forefinger flicked an invisible lighter in the air.

"Need a smoke?" I said.

She snorted. "I can buy my own now. Git this—I'm rich."

"Oh?"

"Lorraine couldn't profit off of all those books and movies they wrote. Legally, anyway. It's called the Son of Sam law. But the money's still there. I found out. She willed it to me before they fried her."

She said it so casually. Maybe it was hard on her.

"Don't beat yourself up over it," I said. "Hell, start a charity. Or use it for the baby. Aren't they expensive? I don't get that. Don't they just suck on a boob every four hours?"

She blinked and shifted her weight. "Yeah. Guess we could."

She moved on top of me, straddling me with her thighs, and cupped my jaw. I tried to focus. I wanted to rip off her clothes. Random gory thoughts droned in the background. I needed to call Lamiel.

I can smell her rotting.

No. No, I couldn't. She loved me, goddamn it, and nothing was going to screw that up. Mallory loved me.

"If I stay alive for another forty-eight hours, we're in the clear," I said. "I know things have been shit lately. Jesus, I've nearly been shish-kebabbed and shot. But Lorraine won't hurt you. Not as long as I'm alive."

She rested her forehead against my neck, then nibbled along my jawline, her boobs grinding into me, and the smell of her—*rotting meat, cigarettes, gasoline*—in my nose. "Really? She won't?"

She bit my earlobe. "What if you hurt me?"

"Never."

"What if I wanna light a fire? You gonna jab me with sedatives again?"

She kissed me. Deep and long and sugar-sweet, her tongue digging in, the sharp edge of her teeth grinding into my lips. *Oh God. Yes. Yes.* I pressed in. So goddamn sweet over the taste of *rot*—I dug my tongue in, fishing for more, more.

"That's not Mallory, mate," Blueing said.

Yes it is.

Both her hands trailed down my neck. She bit down on my lips, harder and harder. *Ouch*, but yes, Jesus, I wanted more so I let her. Warm blood funneled down in a heady rush, trailing pleasure and want. She panted. Her hands returned to my throat.

I was hard, throbbing. *Need it*. I took her hand and gently tried to move it

down, but she didn't budge. Salty blood ran down my chin. My lips burned. Good. Fantastic.
"Do you love me?" she asked.
"I love you. Yeah," I breathed.
Her hands tightened around my throat.
Lorraine's voice grated out of Mallory Worner's body.
"Of course you do. I've blown you more than *she* ever did, honey."
She pulled away, grinning like a mad demon. And squeezed tighter.

TWENTY-NINE

MY HEAD SPUN. I gasped for air. Lungs ached.

No. Nope.

Her face loomed over me in a blurry smudge of hair and pale skin and two empty black pits for eyes. I slumped into the seat. No air. Pounding behind my eyes. Pounding eardrums. Pounding chest.

I bucked and thrashed. She strangled harder.

I got harder. The inside of my scrub pants tickled against me.

An impact, wet-sounding. Then a grunt. Her fingers slackened. I gulped in lungfuls of air, wriggling away as she twisted around. Everything sharpened. Blueing turned back and wrenched a handful of her curly hair. The pocketknife glinted between his teeth. His bad arm hung at his side, useless.

He bared his teeth at me. "Fucking hit her!"

She had to be in there somewhere. Had to be.

"Mallory," I said hoarsely. "Fight back. You're stronger than her—"

She laughed. Tears oozed out from the corners of her eyes.

"Honey, you seen her lately?" Lorraine said. "Mallory ain't good for nothin' but a body to prance around in. Got no spine. No brains. 'Bout as much heart as me. And she wants to piss on back to that desert fuckin' prison y'all been living in." She jerked her chin towards me. "She's even got herself a lil' dog for the road to Oz."

"You said we—"

"Known you for years, Honeydoll. In more ways than one."

Vomit churned. *Years?* All those times Mallory blew me, or kissed me... *for years?*

"You're—you're lying. You're full of shit, Lorraine."

She grinned. Dim light shadowed half her face.

"Bless your heart, Baby Warden. You really should git that lil' black mole removed. Y'know. The one right by your eye hole, makes it look like there's two on your cock."

Jesus fuck no.

"Hated you for years, Baby Warden. Know how hard it is to escape Hell? Even for a little-bitty second? Slip away durin' guard changes, slip into Mallory's body, try to have fun—and what do I git? *You.* Jamming fuckin' drugs down my gullet till I can't stay awake no more. All these years, I've been tortured on a weekly fuckin' basis by *you*."

"All these years?"

"Mm-hmmm. All of 'em."

Lorraine the Immane. She was a serial killer that'd eaten people. The same mouth that ate human fat, chewed it...her mouth, had been wrapped around me and sucked me to oblivion.

More teeth burst through the thin membrane inside my mouth.

Blueing exhaled. He released Lorraine's hair. He twisted his head around, staring at us. Lorraine Worner whipped around to face him, couched in her daughter's body like a malignant tumor.

His pupils dilated. Softened. "Time to go back, luv."

This was still Mallory's body. If he touched her, I'd kill him. I unwrapped the Hands. Lorraine slithered off me. I scooted away.

"Hurt me, you hurt her too," she said, turning to me. "And she can feel it."

"All this time...it's been you, parading as Mallory? Hurting her from the inside? Did I even know her? Ever? And you murdered Blueing? You? You framed me," my voice got higher and higher, "told me you loved me? That I mattered? *How long—*"

She chuckled. "Remember that dead jackrabbit? When y'all were ten? And you took the lighter away from me after I'd slit its throat? And you stood there, about sick to up your fuckin' Cheerios?"

It'd still been bleeding when Mallory—well, Lorraine—dragged me over to fetch wood. Dish soap suds covered my apron. Maqluba day, then dishes, then dusting after Ma stared blankly at the TV for another four hours. I swallowed back vomit, ran back with the lighter, and rifled through my stash of "sleepy medicine." Something mild. NyQuil or Benadryl. Not a Haldol situation yet. At ten years old, I knew the difference.

My Hands shook. "The lighter."

I took it from Mallory every time she had an episode. Those sedatives I shoved down her throat. Babysit. I'd babysat an undead serial killer for over a decade. What the hell did that make me? Her lips on mine. The necrotic patches. Blood-coated hands. *I let her touch me and I liked it. I fucking liked it. I'm still half hard right now.*

"You were the one who drugged me. We murdered Blueing."

Her black eyes bored into mine like soldering irons. "You'd like that, wouldn't you? Ain't that insultin'. Like I'd leave a body rottin' like that, no fire, nothin'? Honey, Blueing was *all* Mallory. I ain't an amateur. Want that, go talk to Eddie here."

"He hurt her," I said, lips numb. "He raped her."

"Raped me, too, Honeydoll."

"You—"

"Sometimes I seduced him," Lorraine said, raising her voice. "And what'd I git for tryin' to be nice from beyond the motherfuckin' grave? Eddie here turned fuckin' traitor."

"Remember how funny you thought it was, luv?" Blueing said. "When I asked for your bloody autograph?"

"Gave you one, didn't I? And you ain't gonna lose it."

Blueing got up onto the center console, one knee resting on it, and the other in the driver's seat. He unzipped his jeans. His greasy hand slid down into the bulge. He pulled himself free. A little bead of something gleamed in the eyehole as it sprang out. He leered, empty-eyed.

Pulse. Pulse. Pulse. I raised the Hands.

"Don't," I said.

"That's not her, you bloody moron. It's Lori."

She lounged on the seat beside me, a hand over her mouth. Over Mallory's mouth.

"But it's Mallory's body," I said. "You got a sample of the Hands earlier, Blueing. Wanna see what happens next, get closer. I fucking dare you."

Heat crescendoed from my spine to my brain. Sweat stung along my upper lip and trickled down. *Pulse. Pulse.* Blueing slowly reached up. I tensed. He flicked on the overhead light. Fat-colored light, like a cadaver's yellowish deposits, filmed over us and cast stark shadows.

"Paralyze her," he said.

"What?"

Blueing's eye twitched. "Wanna help her? Keep Lorraine from using her body."

So Blueing could yank out his cock and rape her again? Turn Mallory into another corpse in a tarp? Hurt her again?

—*Why is the threat alive?*—

How fucking stupid did he think I was? *Pulse. Pulse. Pulse.*

—*Why is it alive? Rip tear kill his stomach, claw his intestines out and WEAR THEM why is it alive?*—

The name tag shone on the dashboard. Reach out and do it. Grab that tiny vertebra, the one jutting like a knob on the back of his neck. Holiday,

Blueing. Was it a holiday for Annie, too? *Pulse. Pulse.* Easy to reach. I curled and uncurled the Hands—

—Yes oh yes it feels so GOOD—

The threat's gaze went up to them. Threat leaned away. Its weight shifted. Coiling for a strike.

Lorraine had no expression. Nothing in her gaze, no sadness or fear or even anger. She sat and stared at the threat. Her mouth tightened for a millisecond.

Threat sprang.

I caught it.

It hit me in the shoulder. Jerked back. I latched onto its limp arm. *The knob. Neck vertebra.*

I snapped forward—

—Yes GRAB IT and HOLD then tear—

Wrapped my Hand around the back of its neck. Good aim. It wriggled briefly. Then it spasmed. Each jerk grew weaker. *Pulse.* I held on. No Mississippi's. I held on and on. Energy cascaded down throughout my arm and into the Hand, sticky, tingling, like a bee-sting and here was the honey, the sugar-sweet honey—*oh yes oh God it feels SO GOOD like lightning like coming—more!*

It threw its head back. The mouth opened and spasmed. No sound came out. To my left came a regular sound, but a good sound. Safe sound.

I released the threat after it went fully limp. It collapsed onto the center console, drawing in shallow breaths. Seared into its neck was a scarlet imprint of my Hand. The good sound continued, nasally and rhythmic. Laughter. My guts lurched. Wait a minute. Good sound? *Oh shit.* The threat—Blueing, its name was Blueing—gurgled weakly.

Lorraine Worner kept laughing. Tiny blisters gleamed like blind eyes where I'd paralyzed Edward Sal Blueing.

I stared down at the Hands. *Monster.*

"...You...b-bastard..." Blueing choked out, his lips barely moving.

His breathing was ragged and sporadic. Every inhale came a little later than the last. I saw myself grab onto his shirt, rolling him face up. Grayout tickled the edges of my vision. He deserved it. He didn't deserve it. He was an undead serial killer...but nobody deserved to be locked in their body, unable to move, waiting for their lungs to freeze up.

Lorraine nudged me. "You be my Honeydoll, you git to do that all the time."

Blueing wheezed. Lorraine whipped out a cigarette, stuck it between her teeth, and lit it. She inhaled.

"Honeydoll wasn't a term in the bargain," I heard myself say.

"Ain't about the bargain. Never was. Bargain's the anchor—for now."

"What the hell do you want?"

"Bless your heart. Tag along, Honeydoll. I got preparations. I got fires to set. Things to do. You can paralyze folks for me. I ain't lazy, but I ain't dumb, either. Work smarter, not harder."

She snorted. "Hell, maybe I'll even follow through. Take away them Hands? I can do that. I got experience."

Go with the serial killer possessing Mallory's body, see the sights, abandon all morality and become a literal monster. How tempting. Blueing moaned. Scarlet lines crawled down his neck like submerged vines.

"Get out of her body," I said.

Lorraine leaned forward and pried the pocketknife from Blueing's fingers, her face blank. The lighter rested on her lap. She ran her thumb along the knife's blade gently.

"I can pretend to be her," she said, and unbuttoned my jeans.

Mallory still feels everything. She can't exactly say yes.

"No."

She put the knife to her arm and sliced a finger-long cut. Blood wept from the cut.

"Ouch. Mallory's screamin' somewhere inside," Lorraine said, voice monotone. "So you're gonna come with me. You act up, I put her hand in a vise and crank it. Or I jam a knittin' needle where it don't go. Hot stoves ain't nice to flesh. Why should I care what happens to her body? Ain't mine—"

"What do you want?"

Nothing but Blueing's choked breathing from the front seat. Cigarette ash fell. The cigarette lay erect between her fingers and smoldered. She studied me, face mask-like. Something malevolent and alien sparkled behind the eyeholes.

"You, Honeydoll."

She slid a fresh cigarette out of the pack and offered it to me. "Smoke? I'll light it."

She picked up the lighter, tilting her head to the side. *She doesn't want you to pick it up. Because Lorraine doesn't want you to light a fire.* If I ignited something, Lorraine had to show up, regardless of whether she wanted to or not. She'd never shown up possessing anyone. Could I forcibly separate Mallory and Lorraine, by igniting a fire, and forcing Lorraine to reappear? It was worth a shot. If I separated them, even for a second, maybe I could help Mallory.

I faked a sigh, letting my shoulders slump. "You said you wanted to chat? What's a Honeydoll, ma'am?"

"Mm-hmm," she said. "I like hearin' you say 'ma'am.' Do it again."

Anyone darker than Wonder Bread has to call you ma'am, don't they? What a fucking shocker. What an unexpected turn of events, Lori.

I smiled my bestest Stepford Wife smile. "Ma'am? What do you want?"

She offered the cigarette to me again. I took it.

"What if I told you that I could live again? In this body, or even another? Said I'd never die, and I meant what I fuckin' said. You think you love Mallory, but lemme tell you—you've probably spent more time around me than her. Think on that. I ain't sayin' 'I love you' or any of that shit, but I know you, Baby Warden, and I know what you want. I call it 'a titty to suck.' You call it 'love.' So. I want you by my side, helpin' me, as I bring myself back to life. Hell, maybe even after that. I dunno. Depends on if I can make you into a good Honeydoll. I've been planning this since before they fried me. Whether you go along or not, I'm gonna make it happen."

"What happens to Mallory?"

"I give her what she's always wanted. Death."

No.

Lorraine's voice grew honey-sweet. "She'll be happier dead. You'll be happy, too, because I'll be alive and well in her body, and then we'll have fun. Do all kinds of things. Me and my Honeydoll, killin' and burnin' across the USA. I'll give you everything she couldn't. I'll say the right words, give ya all the fuckin' blowjobs you want…hell, maybe we even have the baby you knocked her up with."

"Can you sound like Mallory again?" I said. "Please?"

Lorraine beamed, and Mallory's voice came out. "I can do better than that. I love you, Triple-Six. I want to be with you forever."

It was as real as a talking doll.

It sent a gut-jolt of hurt through me.

"See, you don't really love Mallory. She would never say that shit, and she's too fuckin' sentimental to lie and say it to you, Baby."

As Lorraine leaned in, I snatched the lighter off her lap. She startled. I flicked it. With a *click*, the flame ignited.

Two women in the backseat. Lorraine, closer to me. Squeezed against the window was Mallory, curled into a ball. Catatonic. Lorraine snarled, lips curling back. She scrambled for the lighter. I jerked it away.

"Mallory," I said.

A grunt.

Lorraine punched me in the gut. I hunched over, gasping. She scooped up the lighter. Hurled it into the front seat. Blueing wheezed. Each breath bubbled.

"Mallory, please!" I said.

Lori groped for Mallory's arm. I wrenched her back. She whipped around. Huffed. Snapped her head forward. Dug her teeth into my wrist. Pain stung down. My grip loosened. She broke it.

"You said you wouldn't," Mallory choked out. "Said you wouldn't hurt him."

Lorraine disappeared. Mallory's body abruptly relaxed.

"Told you," Lorraine said, using Mallory's lips.

"....L-Lori...it's a...bl-bloody pipe...dr-dream," Blueing said. Her skin flushed red. "Eddie? You got somethin' to say?"

"...C-conniving...bitch."

Lorraine clambered onto Edward Sal Blueing, smile twitching around her mouth. It ripened. Like rotting peaches gone moldy. Her teeth showed, even the pointed canines.

"Eddie. Oh, Eddie," she said. "Been a real thorn in my side. C'mere. See how nice I am."

Nausea roiled in my stomach. Was she going to turn to me? Hurt Mallory?

She got atop Blueing. She centered his head on the console, still smiling. Frantic bubbling sounds came from him. His eyes wheeled. She straddled his chest, thighs encircling him, and put her hands on his shoulders.

She caressed his cheek. "Look. Look at me, Eddie."

She lowered her face until it almost touched Blueing's lips. Her eyes locked onto mine.

She ripped his throat out with her teeth.

Blood spurted up onto her face, daubed her shirt and neck. Red droplets quivered in her hair. *Oh God, oh God!* I froze. *Run. Now.* Lorraine chewed the flesh she'd bitten off, jaw working. She swallowed. Without breaking eye contact with me. Low hyena chuckles came out of her. She dipped down again and mauled more of Blueing. Eating.

Run.

I gagged. Clutched the door handle. Lorraine mauled and mauled, using Mallory's body.

She stared at me the whole time.

Honeydoll, she mouthed.

I ripped open the truck door and ran.

THIRTY

I GOT ABOUT fifty feet away before I threw up.

I ran. I coughed. I hacked and hacked, then somewhere along the line, it turned into dry heaving. Dry heaving became hurling.

Blueing's spasming throat. The crimson gush of gore. The muscles tearing off in strings like raw steak. Lorraine chewing. Chewing the fat. Wasn't that what they called talking? *Oh God. Oh Christ.* A shaking, deep in my chest. It spread to my limbs. Overhead, the sky loomed pitch-black. No moon, no stars, just summer humidity smothering down. Dry grass crunched. Electric lights glowed faintly, far away. Too far away to reach via foot.

The truck engine revved.

I heaved again.

Her eyes, stabbing into mine as she ripped his throat out and ate him. Black beyond shark-like. Black like an empty universe. They weren't angry.

They were ravenous.

For what, I didn't know. I didn't want to know.

I wiped my mouth with my arm and kept running. Couldn't see a thing. I kept running. My legs screamed. I tripped, fell over, panted. Got up. Kept running.

Mallory can't run.

I stopped, breathing hard. No matter what else I was—bona fide freakshow, monster—I couldn't leave her like this. I hadn't left her when I'd thought she'd fricasseed Blueing.

But Jesus, what was I supposed to do? What *could* I even do?

I fumbled in my pocket. No burner phone. It was probably sitting right by Blueing's still-warm body. Great. How was I going to reach Lamiel? Roy Pike? Anyone?

Engine noise. Crunching grass. Up ahead, red taillights burned like twin coals.

The truck stopped.

I froze, heart racing. Was she about to get out? Shoot me?

Lorraine wanted to murder Mallory. She had control of Mallory's body. Unless I wanted to hurt Mallory, it was Hands off. I imagined Mallory, spasming like Blueing, corpse-still except for her eyes, those could look around…if she lived. If I timed it right. Too many ifs.

The truck slowly turned around.

Headlights.

She's going to run me down.

Pulse. Pulse. Pulse. Teeth popped. The Hands itched.

Under my shirt lurked a spread of veins. I felt them. They'd gone past my arms and shoulders, coiling around the submerged outline of my ribs. Like blood poisoning. Yeah, it might kill me. But what would happen *if it didn't?*

A hundred feet away, Lorraine Worner stared at me through the truck's windshield. She reached up. Overhead light flicked on. Blisters marred her—Mallory's—neck.

I stared back. Neither of us moved.

More teeth burst out of the roof of my mouth. How many rows were we at now? Four? Six?

Demon. Monster. I shivered.

She waved at me.

The engine snarled to life. Tires spun. Diesel fumes clogged the air, engine spitting louder and louder. Revving up.

Like a bull about to charge. Time to be the matador. When the truck came, I'd jump off to the side and dodge. But stumbling in the dark wouldn't last long. She only needed to get lucky once, and I'd either die or metamorphose into something that'd make the eels living in the Mariana Trench envious.

I unwrapped the Hands. Smoke from burning rubber darkened the stars above.

What the hell happened with Blueing, champ? You thought Blueing was an it. You didn't even think before you zapped him. Before you—no. Lorraine killed him. He'd been a serial killer. He'd hurt Mallory.

You didn't mind kissing her when she was rotting from the inside out.

"Shut up," I said aloud.

Lorraine shifted gears.

The truck came for me.

Headlights.

Closer.

Too close—

I stumbled, hit the grass, and rolled away into the weeds. The truck surged past, throwing gravel and dirt into my face. I sneezed. Then it was gone. Engine rumbled in the distance.

It felt good to paralyze Blueing. So good. *You're roided up. Who's your daddy, man?*

I slashed out at the air. No portal.

I didn't need to find out. Nope. Because sooner or later, I'd hear that I was actual hell spawn, a real monster, something grotesque, and you know what? Later worked just fine for me. And I had to help Mallory.

Get me out of here.

I clawed again. Membrane slimed in my Hands. I picked at the scab on my wrist, coughing. Warm wetness oozed down.

Truck headlights gleamed. My stomach backflipped. It sped by a couple hundred yards away before turning closer. It passed by, slowing. I laid on my stomach, face in the grass. I didn't breathe until the headlights blinkered out, and it rumbled on.

But she'd find me eventually. I couldn't exactly see in the dark. *Gee, how inconvenient.*

Inconvenient.

If I knew then what I know now, maybe I'd still have my original set of eyes.

I would've guarded my thoughts more. Understood that when your parentage is sketchy, there are certain things you don't get the luxury of thinking. Certain words that trigger change. Obstacles are obstacles, and if that obstacle happens to be your own flesh, well, tough shit. Get rid of it. Change it.

Yeah.

Hell doesn't do inconvenient.

Inconvenient.

The Hands tingled. Already fired up, the thrum of energy in them intensified. Exhaustion slammed over me like a warm lead blanket. Had I heard the truck engine? Not important. No need to run. I suddenly felt relaxed. Stoned. *Pulse. Pulse. Pulse.* I clenched and unclenched the Hands. I needed to be still. *Still? Wait, what?* Had to stay frozen like a statue because the fix would hurt less—

What the fuck? What fix? What the fuck is going on?

My muscles locked up. I tried to move. Couldn't. Numbness crept down my forehead and over my eye sockets, like hopped-up Novocain. Numb. Oh, God, *why the fuck was my face going numb?* Was this a stroke?

My elbows bent. I had nothing to do with it. *No. No, no, no! STOP IT! Make it stop, make it stop, I said that last time and it STOPPED so STOP!*

Tears ran down my cheeks. *Stop. Please. Don't do this.* But my arms kept moving towards my face. I had nothing to do with it. Forced relaxation slammed over me again. Be still. I really had to be still for this, because it was good and it really wouldn't hurt very much—SHUT THE FUCK UP!—and the fix was going to make everything better, please relax and understand. *No.*

The Hands, sharp at the tips, gently grazed my cheeks. *No. No.*

Maybe it wouldn't be a bad idea to sleep, get some perspective on this whole thing. It wouldn't hurt. Give me time to heal after the fix—*She's after me!* Well, I couldn't just escape in the dark, now, could I? What a silly thing to do—*What the fuck are you doing, tell me what, please oh Jesus STOP!*

The Hands continued moving up. I had nothing to do with it. All I could do was mentally scream as the Hands worked. The bottom half of each Hand braced against the sides of my nose. Braced against each cheek. *Stop. Please.*

The bony tips nestled into the crease of each eye. Like a spoon in a bowl. Like an ice cream scoop. The numbness blotted out the pain.

The Hands dug in. Hard. Hard bony edges ground against my eye sockets, still they dug *deeper*, and I didn't move, didn't try, sensation bored painlessly in and in, the Hands scooped cleanly, flicked down, *schlorop*, nice wet sound like mud.

All I felt was dull pressure.

Night darkness. Then a deeper black. *Oh, ha-ha, I get it! If you can't see in the dark, claw those useless fucking eyes out! Great fucking solution!* The Hands snipped two moist cords off and retreated down to my sides, an eye dangling from each. My eyes, gone. Green. Got them from Ma. Never needed glasses. The vial of Ma's ashes swung against my chest as the shakes started anew. A hyena laughter chittered out of me, but I didn't feel it, just fake heavy relaxation, and Jesus God, was this going to happen again? And again? Paralyzed. Hunted. Blinded by my own Hands.

A scream—or a sob—built beneath an artificially-sweet tiredness. Underneath it all, something excited. Something that was *not me* pulsed foreign joy. Like a puppy learning how to sit, large-pawed and eager to please. *Look! I'm helping! I'm so good at helping! I fixed it for you!*

Crickets chirped. Grass rustled. Lorraine hunted.

Eventually, I unfroze. The numbness lifted. My eye sockets ached bone deep.

Engine noise, close again. Vibrations in the air. Strong smell of exhaust.

No clue where it was, other than close. No way to dodge Lorraine this time.

Portal-time.

Whether I liked it or not, the Hands existed. I had to know what that meant. What all of it meant.

"Take me to someone who can help," I mumbled to the Hands, to my body or whatever intelligent thing lurked in me, "Please. I'm blind."

Membrane slid between my fingers—er, pincers. I lashed out vaguely in front of me. Slime caressed my hands. A lush tearing noise occurred. Electricity prickled up my arms. A breeze swirled over me, ozone-tinged.

Grrrrrrr!

Heat.

Headlight-heat.

Close enough to feel the heat baking—

Head spinning, I sprinted into the rift.

Wind screamed by. Engine. Dust polluted the air behind me as Lorraine floored it, missing where I'd been by inches. The rift began to seal. I'd pass out soon. No black spots dancing in my vision, but I felt it.

Prickling in my eye sockets.

A flicker of green flared in the black.

I collapsed. Hit a glazed floor that smelled like varnish—wood?—and a soft voice murmured something indistinguishable. I blacked out.

THIRTY-ONE

"SON…"

Deal or No Deal?

Roy Pike? Here? Where was "here?" *Bed. I'm lying on a bed.*

Everything I'd seen and learned in the past twenty-four hours came rushing back. Mallory might be pregnant via me, oh, hey, she's been possessed off and on by her undead serial killer mother for years, who I've been inadvertently drugging, so now she hates my guts, too, and speaking of, Lorraine and I might've banged, probably had, and there was no way to save Mallory so far, no way out of my bargain.

I opened my eyes. Where the hell was I?

I was lying in a California king with purple silk sheets. Lots of stains on these sheets. White splooge stains. Of course there were. The carved ebony bed frame was gaudy as Marie Antoinette gone goth. A leather ball gag hung off one of the posts. Three blown-glass bongs smoked on an end table. A smell of good quality Kush overpowering chocolate. Wine-colored walls. Dim, warm light.

Roy Pike glowered at me from a leather-padded chair.

"You're goin' back to the desert cell, Project 0666."

"Where am I?"

Roy said nothing. Good old Roy. This was probably fake hallucination Roy, so—

Holy shit! I can see.

I gently probed my face. No more empty eye sockets. It didn't hurt to talk. No sore battered pulp of a mouth…oh, Jesus. What, exactly, did I look like now? A nasty cold sensation chilled over me. I had to find a mirror. I rolled out of bed, ignoring Roy. Dried blood coated the sharp tips of my Hands.

"You hear me, son?" Roy Pike said, and stood to block the door.

"Look, Roy. Mallory's in danger. Lorraine's killing people, for God's sake. I can't let that happen, so can you please move?"

He didn't. His mouth tightened.

I took a deep breath. Calm. Rational. Use logic to appease my lifetime jailer.

"I—you know what?" I said. "I can't even tell if you're real or not, Roy. Because you fucked me up so badly that every time I'm in a dark room for more than thirty seconds, I see shit that's not there."

I balled my Hands. *Pulse. Pulse. Pulse.*

"You let Mallory get hurt. A fucking *seven-year-old, Roy!* You put her in the care of Edward Sal Blueing, and you wanna act like you didn't know what was gonna happen? All these years. You call me every *fucking slur in the book,* you starve me, you slap my Ma, you throw me into solitary at random, you—and what did I do? I tried to be nice."

I swallowed back acid. "I tried. And I'm done."

"Project 0666, I had reasons—"

"Move."

I shoved him aside. I shoved something aside. I didn't turn to see if he'd vanish like all the other fake-Roys.

I had bigger fish to fry.

What fresh horror lurked in my eye sockets? My teeth? I slicked my tongue around my mouth. Lots of Fun Teeth. Great. I padded through a tiny hallway with a couple of closed doors and a bare light bulb. I cracked open doors until I found a bathroom, and went in. A mirror cabinet hung above a sink with faucets rustier than my Spanish. Thanks, budget textbooks. *Gracias.* A nervous laugh burst out of me.

Bloodshot. My eyes looked like I'd just smoked a whole bowl of weed, but… they were still green. Thank God. I leaned closer. I didn't look at my teeth. One horror at a time, please. The red veins laced over my sclerae. Bulged. Weird. Not super noticeable, but definitely not standard-bloodshot. Thicker, knottier veins, coiling around my iris. Lying in wait. Lurid red.

Something icy trickled into my gut.

I closed the bathroom door. I flicked the lights off.

Sharp pain surged through my eyes. I closed them. Opened. Pain gone.

I could still see.

Everything seemed fuzzy, like I'd smudged Vaseline over my eyes, but it was visible. Okay, but I still looked pretty normal. Ish. I looked in the mirror.

What the fuck are those?

Veins.

Veins engorged, emerged, and meshed over my irises, forming thick mats of red over the entirety of my eye. Red like a hooker's lipstick. Like oxygen-rich blood. No more whites. No more irises. No more pupils. Just eyelids holding layers of lacy veins in a ball-shape, step ten feet back, and you'd see red blanks where my eyes used to be. Oh, wait. You wouldn't. *Look on the bright side, champ. Need a job, just show up at the set of any horror flick. They'll save a shitload of money on colored contacts.*

I stared at them.

"Okay," I managed.

Teeth.

I turned the lights on. My nightmare eye-veins receded back to normal-bloodshot-mode. I opened my mouth.

Fun Teeth. Nothing but Fun Teeth now. Needle-like teeth crowded my gums…and the roof of my mouth. Rows upon rows of inhuman teeth ringed my maw, at least four more behind the front set. *Triple-Six, what sharp teeth you have!* The better to—actually, what the hell did these do better?

I giggled. Hysterically.

"If you don't like them, try again," someone said behind me.

Lamiel stood in the doorway, holding a mug of hot chocolate and clad in one of those T-shirts you could personalize with your name. *My name is LAMIEL, and I've got too many KIDS!*, it said. It was yellow as a pencil. Purple lipstick slathered on his mouth. Beneath, energy scuttled. The Hands tingled.

"What?" I asked.

"You can always remove eyes," he said. "Perhaps you'll gain other sights. Vital signs."

"You're telling me they'll just keep regrowing?"

He nodded.

I swallowed. "W-Will they go back to normal?"

"Normal?"

"Human. How do I make that happen?"

Lamiel blinked at me. "They can't devolve. Why would you want that?"

"I'm *stuck like this?*"

He fished in his bathrobe pocket, face expressionless, and pulled out a metal tin. He cracked it open, revealing some very promising gummies, and ate one. Lamiel offered me a gummy.

"What the hell are those?"

"Edibles. Thirty milligrams of THC in each, child," he said, and popped another into his mouth.

Holy shit, this dude was a stoner. A bona fide THC master. One of those edibles would knock me straight into next week, and I'd go laughing all the way. The green gummy sat on Lamiel's palm, like a forgotten fruit from Eden. Tempting—get high, lay back, let everything happen.

But wasn't that exactly what got me into this mess in the first place?

"Need to have a clear head. So—I'm just turning into a literal monster, and I'm supposed to be okay with that?"

"Normally there's a fun tour. Of Hell. You'd have your half-siblings along, they'd show you the crystal spires and the cities, the silver canals…Hell's usual highlights. You wouldn't be going through this alone."

"Half-siblings?" I asked.

"We need to talk. Come."

He guided me down the hall, and over to a table piled with papers. Roy Pike sat, pen in hand, thick work gloves on, and didn't look at either of us. Mugs of something warm steamed between the papers. We sat. I yanked something hard out from under me. A neon-pink, silicone dildo. Jesus Christ. I dropped it and wiped my Hand on my pants.

"What's he doing here?" I said.

Lamiel sipped his hot chocolate. "Roy? He's acting as a scribe. And a witness."

It took me a second.

"Oh, c'mon. Really? You're going to rope me into *another bargain?*"

"What do you know? About Hell, possession, your nature…how, exactly, do you intend to solve the Worner situation?"

"I—"

Lamiel's voice dropped to a soft croon. "Would you like knowledge?"

"No, but I need it. What are your terms, Lamiel?"

"So naive. Barter with me more, child. Never ask someone their terms outright. It shows you're vulnerable. Ask what might interest the other party instead. Let's try again," he said. "Would you like knowledge?"

Polite, but not weak. It made sense. So, I drank my hot chocolate and jutted my chin out like I owned the joint.

"It wouldn't kill me to be more informed. What can I do for you, Lamiel?"

He drummed his fingers on the table. Orange polish gleamed on his nails. "Solve the Worner issue. Hell needs it solved fast. I need…more soft power. Reputation. Influence. Normally, the credit would go to your father, Amalek."

Demon dad?

Lamiel sipped. "Want information? I get the credit. It's very simple. You don't have to do anything besides solve the Worner issue. After that, you'll get a good job assignment…you know, I'm on speaking terms with the Hell Wardens. Not many can say that."

This sounded okay so far. It almost certainly wasn't. Through a nearby window, a sliver of moon rose. The microwave read *10:06 p.m.* Had I been out for over twenty-four hours?

"Are you a demon?"

He grinned. Unpleasantly. "Angels aren't real, Project 0666. Not anymore. All of us got...chained."

"Fallen? Like, fallen angels?"

"Roy, get my Xanax. I'm too sober for this conversation."

Made two of us. Roy Pike scurried off. Fallen angels? Demons? Roy was some variety of psycho Christian, Dr. Hitch had been a Catholic, and Ma never cared about religion. But there had to be someone upstairs who could help put Lorraine back in Hell, or take off the Hands. Right?

"Angels aren't real?" I said. "What about heaven? God? Satan? The Devil? I'm—I'm not like, Satan's kid, am I?"

"Heaven never existed."

"*What?*"

"The clouds and harps? Bullshit. It's simply a...nicer section of Hell."

"My Ma's in Hell?"

"She's in a lovely garden. A palace. We like to keep our concubines happy after they die. Amalek, in all likelihood, will never let you see your mother again—"

My voice got higher and higher. "So God's in Hell? Everything's in Hell? Everyone's in Hell? That's just where they go after they die? *Where's God?*"

"No one knows," Roy Pike said.

He slapped a pill bottle into Lamiel's hand. Lamiel dry-swallowed several, shuddering.

Lamiel tilted his head and leaned in close. "You want an angel, child? *You want God?* Someone to *come down* and *save* and *solve* all your problems? Most of which *you* created?"

"Lamiel. He's a kid—"

"You treat him like a dog and you discipline him like a man," Lamiel said. His gaze glazed over. "There's no God. Not the way you think of it. Never was. We existed, we dominated, we lived without limits, and there was a force birthing, creating, but not...not sentient. It just *was*. And it was good."

A harsh breath. "And then—eons ago, long before the pond scum breathed, before the meteor hit—it vanished. Suddenly we were chained, bound to physical matter, trapped in one plane of existence. For eternity."

"Not Earth, I'm assuming?"

"Hell."

"So, how are you here? Why should I believe anything you say?"

He smiled. "Here?"

"Earth. You can't leave Hell—"

I blinked. "We're in Hell, aren't we?"

"The outskirts."

"What about those other times I saw you on Earth?"

"Temporary. Call it a helping hand from one of my children."

Yeah, not vague at all. Trust the demon with purple lipstick and a million random sex toys scattered on the floor.

Heat, dry and sudden. Something orange glowed in my peripheral.

"Will you bargain, or not?" Lamiel said. "Allow me to sum this up, child—nobody's coming to help from above, you're trapped in a situation you know nothing about, your prayers mean nothing, Mallory Worner's deteriorating rapidly—both body and mind—Lorraine Worner's planning something and can't be restrained, the Hell Wardens despise outside influence—good luck communicating with *them*—and given who your father is, I doubt you'll be able to pass for human in another five years. Now, what are you going to do about it?"

The only thing I could do.

I picked up a pen.

"Let's make a deal, Lamiel."

THIRTY-TWO

"**IF MALLORY WORNER** dies, you can't revive her," Lamiel said.

"Why?"

We'd almost figured it out, after fifteen minutes of opaque lawyer-speak. Roy Pike scribbled every single solitary word down. I'd screwed up my last bargain. I wasn't about to blow this one, too. Not with Mallory's life on the line.

But now I couldn't revive Mallory?

I cleared my throat. "What if I do? Huh?"

"Be a dear and fetch the switchblade, Roy," Lamiel said.

Roy grunted, stood. "Which one?"

"Whichever's the sharpest."

Flies frenzied in the windows. Lamiel sucked a hit off a candy-apple red bong, leaving purple lip prints around the mouthpiece. He exhaled.

I clenched my Hands together on the table. Sweat beaded between bulging veins. I'd bargained. Truthful—no Faustian bullshit—and immediate information on possession, the laws governing it, Hell itself, the Hell Wardens, Lorraine Worner, and my heritage. Other topics? At his discretion. Lamiel wasn't exactly in a chatty mood after gulping down lethal amounts of Xanax and 100 mg of THC per hour. That I'd seen. Go figure. Magic revolver? Still tucked in my waistband, along with its bullets. Lamiel wanted to broker for it. Roy Pike eyed it, lips twitching.

Stagnant silence, broken by the whine of flies.

"What happens if I revive Mallory Worner?"

"You'll be responsible for ending the Worner situation. Fully responsible," Lamiel said softly. "If Mallory's soul leaves her body…and Lorraine sees the opportunity…she'll be able to permanently possess it."

My mouth went dry.

"Do you know how much you'll have to mutilate the body?"

"Stop it," I said.

"After you kill it? Tell me, child. Do you relish the idea of hunting her down? Cutting Mallory Worner's corpse into pieces to evict Lorraine? Because *you'll be doing that.*"

Dead. Her brain, inert jelly. Mallory. At age twenty-two. And she was— *Pregnant.*

If I screwed this up, it wouldn't be just me dead. It'd be Mallory, too. And whatever I'd knocked her up with. I had to throw Lorraine back in Hell, ASAP. Even if it meant I'd have to live with the Hands and the Eyes and God knew what else.

Roy Pike walked over, carrying a baroque tray. A gold-handled switchblade rested on it. Ornate filigree twined in organic webs around the handle.

Lamiel plucked it off the tray.

"What's that for?" I asked.

Snick.

Rust caked the edges of the blade. Old blood flaked off.

"Do you accept the terms I've laid out?" Lamiel asked.

"Yeah. I accept," I said.

"The gun. Would you accept something from me in exchange for it?"

Roy Pike flushed red.

He opened his mouth, but Lamiel cut him off. "You can have it back later, dear. We don't have time for your neuroses."

"Yeah, Roy. We don't," I said.

"Would you like another assistant? Someone more...competent than Blueing?" Lamiel asked.

Roy stood, posture stiff as ruined leather. "No. I ain't doin'—"

"Roy Alexander Pike will be on his *best behavior.* I can assure you. He's quite adept at energy manipulation. His assistance, on the Worner issue, in exchange for the gun. Sound good?" Lamiel asked.

Roy Pike, unstoppable doler of punishment...standing, and silently seething. How the worm turns. He'd worked plenty with both of the Worner ladies. Knowledge in spades.

"He'll have to obey me?" I said.

"Yes. Until the Worner issue is solved."

"No bullshit. No trying to screw me over or kill me?"

Lamiel drawled, "I hope not. For his sake."

"If something happens to Roy—excluding intentional action on my part—will you give me another assistant until the Worner situation's solved? By solved, I'm referring to our definition of 'solved,' which constitutes Lorraine Worner's soul returned to Hell."

He nodded.

"Deal," I said, and placed the revolver on the table.

"Once more, Project 0666. Do you accept the terms I've laid out?"

The Hands pulsed. Something crawled through my guts.

"I agree to your terms, Lamiel."

Sudden heat.

The room itself flickered. Reality flickered.

Taste of myrrh, condensed resinous sunlight, coiling at the back of my mouth. Flash of orange. Energy. There but invisible.

Churning eldritch energy.

I was a speck in a vast sea and the room was there but not there, like the walls and the physical stuff and the illusion-organs of the man-shape in front of me—*oh God what's going on WHAT IS THIS*—would crumble like wet cotton candy if I touched them—

The man-shape threw its arms out, metal switchblade gleaming, it waited for me to step forward, but the man-shape wasn't really *there,* easy-peasy, silly me, the *energy* of Lamiel, whatever sad little arrangement of letters it'd picked to call itself, that *sentient energy* was bigger than a hurricane and rotating around itself—*make it stop I don't wanna see behind the curtain, Mr. Wizard—*

"Lamiel," Roy said. "The kid can't handle this."

"He wanted information. This is quicker than talking."

Pulse. Pulse. The man-shape smiled at me, arms open. Prodigal son, return home. Come. I felt my legs move. In a "room." I was in a sea of sentient energy—*foreign energy*—both truths existed at once. *Bye-bye, brain.* Speck. I floated in the heat. In the house, I embraced an illusion.

The deal is struck.

Pain stung my cheek in a fiery line. A cut. Warm wetness ran down. The man-shape licked my blood off the switchblade—*the illusion of it*—the energy absorbed it. Eldritch matter coalesced around me. Thickened. Heat tickled the back of my skull. My eyes.

"Taste and see. Taste and see," it laughed, and some warm wash of amusement lanced over me.

I closed my eyes. Now there was only one truth. Glowing sentient sea of orange light. I drifted like a rag doll. *Mallory, I love you.*

I don't want to go crazy. Please. I didn't—

Come and taste. Taste and see.

Something warm brushed my mouth, intruded. Aseptic non-taste. *Do you want to know?*

I'll do anything to stop Lorraine, and I forced myself to think, *Tell me what I bargained for!*

Blood. Salty. Metallic.
Taste and see.
Oh.
Quicker this way.

I drank. The laws of possession hummed through my skull as I swallowed illusion-blood, liquid information, knowledge…

I took my Communion in Hell.

PART 3:
SPOOKSHOW BABY

THIRTY-THREE

SOMEONE PRESSED THE burner phone into my Hand. They told me the Hell Wardens recovered it after Blueing got culled.

Okay.

Blood lingered on my tongue. Taste of copper and myrrh.

Someone dragged me off the floor, cut my arm, and squeezed my wrist. *People aren't supposed to do that.* Someone told me to think about Earth.

Earth. Take me there.

Someone sighed, "Goddamn it, Project 0666. Move your arm. What's he—"

"Processing. Give him a few minutes."

Someone moved my arm through the air, muttering.

"He's a kid, Lamiel."

"Like you were, once?"

"I'm human enough, goddamn it!"

"No, my dear. You're not," and the voice saddened, "How many times can I apologize for that? All I have is infinity. My children. The kingship we feign in our gilded cages."

Rift membrane slimed in my Hand. Neon slash hung in the air. Dilated. *Pulse. Pulse. Pulse.*

"How long do you have, Roy?"

"Don't matter. I ain't goin' to—to change. Not like him. I thought…"

"But your little experiment failed. You can't ignore the inevitable. It's like puberty. By the time it happens, you'll welcome the changes."

Someone dragged me to the rift.

"Like hell I will," Roy Pike said.

Lamiel smiled. "See you in three months, *son*."

Roy pulled me into the rift.

DEAD SOULS CANNOT *travel to Earth without something to anchor them there. This can be an item or a person. When alive, a soul's anchor to Earth is their body.*

It spat us out in a flat dead field. Flat as a plate. Cast in sallow golden browns. Tumbleweeds shifted across the earth. Beyond them, nothing. No structures, either man-made or natural. Early dawn blued the sky, and the stars were fading out.

If the anchored item or person becomes destroyed, the bond is broken. Ingestion of bodily fluids creates a temporary anchor point that can atrophy over time, if not used regularly.

Regularly.

As my sanity staggered back in, I shivered.

Possession causes considerable damage over long periods of time. The presence of two souls in one body creates an unstable situation...If abused, the body will eventually disintegrate, and be rendered unusable.

The blisters on Mallory's arms. Those necrotic patches. Her flesh, sloughing off.

"Roy," I said slowly. "Can you summon the Hell Wardens?"

Why hadn't Lorraine just killed Mallory? Taken over her body long ago?

A soul cannot possess a corpse permanently. The corpse will still begin decomposition if not brought back to life or revived.

"I can't. You know how touchy Dunkirk gits?"

"Can't or won't, Roy?"

His cold gaze glittered.

I reviewed the facts. Lorraine had created an anchor point, a gateway through which she'd possessed Mallory for years. She'd slipped out of Hell, maybe found some other patsy to make a deal with while she did it...Blueing? Not important now. She'd done it. I'd probably prevented several massacres before my tenth birthday, with the magic of legal sedatives. Peachy.

"Look, I need the Hell Wardens. I think I can trap Lorraine and turn her over to them, but—"

"You want all five thousand Hell Wardens? Good luck."

I gritted my teeth. "No, Roy Alexander Pike. I want to talk to the head guy. Dunkirk. You need anything to manage that?"

"Gasoline. Lighters."

"Great, so do I," I said. "Can you magic us to a gas station?"

He chewed a piece of grass. A humid breeze played through the air.

"Be easier if you did."

"Give me a second."

His upper lip curled. "Don't it bother you anymore?"

"What?"

"The more you use those hands, the more *you change*," he said, and spat on the ground.

He didn't have to tell me.

It felt good for a *reason*.

The veins would spread. Cover every inch of skin. Spikes on the Hands, growing. Layers of hard bony stuff mounding, burying me alive. Day by day. Would I even care when someone, maybe even Mallory, dry-heaved at the sight? When people were scared of me?

Deep in the meat of my throat, just below my Adam's apple, neoplasmic flesh pulsed. Lamiel's "blood." Emitting energy as it'd trickled down into me, myrrh and infernal Communion. Like some cousin of cosmic radiation…

I made myself focus. Lorraine was hurting people while I stood here having my tenth existential crisis.

So Lorraine possessed Mallory. She slipped out for fun times. At what point wasn't that enough? She hated Mallory. Was it vengeance? She hated me. But she hadn't been lying when she said she'd come out on top. She'd wanted to bargain with me and trick me into removing her safeguards. Blueing had been an unexpected variable, but one that she'd adapted to. So, assume that Lorraine's original plan was to possess Mallory's body, then have me perform the summoning. If Mallory told me to draw a circle on the floor in my own blood, and started chanting…would I have just rolled with it? Probably. Especially if she did it naked.

It would've taken a demon-hybrid to alter the ritual into a bargain, via the pure energy matrixed throughout our physical bodies. Aka "magic."

If I lost the bargain? She'd be free to run around on Earth as a quasi-ghost until she paid up…or until the Hell Wardens caught up to her. But she preferred possessing Mallory. Even if that meant she had to take breaks. Two souls, one body.

What if Lorraine knocked Mallory's soul out? In a way that left Mallory's body intact and empty?

And what if a certain lovesick guy resuscitated said body?

Goosebumps prickled over my Hands as I readied them, and they burned, slow and sweet. Heat hummed through my throat like the raw aftermath of a scream.

Who would come back?

Mallory?

Or Lorraine?

I OPENED THE rift. Exhaustion muddled my steps. For all I knew, Lorraine had possessed Mallory and thrown herself in front of a truck. The bargain acted as Lorraine's anchor to Earth while she wasn't possessing Mallory. Could I force the bargain to end early?

Or.

Light a fire.

Intentionally summon Lorraine. It'd rip her out of Mallory's body. Then I could tie her up or distract her until the Hell Wardens came up with a better solution. Lorraine weighed a hundred pounds, max, and stood a whopping five foot one. What if I just...punched her? Like, actually put force into hitting her?

Punching women. What a great life-path I was on. Totally not the monstrous, steroid-fueled scheme of a demon-hybrid hitting some kind of infernal second puberty.

"Can you find me zip ties?" I asked.

Roy made a face like he'd chugged kerosene.

"She's going to possess Mallory's body. Permanently. Roy, I know you hate me, but can you do a good job for her?"

"I'd do anythin' to keep Lorraine Worner caged."

"Yeah, ditto."

He entered the rift. "You didn't see the bodies, son. The ones she forgot to hide."

We stepped out into the parking lot of a 7-Eleven. We went for the door, Roy Pike shuffling as if in pain. The burner phone vibrated. *Zzzzt!*

I pulled it out.

She'd texted me at 3:03 a.m. *Kid do u wanna another snack?*

At 6:17 a.m., *I love you, Triple-Six.*

6:19 a.m., *Don't let her hurt me. Please. I love you.*

A picture of Mallory's slit-open wrists accompanied the last text. Her blood had puddled on the hard surface below them. Big puddle. Two vertical lines.

Current time? 6:34 a.m.

Shit.

Nausea threaded through my chest. Maybe Lorraine just wanted to pilot Mallory's corpse until it rotted to pieces.

I hunted through racks of gas station lighters while Roy Pike filled a red gas can. I selected two rhinestone-encrusted BICs. Found some zip ties next to the car stuff. I forced a scream back. Jesus.

She wants you to freak out...take another look at that picture, champ. Really look.

I did. Those cuts were shallow. Blood barely pooling up...honestly? I'd seen

Mallory do worse. I'd seen her slice her arms so deep the tendons peeked out like exposed wiring. In this lovely tableau, Lorraine had probably murdered someone, put Mallory's wrists on the blood puddle, cut them, and snapped a beauty shot.

Was she trying to get my attention for a reason?

I fingered the phone. Felt the pleasant hum in my throat.

Time to lure Lorraine.

I called.

"T-Triple-Six?" Mallory said. "God—I'm bleeding out. I'm sorry. I couldn't—"

"No. You're not."

"I—I can't take this anymore. She cut me, Triple-Six. She *hurt me*. Why weren't you there?"

A sob. "I loved you. I loved you so much. And now I'm dying and I don't wanna die, I don't wanna die, oh God, she said she'd kill me because I killed her, and now I'm bleeding…there's so much blood. I'm s-sorry. We could've had a baby."

I took a deep breath. It did nothing.

Mallory sobbed again. "I wanted to have your baby, man. I love you… and now it *hurts. I didn't want it to hurt! I wanted you to love me!* Why didn't you *love me?*"

I flinched. My breath caught.

Her words slurred together. "I love-d you, man. Ss-sorry…"

Very sad.

Very fake.

"Lorraine, are you fake-overdosing or fake-bleeding out? Pick one and commit to it. Jesus."

A single grunt.

"T-Triple-Six—"

"That's a shitty impersonation of me after two-fifths of vodka and a rewatch of *Edward Scissorhands*. Not someone dying of an overdose. Or blood loss. I've seen my Ma try to overdose three times. I crammed a finger down her throat to force her to vomit when I was twelve. I watched her bleed out on the kitchen linoleum after she slashed her wrists, and I tied the tourniquet that saved her life at the tender fucking age of six. So you know what? Talk to me like an adult, or don't talk to me at all."

I hung up. Turned towards the cashier.

He was already a pale kid, but he'd gone *white*-white. He clutched at his *Insane Clown Posse* T-shirt like a maiden aunt having a fit of the vapors. His hair looked like someone had opened a package of Top Ramen and glued it to his scalp. Sweat trickled down a column of neck tattoos.

"How's it going?" I said and smiled. "It's hot out today, isn't it?"

His mouth dropped open.

Shit! My Fun Teeth.

"Yeah, so that was, uh, my director. We're, uh, doing this new rendition of *Hamlet,* y'know, the one with the dude that makes all those whiny monologues? We're revamping it. Hamlet's a struggling dude exiled to the trailer park, kinda like Eminem, y'know, where he, uh, he's got all this talent but he's super raw? It's like, uh, if Shakespeare and *8 Mile* had a baby. So that was my monologue. They got me in a side role. I was just running over to my other play, so I'm wearing my prosthetics to see if they're good enough to last through a play. That one's in October, it's kind of a freakshow love story thing, takes place in a haunted circus? Yeah, so I'm playing the Lobster Boy role, and they thought it'd be cool to see if they could give me these teeth, maybe add like a piranha-kid backstory, but the director was thinking, *hey, what if the CIRCUS makes Lobster Boy put the fake teeth in?* Uh, anyway, it's a charity thing. We're donating the profits."

I placed the lighters on the counter. Cashier didn't move. He gaped at my teeth.

I could almost hear his thoughts. *Those aren't fake. That was the shittiest lie I've ever heard. Those pincer hands aren't fake, no way.*

I scooped up the lighters, threw a twenty on the counter. "You know what, buddy? You keep that change."

I met Roy Pike outside. *The field?* I mouthed. He nodded. I pocketed the lighters. *Pulse. Pulse.*

The phone vibrated. I answered.

Lorraine rasped, "Just tryin' to prove a point, kid."

"What do you want?"

"What do you want, *ma'am?*" Lorraine said. "Honeydoll. I wanna use them Hands. What demonspawn brand are you, anyways? I know some 'bout that."

"Lorraine—"

"Ma'am. It's Amalek. Ain't it?"

She knew about Demon Dad?

"Yeah, so?"

She giggled, horribly girlish. "Ever wonder why you can't git Mallory out of your mind, Honeydoll? They call Amalek 'The Guardsman.'"

"Okay?"

"Amalek's kids," she said. "Baby Hell Wardens. Y'all latch onto one or two people to protect." Her voice hardened, "You thought you really loved her? Honey, you love the *me* in her. Not Mallory. Mallory's barely a fuckin' person."

"Shut up!"

The Hands shook. Plastic crunched on the phone's case.

"She doesn't have to die," Lorraine said.

"You said—"

"Y'know, I reviewed my plan. Only need one body. It don't have to be Mallory's. So I been callin' you, Honeydoll, 'cause I know you think you love her, and I reckon, what the hell, maybe I let the kid save Mallory. See how nice I am? See the issue I'm havin'?"

I squeezed the package of zip ties. Lure Lorraine. Play by her rules. Then I'd hand her over and hurl her into Hell.

"You're a lot smarter than those movies and books made you seem."

She snorted. "Gonna do it, or not?"

"What, exactly, do you want?"

"Work for me till the bargain's up. I'll kill you. But not her. Honey, you git to guard Mallory's body. You'd like that, right? I'll even let you bandage her wrists up, just like every other fuckin' time."

"Lorraine—"

"You can even kiss her goodnight. When I ain't in her."

"Where are you?"

"Summon me. I'll take you to her."

Blood. Sweat. Cum. Tears? Spit? What if she'd found some random person's bodily fluids? Possessed them? Couldn't she keep doing that? There was so much I didn't know.

But she needed to buy that I'd given up. Yes, ma'am, I'm a weak loser that wants you to blow me. Pretty please? Sure, I'll let you incinerate innocents. Lorraine the Immane, here are your offerings. Blood, sweat, cum, and bedazzled lighters.

I whined, "Okay. You win. I found some, uh, lighters I think you'd like. Ma'am."

"That's the shit I like hearin'. Be seein' you."

Click.

I opened the rift. Back to the dead field. Sun peeked over the horizon. Each step crunched on dehydrated grass.

"How long will it take?" I asked Roy Pike.

"Fifteen minutes."

Wordlessly, I pulled a few zip ties out. Roy Pike scattered gasoline around the field, sweat beading on his scalp. He burned symbols onto the grass, using laser-like flares of flame. Occasionally, he stiffened. Hunched over.

"Roy," I said. "Are you okay? Do you need me to do this?"

He stumbled.

I ran, caught him before he hit the grass. Unbuttoned section of shirt shifted, exposing white chest hairs. Age spots. A plastic chemotherapy port.

Cancer.

"You have—"

"Don't touch me."

I let his shirt go. The Hands weren't bandaged up. Made sense.

But he stared at the Hands, upper lip twitching up. "Never touch me. You're an abomination, Project 0666. I don't take kindly to 'em."

"I'm also a disappointment on two planes of existence. How long do you have, Roy? Huh? Earlier. I heard that conversation. You're Lamiel's kid?"

His fist flashed towards me.

Pain. Burning through my nose. Blood streamed down, I licked it up. Swallowed. Something in my throat shifted. Felt nice. We stood there, both breathing hard and staring at each other. Then he picked up the gas can and sidled away.

"Take me fifteen minutes," he said.

I nodded. Took the rhinestone-encrusted lighter out of my pocket. If Roy Pike had three months left to live, why bother him? *Eat it again, raghead.* Nope. He had cancer. He was old. He could pretend to be human. Lucky him. I didn't have that luxury anymore.

All done, something inside me thought.

Lorraine knew about demon-hybrids. What did I know? I assessed my inner cache of knowledge.

As a hybrid, you bridge the gap between inert flesh and pure energy. You embody part of your father's Self, His energy, His purpose...to protect, to explore, to delight....It varies between demons.

So? Thanks, Creature-Feature Body. Fun Teeth, Fun Eyes, and what else? Fun Throat?

Your flesh adapts to the environment.

Lamiel? What was that guy's purpose? To collect dildos? Be weirdly pervy?

The Explorer. Offspring of Lamiel are driven by the core need to explore new sensations and experiment.

Amalek?

The Guardsman. The Protector. Offspring of Amalek are driven by the core need to protect the vulnerable.

What was Lorraine talking about earlier? Why would I ever be driven to guard her, even for a day or two? She had all the innocence and vulnerability of an industrial crematorium.

I flicked the lighter.

She came.

THIRTY-FOUR

LORRAINE POINTED AT Roy Pike and asked, "What's he doin'?"

"I don't know, ma'am."

She'd appeared a few feet away from me. I could smell Eau de Lori. Gasoline. Cigarettes. Mold. I wadded the zip ties up in my right Hand. Distract her. Lure her over.

"Ain't he the one that kept lockin' you up? In solitary?" Lori asked, and tilted her head, "Ain't solitary a real bitch? Me, I'd jack off till I rubbed myself raw. Just to feel somethin'."

Heat flushed over my face. Okay, maybe that happened to me. Once. Twice. A lot.

I held up the rhinestone-encrusted lighters. They glittered in the sunlight. Lorraine's bangles and silver eyeshadow sparkled. The sunlight brought out the crinkled burn scar on her cheek and her freckles. Roy Pike chanted in the background, but it sounded faint and tinny. Early morning quiet muffled his voice like a blanket of unseen snow.

She smiled. Her black eyes flattened.

"C'mere. Give 'em to Lori," she said.

I took two steps closer.

"I don't bite, honey."

I swallowed. I took another step. *Pulse. Pulse. Pulse.*

"Is Mallory okay?" I asked.

"Nobody did nothin', did they? 'Bout your mama. I seen it in Mallory's head," and her voice softened like a lullaby. "She could've killed Roy Pike. But she didn't. She waited till you could kill someone else for her."

Bullshit. Mallory wanted to. I slapped the lighters into her open hands. I lunged out, zip tie already looped. Got it around her wrists. Pulled it tight.

Grabbed her bound hands.

Lorraine stood, still smiling her closed-lip smile, head cocked, expectant.

"Your mama ever feed you? Care for you? What'd Mallory ever do for you, besides use you?"

"Shut up!"

So soft. So small. Her voice.

"Kid...you ever hate her? Your mama?"

"Rot in Hell, Lorraine."

"What was it like? Watchin' her kill herself, over and over. I don't mention this a lot, 'cause I don't believe in bitchin' about my childhood, but you think I got a white picket fence?"

She laughed. She phased her hands out of the zip ties.

Shit.

"She bled. Tell me, kid. You cooked and cleaned and loved on her, and the bitch wanted to die? Instead of takin' care of her kid? Of you? I kept my shit together for Mallory. Wasn't easy, but I put food on the fuckin' table. Why couldn't your mama?"

"You—"

"Sssshhh, honey. It's gonna be okay."

Something shook in my chest. Gray fuzzed the edges of my vision. Not there. Oh, God, where the hell was I? A field? My lips felt numb. Blood. Bleeding, expanding puddle on the linoleum, *oh Jesus, Ma, what are you doing why are you doing this. Am I not—is it because I'm wrong?*

"Don't," I said. "You're making me—"

"Where was she when you got thrown into fuckin' solitary? *Where was anyone?*"

"I don't know," I heard someone say.

Wetness ran down my cheeks. Lump in my throat. When had I put a Hand in Lorraine's hair? It tickled. Old hairspray filmed over my skin.

"You hated her. Deep down. You wanted her dead."

"No I didn't. I—I just wanted..."

I just wanted her to fall asleep and not wake up so Dr. Hitch could be my parent and make cookies with me and not scream that I was a fucking pincered freak if I did something wrong or threaten to kill herself because—

"It's okay, honey. I know how it feels."

Lorraine ground into me, tilted her head up. Her mouth dropped open a little, soft tongue and soft lips—*pink the same pink as Mallory's*—and something warm caressed the back of my neck. Her pupils dilated.

"Anyone ever loved you? Just for bein' you? Not for nothin' else?"

"N-no."

"She bled. She bled and moaned and cried while you saved her. What'd you say? You said 'Ma, I love you.'"

I love you.

Ma.

Ma—

"Ma?"

Back from Dr. Hitch's. We'd baked snickerdoodles that day after lab stuff. I opened the door, and my house was dark. Yeah, okay. I wandered in, the stench of mouse crap and cockroach and stale old Fritos strong everywhere. Floor-popcorn crunched under my shoes. The A/C growled. I gnawed a snickerdoodle, saving half for Ma. She'd like it. I could cheer her up. I left the cookie on the coffee table. For some reason, Ma made a funny sad face if I handed her something, so I didn't.

"Ma!" I yelled, "I'm back!"

A garbled sound came from the kitchen. I walked over, flicked the light switch on, and—

Not bright red like paint, it was dark red, but there was too much and it kept dribbling out. Ma curled up on the floor, blood flowing from her slit wrists, her hair spread out on the linoleum, flies crawling down her skin. The knife lay next to her.

I ran over.

"Ma!"

She made that sound again. Did nothing. Her eyes were closed. White pills littered the floor. The orange bottle was open. Dribble, dribble, flow. Too much blood, oh Jesus, too much blood, what did I do? Get a Band-Aid?

Call Roy Pike. I sprinted over to the landline phone and dialed.

"Emergency, son?"

"M-my Ma's bleeding out, and I don't know what to do. I—I don't k-know—"

I clamped the phone under my jaw. Ran back to Ma. Blood flowed. I almost slipped in the puddle—*Jesus what a mess*—pills grinding under my shoes. She wheezed. Foam dried around her mouth. I ripped a paper towel off. *Please, oh God, don't let my Ma die. Please.* Blood soaked through the towel. Soaked the whole thing.

"Ma. What do I do? Ma, I love you, please don't die, *you're gonna die, please. Wake up! I can't—*"

I kissed her cheek. Love worked in movies, right? Why wasn't anything happening? Why was she still bleeding? Why was everything so blurry?

"You can't die," I said, pressing more paper towels to her wrists.

I tried pulling her up to a sitting position. She smelled wrong.

She tried to hit me. I kept pressing paper towels.

Oh God, was this my fault? Was she doing this because of me? What could I do? The paper towels weren't working and Ma was gonna die and I couldn't do anything, never could do anything but sit and watch the blood puddle on the linoleum and smell the chemical odor of the pills on her breath and the sickly-sweet Fireball she'd downed with it, me, the pincer-monster boy, the mistake—

"Sit down, honey," Lorraine said.

Deep chattering, deep shaking. A field. *You're twenty-two, and Lorraine's screwing with you! Get a grip!* But I shook. So cold. She was so warm and she smelled good—*just like Mallory*—and her hair was soft so I half-collapsed down and sobs burst out through my clenched teeth, barking sobs, Jesus Christ, why couldn't I calm down, but the grass felt okay and then she—*this is Lorraine it's NOT MALLORY*—kneeled down on the grass with me. Put my head in her lap. Something nice stroked through my hair. A man was walking around the field. What a funny thin man.

"He's summonin' the Hell Wardens, ain't he?"

I made a sound. Sweat beads trickled down my arms. My Hands. Everything.

"They'll hurt me," she said.

Hurt her? Why?

"You wouldn't want that, you're a good kid," she said, and her nails trailed down my cheek. "I'm just like her…Mallory. You love her, wanna protect her…I am her. Here I am, Triple-Six. You love me. You wanna protect me from them Hell monsters."

She's going to hurt Mallory! Wait, what? Wasn't she Mallory?

Her too-warm hand touched mine. Skin on skin. So silky.

She held my pincer. "Don't that feel good, honey?"

"Y-yeah."

She guided my Hand to her lips, rested it. Her tongue flitted out. Lapped up the sweat, and then she plunged the tip of my Hand in, sharp tip, sensitive tip, and her wet mouth worked. Sucked. Slick. Oh so good. Sweet soreness.

Wetness blurred my sight. Mallory. Was that her? Was I being loved by her, finally?

"Mallory," I slurred. "I love you. Babe, it feels so good."

"You're hungry, ain't you?"

"Keep touching me. P-Please," I said, head spinning. "Nobody's ever…"

The world was gray. She was gray.

"Feels better than a blow job? Alright, honey."

She delicately shifted, grabbed the edge of her tank top, and slipped it off. Unhooked her bra. Her nipples—*so hard*—engorged. She raked her fingers through my hair. She leaned in, kissed my forehead.

"Protect me, Triple-Six."

"Yes, Mallory."

"You love me? You'd die for me?"

"Uh-huh."

Hand supported my head. She nudged my head up. Her boobs. Sweat-smell, faint nicotine smell. Soft sweet skin. Round.

"You can bite a little bit," she said.

Someone was walking across the field. Thin old man—

Why are you hurting me? I remembered, sudden as lightning, being small and unable to move, body so heavy, crying and crying because I was *hungry* and it hurt and nobody could understand me when I cried but I kept crying and I was *thirsty* too and sitting in something wet and *cold* and now my skin *hurt* and *burned* so I kept crying but nobody came and then it took too much work—*tired*—so I stopped crying.

Someone found me, I remembered. Thin old man, looking down at me and it made my tummy hurt—*unhappy?*—the look on his face but I tried to cry again and nothing came out but a little sound no matter how much I tried so I tried to smile at him, couldn't reach for him—*hungry*—and then he grabbed my face and *twisted* it and it *hurt* but my nose squished against soft, mouth was squished up no breathing. Tried to breathe. No breathing. Couldn't move, body too heavy so I tried and tried—

Holy fuck, Roy Pike tried to smother me.

He said Ma left me for four days before he found me. Four days. Unfed, dying, sitting in my own waste. A three-month old baby.

"Oh God," I sobbed. "I—"

She tilted my head up to her boob. Brushed my lips on her nipple. Her other hand stroked my face. "Sssshhhhh."

Hazy. Her skin. Pink nipple. The soft taste. Sucking. Nothing coming out.

"Bite a little, honey."

I did.

Salty blood. Four rings of tiny puncture marks circled her breast, concentric rings. Teeth marks.

I think it's blood.

Her freckled face—*which one is it?*—barely touching mine, looming over me, her hot breath across my skin. She kissed my cheek, stroked it. I suckled. Blood. Soft lady kept feeding me, crooning that I was a good little baby and loved and that I should really eat more, grow up big and strong and didn't I wanna protect her? Didn't I wanna? Warm liquid flowed into my tummy.

"You should've seen how much Mallory liked this," she said. "Y'all are some weird fuckin' kids. I kill a dozen folks in front of her, she don't react. But give her a titty to suck. Same as you. Tell I love her, oh, *Mallory, I love you?* Stroke her hair? She cries."

Mallory?

"She couldn't drink as much. Gave her a bellyache."

Mallory hurt? Wait, what am I...doing? Roy Pike was walking over. His boots had bits of broken grass on them.

"But it's good for you, ain't it? Blood."

Oh my God. I'm sucking her—I stiffened. Took my mouth off her—

You're being breast-fed! Blood! By Lorraine Worner, champ! How the FUCK DID THAT HAPPEN?!

Roy Pike stood over us. "You—"

Lorraine sprang.

I fell off her, hit the grass. I scrambled up. *Shit. What—what had happened?* Lorraine knocked into Roy. He stumbled, grunting. She punched him in the gut. He hissed. Clutched himself, doubling over. Lorraine lashed out at his knee. *Crack.* It twisted like old rubber. Roy crumbled to the ground. Fell on his knee. Made a choking rasping sound.

I seized Lori's hair. She turned. Looked. Punched me in the throat. *Jesus*—I gasped, unable to catch a breath.

She pounced on Roy. Wrapped her hands around his neck. Throttled. A bloody, round cut gleamed on her arm, as if she'd worn a razor blade-lined bangle. It hadn't even scabbed over.

She throttled methodically, leaning her weight into it. Roy gasped, face beet-red. His hands punched but met nothing. His blue eyes bulged. Sweat glistened on his face. His mouth worked soundlessly.

Eat it again, raghead.

Roy Pike. Sixteen solitary stays. The sickly-sweet, acidic burn of my own vomit as I ate it. In front of him. Like a dog.

Dog. That puppy—the only pet I'd ever been allowed—*Hannibal*, I'd named him Hannibal and I was twelve and I'd begged for a year for Hannibal and read all these books on dogs—Roy kept saying I'd get a puppy for my birthday but then I didn't, so Dr. Hitch put her foot down and presto, a cardboard box with a tiny chocolate Lab inside appeared in my kitchen, Hannibal, and he gnawed at my bandaged pincers with his sharp little puppy teeth and licked my face and smelled like puppy and he loved me. That dog fucking loved me. When I woke up early the next morning to feed Hannibal, Roy Pike stood in my kitchen instead. *W-Where's Hannibal?* I asked but I knew. *Gone*, he said. *You ain't fit to have a dog. I told Judith.*

What?

Dog's gone, Project 0666.

You didn't—

Dog needs a normal kid, not someone cooped in facilities every two months...your mother can't take care—

Mallory said she'd care for him if I was gone, YOU—YOU OLD FUCKING—

He'd slapped me mid-scream. One of my teeth got loose. I'd already started crying.

Eat it again, raghead.

"You likin' this, Honeydoll?" Lorraine asked.

Roy's face purpled. His hands dropped. His body went limp...powerless. He'd die in a few months. He already had cancer. He was seventy-something, old and drained of malice and now here he was...*You used to beg him for food, water, even to turn on a goddamn light.*

Her knuckles whitened. *Raghead. Camel jockey. Son, you might want to wear sunblock...you git any darker, you'll blend into the woodworks.* His face, darkening into black. Death—

No.

This isn't right.

How? How did I get her off him? I lunged. Then stopped. *Her arm's still cut from your rift!* The Hands. Of course. Stuff from Earth wouldn't touch Lorraine—*because she's dead!*

Stuff from Hell?

She had to bargain to get immunity from the Hands. Remember?

A horrible crackling noise. Her grip crushed Roy's throat. Harder.

Pulse. Pulse. Pulse.

"Mama?" I said, and forced a wobbly sob out. "You said I'd get my snack. I'm *hungry*."

Lorraine blinked. Calculated.

"You wanna eat it raw?" She said, in a singsong, strychnine-sweet voice.

"Yes, ma'am."

She dropped Roy Pike, lickety-split. He slumped to the ground. She slowly turned to look at me. She licked her lips. Her teeth.

Hands, go crazy. I poured my fear, the wave of cold nausea, into my arms and Hands, and energy electrified them, a nice *pulse-pulse-pulse-pulse*. Paralyze her? No, but I could punch her while she jerked off to mutilating me.

Lorraine beamed like she'd just discovered a fire sale on lighters, kerosene, and stainless-steel chain, and all in the same building. "C'mere, honey."

She whipped out a pocketknife.

"C'mere," she said.

I did.

"If you hold real still, I'll let you see her. After you eat your snack. Wait." She snickered. "I got a better idea. Let's share your snack with Mallory."

Acid skyrocketed up my esophagus. I forced it back. I put on a dopey grin and tried not to think about my last snack. Seasoning salt. Grease from the—

"Wanna share it with Mallory?"

I shook my head.

"You sure, honey? She must like how it tastes. She's had it in her fuckin' mouth often enough."

Roy Pike made a choking sound.

I nodded. "Uh-huh."

She hugged me. Warmth radiated off her wiry body. One of her hands fished for my fly.

Still using her singsong voice, "You wanna feel somethin' real nice? Before you eat your fuckin' snack?"

"Uh-huh," I said.

Her hand creeped into my pants. Wrapped around me. Stroked.

Roy Pike wheezed. His face? Lightening to navy. He seized, jerking like a fish on a beach. Urine stain spread across his jeans. That couldn't be good. He'd need a hospital.

She's a killer of innocents.

Manic energy quickened, *pulsepulsepulsepulsepulse,* zinging through the Hands. It hammered my eardrums. Yeah. I breathed. Reflexive rush of blood downstairs. The Hands quieted. Focus. *Keep going. More!* I balled my fists, still holding Lorraine.

Break her nose. When she pulls away.

What the hell had she done to Mallory? All those years?

Lorraine the Immane. *Where are the bodies, Worner?*

Her, all smirking silence.

Lorraine, you fucking bitch.

I worked a Hand into her hair. Clutched a fistful of her curls.

I made a horny noise.

"It feel good?" Lorraine asked.

"Yeah."

Pulsepulsepulsepulsepulse—

"But not great, Lorraine."

She hissed.

I grabbed her hair. Wrenched her head back. She twisted, I held.

I pulled my free fist back, aimed for her head, and swung.

Crunch!

Her nose gave. Blood streaked my Hand. She grunted softly, both her hands clawing at mine. Sharp sting. She'd landed a cut with the pocketknife.

"This does," I said.

Again. I threw all my weight into the punch.

Squelch. She spat blood onto the grass.

"Go back to Hell, Lorraine. *Now.*"

Crunch!

Her black eyes dulled. Her weight sagged. Her nose was crooked and dribbled blood. Pain ached through my Hand. *She's a predator.*

She did the same fucked up shit to Mallory.

I opened my Hand, curved it. Grazed the claw tips down her face. She exhaled. I twisted her hair more, almost ripping it from her greasy scalp. Touched my pincer to her burn scar. Sharp tip.

I dug in.

A bead of blood formed. I dug harder. Pressed into bone. She'd gone still and expressionless, gaze fixed on mine.

Roy Pike made a rattling gasp.

Shit.

Get him medical help.

I balled my Hand. I punched her again, releasing her hair right as it connected. She flew back. Hit the ground.

I ripped the burner phone out of my pocket. Flipped it open. Dialed 911.

"911, what's your emergency?"

Lorraine pushed herself up.

"My—my, uh, grandpa and I were on a—a fishing trip and some guy came out."

"What's your address?"

"We're in a, uh, a field. I don't know where."

"Judging by your call location, emergency services will arrive in about thirty minutes—"

"*He's dying!*"

"Sir, please calm down—"

"Someone strangled him. He's wheezing. He can't breathe right."

Every time Roy Pike strained for air, he rattled. Bluish skin. He coughed. Blood splattered around his mouth. Flyspecks of it dotted his shirt collar. His throat pumped and choked, malformed like abused putty.

Thirty minutes?

"Sir? Do you know CPR?"

"His throat's crushed."

The operator babbled until it became gray noise.

Lorraine Worner wiped the blood off her face with her hand. She stared at me.

And vanished.

THIRTY-FIVE

I KNELT BY Roy Pike's head. He couldn't just...die. Not here.

His chest wasn't moving.

No time to wait.

"Roy," I said. "I'm taking you to a hospital. I'm going to pick you up. Okay?"

A deadened rasp. His eyelids drooped.

I put one arm under his shoulders, and the other under his thighs. I braced. I lifted. Very faintly, his pulse worked. Out-of-rhythm. He felt so frail. Like a baby. His bones dug into me. *How long were you sick, Roy Pike?*

Hospital.

Any hospital, please. Close by.

Pulse. Pulse. Pulse, went the Hands, so I shifted, got one of my Hands free, went to slash. A cut bled. Her pocketknife.

Rift membrane slimed invisibly in my Hand.

I slashed the rift, a yawning red blot lacking a visible destination.

I took a step forward—

And Roy Pike, without fuss or fanfare, or a last word, or a nod or any kind of Hallmark sentimental forgiveness-all-is-well stuff, or even any sign that he'd heard me at all, spasmed once, and died.

GRAYOUT.

I think I placed his body on the ground at some point.

Eat it again, raghead.

But Jesus...he looked so small, lying there on the grass.

He let Mallory get raped. He was a screwed-up old guy with a billion neuroses. Another demon-hybrid. Terrified to change, convinced I was an abomination for it.

I shivered in the summer heat.

When Roy Pike looked at me, did he see his future?

I rubbed my Adam's apple. Faint residual thrum of energy nestled there. My shoulders ached. I felt between my shoulder blades. Thick knots of muscle were forming. Hunger gnawed in my gut.

In the midst of all this brain-scarring carnage, *I was still hungry.*

Fuck demon puberty.

Fuck this.

I lurched over to the half-charred symbols on the grass. Not even close to finished. Peachy. Roy Pike had died for absolutely nothing. The Hell Wardens weren't coming. Lorraine Worner? Probably about to finish Mallory off.

I dug around for a lighter and found none. She'd taken them.

I held up my Hands. *Babe, I never got the chance to ask...is it them? Is that why you don't—*

I glanced at Roy's corpse.

If it took a demon to drag Lorraine Worner back into Hell before she hurt anyone else? If nobody loved me? If Mallory saw me as a monster? And if I had to become that demon to do it? To keep people safe?

I sighed.

Then I'd grow a pair of horns and buy a discount pitchfork. Demonoid phenomenon on a budget. Current worldly possessions? A hundred bucks in my pocket, no guns—the .45 wasn't in my waistband anymore—no lighters, no knowledge of summoning the Hell Wardens, and an appetite whetted by two days of the Vampire Bat Diet. Random blood, adrenaline, and half an orange.

Dizziness.

I half-sat, half-fell to the ground.

If the Hell Wardens couldn't get their lazy asses up top to drag Lorraine back into Hell, why couldn't I drag her back myself? But how would I find her? I couldn't even *summon* her right now.

Wait.

They call it gunfire, honey. I could fire a gun, sure, but where could I get one?

Roy Pike's shoulder holster bulged through his thin jacket.

Like Blueing, I kept seeing his chest move. I'd blink, hard, then it'd be fine, dead was dead, alive was alive, dead chests didn't move. Yet part of my brain screamed silently, *He's not dead. Look! Isn't he moving?* Like it was trying to fix something horribly, horrifically *wrong.*

My Hands shook. Godawful lurching in my stomach.

"Roy," I said. "I'm sorry."

I opened his jacket, feeling for the holster. Found it. With a gun inside. I grabbed it, pulled it out. A modern handgun. I fiddled with the magazine. Bullets glinted inside. Loaded.

I breathed out.

"Thank you," I said.

I buttoned up his jacket, and gently crossed his arms over his chest.

My voice grew thick. "People are coming. You aren't—oh God. I don't want to leave you here like this, but I have to. I'm gonna make sure they find you. If you have a family, I'll tell them."

What happened to demon-hybrids when they died?

Children of the Lords of Hell return home, to continue working. They're bound to Hell, instead of Earth, and cannot easily travel between the two realms. Hell Wardens and a few other professions are granted travel privileges to assist their work.

So Roy Pike was just chilling in Hell? With Lamiel and his plethora of sex toys?

Could I go find him? Convince him to possess me? Why couldn't he use my body to finish summoning the Hell Wardens? *Yeah, champ. Go find the guy who just died because you zoned out while Lorraine strangled him. Go knock on Lamiel's door. Tell him you got his kid killed.*

I'd cut Lorraine's arm in a rift. What if more than her arm got caught? Zip ties from Earth failed. What about a zip tie from Hell?

If you don't have store-bought zip ties from Hell, homemade is fine.

The Hands pulsed.

Yeah.

I felt a grin spread across my face.

Lorraine...how about a little Texas hospitality? Complete, of course, with a glowing, neon lasso.

I aimed the gun at the sky and pulled the trigger.

Crack!

Gunfire echoed.

Eau de Lori burned my nose.

"Lorraine?" I said, without turning around.

"The hell you want, kid?"

Pleasant tingle in my throat. Cold, eager rush. Take the prisoner back. Protect others. Keep them safe.

I turned to face her, baring my Fun Teeth in some parody of a smile, something nice went *click* in my throat, and a voice that *was not mine* snarled out, "Lorraine Worner. You've escaped the bounds of Hell and murdered innocent people."

God, it felt *good*. Right. I had a shiny, new Fun Voice, and it was a deep, demonic growl. The culmination of every Hell creature ever committed to film.

"And?" Lorraine said, crossing her arms.

"I'm going to *drag you back, Lorraine.*"

THIRTY-SIX

SHE TENSED. BLACK, ashy flakes appeared on her skin. Her curls melted away into charred puffs. Those dark eyes suddenly seemed half-there. As if they longed to vanish from her skull.

My Hands itched at the sight. *Pulse. Pulse. Pulse.*

Rip threat apart. Exterminate it. Annihilate it.

Lorraine edged back, clutching her injured arm. Blood slicked her fingers, still fresh. *Yeah, bitch. I did that.*

"Saw Mallory, kid."

I stalked towards her.

She licked her lips. "She's beggin' to go git Plan B. I ain't lettin' her."

Of course she wouldn't. She'd hurt Mallory in a million ways already. Heat built in my chest, and I stopped breathing for a split second.

"She don't wanna have your pincer-baby."

I was about three feet away from her.

"You think she banged you 'cause she loves you? Please. Mallory would've sucked a red-hot brandin' iron if it kept her safe. I seen her memories, honey. She ain't capable of love."

Lorraine grinned. "There's too much of *me* in her."

What if she's right? Mallory's eyes. They go so dead when she's angry—

No. Worry about personal bullshit later.

Hell. Take me to Hell.

Rift membrane filled my Hands like oil-drenched silk, like the velvety inside of a mouth, the pink flesh behind lips. Lush for tearing.

I sliced open a rift in midair. *Pulse. Pulse.* Energy sang down my arms. I could taste Mallory's strawberry nicotine gum. The rift dangled into Hell, a yard-wide crimson slit leaking lighting-struck air that still reeked of ozone.

I grabbed Lorraine by her throat. I twisted my other Hand in her hair. She squirmed, kicking out, but I held her away from my body. She didn't land a hit. I dragged her to the rift, easy. I kicked her in the gut. She doubled over, retching. In that split second, I wrapped an arm around her waist, hoisted her up, and chucked her into the rift. Feet-first. Her head and upper body stuck out. Blackened skin flaked off onto my arms. Red, infernal light glowed along my veins like neon rivers. *Pulse. Pulse. Pulse.*

"Close," I said, still using my Fun Voice.

The rift—my rift—sealed up on Lorraine's torso. Cut through her shirt. It sliced into her skin.

"Stay."

And grazed it. Lorraine writhed, then winced. Blood seeped into her tank top.

It was sharp. Like a round guillotine. I *felt* her try to disappear. And fail. Whatever the hell this rift was, it had her caught…

I clutched her wrist. Closed my other Hand around the far edge of the rift.

Solid. Like touching an electrified neon tube. I pulled it a little. It moved, bobbing in midair with Lorraine. Fantastic, I could move her. I turned, released Lorraine's wrist, and moved to open a rift to the Hell Wardens.

The Hell Wardens. Take me there. Hell Wardens.

Black spots darted around in my sight. I gagged. Head spun. Who put an invisible lead blanket on me? *Pulse. Pulse. Pulse.* It blotted out my hearing. I turned away from her, ready to slash open the rift.

"Knew I'd go to Hell before they fried me, Baby Warden," she said.

Hot hand grazed my stomach. Spidered down.

This shit again? I looked back, about to make some snappy comment. Poor Lori. If she couldn't sexually assault people and be a rapey piece of shit, the other serial killers were going to gossip in the prison yard.

Lorraine smiled. Her charred gray lips split open, revealing hot-dog-pink flesh. Cooked flesh. Empty eye sockets. Black, shriveled optic nerves dangled down her face. A sac-like bag—*is that a fucking eye*—was still attached to one.

Lorraine struck.

If I knew then what I know now, maybe it wouldn't have happened.

Mallory could've told me that Lorraine Worner could waltz into a room and pick up anyone's darkest secret in ten seconds. That the lady staked her life—literally, as a tiny female serial killer—on mentally tearing potential marks apart like clockwork, analyzing, probing. Making judgments in the blink of an eye. They a mark? If so, what kind? The hero that'd give a poor single trailer park mom a ride? They screamers? Loud? Or do they freeze up like deer? Will it be fun? Can they git fucked? Burned? Will they move like paper dolls in a fire? Will they try the doors? Do I gotta bar 'em up before I set the gas on fire, or are these folks passive? Nice prey? Wannabe predators? Can I bait 'em?

She was a pack of firecrackers tied to a bayonet. See the blood-red loud things. Ignore the sharp edge coming to cut your throat.

And like a seasoned carny, she'd seen me for the mark I was.

"Blood. Sweat. Cum," she said.

Blood. Sweat. Cum.

The ingredients to possess someone.

Oh God no.

Lorraine started jerking me off. My guts filled with ice. No. No, not this. Anything but this. I flinched away. She squeezed. Dug her fingernails in—*Jesus fuck!*—and little breaths hissed out from between my clenched teeth. Rift. Open one. Drag her to Hell.

I slashed the air. Nothing.

"I wanna use them Hands," Lorraine said, barely audible.

Is this a bad porno? Hysterical laughter bubbled out of me. The hand job earlier…wait, the other one, there'd been one while she pretended to be Mallory, too, and oh sweet Jesus, she'd wanted to possess me this entire time, she'd slurped the blood off my bashed face, sucked sweat off my bare Hand in the field, and now this and then she'd possess me, use my body to hurt and rape and kill innocent people.

I'd thought she wanted to possess Mallory Worner. Not me.

Mallory.

Holy fuck she's going to use my body and murder Mallory because Mallory trusts me—that's how she's going to hurt her. That's the worst thing she could do to Mallory.

No. *No.*

I dry-heaved. Lorraine rubbed and stroked.

"I love you," she said in Mallory's voice. "Let me make you happy, man."

I got hard.

This was *so wrong*. Foul. Like eating rotten, slimy raw chicken. Every muscle in my body locked up and tensed, and a quaking came from deep inside my chest. *Jesus God, no.*

This fucking predator can't keep her mitts off me, can she?

I punched her in the jaw. Hard. Lorraine stopped.

Hell. The Hell Wardens.

Rift membrane.

But—smooth *stroke-stroke-stroke*, pleasure, and I lost it.

Claw her face and bolt?

No.

"Close," I mouthed. "Close on her. Kill her."

The rift began to close. Lori narrowed her eyes and picked up the pace.

I grabbed for her. Missed. She pinched. Pain. Grayout. *Throb. Throb.* She dug in, knuckles white. My knees buckled. I tried to crawl-walk away, but she yanked my cock, almost uprooting it—

A white-hot spike gutted me from the dick up. Pain. Make it stop. Make it stop, make it *fucking stop*—

Lorraine hissed.

The rift was an inch deep into her torso and still closing. We were bound together like a Chinese finger trap—her, trying to jerk me off, and me, trying to cut her in half before she could.

She bared her teeth. She molested me faster.

Squelch. A godawful wet noise, then a grinding whine under it. The rift cut into her undead ribs and spine. Her eyes blazed. Her skin flushed cherry red.

Lorraine threw her head back as if to scream.

But her hand continued jerk, jerk, jerking.

Hell, take me to Hell, and I almost blacked out right there, *Hell, oh God take me to Hell let me feel anything, don't let her use me. Don't let her carve me out and use my body, oh fuck, please, not that oh shit I'm almost there oh God oh oh oh—*

(!!!!)

I came.

Semen dribbled out and down. White jizz coated Lorraine's fingers, she'd exposed me and now it was everywhere—she thrust her hand up to her lips and lapped off my cum like a bad issue of Hustler or Playboy, ha-ha. This was funny, man. Real funny. Wasn't it fucking hilarious?

A half-sob, half-laugh clawed its way out of me.

Blood. Sweat. Cum.

Lorraine Worner swallowed my semen.

Then she raped me.

THERE'S NO OTHER way to describe it.

Her, *inside* me, alien and foul and horrifically *smooth*, forcing in bit by bit like the tide creeping ashore, inevitable and unstoppable.

GET OUT! I screamed, *GET THE FUCK OUT!*

It did nothing.

She stood. In my body. The rift dilated for her, open sesame. She climbed out. The rift closed on nothing. I could see through my eyes, but I couldn't do anything. Encysted in my own body. Something like rift membrane separated *her* and *me,* and it felt—as much as it could be felt—like a fleshy doorway.

This is fun! Lorraine thought, and savored the rush of power in the Hands. Her thoughts.

I could hear them.

I'd given a five foot one undead serial killer full control of my six foot four male body. Add paralyzing demon pincers and the power to teleport. The worst part? I could feel what she felt. It was nasty. The psychic equivalent of food poisoning mixed with tetanus. Rape, kill, fun stuff, fire, all animal sensation strung over a void…mentally, I flinched.

I visualized the mind membrane. Pink. Like Bubblegum Hell, another cell—and instantly, I was there…not quite Bubblegum Hell, but some imaginary amalgam of every solitary confinement cell I'd ever had the pleasure of staying in. Home sweet home.

My body's field of vision played out on a wall, like a movie screen. Far wall? That weird membrane. In the mind-space, I walked over and touched it. Something buzzed on the other side.

Could rape. It'd feel good. Fun, Lori mused. *But first I gotta eat somethin'.*

I went back to looking through my body's eyes.

Lorraine immediately figured out how to open a rift. Maybe she'd seen me do it enough. Or maybe she was a hell of a lot smarter than I'd thought, and now everyone was going to pay the price for it. But she concentrated.

Mallory, she thought, and visualized her in a car.

"Lorraine, please," I said. "Don't hurt her."

She tore open the rift. Mallory sat in a rust-spotted junker car, her face gray beneath her freckles.

You try jack, I rape her. I squeeze her throat and imitate your voice, kid. You reckon I care? Lorraine thought.

Try something? What, was I going to graffiti the walls of my imaginary cell? Get my imaginary privileges taken away by imaginary prison guards?

My body entered the rift and dear old Lori thought, *Y'know, this body's a good gig. Maybe I'll choose this one.*

This might be better than using Mallory's body.

Maybe I'll stay a long *while.*

Maybe I'll stay forever.

THIRTY-SEVEN

WHEN MY BODY materialized in the car, I immediately understood two things.

One: The car's backseat had more flammable chemicals than a gas refinery.

And two: I made Mallory Worner feel safe.

Her shoulders were tensed like tripwires. When Lorraine showed up in the driver's seat, possessing my body, Mallory whipped around to face me. *Not catatonic, thank God.*

Her lower lip spasmed. Her gaze flew to the car windows, then back to me.

Then her shoulders finally relaxed.

"Oh my God, Triple-Six," she said, voice breaking.

Bruises marred her neck. The white of one of her eyes gleamed red. Blisters bubbled across her bare forearms and hands. Five necrotic patches rotted on her neck. She reeked, like gasoline and stale cigarettes. Two parts of Eau de Lori.

Lorraine thought, *Wouldn't it be fuckin' hilarious if I clawed open your face? Look at her. Like a lil' guppy.*

Oh Jesus no.

Mallory leaned in, wetting her lips. "You *have* to get out of here. She'll find you. She'll *kill* you."

Lorraine thought, *Oh, she will now will she? I gotta see where this goes.*

And she said, in my non-Fun voice, "Mallory. Follow me. I can protect you."

She extended an unwrapped Hand to Mallory.

Mallory froze for a second. Paled.

"You don't know him very well, Lorraine," she said softly.

"Knew him well enough."

Lori dropped the imitation. My voice drawled out, now flatter and duller and Texan.

"Git me a Sno Ball from the glovebox, kid. And a beer. And light me a smoke. Got a few hours to burn on the road. How's the map lookin'?"

Mallory threw Lorraine a half-melted Sno Ball. "Five more hours to the lake."

I tasted the sugary mush as Lori ate. Map? Lake? What, was there a camping trip on the itinerary now? July heat blazed through the car window. We were parked on the shoulder of a gravel road and tree branches dangled overhead like hanged men. A humid jungle wasteland. All I could do was watch as this undead fucking incubus piloted my body.

"Be quicker to use a GPS, ma'am," Mallory said. "Or a smartphone."

"Oh, so you can screw me over again? Find a way to call someone, tell 'em you're on the loose or whatever?"

She lashed out. Grabbed Mallory's tank top. Fabric tore, cut by the sharp edges on the Hands.

Mallory didn't even flinch.

"I'll kill 'em. You git to watch while they beg. Then I rape you till you bleed. 'Cause we ain't doin' this again, Mallory. Ain't goin' to the chair again because my dumbass kid decided to run up to a cop and say 'my mama kills people.'"

Mallory cracked open a bottle of IPA, not looking up.

"You never told your lil' boyfriend about sellin' me down the fuckin' river....why's that, Mallory?"

Silence.

Lorraine took a lit cigarette and started the car, apparently satisfied for now.

Did you know, Baby Warden? She thought, *C'mere, honey. Share a memory with me.*

"Mallory deserves a goddamn medal," I said inside my head.

The Hell Wardens never told you? 'Bout the other torture? They just let you bother the tar outta me all these years and they never told you? Bull-fuckin'-shit, honey.

"Other torture?"

I fuckin' hated you.

"What are you—"

You HAD TO KNOW!

Lorraine eased the junker down the road. She took a draw of the cigarette. Immediate nausea surged through my body. I'd never been able to smoke without gagging. She growled, stubbed it out, and flicked the butt out the car window.

"You still like it, Lori? My shitty body?"

In response, she flexed the Hands. *I like it fine,* she thought. *Can't wait to give these puppies a test run.* Veins inched down my stomach. *Pulse.* She scanned the backseat. Red plastic jugs of gasoline rested on the floorboards, half-drunk bottles of vodka, a can of kerosene, a busted pack of cherry bombs, boxes of Diamond matches, three BIC lighters, and even a used jam jar with a hunk of white-silver metal, preserved under oil. Sodium. So explosive that it got kept away from moisture in the air.

Show me. Did you? Did you know?

"How?"

Touch it and think, you fuckin' moron.

Mind membrane. I went over to it. I touched. Moist. Warm.

Something pushed back. Memories of finger-painting the ground with my blood, summoning her, the shock of seeing Lorraine goddamn Worner in the flesh—flashed briefly through my mind.

Oh you gotta be fuckin' kiddin' me, Lorraine thought. *Baby Warden?*

Okay. We had a weird mind-exchange thing. How could I get Lorraine out of my body? Dredge up my shittiest memories? Wild thought—what if I could cure her? Yeah. What if nobody had ever loved Lorraine, and that was why she killed people? I could totally cure her. Love always worked! It cured everything! Just ask my dead Ma! Or Mallory!

I'm so fucking screwed.

I burst out laughing, laughing until it hurt.

Honey, I went through three shrinks on Earth and two in Hell before they gave up on that shit.

"Show me, Lorraine."

Oh you wanna see? You wanna see my sparkly shiny memories?

"You said I tortured you?"

Git on over and take a gander. C'mon. Look at Lori's sparklies. C'mere, she thought. She licked crusted sugar off the corner of her—no, *my* mouth. Tasty. Lorraine mentally perused images of charred buildings and people. The delicious sweet chemical tang of gasoline and fire set free to gorge itself. Fun things to do and eat. Fun sights to see.

"I'm not seeing anything," I said.

Those ain't my sparklies. We're goin' deep for those, kid.

"Don't hurt Mallory. Please."

Oh, Honeydoll, she thought, *wouldn't dream of it right now. Keep touchin' that link.*

I slapped my Hand on the mind membrane. "Really, Lori?"

I'll hurt her while you watch, she thought coldly.
Watch.
Sharp poke through a fleshy door, flesh and ignition, warmth. Buzzing. Couldn't move my Hand—
Watch, Baby Warden.

THIRTY-EIGHT

THE DREAMS STARTED a year before they fried Lorraine Worner in the chair. Big red devil looming over her, fancy pitchfork in hand, snarling, *Lorraine Worner, you will burn in HELL!*

She stood waist-deep in flames and said, *Bless your heart, Beelzebub.*

Beelzebub didn't like that. He kept trying and trying to get a rise outta her, and for the first few nights, she didn't flinch. Mr. Beelzebub was too fuckin' persistent about it, too scripted...Not a real sadist. *Honey, if you got a pitchfork, flames, and ain't gettin' so much as a flinch, you stab 'em through the guts and find somethin' else to play with.*

On the third night, she screamed. Crying out questions—desperate only on the surface—*Oh Lord, why? Ain't there a way out? Ain't there a way I go to Earth? Well, why not?*—And Mr. Beelzebub had a fuckin' ego like every other cop, so he ate that shit up.

By the time they walked her to Ol' Sparky, Lorraine Worner had everything situated as she liked it.

SHE SLID A hairball into Edward Sal Blueing's shapeless mouth—hair, menstrual blood, her spit—right before they took her to the chamber. *Blueing, you better take real fuckin' good care of that anchor point.*

She'd paid him well enough for it. Gave him Mallory.

Last kiss. Last visit. Fuckin' moron thought it was cute, some Victorian shit like them rings of human hair lovers gave one another. Months of writing her biggest fan—some reject two-bit killer who wanted a lil' blood and sparkle—and painting on emotion as needed, months of interviews with yuppie fucks and shrinks and the sheer fuckin' indignity of hearing, over and over—*Do you regret any of it? Have you accepted Jesus into your HEART? Oh, Lorraine, HOW DO YOU FEEL?*

Like stabbin' your throat with this pen, honey.

She walked down the hallway for the last time. Six guards. Cameras rolling, their glassed eyes like a whore on heroin.

She sat in death's throne, head held high. There wasn't no room for bawling here. Leather straps bit her wrists and ankles. Someone crowned her with the standard issue steel bowl. Dry sponge underneath. Thick snarl of curls below that. *They should've shaved 'em off.*

But they hadn't. And the sponge crunched, arid as death, as she fumed, and cameras whined like mosquitoes hankerin' for her blood.

Lorraine Worner gritted her teeth.

Mallory, you fuckin' bitch.

EVENTUALLY SHE SLIPPED away from Hell and went to git the fluids of a certain Mallory Worner.

She concentrated, curled up on her paper-thin cot. Solitary confinement for the first year. Something stirred in her—

Darkness.

Then, light.

She was in a trailer. A bunny-ears TV glowed blue. Bad color-setting blue, and it threw light over the whole shebang, but nothing else was on.

The kid was maybe ten or so, sittin' cross-legged on the carpet in front of the TV. She was watching video footage of the execution, crunchin' on—git this—a bowl of fuckin' popcorn.

On-screen, Lorraine Worner spasmed in the chair like a rabid dog.

In real life, the lady lurked behind her still-living spawn, kneeled down, and snarled, *"Mallory."*

The kid didn't move.

Lorraine felt for her hair. Gone. Blackened patches of skin carpeted her arms. She leaned, putting her dead charred hands on each side of her spawn's face.

"Howdy, kid," Lorraine said.

The kid stiffened. "You're not real. I'm hallucinating."

"Oh, really?"

She dug her fingers *in*.

Shuddering little breaths came out of the kid, still staring at the TV. Locked into place.

"Y-you're not—"

She brushed the kid's curls back and breathed, "I ain't mad, honey. *See how nice I am?*"

On-screen, smoke clouded the cameras.

"We're gonna have *fun,* ain't we?"

Blood, sweat, tears—blood and two other fluids.

Kid didn't feel a fuckin' thing. She was long gone, dead to the world, and Lorraine kicked the limp small body several times before she slipped back on down to Hell. Nothing. *There's more'n one way to travel, Mallory.*

It wasn't sadness, exactly, but a brutal kin-feeling.

You think I didn't know how when I was your age? Dissociate? Travel outta your own body and hover up by the ceilin'? I done it before I was four.

She smiled.

I travel through better doors now.

WHEN LORRAINE FIRST slipped into Mallory's skin, she hadn't figured on a baby Hell Warden—*what the fuck else could it be?*—but death hadn't stopped her, so why the hell was some ten-year-old demonspawn gonna?

She dug the broken glass deeper into the jackrabbit's panicking throat. Blood spurted. Some landed on her face. Cold, almost sexual tension thrilled through her. She licked. Salty. Tasty. *Look it jerkin'! Like a broken dolly!* And oh, did it bring back memories. Hunting up quarters for pet shop mice. Watchin' 'em struggle.

"*MALLORY!*"

Lorraine smirked. Rabbit-guts spooled out onto desert sand. Red dust caked the gore.

Kid, you likin' this?

But Mallory didn't answer or react. Mallory rarely did.

Time to git a lighter. Torch something.

"Mallory!"

And like a ghost straight outta Hell, Baby Warden ran over, big black poof of hair bouncin'.

Motherfuckers found me already? This was one brown fuckin' kid, maybe ten years old, and a real beanpole. Hell-energy tingled off a pair of lobster-claw hands, bandaged up nice. Was this a trainee?

He got close, saw the rabbit, and dry-heaved. Paled. Sweat beaded down his bony nose.

"M-Mallory? What—what are you doing?"

"Killing."

He bit his lip. "Are you, uh, sick? My Ma gets sick a lot—"
"I don't fuckin' care."
Baby Warden reeked like rose-scented soap and cumin. He had bags under his eyes, and dark circles blacker than sin.
"You—you want something to drink?"
She nodded. He ran off.
An isolated Baby Warden? Could be pliable.
Baby Warden came sprintin' back, glass in hand.
"It's strawberry milk, he said with a weak smile. "It'll make you feel better."
Lorraine chugged the whole thing down—*I can eat! I can drink here!*—before she realized what the pink residue at the bottom of the glass was. Why her mouth tasted bitter beneath the artificial strawberry.
Her lips numbed.
"Hey—hey, kid," she slurred. "What the hell's this?"
"Sometimes my Ma tries to do dumb stuff," he said, shrugging. "So I make sure she can't."
Fog filled her skull. Her knees buckled.
Baby Warden caught her before she hit the dirt. "Don't worry, Mallory. I've got a couch. It's like a mini sleepover!"
He started dragging her by the shoulders. "Sweet dreams, sleepyhead!" he said cheerfully.
Mallory what the shit is this?
Lorraine slipped out.
After five more trips, Lorraine Worner could only conclude that *this was also Hell.*

ON THE SIXTH, Baby Warden was gone.
She set cacti ablaze. Noon heat dried her lips. Unbroken sky arced overhead. She broke bottles and hoarded the best shards of glass for future use. See Baby Warden steal them *now*. He'd hold her nose if she tried to struggle, and when she opened her mouth to breathe—in sloshed thick blue NyQuil, or pills, or the needle or whatever else the fuckin' kid had, and he'd rub her back. *Mallory, you can't hit people. Mallory, you can't set stuff on fire.*
She lunged for his throat last time. Her teeth snapped on nothin'.
Mallory, where the fuck is Baby Warden?
Mallory thought, *They put him downstairs, in solitary confinement.*
Lorraine passed by his shack. Muffled crashes mixed with the keen of glass breaking.

Sounds like he's home.

Mallory thought, *It's his mom. She breaks shit a day or two before he comes back. Makes it look like she can't—*

Like she can't do jack?

Yeah, Mallory thought, *does it to punish him. She's—she's really fucked up. I don't know how to tell Triple-Six...*

Tingles spread over Lorraine. Hell. A summons to work.

She went.

Years slipped by.

...SHE CAUGHT HIM, bone-thin, sitting on the floor, rocking. Eyes rolled up completely, showing only blank whites. He hummed, chewing. A package of raw chicken breasts lay by him. Soft grunts. Wet smacking. The package of meat only half-eaten.

Baby Warden, you gonna sick that up?

...A DULL RAGE gestating deep in Baby Warden's eyes. *It's fine, Ma.*

It's totally fine.

Hey, I needed to lose weight anyway!

Everyone's great here.

Him, laughing—the high-pitched laugh she'd sometimes hear before she threw the match, some last squeeze of feel-good chemicals released before death—and laughing.

...SITTING ON THE couch, listenin' to Baby Warden cry as he jerked off in the bathroom for the fifth fuckin' time that day—*Mallory, I gotta pee, I'll be right back*—and the dull thuds of something hitting flesh. Baby Warden was eighteen, wantin' to watch some dumb romance, but he couldn't git his eyes off Mallory's tits.

Would you just fuck her and git done with it?

Mallory thought, *Dude. I want to bang you. All you have to do is ask.*

I CAME OUT of Lorraine's memories, hyperventilating.

Holy fuck.
Was my life really that shitty?
I got another one for you, honey, Lorraine thought.
I couldn't have tortured Lorraine Worner better if I'd tried. I took my Hand off the wall. Looked through my eyes again.

We were screaming by on the freeway. Off it, a splintered red stand came up. Two plywood signs leaned against the peeling paint, one reading *Fruit. Peaches!* And the other, more faded, *Fireworks.*

Mallory glanced up. "Looks like they have old stock."

Tons of fireworks, almost two weeks after the Fourth? But Lorraine hissed. She slammed on the brakes. She careened the car into a matchbook-sized parking lot. A few people milled around. Lorraine thought, *Two couples here, no kids in sight, females seem distracted. Males sizin' me up. Shit, I ain't a chick no more. Better lug Mallory along.*

Peaches, plums, and ripe nectarines filled half the stand, and dusty fireworks lined the other half in faded paper wrappers. Lorraine jerked her head to Mallory. They both got out. Prickly, almost sexual tension tingled through my arms and chest. Jesus Christ, lady. These were fireworks, not vibrators.

Lorraine caressed the Hands over everything. The smell of sulfur mixed with chemicals and rotting paper. *Gonna wait to blow it up. Freeway's whizzing by, mostly,* she thought. *Cashier won't see it comin'. They'll call it an accident.*

And I couldn't do a goddamn thing about it.

"Lady, don't you have a body to possess?" I asked.

She rolled a red firecracker between my "fingers." *I got time.*

Blisters lined my wrists. A few necrotic patches stank between red veins.

I'll switch off to Mallory soon, she thought. *Baby Warden, you best be behavin'.*

Maybe I could tie up Mallory's possessed body, throw it into a rift, and sit tight in Hell. Okay. All I had to do was wait this out.

I love fireworks, kid. Gotta love the Fourth, Lorraine thought, treating me to a series of lovely images. Frogs from a pond of industrial runoff, vivid blood-red firecrackers taped to their bloated bodies. Striking a match, loving the flame, laughing at the fun squiggling things before she lit the fuse. The wet explosion. Frog guts. Mice guts. Rat guts. Everything Lorraine Worner could catch. I saw her at seven, stealing change to buy thirty-five cent bottle rockets.

If I had my body, I would've thrown up.

She stood there until everyone left.

"Can I leave these here a second?" Lorraine asked.

The cashier blinked when she sidled up to the counter, arms laden with firecrackers. Sweat gleamed off his balding scalp and in his wrinkles. He had a brutal prizefighter's face and no neck at all. Skin like greased orange peel. Though aged enough to have steel-gray hair, he had barely any wrinkles.

I don't want to see this.

Lorraine thought, *Lemme show you somethin' else then.*

"Yup. Wanna bag for 'em?"

"Wouldn't mind one," she said. "My girl needs help carryin'."

As if summoned, Mallory appeared at Lorraine's side. The cashier's gaze fell to her blistered arms. His eyes narrowed.

Mallory shrugged. "Got too close to a bonfire."

"Horseshit," the cashier said, leaning closer to her. "Who burned you?"

"Kitchen accident. Boiling water. I was making pasta."

He jabbed a finger like a beef stick at me. "This guy's not from around here, is he? He hurt you?"

"This is my boyfriend. We've been together several years. In fact, he's been nagging me to see a doctor. Haven't you, man?"

The cashier stared at me, lip curling, fingers drumming on the countertop. "Maybe back in Arab-land they burn their women, but we don't do that here in America."

Lorraine thought, *Damn, Baby Warden. This really what you gotta put up with on a consistent fuckin' basis? Someone talked to me this way, they'd've been dead before the next sentence. Or I'd be plannin' their death. I ain't done so much as blink at this motherfucker and he's itchin' to call the cops.*

You still like my body, Lorraine? I thought. *How are you going to murder people like this? It's a sad state of affairs all right.*

"Don't call anyone," Mallory said slowly. "I wouldn't want them to get the wrong idea. About who's harassing me."

"Nobody'd believe you."

"They'll believe *me* over *you*. You look like you drink. I can see the broken blood vessels on your cheeks. You the town wino?" Mallory asked.

"Take your fireworks and git the hell off my property."

"Yessir."

"Lorraine—I'm sorry," I said. "Okay?"

All you want is a titty to suck. A way to git out, she thought coldly, *and you ain't seen the best one yet. So see that. Then you don't gotta see what I'm about to do to this cashier.*

What else could I do?

I went into her memories again.

THIRTY-NINE

"BABE!" BABY WARDEN yelled from the kitchen. "C'mere!"

Then a long, half-sobbed string of sound. Laughter? Choking? Hell if she knew. Baby Warden sounded blackout drunk.

Lorraine piloted Mallory's body through the living room. Old mama's door was closed. She poked her head inside. Empty. Tomb-still. A white hospital bed gaped. IV, dangling but drained. Dead medical monitors gathered dust.

Mallory, is she—

Yeah, Mallory thought, *died two days ago. He found the body.*

"Mallory, babe! I finally did it!"

Another manic laugh. It degenerated into choked grunts.

She shut the door, turned, and went over—

Blood.

Gleaming red puddles across the Formica. Dripping down onto white linoleum. Tasty-iron smell, mingled with booze. A wet utility knife, blade out, lying on the counter. Baby Warden hunched over the white sink. Used to be white, anyways. Now blood decorated the basin in pinks and red, filled the bottom few inches. *Gotta git me a straw.*

Baby Warden's back was to her.

Didn't have nothin' on below the waist.

"Look," he said, and faced her, cock swingin'.

He grinned. Bloodshot eyes and mania. He held up his hands. He giggled. Each pincer was crudely sliced into four "fingers" and some parody of a thumb. He didn't have the bones for it, but that didn't stop Baby Warden.

He'd sliced around the bone.

The "thumbs"? Flaps of meat. Three boneless flaps on each hand, thumb and pinkie and index.... Bits of flesh flopped over and out like meaty flower petals. From the center, two bony spars jutted. White bone peeked through pulsing, living flesh. The blood flow slowed. His arms quivered. The fleshy "fingers" jiggled along.

"Look, babe. I'm normal."

Another laugh.

"I did it. Now you love me. Right?"

Oh my God, Mallory thought, *Triple-Six.*

A squelching, fleshy sound, then the bleeding stopped. Mutilated flesh resealed, bits of muscle knitting together.

Baby Warden burst into sobs. "Are you *fucking kidding me?*"

Then, still crying, he stared at Mallory's body. His unfocused gaze lingered on its hips, lumbered up to its tits. Stayed there. He staggered in place. His cock got to twitchin' up.

"I used to have nightmares. About her."

"Who?"

He glanced at his hard on. "I used to—I used to dream that she'd—she'd crawl through the fucking walls and try to cut it off."

"She ever succeed?"

Fresh, hitching sobs. "I hated Ma. Okay? I'm—I'm a monster."

I wanted to kill her, Triple-Six, Mallory thought.

Baby Warden loomed over her. Alcohol on his breath. Warm weight settled on her shoulders. Fluids from his ruined pincer seeped into her shirt. Metallic smell of raw meat, salt, septic smell like an open blister. Hard bone stroked along the outside of her tit. The flaps of flesh splayed.

"Mallory?"

Baby Warden's got a fuckin' foot and half on you, Mallory. You think he takes no for an answer?

"Yeah?" Lorraine said.

"I—I thought about killing her," and he sniffled. "I was fifteen years old and I had the—I had the pills I always put in her food and she'd screamed at me and oh, fuck me, I thought—"

"Thought what, honey?"

I used roach poison, Baby Warden, when I was that age.

"I thought, shit, maybe I'll throw in twelve instead of six. Oh, God—"

He let out a rattling breath. "Sometimes she made me sleep in her bed with her after I turned fifteen and she'd get me drunk and—and talked about how handsome I was getting, uh, how lonely she was and she'd start stroking me and ask why I was wearing—because she was my Ma, so why was I wearing clothes in the bed with her and she—oh, God, she did it—fuck, I didn't want—I didn't want her to—*I didn't want her to fuck me! I wanted to fucking kill her and MAKE IT STOP!*"

He sobbed. Did Baby Warden do anything besides cry? But oh, was he pliable. Moldable. Able to kill. How easy would it be, to git his fluids and possess him, or git herself a custom-broken demonspawn as a guard? His fuckin' hands. How many more folks could she kill if he paralyzed 'em first? How many more to burn? Escape Hell, live again, and have a broken slave to fuck whenever she pleased. *Eat your heart out, Dahmer.*

Baby Warden leaned closer and stooped, his forehead almost touching hers. His hair tickled her face. He fumbled his arm 'round her waist, pulled in. His cock pressed into her. Ground into her.

"Tell me you love me," he said.

Mallory...you git to be a fucktoy again. Ain't that nice?

"Tell me. You love me. Tell me..."

Lorraine smiled as she slipped back to Hell.

Have fun, Mallory.

I JERKED OUT of the memory. *Shit, she knows about how Ma*—I couldn't finish the thought. Jesus God, she wanted to—had I hurt Mallory? Had I—

No.

I'd been blackout drunk. A blank of time between drinking Fireball in the kitchen and waking up in my bed.

I peered through my eyes. The cashier grayed on the floor. Blood haloed around his head in a crimson puddle, seeping into the cracked linoleum and mapped red raw lines, probably a hemorrhage or a hematoma, oh Jesus, oh no.

Cars sped by on the freeway. Nobody stopped.

Flies droned around rotting peaches. Striped horseflies buzzed on the puddle of blood.

The Hands throbbed. Lorraine panted, sated like an incubus after an orgy.

Mallory already had the gas can out. She presented it to Lorraine, her face expressionless. Lorraine seized the gas can, guts a-quiver, and licked her—no, *my*—lips. This was still my body. But what the hell could I do?

She drenched the cashier in gasoline. Baptized the countertop and the pile of firecrackers on it.

"Git some firecrackers," she said, nodding to Mallory. "No mortars—"

"M-80s, Cherry Bombs, and Black Cats. I know."

"And Moonrakers," Lori said.

Mallory tucked bricks of firecrackers under her arm. "I know what you like, Lorraine."

Lorraine threw gasoline over the peaches. She stormed around the perimeter of the fruit stand, dousing it. Chemical fumes overwhelmed everything. My throat burned.

"I didn't like bein' hurled into the fuckin' chair, kid. But you did that," she spat.

No response.

Nasty, low heat bubbled in my skull. Lorraine clenched my Hands into fists, thinking, *Calm down. You bash her skull in, you ain't gonna live again.*

And miraculously, she settled. I watched her concentrate on the burning preparations. Mallory sat in the car. Lori ran a path of gasoline out the door of the wooden stand and entered the junker. She fired it up.

The cashier had stopped breathing long ago.

Thank God. He wouldn't feel it now.

Mallory struck a match. Lorraine took it. She eased the car away slowly, and "Hotel California" blared out from the radio.

You can check out anytime you like, kid. Keep lookin' at memories. Have another fuckin' flashback. Hell, you do and I'll even fulfill my end of our lil' bargain. Remember that?

"Screw the bargain. I forfeit."

"Tough shit, honey. It don't make a difference," she said.

You can check out anytime you like but you can never leave, she thought. *We didn't have no forfeit clause.*

Lorraine threw the match out the window. Then she floored it onto the freeway. Fire flared down the path, lightning quick, and gobbled the edges of the stand.

BOOM!

From far off, the explosion rattled the car windows. Mallory cringed. A fireball flew up towards the sky like a dying gasp.

You can check out anytime you like but you can never leave...

Two could play at this mental-bullshit mind connection stuff. The Hands could tear rifts. Sharp. Great for tearing...*but they aren't real IN HERE. All of this is imaginary.* Sure, but wasn't the mind membrane itself? I crept over to it.

Lorraine.

Yes, Baby Warden?

I grazed my Hand over the mind membrane. Soft. Tearable.

"Where'd you hide the bodies, Lori?"

Don't you fuckin' dare—

I pierced it.

FORTY

INJECTED INTO MY tender Demonspawn brain? A psychic hypodermic of Lorraine Worner's subconscious.

Smoothness.

Nothing.

I recoiled from the sensation of her, unnaturally smooth and empty, like the sexless crotch of a Barbie doll. Like a gory *nothing* where a face should exist, a horrific mash of crimson, the aftermath of a tragedy.

Jesus fucking Christ!

No right. No wrong. Nothing stopped her. There existed no deep emotion, except maybe primitive rage. Lust. Hunger. If she wanted to do something, *she did it.*

Memories. You're looking for the bodies, champ.

They formed and disintegrated, flickered like fire—I concentrated on finding her hiding spots, *The bodies, the bodies where did you hide the ones you hid—*

OH YOU WANNA SEE MY FUCKIN' MEMORIES!

—Hitching a ride at a truck stop and knowin' the fucker was gonna want a blow job but kill him later, pull the rubber bands off her braces, listening to him grunt *Keep 'em on, Missy…your parents looking for you?—*

—Loading the Body into the trash incinerator. Mama was slack like a dolly and her face didn't look right cause of it, doughy…asking Rape-A-Daddy, *You gonna forget her ring? We gotta pawn it—*

Where are the bodies, Lorraine?

She mentally pushed back.

I broke through.

A deluge of locations—grassy abandoned fields, derelict fuel stations, corrals, burn pits and addresses, burnt bone fragments hidden in ruin—flooded me.

Lorraine was silent.

Back in my imaginary prison. I forced myself away, and the puncture hole healed immediately. What was she doing?

She took the first exit off the freeway.

"Lorraine?" Mallory asked.

I fuckin' warned you, Baby Warden.

Lorraine parked the car behind a dingy 7-Eleven. Shadows stretched long in the afternoon haze. Heat roiled up from cracked asphalt and cast mirages in the distance. She placed an unlit cigarette between my teeth and gnawed it. Bitter tobacco mixed with the taste of copper.

"Lorraine? What are you doing?" I asked.

Radio silence.

Lori unbuckled her seatbelt. Sweat shone along Mallory's forehead, and her jaw worked. Lorraine unzipped my fly. Spidered my Hand down and in. Started jerking, a slow deliberate rhythm. Low, sweet heat curled up in my guts. Arousal.

Mallory's throat worked.

NO. Not this. Jesus, Lorraine, don't rape her please—

I fuckin' warned you.

"Panties off," Lorraine said. "You know the drill."

Mallory's eyes deadened. "Okay."

Mallory robotically removed her shorts and lace thong. She let them drop onto the floorboards. Bristly pubes peeked out from underneath the edge of her shirt. My dick hardened.

NO!

"Lemme make this clear," Lorraine said, voice low. "Y'all are broken fuckin' kids. Both of you. And y'all gotta accept it sooner or later. Let me work. 'Cause if you don't…I will *break you* till you do."

"Please. Don't—"

"You fucked with me. So I'll take somethin' else from y'all."

The Hands were bandaged. She grabbed Mallory's shoulder and pressed her limp body into the seat. She climbed over. Onto her. Mallory's breathing remained calm. The external world grayed out as I retreated in, dissociating. Inside the mental cell, I tried to run and claw at the mind membrane, something, anything but this. I froze. *Such a lovely place, such a lovely place.*

"Love? There's only this."

She raped Mallory Worner.

BETWEEN THRUSTS.

Loosening, a familiar disconnect with my body...*like going to Naamah's... Hotel California...*

Grayout. A disembodied feeling, like floating. Being sucked towards something...*you can check out anytime you like but you can NEVER LEAVE.*

Mallory's head thumped against her seat, *thump-thump-thump,* and my body uttered a grunt, *thump-thump-thump...*

She's right. You're broken beyond repair. You probably rape-fucked Mallory when you were blackout drunk, too, champ, so why the fuck does this make any difference? You don't deserve to touch her. Monster. Who'd ever love you? Now you're back in a cell. You can't leave—

No. Enough of this self-pity spiel...I *could* leave. Because I was broken. Because I'd been doing it my whole goddamn life. How many times had I gone to Naamah's? How many times had I saved myself from actual starvation?

I concentrated on the disembodied feeling, shut out my thoughts and outer stimuli. *I know where she hid the bodies.*

Then I stood in the parking lot, inches away from the passenger door. I could see everything happening through the passenger window.

My body rutted with a mechanical pace. The car gently rocked. My body had climbed atop Mallory and pressed her into the passenger seat as it rutted. Sweat had soaked the *Blue Lobster* T-shirt. The indigo lobster logo rippled as my body thrusted, fabric crinkling, flesh slapping against flesh, damp from sweat, at the nexus where the two bodies met it was red, raw red, flesh penetrated in and out, came out of her, glazed in blood, blood had stained the gray car seat, *Mallory's bleeding, she's being hurt she's bleeding she's—*

I screamed.

Nothing happened. My body continued. I hit the car window, but my fist passed through it like a ghost.

Mallory's eyes were dead and half open. She remained limp. My body had wrapped both arms around her shoulders and pressed her into itself with each thrust, veins bulging over its forehead, skin flushed reddish. A thin line of spittle oozed out of Mallory's mouth. Her head flopped back and forth. Rug burns reddened the outsides of her thighs.

Thrust. Thrust. Thrust.

Lorraine rasped softly, as if to herself, "This how it feels? To fuck like a man? No wonder they did it to me so much before I..."

I screamed.

I love you, I'm sorry, I'm sorry, it's not me, I'm not doing it—but it was my body, so it was, and I couldn't do anything.

An invisible weight tugged me down. *Hell. No body, no anchor to Earth… so I'm going home. To Hell.*

Hell.

Could I control where I went in Hell?

The Hell Wardens. Take me to Dunkirk, Head Warden!

I sank into the asphalt.

Before it engulfed me, something flickered out of the corner of my eye. Mallory Worner, separated from her body, peering in through the driver's side window at our tangled-up bodies.

Mallory! I tried to say, but all that came out was a whisper.

She must've heard me, or seen me, though, because she sprinted around the front of the car to where I was. She cast no shadow. The pebbles didn't move as her feet hit them. The car continued rocking. Lorraine continued raping.

Triple-Six, Mallory mouthed, grabbing for me.

She caught my hair, but then the ground swallowed me up and it slipped through her fingers.

A SMALL OFFICE, painted beige. Well-lit. Faint scent of dry paper and coffee. A granite desk dominated the space, flanked by filing cabinets. Snow piled outside a narrow window. Nighttime. I'd seen Christmas cards more demonic than this.

Except, of course, for the Head Warden imprisoned behind his desk.

I'd blinked into existence right in front of Dunkirk. He was hunched over a massive pile of paperwork, head resting in hand, absently stroking one of his horns. A percolator bubbled on his desk.

He dragged a talon down the paper. "No way around it…"

He sighed. Diagrams of the human body covered an entire wall, marked off in red arrows and diagrams. Torture guides.

I cleared my throat. "Uh, sir?"

His gaze flicked up. His eyes widened for a fraction of a second.

"Look, I don't know why you guys haven't taken care of Lorraine Worner—"

"Kid," Dunkirk said, voice dangerously soft. "And you *are* a *kid*. What did she offer you to help her? Money? Sex? Did Lorraine Worner send you here to mock me for my failure?"

"What?"

"It's not worth it. Human lives are at stake."

"I'm not in cahoots with Lorraine! I'm trying to hurl her back into Hell *because you lazy fucks won't do it!*"

He stood. "You mean to tell me that you summoned Lorraine Worner, put a target on yourself—by accident—managed to bargain with a sociopath in such a way that we can't touch her...and now you're here, rubbing it in my face. How convenient."

"What do you mean, can't touch her?"

"How many times did you engage in intercourse with Lorraine Worner?"

Vomit churned in my guts.

"You can't touch her?"

He read from a paper. "'...Them Wardens in Hell, honey. You don't want them out. So. I do this, they can't interfere, kid.' You agreed to those terms."

"How do I break them? Please. Blueing set me up. I didn't know I'd be the target—"

"How many times did you allow Lorraine Worner to possess her daughter's body and perform oral sex on you?"

Heat burned across my face. I stared at the carpet, blinking away tears.

It came out in a choked, "I didn't know."

"She's possessed my body. She's hurting Mallory with it. You have to kill me. Hell, anything. I can—"

I took a deep breath. "She's trying to possess Mallory permanently, and break me into being her slave. I'd rather die than let that happen. But if I kill myself before the bargain's up, she gets free rein on Earth while I'm stuck in Hell. You think I didn't try?"

Pain tingled below my collarbone. I slapped a Hand over the spot.

Dunkirk studied me. I stared back. He was old, unamused, and not sadistic. Not a warm-fuzzies guy. Someone running on fumes and pulling double shifts.

"She's possessed my body."

"You traveled out?" Dunkirk asked.

Everything in the room grayed again. More pain—what was going on?

"Yeah. I thought you'd help."

"Why should I believe anything you've told me?"

"Talk to Lamiel. I made a bargain with him."

"My God, *another* bargain?"

"Talk to Roy Pike. They'll tell you I'm honest...and Dunkirk?"

I was fading fast. Back to my body. More pain.

"I found where Lorraine hid the bodies. Blueing—he killed a girl, her name's Annie or something, but he killed a girl and threw the body in a field. Fifteen minutes away from where Lorraine killed him."

Dunkirk's hand tightened around a coffee mug. "Annabel Claire Smith."

"After this is over, we need to find Lorraine's victims. And if you don't want to help, fine. I'll do it."

I blinked out before I saw his response.

CLOSED EYES.

She wasn't *in me* anymore. Thank God, yay me. Eau de Lorraine, close up and strong. Burning flesh. Fever-hot weight pressed into my shoulder. Pain seared in a white-hot line under my collarbone.

I grunted. A rag had been stuffed in my mouth. I opened my eyes.

"Back again, honey?"

Duct tape strangled my wrists and ankles. I laid, half-curled up, in the open trunk of the junker. Next to a Styrofoam cooler. A sun like a ball of blood kissed the horizon. Lorraine smiled. Mallory held my shoulders flat against the floorboards.

"It ain't gonna look right if you don't hold him good."

Mallory's eyes glistened. Her lips pressed together.

Lorraine bent over me, holding a thick, white pen. Wire glowed in place of a nib.

Oh, fuck, is that a cautery pen?

Pain again. Burning meat. *Maybe she's drawing a dick on you.* I snorted. Ha-ha, I was being branded like a cow. Funny, right?

"Just gotta do the 'i.' Then you git your medicine."

"It's getting dark, ma'am," Mallory said. "We sleeping in the car?"

"You got a bedtime now, Mallory? Drink some fuckin' coffee if you can't drive."

Lorraine finished. She sent Mallory to get a pocket mirror from the glovebox.

"What was I supposed to give you, anyways? If you won?" Lorraine asked, smile splitting across her face.

She cocked her head a little bit and tapped my lips. She knew exactly what she was supposed to give me. She just wanted to hear me say it. She removed the rag from my mouth.

"You said that you'd take away the Hands and give me normal ones. Human ones," I said.

She burst out laughing. Belly laughing, shaking while hunched against the side of the car. How screwed was I now? The wording didn't sound too bad. I thought I'd get normal hands from an undead serial killer.

"Aw, poor lil' Honeydoll. You're almost cute. I reckon you'll be downright adorable after we operate on you a bit more."

Operate? What?

"Mallory!"

Mallory slammed the car door and walked around. She picked at one of the blisters on her wrist and handed Lorraine a hot-pink hand mirror.

"Yeah?"

"Go check the cooler for me. Don't show him."

Mallory nodded.

Lorraine grinned devilishly and angled the mirror over my chest. "Can you see it, Honeydoll?"

"I'm not a fucking doll, Lorraine."

"Take a look," she said.

Lori was branded below my collarbone in neat lettering. A tiny heart dotted the i.

"Had to celebrate somehow. You're about to win our lil' bargain. How'd you feel?"

I said nothing. She leaned in. She bit my earlobe. I barely felt it. She drew back, lips and teeth coated in blood. Warm blood trickled down the side of my head.

"He tastes like a winner, Mallory."

Mallory grunted, head tilted low over something in the truck. Purple nitrile gloves covered her hands. She held a Styrofoam lid—a cooler's lid. She replaced the cooler's lid, grim-faced.

"We got two bunches of bananas in the cooler?"

"Yes, ma'am."

"Not too rotten?"

"Naw, they're good. The ice should last another few hours."

I almost giggled. Who put bananas on ice? What, was the serial killer clan guilty of icing random fruit now, too? Oh God. I was branded for life and even the Hell Wardens couldn't help me now.

"Now, take your medicine, Honeydoll," Lorraine said.

She jammed two Vicodin into my mouth. I pretended to swallow.

"I'll follow through on my end of the bargain," she said, licking her lips. "Don't worry, honey. You're in for a real treat."

She slammed the trunk shut. *Clunk!* Blackness engulfed me. It immediately got hot and dank inside. I spat the pills out. My brand pulsed with pain.

They entered the junker. Doors clunked shut. Engine roared to life. With Mallory, me, a backseat of pyromaniac toys, and a Styrofoam cooler in tow, Lorraine headed down the interstate.

From a pragmatic standpoint, none of this made sense. Why hadn't Lorraine just pulled over and strangled Mallory, or smothered her with a pillow, then possessed her permanently? Why was she so dead set on this lake? I could ask my cache of knowledge, but how to phrase the question?

Could a soul possess someone while a bargain was unfulfilled?

Possession can occur regardless of the status of a bargain. Exceptions may occur when the possession itself—or the ability to possess—is the subject of the bargain.

If someone died and got resuscitated, how long did it take their soul to rejoin the body?

Times vary, depending on several factors. There are physical factors, such as cause of death and condition of the body, and also psychological factors, such as the strength of the soul's desire to rejoin its body. In suicides, this tends to double the amount of time.

Suicide. Of course.

Lorraine didn't want to smother Mallory. She wanted to break Mallory so thoroughly that she'd be ready to kill herself. Revenge. Sadism to sate dear Lori's appetite. And if it gave Lorraine more time to hijack Mallory's body, then all the better. Dried semen crusted inside my thigh. Everything down there was raw and brutalized. If I was in this much pain, how badly hurt was Mallory? I hoped she wasn't bleeding too badly. I didn't think about how much worse everything was going to get.

Lorraine drove on. Lake bound.

FORTY-ONE

IT WASN'T REALLY a lake.

At some point, she stopped, possessed me, and continued on. By the time we pulled up to the rusted chain-link fence, the night air had cooled to a low broil. Lorraine parked the car and gestured at a person-sized hole in the chain-link. Broken ends of wire stood out silver in the rust.

Lorraine smiled. "Go on, now. We snipped that hole just yesterday. Remember how nice the lake looked? Blue from the limestone?"

"Yeah," Mallory said.

"Told the guy from yesterday to park close by. I see his truck. He loved gettin' a blowjob from the famous Mallory Worner, didn't he? Even asked you how killin' a person felt. Said you grew up lookin' just like me. Ain't that right?"

"I get the message, ma'am."

"Just so we're clear. You try to run, and manage to git past that fence, all I gotta do is jump into his body and keep you from going further. Blood, sweat, and cum, honey. So load up and follow me."

She walked my body through the chain-link, through cheatgrass and vegetation, until she reached the lip of the flooded, abandoned quarry. Mallory followed close behind. Dusk cooled, sludgy around us. Mosquitoes bit every inch of my skin. A bullet-riddled sign warned us *No Swimming*. Quarries had cold water and steep drop-offs. Chemical contamination. Debris. The "lake" reeked. Like bleach, rotting dead mouse, and herbicide.

Even in the dimming light, the water was poison blue.

Lorraine pointed to the far edge of the shore, about a quarter-mile walk. Thick trees and vegetation guarded a corrugated tin shack, half-rusted and half-glinting in the scant light of an eyelash moon. Part of the roof sagged.

It looked like a place Mallory or I could die in. Actually, I'd be shocked if there wasn't already a dead body chilling in the goddamn thing. *Single white female, age thirty-nine, seeking demonspawn bodyguard/slave/toy to help murder daughter—and possibly more. Must help murder victims. Hobbies include arson and bedazzling.*

Okay, think. If Lorraine possessed Mallory…could I restrain her body after she'd paid up on our bargain? Could Lorraine exist on Earth, sans bargain? Or would she have to be possessing someone?

Without an anchor point or a body to possess, a deceased soul will return to Hell.

Then I remembered. She did have an anchor point. I'd even seen it, in her memories. That ball of her hair, blood, and spit, the one she gave to Blueing so long ago. When our bargain ended, she'd be vulnerable if the Hell Wardens found us, and she wouldn't be able to touch anything, but she wouldn't be confined to a body.

"Gotta walk over to it," Lorraine said.

Far behind us, a cop car prowled lazily on the road.

Mallory inhaled sharply. "You see—"

"Please. Lights ain't even on. He's just cruisin' for nookie or doughnuts."

The cop car passed. I couldn't scream.

She was carrying a plastic shopping bag. All the essentials, of course. Duct tape, three new bricks of M-80 firecrackers, zip ties, an honest-to-God machete, the BIC lighters, a whole box of matches, a bottle of vodka, and a fresh pack of Camel Lights.

Mallory clutched the Styrofoam cooler. Her hands shook. The cords on her neck stood out.

"Don't hurt him," she said. "You can possess me forever. I don't care. Lorraine, *please*."

Lorraine's voice chilled. "I gotta pay up. We all do."

She lugged a red gas can with my free hand. Grass crackled under my feet. Mosquitoes plagued us, itching and draining. Maybe if they drank enough of my magic blood, it'd form a rift. Or something. *C'mon, guys. Work with me here!*

No dice. Lorraine swatted at the mosquitoes. We walked towards the shack.

As she neared it, the grass thinned out. Blackened, bare earth surrounded the shack and long streaks of black marred the trees. Even after twelve years, the place still bore scars from Lorraine Worner. The tin darkened closer to the ground. She went up two charred steps. I prayed for them to collapse and twist my ankle.

They held.

The doorframe gaped, empty and black. She ran my Hands over the frame, chuckling.

Lorraine pointed to a brown stain on the wood. "I bashed his face against this as he cuffed me. Even heard his nose break."

"I saw it, Lorraine."

She whipped around to face Mallory, something ugly and hot flaring in my chest.

"Your cop buddies told you to lure me here, huh?"

Mallory swallowed, throat working.

"Git a bonfire goin'. Gonna need some light to work," Lori said.

Mallory entered the shack, silent as a ghost. Darkness immediately engulfed her. Backed by plywood, the tin walls muffled her steps.

What the hell was Lorraine going to do to me? Hack off my Hands with the machete? Some arcane magic ritual that'd give me normal hands and then explode my head? Judging from the icy, practically sexual rush of excitement running through my body, it would hurt. A lot. I mentally screamed, something wordless. It did nothing.

And then she'd kill Mallory. And someone would bring her body back to life…allowing Lorraine to live again. I couldn't let that happen. But I couldn't watch Mallory Worner die and do nothing.

Wood broke. Rocks scraped. Twigs snapped, from deep inside the shack. Lorraine entered it. Charred wood-smell and gasoline replaced the odor of the "lake." A lone flame danced in the blackness. A second later, flames curled along the edges of paper towels laid between broken planks. Campfire light, like a caveman's lantern, lit everything in a primal glow and threw shadows into sharp relief. Rich light glinted off Mallory's curls. She crouched by the fire, her bruises and blisters barely visible. Her eyes caught the glow, burning like candles in an ocean of black.

Stones caged the bonfire. Smoke stung my nose.

Lorraine set everything down on the ground. She batted away a few wood ants, then sat on the ground. *Oh God oh God oh God Lorraine, please don't.*

I thought, *You can't do it. Lady, you had it pretty good in Hell. All you had to do was kill a person every once in a while. Lorraine, let's make another bargain.*

"Oh?" Lorraine asked, plucking a zip tie out of the bag.

If you turn yourself in to the Hell Wardens, right now, I'll tell them it was my fault. I baited you. I don't care what they do to me, just don't kill Mallory!

"Be a rat in a fuckin' cage again?" she said. "Naw, ain't worth it."

She unwrapped the duct tape. She wound it around my ankles, fumbling with it a bit. Thank God for my pincer Hands.

If you want my body or for me to be your Honeydoll, why the hell are you doing this? Aren't I more useful with the Hands?

"That's the fun part, Honeydoll. They'll grow back. Everything you got grows back…you're gonna be a fun toy when the killin' runs low. I'll even feed you right. Raw meat? Hell, I'll feed you the fuckin' corpses. See how nice I am? I'm treatin' you better than your real mama, 'cause you ain't gonna starve."

I legitimately tried to come up with something nicer that Ma had done for me. I failed.

I'm not a goddamn toy! I'm a human being!

She laughed. Grabbed another zip tie. "Mallory. C'mere."

Mallory padded over, her face expressionless. Lorraine threaded the zip tie, keeping the loop open. She thrust both my wrists into it and nodded to Mallory.

For a brief second, pure rage stiffened Mallory's face.

Do it. Mallory, hurt her. Attack her! But she yanked the zip tie, tightening it around my bound Hands. No opening a rift for me. The hard floor dug into my spine.

Deep nausea roiled up. My body gagged.

It threw up Lorraine.

I screamed out, throat raw from smoke and frustration. Lorraine vanished and presto, possessed Mallory. She blinked at me coyly, puppeteering Mallory's injured body. She cleared her throat.

She checked the time on a burner phone.

"The bargain expired seventy minutes ago. Project 0666, you won. I didn't kill you in the allotted time span, so now I gotta pay up—"

"*I don't accept.*"

"It don't make a difference," she said. "Anyways, I understand that this means I gotta pay Project 0666 what I owe him. Precisely, I'm supposed to take away his Hands and give him normal ones."

Energy filled the air. Static forced my hair on end. Tingles ran up and down my spine. The bonfire darkened into a low red, like blood. Like firecrackers.

"W-where the fuck are the normal hands, Lorraine?"

She grinned.

Shit.

She wound duct tape around the sharp parts of my Hands, dodging the bony spikes. Mallory's body still wore the nitrile gloves.

Lorraine blew a kiss at the Hands. "Gonna miss these puppies."

Then she unsheathed the machete.

Oiled, the blade gleamed in the firelight. Razor-sharp. Well taken care of. She tickled the edge against my wrist. Oh God. Oh God. She'd dig in and then it'd hurt and I'd scream and bleed out and die and then Mallory would die. My stomach tightened. I retched. A hyena giggle burst out of me. Ha-ha, no Hands, ha-ha, no life, *real fucking funny*. Lorraine pressed. Warmth. A red gash opened, like a bracelet made of raw sirloin, oh God, was that muscle? *Was that muscle?*

"That's for my fuckin' arm, kid," she said. "You sorry for that?"

I nodded, teeth chattering. *Was that muscle? Oh God is she gonna skin me alive?* Her black, flat eyes scored into mine.

Then she laughed.

She threw the machete away. It landed on the floor with a *clunk*.

"You've been watchin' too many horror flicks," she said, still snickering. "I gotta give you your present first."

I took a shuddering breath.

She found the Styrofoam cooler, dug around in the shopping bag for a minute, and came up with a red sticky bow. The kind that come in little bags at dollar stores. Pre-tied plastic junk with sticky backings. Lorraine slapped the bow onto the cooler.

What the fuck?

"I—I don't want a gift," I said.

She plopped the cooler into my lap. Something red and dried was crusted on the side of it. The bow fell off. She reattached it.

Her nipples—Mallory's nipples, technically—hardened underneath her shirt.

"Tough shit. You git the gift. I'll even open it for you."

Lorraine lifted the lid off the cooler.

The first thing to hit me was the smell. Bad meat and synthetic foam. Like the meat section at a supermarket in midsummer. I peered down, nausea welling up. Hands. A severed pair of hands lay at the bottom of the cooler, placed on ice. Pale and sterile, the skin eggshell white and the nails bloodless. Men's hands, lacking a wedding band or wrinkles. Pre-vomit drool pooled in my mouth.

"I said I'd give you normal hands," she said.

She took each one out and placed them in my lap. I flinched back. Tried not to look. Tried not to think about the fact that some poor bastard's severed, rotting hands were now smack-dab in my lap. Right next to my balls. *Shit, what if they're haunted? What if they're haunted and the guy's mad and they come to life and oh shit, what if they start ripping my balls off—*

What the hell's she gonna do to my *Hands?*

In my lap, they weighed more than I expected.

Lorraine rifled through the bag again, crinkling plastic. The shack was hot now. Sweat beaded on my face.

"W-what a-are you—"

"Doin'?" Firelight glinted off her teeth. "Honey, those Hands of yours gotta come off. I said I'd take them away, didn't I?"

Oh fuck no. Maybe she's looking for the machete. Maybe she can't find it.

She laid out the bricks of firecrackers, blood-red and fresh. She tore open the plastic. Put a twined row of them around her wrist, firecrackers dangling from it like charms on a bracelet. She waggled her fingers.

No.

Gotta love the Fourth, honey.

I forced out, "The machete's over on the floor, Lorraine."

And like a nightmare come to life, Lorraine licked her lips and beamed at me.

"Gotta love the Fourth," she said. "You ever seen what happens when you hold a firecracker after lightin' it?"

No.

"Please," I breathed. "Please. Not that. Don't blow them off, fuck, use the *fucking machete,* don't *blow them off!*"

She reached for me. I jerked back. Tried to scoot away on my ass. She kicked out. A crimson bolt of pain shot through my ribs. I gasped for air. Lorraine grabbed my forearm. Veins burst, dripping red, making my arm slick. I wriggled—but she dug her nails in.

"They stay lit even when they're wet," she said.

Oh God no.

I shrieked. No pride here.

"HELP! HELP ME!"

Lorraine tore off a strip of duct tape.

"SHE'S GONNA KILL ME—"

She slapped it over my mouth, mid-scream. She pulled her arm back. Punched. Pain hitched down my throat, left me sucking in fruitlessly against the duct tape. Shit. If my nose stuffed up—*If you die of suffocation THAT'S STILL BETTER THAN THIS!*

I was half-sitting up. She stomped. On my bound ankles. I froze, eyes tearing up. Lorraine lashed out, hands full of strung firecrackers. She flung them around my bound wrists. Lightning quick, she wrapped duct tape around the mess.

The fat main fuse was uncovered.

Fire crackled. Duct tape stuck to my stubble and hurt when I twitched. Lorraine's face—no, Mallory's face, it was Mallory's body—remained serene. Moderately expectant. The face of someone when the waiter came with bread.

She froze.

"Mallory," she hissed, "quit it."
Don't stop. Mallory, if you're fighting her...keep it up.
I love you.
You're better than her.

In a Hallmark movie, that shit worked. Possessed person resists, ousts the invader, guy gets girl, they bang, all via The Power of Love™.

In the real world, Lorraine composed herself. Pounced on me. I writhed. She wrapped another layer of firecrackers around. Main fuses close together. Oh God, two layers of explosives. Christ. Fuck. Images flashed in my brain. Bloody mess. Cherry pie filling. A coyote gnawing its leg off in gory splendor, chewing chewing. I smelled, vivid as day, the cedar sawdust of the wood shop I'd broken into when I was ten, thrusting my left Hand under the safety guard of the buzz saw, the cool plastic grip before Roy Pike caught me.

Getting what you always wanted, champ. The Hands are going bye-bye. Oh, they'll regrow, probably worse than before, and that's assuming you live. And the arms can paralyze people, too.

I gagged. I didn't fight it. *Hurl. Choke on your own vomit. Quicker death.* Deep shaking from my chest, cold and somehow gray. But I'd upchucked all I had. Grayout grew over my sight like mold. Good. Let it come. It'd hurt less, maybe.

She added the third layer of firecrackers. Three fuses hung out. She twisted them together. She fished a BIC lighter from the floor. Grabbed a Camel Light, held it between her teeth and stared at me with those void eyes.

She lit her smoke.

Burning ember.

She touched it to the fuses.

Snick! Fffff...

Jesus fuck no no no, make it stop make it stop please oh God don't let it blow up don't let it don't let it—

!!!!!!

FORTY-TWO

HEAT.

Dull vibrating in my ears, white noise cranked up to ten, the reek of blood and sulfur and spent smoke, *Who burned bacon?* Numb Hands *(where the fuck are my Hands?)*, good, it could stay numb but already the fucking crescendo was sizzling from here to there—

White-hot pain—

MAKE IT STOP! STOP! FUCK!

It blotted out my thoughts in a white acidic flood.

Warm piss dribbled down my thighs. The pain consumed. *In a forge, they're in a fucking forge why did I stick my Hands in a fucking forge.* Gasoline smell. Charred bacon, sulfur, iron-rich blood piddling onto the wood. Duct tape softened from heat. Flailing. My Hands—*no where are they*—the stumps came apart. Blood gushed.

Pulse.

Pain arched through. Life bled out. Everything blurred.

Make it stop I wanna die I wanna die let me die—

And a voice that was *not mine* cut through the pain and haze. The thing that pulsed with foreign joy when it clawed my old eyes out. *Go to sleep! I will REBUILD but sleep you must rest.*

Too much pain? Okay, champ, let me take over from here. Rebuild from scratch. The whole shebang. Numbness, sweet numbness rushed through my body. Go to sleep. Sounded nice.

Suddenly, I saw the whole shack and Lorraine, but from outside of my body. I saw the broken, mutilated thing bleeding out on the floor, twin red streams pouring from its two stumps. It lay face-down. Its black mop of hair frizzed out. Mangled stumps, part blackened char and part tattered meat. The white edge of a bone, couched in stump. Spent firecrackers rolled on the floor. A tear glistened on Mallory's freckled cheek.

Mallory!

Lorraine pried up one of the floorboards. It crumbled apart, revealing something glittering within the underfloor space. She thrust her hand in, drew out something black and floppy, dropped it in front of my body. Two somethings, jeweled in plastic rhinestones.

Tourniquets. EMT-style, premade tourniquets.

The rhinestones spelled out *Honeydoll*.

Back in my body—*no make it fucking stop make it stop*—I forced my head up. Chunks of meat littered the floorboards.

Get up, champ.

I staggered. Used my elbows to prop up my chest. Fresh wave of pain came. I gritted my teeth. Lorraine was about to kill Mallory. I'd save her, or I'd die trying. *You're gonna bleed the fuck out if you don't get those tourniquets on something!*

"Uh-uh, Baby Warden. Let's chat for a minute."

Lorraine possessed me. Mallory's body slumped into a sitting position, eyes open but glazed over.

You see those tourniquets? See how nice they look? Want me to put 'em on for you?

I didn't answer.

Here's what you're gonna do. I'm gonna pilot her out to the lake. You put on my fancy-dancy tourniquets and come on out. I own you now. I've been directin' your every move...she'll believe you betrayed her, and when I speak, you better fuckin' play along.

"What if I don't play along?" I said in my head. "What if I don't come out?"

I'll give you about five minutes before I possess you and walk you out myself. This way, you'll git to see her one last time, say some goodbyes. See how nice I am?

"You're trying to make Mallory think that I—that I've been working for you the entire time?"

You have, Baby. You just didn't know it.

She flickered out, re-possessed Mallory, and ran out of the shack.

Blood spurted from both arms, spraying the desiccated floorboards. I got my wobbly legs under me. I stood. My knees buckled. *Shit.* Caught myself before I stumbled. Sweat trickled down my back. Every breath stung. I coughed. Stop the bleeding, okay, but how? No duct tape left. She'd taken the bag with her. If I used the Honeydoll tourniquets, I'd be admitting that she owned me, and it might even make Mallory think that I was working with Lorraine. Fuck that. I'd been through indignity after indignity, I was a burned up mess, and my body was no longer something I had any control over, but *fuck that*. I could make my own tourniquet, then, but oh God, I had to get something tied around my wrists before I bled out, but if I moved it'd get worse and how the fuck was I supposed to tie anything without *fucking* hands?

You don't have to tie anything.

The bonfire raged in its ring of stones. At the heart of it, coals glowed white hot.

There was a third option.

No. Not that. Anything but that. I lurched over to the fire, everything swimming by in a dreamlike haze. With my stumps still bleeding. The pain would probably kill me by itself if I actually—

Don't even think it.

But what the hell else could I do? Sit on my ass and wait for Lorraine to possess me? Let her kill Mallory?

I swallowed back bile.

I lunged forward, jamming my bleeding stumps into the bed of coals.

O fuck why—

I couldn't scream but my mouth worked against the melting sheet of duct tape, panic-breaths steaming out, the coals searing and searing as the charring stench of meat filled the air and bred with the smoke, *sssszzzzzsssss* as blood sizzled on the coals, *sssszzzzzzzsss*, shushing me, and all that below PAIN, PAIN exorcising thought like a gunshot to the *fucking* head—

Make it stop Christ make it STOP!

I held them in. *One Mississippi.*

Fire licked up my arms and lapped at my face. Blisters bubbled. *Ssszzzzzzsssss*, still shushing, still flowing out, as the smell of burning hair curdled in my nose with the meat and smoke, duct tape over my mouth superheating into molten marshmallow—

Scorching like a fucking marshmallow, ha-ha.

More blisters formed under the duct tape, *claw it off*, but I couldn't so I sat there and let the fire eat me. *Two Mississippi.*

Ssssszzzzsss…now it trailed off. I flinched, and the melted duct tape flew into the bonfire, burned into chemical stench on the coals, PAIN as skin ripped off with it, hot salty blister-fluid dribbling down into my mouth, steaming into vapor, PAIN—then nothing on the stumps. No pain. *Three Mississippi.*

"AAAAAHHHHHHHH!!!!"

I tore myself out of the bonfire, voice ragged.

"I'm ALIVE!"

Adrenaline chilled through me. It numbed the pain shooting up my arms, my blistered neck, and my burned face. Evidently, my body had one last stash stowed away. One of the Hands, now blown off, lay smoking on the floorboards. Ragged flesh and skin cocooned bone. The edges of the skin smoldered, blackening. Splatters of blood trailed to the Hand.

I'm sorry.

I jumped up and bolted out the door. The air outside felt blissfully cool. Every breath stung deep in my throat and lungs. Probably permanent damage. I reached for my face—oh, shit. No Hands. And my Stumps? Blackened ends capped my wrists, like burnt edges on barbecue. I pressed them against each other. Savage pain flared up, deep in the flesh of my arms. A mostly-blackened strand coiled in one of the stumps. *Is that a nerve? Or a tendon?* Was I even going to make it? I panted. All Lorraine needed was a second to get Mallory to kill herself. And here I was, Handless.

I grazed an arm against my face. Why couldn't I feel the hair on one side of it?

Blisters. They carpeted the skin over my face. As I groped it, nausea welled up again. Why the hell were there numb spots along my cheekbone? Over my neck? I couldn't see how bad the burns were, but there had to be a few in the third-degree range. On my face. I was lucky to have my eyesight intact. Half of my hair had burned away. Bits of burnt hair crumbled off, coating my shoulders in ash.

I lurched like a zombie. Or a demon on Valium.

Gravel crunched as I half-ran, half-staggered over to the other edge of the algae-green "lake," where the figures of two women lurked, visible but devoid of color.

Lorraine. Mallory.

FORTY-THREE

THEY FACED EACH other like dueling desperadoes. Mallory's back was to the "lake." Her black eyes looked flatter than Lorraine's. I tried to keep my footsteps quiet. But if her eyes looked like that...Jesus, how pissed off *was* Mallory?

Mallory pressed a gun to her temple.

Oh.

"I finally figured out how to break you, Mallory," Lorraine said. "Baby Warden? Why don't you c'mere and tell her what's what?"

Lorraine smiled. My Stumps pulsed. Her skinned arm cradled across herself, holding her torso shut. A gaping cut bisected it. Torn fabric exposed the inch-deep slice. Maybe two inches. A glimpse of pink viscera peeked through. Gleaming vertebrae poked out, not quite severed. She smoked, cigarette held in her other hand.

Mallory bared her teeth. "You hurt the only person I ever loved."

"Quit pitchin' a fit."

"You raped him, Lorraine!"

My throat went dry. *The only person she ever loved?* Me? What, were pincered freaks in vogue for the budding serial killer? I froze. If I didn't stop this, Mallory would put a bullet through her skull, but Lorraine couldn't use a meat vehicle with pureed brains. Why was she letting this happen?

Lorraine leaned closer to Mallory, grinning. "You turned out just like me. Ain't that some shit?"

"I never raped a person."

"Oh? I seen your shiny, happy memories of drugging Baby Warden and jerkin' him off before y'all killed Blueing. Y'know, he never had the guts to tell you he thought you were a freak, but he told me. He told me so many things 'bout you."

Mallory's mouth opened. Nothing came out.

I got closer, steps crunching in the dry, brittle grass. Calm Mallory. Restrain Mallory. Punch Lorraine.

I wheezed, "Mallory. Don't listen to her. If you kill yourself, she'll get to possess your body forever."

They both whipped to face me, Lorraine hissing. Mallory didn't lower the gun.

"What the hell did you do? I gave you those fuckin' tourniquets!"

I forced a smile. My scorched lips split open, oozing blister-fluid.

"Didn't like them, Lori. Sorry."

All expression slipped off Lorraine's face. She scrutinized me.

"Oh my God," Mallory said, face milk white.

"He wanted new hands. He wanted the old ones off. I got experience with both procedures."

"Babe," I said. "Put the gun down."

Mallory set her shoulders and bared her teeth again, sneering like a cat. She flicked the safety off the handgun, eyes fixed on Lorraine. I wobbled. The reek of the "lake" roiled up. Mutated grass itched at my feet.

"Please don't do this. Mallory, I love you."

"Only one way to end this. You wanna keep me alive. So I can keep being Lorraine's meat vehicle. Your baby incubator? God. No matter much I hurt you—"

"That wasn't you."

"All you ever do is save me. Fuck the consequences. If Lorraine keeps using me to hurt people, so what. God, I—"

The flat rage left her eyes. She didn't look like *Mallory Worner, Born Evil?* Now she only quivered in place, gun pressed hard into her temple. It made her tiny hand seem like a doll's. Spent and used and broken.

"I'm not even sad. I'm just tired. Tired of her hurting people."

Lorraine's gaze flicked to my vein-covered Stumps, then away. The corner of her mouth smirked up, a half-second expression. *You wanna fight me?* It said silently. *You reckon I drove all this way to a lake without usin' it?*

Death via drowning would leave a nice, intact corpse. Easy to revive.

"If you die, Lorraine will bring herself back to life. Look, I know it seems crazy—"

Lorraine laughed. "Baby Warden? You don't gotta keep actin' anymore. We've got her where we need her."

Mallory white-knuckled the gun. Her jaw worked.

"She's lying. Put the gun down."

Instinctively, I reached for her. She recoiled. Along the Stumps, vivid red veins pulsed. "Mallory—"

"Lorraine is never, *ever* going to hurt people using my body again," she said. "As for yours—I don't know what you want."

She lowered the gun. I didn't understand, but thank God, she didn't have a gun to her head. Her shoulders relaxed.

"What do you want? She can possess you, too."

I took a step towards her, mostly shirtless and burned. At least half my hair was scorched off. Fresh burns blighted my face. It wasn't like I'd be able to kiss her, unless she dug the taste of blister à la flesh. Me, with my mouth full of Fun Teeth.

She opened her arms to receive me anyway. I stumbled in.

Maybe The Power of Love worked after all. I drew Mallory to me, not touching her bare skin. Her tits squished against me. Her breaths came in hitching, wet sobs. She buried her face in my chest. *I love you. I can make us safe. We're together again.*

Click.

Something cold and hard pressed against the base of my skull.

"It'll go through both our brains. Shouldn't hurt," Mallory murmured.

What?

This was some kind of joke, right? Some horrific, shitty joke. Mallory wasn't really about to shoot me. Hysteria bubbled up in my chest. I giggled. Okay, then. I could match her for black comedy.

"Is that a .45, or are you just happy to see me?"

"It's a .45. You'll be gone before you realize I pulled the trigger. The least I can do. It'll be longer for me to bleed out."

Holy shit she's not kidding.

Mallory curled her other hand around the back of my head, and gently pulled me down. Our foreheads met. Her back arched up. I stooped. Two burned, used things meeting, sparking again. Artificial-strawberry nicotine gum on her breath. *Pulse. Pulse. Pulse.* The Stumps went haywire. At this angle, the bullet would careen straight through my brainstem, explode along the way, then plow through Mallory's forehead. Probably beyond that, too.

"Never again, Lorraine. Fuck you."

Why was Lorraine letting this happen? I squinted past Mallory. Lorraine crossed her arms, grinning like a kid about to open a birthday gift.

Fun times at the toxic quarry, you know, fireworks and a nice double suicide to round out the evening. Why was I so stupid? Mallory had basically outright asked me if I wanted to kill myself with her, and I'd jumped right in. *You knew. On some level. Because you're tired, too. Would it really be so bad to die with Mallory? It wouldn't stop Lorraine, but she'd move on to some other victim.*

Exhausted. So exhausted.

C'mon, dipshit. Think! There's gotta be something. How hard would it be to wrench the gun away from Mallory? Or zap her with the Stumps for a Mississippi? Lorraine hadn't possessed me yet.

So, gun to my head. Cool. I ignored the panic-bile churning away in my guts.

Mallory whispered, "Okay, this is really starting to hurt my wrist. You're a giant."

"Wait. Please."

"You wanna...kiss me? One last time? Before I pull the trigger?"

Unhealthy relationship dynamic, don't fail me now!

"Yeah, but—"

"But what?"

"I—my face is a little fucked up, Mallory. I'm gonna taste like blisters."

"You taste like you. C'mere," she said, lips parting.

I kissed her. Raw, tender skin stung. Blisters burst, weeping lymph. For a second, only her, sweet fruity saliva and soft boobs grinding on me while the chilly gun barrel ground into the back of my skull. I slipped into her mouth, tasting. She tasted back.

And I eased one of my Stumps closer and closer to her gun hand.

She went still. The gun wiggled, just a little. *Oh God she's curling her finger around the trigger. She's steeling herself.*

I jerked the Stump forward. Hit her wrist.

Contact for a millisecond.

Her gun hand spasmed.

Pulled the trigger.

Click.

A dry click. The .45 wasn't loaded. Had never been loaded.

I knocked her arm away. The gun dropped out of her hand and fell noiselessly to the grass.

She jerked back. *"What are you—"*

She tried to slither out from our little death-embrace. I tightened it. No gun for you, babe. Mallory clawed at the side of my neck, tearing open the burned skin. The gun lay a foot away. I went to kick the goddamned thing into the "lake," but Lorraine reappeared. She touched the gun. Her hand phased through it. She loped back a few steps.

"We planned this the entire fuckin' time, you know. Me and Baby Warden. Thought I'd ever let you around a loaded gun?"

Then she was *in me,* possessing me.

Mallory spat in my face. Fever-hot saliva dribbled down my left cheek. Her forearm and hand dangled uselessly. Dead weight over my shoulders.

Her eyes flitted round like a meth-crazed spider. Dead eyes, and long dead at that. Logic? Reason? We'd gone past them eons ago.

Howdy, Baby Warden.

"Didn't have to offer him much, Mallory," Lorraine said, using my mouth. "He gits to bang you a few times a week, that sorta thing. Ain't that familiar?"

Mallory froze, mid-claw. "You're possessing him. He'd never..."

"Ain't never done somethin' without a backup plan." Lorraine grinned. "Now Baby Warden gits to make sure you don't go slittin' your wrist. Or chewin' a bottle of Xanax. I fixed it with him. You're gonna stay alive *forever*. Didn't I tell you we'd have fun?"

No.

Mallory stared up at me, voice growing softer with each word. "Oh. Oh. Okay. Am I gonna suck your cock or not? Know you can hear me. Did she offer to have me fuck you? How many times? Bet it wasn't too many. You can't lie for shit. Did she tell you to lead me on like this?"

"Babe. I—I didn't think about it that way. Just let her kill people. She'll let us have time together, Mallory," Lorraine said.

"You keep me alive, and she gets to possess me whenever she wants. God—"

Mallory's voice broke. "I'm getting used twenty-four seven now. No matter what I do, no matter who I 'trust,' that's all I ever get. I'm just... fuckable meat. An *it*. It can make a baby. It came from Lorraine. You—you were the only person I ever loved, Triple-Six. So tell me. What's the bargain now? I have your baby? You have to watch me pee, too? Make sure I don't slit my wrists with a bathroom mirror?"

Jesus Christ! Lorraine's been trying to kill me for the past three days. She blew off my fucking Hands! You think I'm working for her?

"He jumped at the chance to babysit you all over again. I offered him that. He don't really care whether he sticks it in you or not. Likes me better, anyway."

I saw the mind membrane. I ran over. I clawed.

Stop it, kid!

Mallory sagged like a rag doll. Used. Lifeless. Something to be moved around and discarded at will, a non-person occupying space. I had her clutched in a bear hug. Imprisoned. The air felt thick with humidity and static. Hairs on my scalp tingled. Heat built on the ends of the Stumps. Power. Lorraine eased a Stump closer to Mallory's neck.

In the mind-space. I had Hands here.

I dug, tore, and mutilated the membrane, shredding pink flesh—her memories flooded me again—I screamed. Poured every bit of rage and fear into that scream, exorcising it from some place deep in my ribs, *You fucking bitch! Get out of my body!*

I like it fine, honey.

But she shivered.

Pulse. Pulse. Pulse. Mallory breathed. The Stumps tingled.

I could've made it hurt more, Lorraine thought.

She touched Mallory's neck, soft freckled skin, fever-hot, and a *pulse-pulse-pulse* flowed down, Mallory's face twitched once and froze, went slack, oh God, oh God not her, *why the fuck couldn't I stop it,* her head slumped onto my chest and her knees buckled, weight sagging into my arms as Lorraine caught her, *pulse-pulse-pulse,* Mallory's body slackening like something dead—*Lorraine, please don't*—and Lorraine removed the Stump.

She crushed Mallory's body to mine, fell back, and we collapsed into the "lake," with Mallory Worner in tow.

FORTY-FOUR

ICE-COLD IMPACT. I inhaled lake water. My lungs hitched. Gagged. I sank, bubbles trailing up. Mallory wasn't moving. *Is she alive?* It was like holding an anchor. The water was deep, colder near my feet. Goosebumps prickled my skin. Lorraine forced my legs to kick away from the light.

Down. Cold water filled my ears. Pressure crushed from overhead.

Mallory inhaled. Her chest filled. Lake water.

Oh God.

GET OUT!

Rusted bicycles rested on silt, rusted cars, forgotten beer cans. *C'mon, shitty body. Grow gills! Grow the Hands back!*

Lorraine left.

Lungs burning, head screaming, I turned, kicked upwards. Everything screamed at me to *inhale, breathe,* and my heart thudded in my ears. I kept going. Arms around her, I kicked up and up. *What if she's dead? What if she's dead, what if she's drowned?* The lake water felt like honey, or half-set Jell-O. Too thick. My mouth worked, trying to breathe, so I let out some air, shit, Mallory was heavy, she hurt, and the surface—so far away. *Do you even know CPR?* Dizziness. Keep fighting. Black spots danced in my vision. I pressed my raw mouth shut so I wouldn't inhale—

Broke the surface.

Sweet, sweet air. I sucked it in. Hoisted Mallory up.

Is she alive?

She wasn't breathing.

She sagged like a dead fish.

She was dead.

No.

This couldn't be happening. Lorraine wasn't—

I towed Mallory's body, swimming to the lip of the shoreline. CPR. Dr. Hitch had taught me CPR. Thirty chest compressions—*probably break her ribs in the process*—two rescue breaths. Reached the lip of the lake.

You can't resuscitate her.

Fuck that.

Tried to shove Mallory's body—no, *Mallory, she's not dead yet*—I tried to push Mallory up onto the shore, but kept slipping, couldn't put any pressure on my burned Stumps without screaming. Without Hands, I couldn't grab her. I clambered up onto the shore. Scooped her up with my arm.

Did I touch her? Shit, did I accidentally zap her more?

No time. I lugged her out of the lake. Sand and gravel dug into my raw skin. Every part of me shook. My teeth chattered. She flopped onto the grass. Still not breathing. *What if she's brain-damaged? What if I can't?*

I put the Stumps over her chest. Right onto the center of her breastbone. I pressed down. Hard. *One.* What the hell was the rhythm here? Oh, yeah, *Stayin' Alive*.

Well you can tell by the way I use my walk—

Press. Press. Press. Press.

Her ribs crackled. Had to press her chest two inches down. I cringed. I kept going, ignoring the godawful sound.

I'm a woman's man, no time to talk—

Press. Press. Press. Press. Don't be dead, don't be dead, please oh Christ don't be dead.

Music loud and women warm, I've been kicked around since I was born—

Press. Press. Press. Press. "Mallory, please. C'mon."

And now it's alright, it's okay—

Press. Press. Press. Everything hurt. Black spots filled the edges of my vision. Felt like I'd just sprinted a mile.

And you may look the other way, we can try to understand—

I leaned over, used my elbow to tilt her head back, but how the fuck was I supposed to open her mouth without *hands?* I tried to nudge it open with the Stumps. Her face spasmed.

You touched her bare face with the Stumps, oh God, what if you paralyze her lungs?

Awkwardly, I pinched her nose between my elbow and knee. Contorted myself as I tried not to put my weight on her. My neck ached as I craned down, planted my mouth over hers, and breathed in. Her chest rose. I breathed. Gurgling noises came from her throat. *Again.* I gave another breath.

Water bubbled out of her mouth. I rolled her onto her side as it streamed out. Was she breathing? I strained to hear. Another gurgling sound. *Is she breathing or not?*

She gasped.

Thank God.

Another gasp. I leaned over her, laughing.

"Mallory?"

She opened her eyes.

They were black. Empty.

"No, Honeydoll," she said.

Now she could move, and she reached up to stroke my cheek.

No.

I didn't—

Little sounds came out of me. Numb. My Stumps and face and everything, numb. *Oh fuck no. Mallory. I didn't mean to.*

Lorraine stood and picked up the gun. She loomed over me, pulse throbbing in her neck. Alive.

A faint *pop* echoed nearby. I turned. Through the waist-high grass, lurid shapes flickered like infernal ghosts. They approached, moving through the vegetation without a sound.

Demons. Or, more accurately, demon-hybrids.

Lorraine bit her lip. Leaned on one hip.

"Git up. You gotta c'mon up."

"No," I said.

She whispered, "The fuckin' Hell Wardens are here. They'll drag her body downstairs if it means takin' me. C'mon."

"No."

I didn't move.

She knelt, and tried to imitate Mallory's voice. She told me loved me. She told me it wouldn't hurt after she used the big needle on me. She told me that Mallory was better off. She wanted her Honeydoll. C'mere and let's git out of here.

Something oozed towards us from the right, an indigo jelly, blue as midnight and veined with silver. The veins thickened towards the center of the jelly, solidified into a mass.

Shhhhhfff. Shhhffff…crunch.

An arachnid leg—thick as a man's hand and armored in gold chitin—probed the grass to the left. Another leg followed. Hairs on the legs quivered, tasting the air.

Barely audible, someone tsk-tsked behind me. An eight-fingered humanoid hand came out of the darkness and clacked its sickles together, obsidian sickles instead of nails, and an eye blinked on the back of said hand. Caucasian skin clothed the hand. They'd been a white person. Before whatever they were now.

A faceless, dark-skinned head thrust through the grass and wormed forward. Its body stretched endlessly behind it—behind *him*. He'd been male. Human mouths lined his arms, working silently. He had segments, and human limbs jutted from those segments in something akin to a centipede. Centipede Dude still had hair. It was textured. It'd been formed into locs and tied back and I could something coming off that hair, not blood or sweat or something gross…a pleasant synthetic citrus smell. Some kind of hair wax. Centipede Dude styled his hair.

How does he see his hair, without eyes? Where the fuck are his eyes?

Between the arachnid legs, two head-sized pincers shot out and touched the ground. A scorpion stinger lashed up, out of the grass. Yellow phosphorescent swirls glowed along it, limning spiny chitin. A droplet of some venom oozed from the tip of the stinger, maybe twenty feet above the ground. It emitted that same light—a tingly energy, a yellowish foul color that was somehow the exact shade of a cadaver's fat—my mouth got greasy looking at it.

Ahead, Dunkirk's eyes blazed through the night. The light of them glinted off his horns.

Lorraine paled.

"Need a distraction," she said. "Need some time."

She stood. She raised the gun. Aimed it at my stomach. Took a step back. She squinted.

I stared up at her, with the blissful realization that nothing mattered anymore, that I was tired, that the only girl I'd ever loved was dead, because of me, and that if I'd done nothing, she would've died, too. There had never really been a way to fight.

The gun barrel gaped. A doorway to oblivion. Sleep.

"Please," I said.

She pulled the trigger.

I didn't hear the shot. A sting of pain. Slipping into soft fuzzy gray—*that blanket in the closet*—and it smelled like my old blanket, warmth and deep rest, and somewhere here, the gray deepened to black.

Lead-heavy bliss.

Sinking.

Heat squeezed around my Stump. Lorraine was gone. Mallory appeared in the haze. *I love you,* I tried to say. But my mouth wouldn't move. *I'm sorry, Mallory.*

Sinking. Deeper.

"Worner," someone said, and there were sounds of flesh bumping into flesh. "Miss Worner, wait."

Scuffling, crunching footsteps.

Mallory touched my cheek, then faded.

Something is in me, something is INSIDE ME—

The small, hard something nestled in my guts, as it had many nights before, when it had dragged my body to the sink in Bubblegum Hell, filled the basin with water, and looked at the reflection to see—

Babe? Is that you?

Mallory Worner's eyes.

Mallory thought, *Triple-Six? Oh fuck.*

She'd possessed me. In intervals. She would leave her body, maybe when Blueing was hurting her, the same way I had left mine, and gently—so gently—settle into mine. Oh God. She'd eaten all my fluids.

The revelation changed nothing. I was sinking, sinking fast, and I didn't fight.

Get up, Mallory thought.

She struggled. The pain of my burned, mutilated body almost obliterated her train of thought. The Hell Wardens were getting closer, moving slowly, scanning the area.

She tried to scream.

My body gave a weak croak. Soothing gray haze swaddled everything. Sleep. Didn't even feel the heat of the bullet wound as blood trickled out. It tickled as it bled.

"Help," she managed.

It was enough. They surrounded us in an instant, blocking the stars overhead. Muted sky. Something picked me up like a rag doll. I sank.

"**...WE CAN'T FIND** Worner, sir..."

Someone had an arm under my head and another under my knees, and they were lurching. I didn't open my eyes.

A sharp inhale. "Look at his arm."

"Necrotic. Who possessed him?"

Warmth bloomed across my chest. It pressed in, below the skin. Tingled. A ghost-hand groped along my innards.

"Oh. You. *There* you are, Miss Worner. You're not supposed to be here."

Pressure. Tearing. Something wrenched out.

I sank. It all became nothing eventually, but before it did, she squeezed what remained of my Hand.

PART 4:
SONG FOR THE DEAD

PART 4:
SONG FOR THE DEAD

FORTY-FIVE

DUST.

Pain.

Metallic-tasting dust rasped down my windpipe as I breathed in, tickled the hairs in my nose, dehydrated the raw pained cavity that used to be my throat. I swallowed. Felt like sword-eating a rusty steak knife. I was lying on my back. The skin there screamed at the weight pressing down on it. Raw. I shifted a little—

Jesus!

And hissed. Tears gushed, ungluing my eyes. My arm twitched. Hit a soft plastic hose. An IV. Pumping God knew what into me. Wait.

Wasn't I dead?

And Mallory?

Oh God, is she dead?

The "lake." The red gleaming gas can, the red firecrackers coiled around my wrists, the cold lake water. Mallory's drowned corpse flopping onto the grass. Lorraine's smile. Smell of charred meat and gasoline.

My eyes flew open. I bolted upright, hyperventilating.

Fresh wave of pain.

I'd been laid out on a hospital bed with crisp white sheets. New plastic everything. IV drips and wires, EKG monitors all hooked up to me. Machinery beeped. Bandages wrapped neatly around my arms. Clean jagged bones grew out of cloth on the Stumps, shredding it. The Hands were already making a comeback. Great. A catheter. A steadily-filling bag of piss dangled beside me. A battered textbook—*DBT for Dummies*—rested at the foot of said hospital bed.

But I wasn't in a hospital.

I was home.

In desert-hell.

Not a speck of dust to be found. Someone had set this hospital bed smack-dab in the middle of the living room. Stains dotted the brown shag carpet, sans Fireball bottles. A stack of DVDs, bottles of booze, and my bong cluttered the coffee table. *Mallory Worner, Born Evil?* topped the lone stack of DVDs and the rust-colored velvet couch was shoved up against the wall. The A/C droned on. Same old picture—smiling Ma and fifteen-year-old me, cooking rice—tacked over the TV.

Was it me? Was it my fault? Is that why you hurt—

Is that why you raped me, Ma?

Nausea. I forced the memory away. Pre-vomit spit filled my mouth. What a pathetic loser I was. Raped? What kind of guy got raped by a woman? His own mother? *Thanks for unlocking that Pandora's box, Lorraine.* I really needed more traumatic memories to liven up my day-to-day existence.

Ma's picture.

I dry-heaved.

You never even told Mallory about that, did you champ?

I swung my legs over the side of the hospital bed and braced against the rail. Gritted my teeth. Then I stood. I almost bit it a few times, but managed. Awkwardly, I batted the IV stand with the Stumps. It wheeled across the carpet. I stormed up to the picture. Even now, Ma's beady eyes watched me slave away.

I skewered it with a Stump and ripped it off the wall.

"Triple-Six?"

I jolted.

Mallory!

I slowly turned.

Mallory Worner stood outside the kitchen, holding a bowl of raw hamburger and a spoon. Sunlight from the window backlit her curls. Clean. Unhurt. No blisters or necrotic patches. Skin like vanilla-speckled cream. Shell-pink lips and burn scar. Stains dotted her apron and jeans.

Her gaze softened as she studied me. "Hey."

"What—where are we?"

"Let's sit at the table," she said.

I stared at the carpet. My stomach grumbled. *Are you alive?* Shit. What if this was Lorraine? No. Too much life in her eyes.

But how?

She held out the hamburger. "You should eat."

"You gotta cook it, babe."

"You like it raw. You've been sneaking it out of the fridge for years. C'mon."

I hobbled over to the dining room table and sat. She plonked the bowl in front of me. I reached for the spoon, and almost shanked Mallory.

"Where the hell are we?"

She shrugged. She held a glass of water up to my mouth. "Drink."

I sipped. Something caught my eye on the table.

"Is that a burner phone?"

She seasoned the raw hamburger. "He said he'd call once you woke up. It's been a week. I think."

A week?

"So I'm dead?"

"No."

I swallowed. "Are—are *you* dead?"

Mallory stared out the window. She stirred the hamburger.

"You need some solid food. Burn victims need protein. They told me that."

"Mallory. Are you dead?"

"There's weed under the sink, booze in the fridge," she said, still not looking at me. "They resupply after a while. Think he just wanted us to get high. Be happy."

She spooned hamburger into my mouth. Sweet pain arced through my jaw. Shot of warm saliva, out of commission salivary glands waking up.

"Mallory—*are you dead?*"

She barked a laugh. "We don't need to worry about birth control anymore."

Holy shit.

"Are we…in Hell?"

Her eyes glistened. "I tried."

"Lorraine—"

"She won," Mallory said softly. "She fucking won, Triple-Six. I'm dead. You know what? Being dead's not bad."

"Babe—"

"Don't say you love me. Just don't."

What could I even say?

She fed me the rest of my raw hamburger. Quiet settled over the house. She didn't eat. She checked my bandages and my IV fluids, and like a scene out of my worst nightmares, had to literally wipe my ass for me. I wanted to die. We shambled a few laps around the house before Coach Mallory decided I'd had enough exercise.

We tried to have sex on the couch. Why not? We were too broken for anything else. At least something would feel good.

She leaned over me. Mallory. Jasmine shampoo. Her hair moved, sending a wave of scent, cigarettes—

Oh God, Lorraine.

Nausea surged through me. *There ain't love. There's only this.* Grayout. I bit my lip, focused on the pain. On reality.

This was Mallory. Boobs. Soft boobs—

Lorraine.

"You remembering, too?" Mallory asked.

Gray-green tinged her face. Cold sweat ran down her cleavage.

"Jesus…Mallory, I can't get hard. I can't—"

"Yeah."

Lorraine really had broken everything. Neither of us could love each other. At what point did you get too broken for that? I'd killed a guy with Mallory and liked it. I'd killed Edward Sal Blueing and liked it. I'd watched Lorraine kill Roy Pike and liked it. Was it trauma, mental illness, or demonic blood?

Now nobody will ever love you.

"It's too much," Mallory said. "I'm sorry, Triple-Six."

We sat back at the table, waiting for the phone to ring.

It didn't take long.

BZZZT!

It vibrated. I reached for it, then remembered.

Mallory answered. "Hello?"

"Let me speak to Project 0666…is he sober?"

She held it up to my ear.

"Yeah," I said. "I'm sober. What about our bargain? I resuscitated Mallory Worner. I violated the terms we laid out—look, I'm sorry about that—"

I'm not, I mouthed to Mallory.

"But I did. Okay? Why am I here? What about Lorraine Worner?"

"Allow me to explain. If you have questions, ask them later."

Yeah, go mutilate Mallory's body. Evict Lorraine.

I traced circles on the table with a bony Stump while Lamiel talked, and Mallory scooted over, head tilted towards the phone.

"Lorraine Worner has dropped off the grid. Because of the terms of our bargain, the Hell Wardens can't handle her—"

"Kill her, you mean?"

Lamiel sighed. "They'd avoid it, if they could. Hell Wardens wrangle souls for a living. They have…abilities, shall we say, that limit the damage done to humanity."

I nudged up one of the bandages on my left arm. Gleaming, fresh skin mostly covered the burned areas, threaded with red veins. Something was wrong with it, though. Too shiny. Like fish skin.

"Do you like this place?"

"Hell?"

"It's a small pocket of Hell. I designed it. What if I told you, Project 0666, that you could stay here forever? With Mallory Worner? Normally, she'd go through a punishment regimen upon death..."

For being Lorraine's kid? I set my jaw. Mallory didn't blink.

"Let me guess—I have to go kill Mallory's body, hack it into little pieces, send Lori back to Hell, and then I get to stay? Is that it?"

Did I even want to stay here?

"No," Lamiel said, laughing. "It's simpler than that—you don't even have to handle Lorraine. All you do is exist. I've solved all of your problems. Your body won't change much after it heals...there's no stress, no environmental triggers—dear Roy's experiments taught us something—time won't seem to pass, not the way it would on Earth. Neither of you will age. Everything would be provided for."

Another bargain? Really?

"What's the catch?"

His voice chilled. "You can't leave."

Just like real desert-hell.

"So who's handling Lorraine?"

"She'll die...eventually."

"Uh, you are suggesting we do nothing? At all?"

"How long are human lifespans now? A hundred years or so?"

"She'll just find another person to possess, kill, and revive," Mallory snapped. "Not hard to get body fluids."

Ice prickled down my chest.

"Jesus fucking Christ, Mallory."

"She'd do it."

The A/C sputtered to a halt.

"Children," Lamiel said. "Does that really concern you?"

We looked at each other for a long minute.

"What happens if I say no, Lamiel?"

"No? You'd say *no*?"

"Just hypothetically. What happens?"

"You'll have to fulfill your obligation, Project 0666. Solve the Worner situation. *By any means necessary.*"

"I understood the first time you said it."

"Did you?"

Silence.

"You won't get this offer again, Project 0666. This pocket of Hell will cease existing if you leave."

"Lord Lamiel," I said quietly. "I understood the first time you said it."

Mallory rubbed her palms. She got me a glass of diluted Pedialyte with a straw. I sipped. Strawberry flavor. A solid for hangovers.

"Is Roy Pike doing okay?"

Electricity tingled where my skin touched the phone. Increased. I gritted my teeth. Blisters popped on my lips and oozed fluid.

"I'll be by later, *child*."

Click.

FORTY-SIX

WE SAT AT the table for ten minutes, silent as severed vocal cords.

"This isn't so bad," Mallory said.

I grunted.

Could we do this all over again? Sit here for an eternity and do this? She could freak out, I could take care of her—*God that sounds nice*—and vice versa, keep up the nice mesh of codependency and hidden secrets. Pretend Lorraine Worner never existed. Pretend I was completely human. Pretend my teeth weren't sharp as sin. Pretend we hadn't killed Blueing and then fucked afterwards. Pretend Mallory hadn't drugged me with trailer park GHB.

And maybe, just maybe, after we'd pretended and lied and brushed over the raw traumas, she'd spackle concealer over her burn scar, and I'd wrench out every last Fun Tooth, bandage up the Hands, and then we'd say—because who could ever love freaks like us otherwise?—

I'm fine, Mallory.
I'm fine, Triple-Six.
I love you.
What a great life to live.
What a great *existence*.
I couldn't live like that anymore.

I cleared my throat. Mallory lifted her head. I hooked a sharp bone underneath my arm bandages and sliced them off, one after the other. Soiled cloth fell to the carpet. New skin shone. Cherry veins pulsed. They'd retreated to my arms. Blackened char coated the ends of the Stumps. Bones broke through like sprouting saplings.

"Mallory," I said. "We need to talk. I don't know what you want, but I'm not staying in fake desert-hell while Lorraine kills innocent people."

"Neither am I."

"They want me to kill your body and cut it into pieces," I said, sweat forming under my arms. "You'd watch me?"

"I'd help dismember my corpse. I know how."

"That's fucked, Mallory."

She narrowed her eyes, grim-faced. "Wanna stop Lorraine? We're gonna have to do some fucked up shit."

I took a deep breath. It didn't help. "I need to tell you something. I'm not human. I'm a demon-hybrid. There's—there's a really good chance I'll, uh, mutate. If we leave here. Did you see what the Hell Wardens looked like?"

"Is one of them Demon Dad?"

"No," I croaked. "They're demon-hybrids. Like me."

"Okay?"

"They've been there longer. That's what happens. Your flesh goes full-on horror flick, and you can't do anything about it…look, I'm saying this because—"

I swallowed. I ran my tongue over my Fun Teeth.

"I don't want Lorraine to take our ability to love each other away. Fuck her. She's taken enough from us. I…want to try again."

She got up and stood by me, heat radiating off her.

"But if you don't want to because I'm certified demonspawn, I understand," I said.

"I want to, man."

Mallory felt along my bandaged arms. It stung. "Got an idea. Can I run you a cool bath? For the burns?"

"I'm a little musty."

"You're six foot five now, Triple-Six. Grew a whole inch on me. Couldn't throw you into the tub myself. Had to work with these discount baby wipes."

I blinked. *Ew.* "Every nook and cranny?"

"I ate a man once. I've seen some shit."

I held up the Hands. "Look, babe. Now I can wipe my own ass."

She snorted, stood, and went to run the bath. I thought I saw her smile.

I hobbled over, trying to bend the Hands. Limited success. They could sort of twitch, but open a rift? Not happening soon. *Hey, champ! You really feel like opening a rift to Lorraine right now? Considering what you have to do?*

But there had to be a way to get her out of Mallory's body without hurting it. Hadn't Lamiel mentioned something about the Hell Wardens? The faucet hissed lukewarm water. Mallory periodically felt it, adjusting as needed.

"There's a bathrobe behind the door. I can put it on. To start," she said.

"It's the cigarette smell."

She nodded. Turned the faucet off. I peeled off bandages. In the dust-filmed mirror, a horrific patchwork dude stared back. His hair—coarse black corkscrews—was half-burned away. Burned patches blistered up past the ears. Fingers of new skin curled up his face, unnaturally shiny. Vaguely metallic when the light hit them right. *Lori* was still seared below my collarbone.

I looked like something straight out of the fucking Exorcist.

My chest wound? Already scar tissue. New, fish-shiny skin covered most of my burns. Pus oozed around the edges. Dead skin rotted here and there.

I couldn't breathe.

"It's okay," she murmured, putting on gloves.

Is it?

She peeled off my crusty bandages. Barely any smell came out. *Folks, we have ourselves the DEAL OF A LIFETIME! ONE BURNED FREAKSHOW! All yours, ladies—JUST THREE PAYMENTS OF $2.22!*

A laugh clawed its way out of me. My eyes got wet. Who'd ever want to love me now? Who'd ever even want to *touch* me, now? Was I doomed to an eternity of jerking off? Was it just me and my Hand, now, forever? *And that's if your dick doesn't fall off or become sentient and crawl up inside you like a spider, like a centipede.*

I considered sex.

Sex.

If I show you who I really am, will you still love me?

You had porn, with its fluid-less sterilized pleasure, vacuum-packed for viewing. Don't like it? Try romance, sex neutered into vanilla-scented *I love yous—but you can't get sick or die, honey! Jizz doesn't stain!*—Wear your costume, perform your role—*you're a "woman," so wear the lace and blink demurely, you're a "man," better not cry or get angry or wear the fun lace*—utter snarky remarks, giggle, jam the right things into the right holes, have your fun, mop up the fluids before they decay or smell—*God forbid!*—but above all, avoid intimacy. Never ask the question.

If I show you who I really am, will you still love me?

The answer could kill you. Better to never ask. Wear the mask. Make appropriate sounds. Call it love. Be Normal. We're Normal People. We have Normal Sex. Please, am I doing it right? Am I a Normal Person? Am I acceptable? Unbroken? Salvageable enough to have sex with?

And the endless internal chant.

Please, oh God, tell me I'm not too broken to be loved.

I EASED INTO the bath—*ouch, Jesus*—but the sting faded after a few seconds. Clean water. The familiar scent of shampoo. Ivory soap. I sighed. Bits of skin floated off.

"Can I?" Mallory asked.

"Please."

She stripped off her top, unhooked her bra, slipped her cotton panties off, and a slow half-smile appeared on her face. Her boobs perked up. Nipples hardened.

We can do this.

Smooth pleasure, warmth down below. Mallory. She stepped into the bath, sitting between my legs. Those were in good shape, thank God, so I wrapped them around her—*how is she warm?* She leaned down, closer—

Cigarettes.

My heart sped. Not in a fun way. Short-circuited pleasure. *This is Mallory! She's not going to hurt you.*

She'd noticed my deflating boner. "You need me to leave?"

"No. I like this, it's just—"

"Pretend we're not even having sex. We don't have to. Need to scrub this dead crap off you anyway."

Mallory cupped water into her gloved hands and poured it over my hair. Unruly, disgusting foreigner hair—according to Roy Pike. She leaned in. Pressed her lips into my eardrum. Oh so good zinged down. She anointed me with shampoo and treasured my hair with her fingers, strong fingers, her hips grinding into my side as I half-sat. Thighs around me.

I felt safe. Secure. I closed my eyes. I talked.

"I wasn't working for Lorraine, Mallory. I don't want you to be some baby incubator. Or a blow-up doll. How could you think I'd ever want that?"

"She blew off your hands. Using my body. After she raped me. Using your body. I was having a *mental breakdown.*"

Her fingers massaged into my scalp. Rinsed. Soapy water trickled down me, burning.

"I watched her kiss you as my body rotted from the inside out. You knew. I saw it in your eyes. You wanted to feel loved so much you ignored it. What else would I assume?"

She blinked and wiped her eyes with her hand.

"I told her she could do whatever she wanted with me. As long as she didn't hurt you. She did anyway."

The Raspberry Zinger. The Sno Ball. Both cut in half.

"You made a bargain with Lorraine?"

"What else could I do, man?"

Warm body, nudging into mine. Dark hairs, fingernail-long, carpeted her legs. Bush of pubes. Hair peeked out from under her armpits.

She blushed. "Shit. I forgot to shave."

I kissed her, softly.

"It's cute. You're fuzzy."

She scrubbed me. Old skin sloughed off. Pus. I shed my dead skin bit by bit. Her shoulders loosened as she worked. She pulled the drain, ran fresh water. I stared at my neo-Hands.

"Did I try to cut my Hands apart?"

"Yeah."

I swallowed. "Did—did I hurt you? Lorraine showed me—"

"Oh my God. Triple-Six, you're taking *Lorraine* at face value?" Mallory said, rolling her eyes. "Dude, you were blackout drunk and horny. Not a budding rapist. I said no. You immediately stopped. Then you pissed yourself and started crying, and then you wanted to watch *Edward Scissorhands* again. We'd already watched it three times. You were so stoned you kept forgetting we'd watched it and—"

"Okay, Mallory, I think I get the picture."

"You didn't have to clean up that pee, man."

Mallory continued, "I found a gun in my pocket with a note that said it was from my guardian angel. Was trying to figure that out. Then you cried about your Ma."

Mallory paled, jaw working. "We could've killed her. If I'd 'ave known she hurt you…"

Oh not this. Not this. She can't know I got—

"You can't just kill everyone, Mallory!"

"I should know," she said. "I killed Lorraine, and that didn't fix everything. I didn't care, Triple-Six. Nobody was ever going to help me but me. So I did. That's me. I didn't feel empathy until I was eight years old…you cried about something. It made me cry."

She laughed. "Thought something was wrong with my eyes."

Pulse. Pulse. Icy-hot fear lit through my chest. How could she think like that? Like Lorraine? Like a monster? Where was the Benadryl when you needed it?

"So it's okay to do fucked up shit to people?"

"Lorraine's not a person."

I mimicked a therapy voice. "Do the feelings fit the facts?"

She jerked away from me. "Quit bringing my BPD into this. I handled Lorraine the best I could."

Oh, the way you handled Blueing?

"What the hell was I when you drugged me, babe? Your pet freakshow? A bodyguard you paid in blow jobs and laced booze?"

She leaned closer, eyes blazing. "When have I ever treated you like a freak?"

"How long were you planning on using me?"

"*I was trying to give us an opportunity to escape!*"

My throat *clicked,* and my Fun Voice burst out, "You USED ME to KILL SOMEONE!"

Shit.

I flinched at the sound. Mallory didn't blink. She drained the bath. We sat in silence as it emptied. She ran clean water in. She grabbed a conditioner bottle, fiddling with it. She stared at the label.

"Yeah. I did," she whispered. "I'm sorry, Triple-Six. I wanted us to escape. You were there. I had a plan. It involved your hands. Can it be both?"

My throat ached. I balled up on the opposite end of the tub, shaking.

"Did you ever actually love me, Mallory?"

"You think I don't love you?"

"Gee, babe, I can remember all the times you've ever said it. Oh, wait. That was when Lorraine possessed you."

Mallory squeezed a giant dollop of conditioner into her hands. "C'mere."

I tilted my head. She raked it through my hair with her fingers, sighing.

"You never use enough. You never take care of your hair. Always wanted to do this for you."

Wait…so you love me?

My heart pounded. "You didn't—"

"I don't say that shit twenty-four seven," Mallory said, exhaling. "Doesn't mean I don't love you. There's more kinds of love than Hallmark stuff."

"You could've said it when I did!"

"I wanted you to find someone better. Was trying to keep you—look. You weren't raised by *her.* You weren't possessed by her, off and on, for years. Didn't know when she'd do it. I thought I had an alternate personality. It seemed to hate you."

Fever heat from her hands leached into my scalp. I slumped. If I'd had a bizarro sociopath in my brain, and it wanted to mentally break Mallory, or kill her—well, shit. I wouldn't exactly bust out the roses and Valentine's candy.

But you busted out the lorazepam, champ.

"I'm sorry I kept shoving drugs down your throat. It was fucked up. It was wrong."

"You only did what you knew how," she said. "Don't worry about it."

Mallory snatched up a roll of waterproof bandage and rebound my arms. She looked at me. Leaned into me. Warm body. Soft boobs. *Oh God, watch the Hands, Jesus, I'm disgusting, she's got to be holding back vomit, she's quiet, something's wrong—*

No. Fuck this self-hating bullshit. Did I really, honestly give a shit about my pincer Hands? If I knew it didn't matter—Hands or no Hands—would I even care?

If you get rid of the Hands, someone will finally love you.

"Do you love me?"

She leaned in, lips parted. "Yeah. I do. I also don't want to be in a romantic relationship with you. Or anyone. I'm dead, man. Got shit to figure out first."

Unexpected relief flushed through me. I took a deep breath.

"Is it bad if I feel the same way?"

"No. I'm glad you do. Seriously, we need to start actual lives."

Pressure against my lips. Her saliva. Tongue slipped in, working—*closer, babe,* and I wrapped my arms around her, pressed her into me—*Jesus, I'm hard as a rock!*—throbbing heat, her, lubricated skin slick on mine, jasmine scent and faint smell of sweat, yeah, no Lorraine no disaster just her, Mallory, safe and wanting me, me, my skin and hair and Hands included, then her mouth worked down my jaw.

"I love you," I said.

"I love you, too."

Holy shit.

She'd loved me all along. The Hands—who cared about how they looked? They were good Hands. I'd had exactly one accident with them over the course of twenty-two years. And they weren't the Hands. They were *my* hands.

She kissed my jaw. Neck. Tingling *good,* trailing down, so I grinned—she laughed a little, humid heat against my neck.

Shit, my Fun Teeth!

"You look so happy when you smile," she said. "It's real. You put everything into it. God, I wish I had expressions like yours."

"You don't care about the teeth?"

"They're just teeth. I'm happy you're smiling."

A lump formed in my throat. "Yeah. Me too."

We looked at each other for a long minute, naked and warm. Mallory Worner, Living Dead Girl. Project 0666, certified demonspawn. We were just…human. Human as anyone else.

"I can't let Lorraine do this again. You understand?" Mallory said quietly.

"Babe, you can't just—you can't just die. You're twenty-two. You can't…"

Her eyes gleamed like hard enamel. "If you can't kill my body, I will."

Jesus God.

Someone knocked on the front door.

Lamiel.

Mallory and I rose out of the tub like baptized converts. Dripping, we ghosted out of the bathroom.

The fun part was over.

FORTY-SEVEN

I NEEDED THIS conversation like a strychnine sundae.

Mallory's face smoothed into its usual mask. Black eyes. I wrapped a towel around me, thinking. The gun. Guardian angel.

My name is LAMIEL and I have TOO MANY KIDS!

But only one favorite.

I went to answer the door.

It sprang open before I touched the knob.

Lamiel. A sentient, genderless ball of energy.

But today, he wore red lipstick. Maraschino cherry red, overdrawn into an exaggerated Cupid's bow. Same body—same illusion.

He clutched a handful of heart-shaped Mylar balloons and a bong.

"It's great to see you again, Lamiel," I said.

Lamiel smiled, exposing lurid white teeth. "I brought you a gift."

The same gift you got dear Roy?

"Wow, thanks."

He stalked into the living room, releasing the balloons. They rose and bounced on the ceiling. Mallory tensed. Froze. She didn't move to cover herself. He stepped towards her.

"Oh, there's no need for that. You won't go through the usual punishment regimen for killing someone. You can stay right here!"

Mallory flinched away. Her back mashed into the couch. Lamiel leaned in.

"No need to experience...the things your victim went through, Miss Worner. Didn't you slash his throat? My, my. But there's no shortage of torturers in Hell..."

"I had to."

Something cruel glinted in his eyes. He kept smiling.

"But there's no need to discuss any of *that,* children," he said. "Or is there?"

Mallory's gaze fixed on Lamiel.

Time to play my cards.

"How's Roy Pike doing?" I asked.

"He died a virgin," Lamiel said, not bothering to look at me. "Very sad."

"My condolences. You really liked Roy, didn't you?"

His voice tightened. "I care for the children I produce, yes."

"You spoil them much? Give them gifts?"

"I don't have time for a long chat," he said, still leaning over Mallory.

I grinned. Bared my Fun Teeth.

"Neither do I, Lamiel."

He finally turned. Stared.

I gestured to the dust-caked dining table. "Let's sit. Let's talk *bargains.*"

"There's no need for that."

"Did he like his desert-hell dollhouse, when you gave it to him?" I said, raising my voice. "Or did dear Roy Alexander Pike like playing with his dolls more?"

He sat, rolling his eyes. Great.

"Let me show you something, child."

I didn't move.

Lamiel tilted his head. "Please. Sit down."

"Ach!"

Shit. What was—

Mallory writhed on the couch, hands pressed over her belly. Her mouth spasmed. No sound. Reddening skin. Tears streaked down her face.

Oh God, he's—

"Sit. *Now."*

I sat.

"Don't look at her. She's fine," he said, and chuckled. "She *is* dead, you know."

Fuck this guy.

He slid his hands across the table. Towards me. He grabbed my wrists. I couldn't feel it. Translucent nerves were twining over the bones of my Hands. Muscle fibers stretched like pink cobweb. Lamiel's hands closed over mine.

Electricity tingled.

Stopped.

"Look at them now, Project 0666."

His red lips moved. How much time did it take a sentient ball of energy to draw those? Was there a makeup store for the Lords of Hell? *Sephora— no, Sep-whore-a! Ha-ha!*

"They're lovely hands, dear," he said.

Warmth. Pressure. On my hands. Real hands. Actual, normal human hands.

I didn't look.

He leaned in, murmuring, "Would you like to touch her?"

My throat got thick. Touch Mallory. No paralyzing freakazoid pincers.

I couldn't resist.

They were sturdy hands. Clothed in my dark skin. No freaky red veins, no claw tips. Just hands. Little black hairs curled on the knuckles. Half-moons nestled in the beds of the pink fingernails. *They would've looked like this.*

Wetness filled my eyes. Everything blurred.

"You can keep them, Project 0666."

"If I stay."

"Precisely. See how nice I am?"

I inhaled.

See how nice I am?

I kept my voice cheerful. Calm.

"Yeah, Lamiel. You are. You made a bargain with some random demon-hybrid and all you wanted was credit for something. You added one stipulation—pretty reasonable—and I blew it. Your own kid got killed. Instead of making me fulfill my end of the bargain, you heal me, haul me to this nice pocket-dimension, and even bring in Mallory. You give me endless weed...you give me normal hands—the thing I've wanted since I could toddle—and all you want me to do is stay?"

I clenched his hands.

"It's almost like that's the entire point," I said.

Expressionless, Lamiel studied me. He didn't respond or move.

"Mallory, babe—why don't you come over?"

She did. Her arms wrapped around her chest. Her knuckles gleamed white.

"I wonder how Lord Amalek feels about the fact that I'm a stunted, mentally ill freak? A late bloomer? Do you think Roy asked him? Or did precious Roy kidnap one of Amalek's children for his experiments?"

Lamiel's voice was barely audible. "You expect me to hurt my own—"

"Why was Mallory Worner involved?"

He stared at me for a long moment. The fridge hummed.

"Fertility experiments," he said.

Mallory paled. "I was on birth control."

"Placebos, Miss Worner."

I took a deep breath. I jammed down the scream building in my throat. Okay. Scream later.

"And now you can't kill me—"

"I can indeed."

"But it doesn't matter in Hell. I just can't go to Earth. Still exist here—man, how pissed off do you think Amalek's going to be? Technically, I'm his property. That's pretty fucked, but hey, when in Rome. So you—or your precious Roy—damaged Lord Amalek's *property*. Now you need to cover it up—but how?"

Mallory shook, white with rage.

"Easy," I said. "Set up a situation, make Amalek's spawn bargain with you, and when he fails? Swoop in, offering forgiveness. Bread and circuses. Put the experiment in another goddamn Skinner Box. Take away his Hands, so he can't go anywhere. And if push comes to shove—well, you've got his girlfriend's soul here…"

Sharp pain throbbed in the left side of my skull.

"Perhaps I'll gift you a brain tumor," Lamiel said.

The pain made me wince, but I forced a laugh. "I've gotta have brains for that first."

"Don't," Mallory snapped.

I tried to ignore the pain. I made eye contact with Lamiel and maintained it as I released his hands. The Hands tingled into existence—but I didn't look.

"I could make this dimension the size of a coffin," he said, still smiling. "A black void. There wouldn't be an end, Project 0666. I wouldn't let you die. Would you prefer the tumor?"

"Well, Lamiel. It's like I said before—I'm *such an idiot*. A dumb bodyguard grunt. Christ, I'm probably wrong about all of this. And if I weren't…who'd ever actually believe me? Think I'd go tattle to Lord Amalek? Please."

He blinked. The pain dissipated. Dust motes danced in the air. Only Mallory's ragged breathing broke the silence.

"I don't understand, Project 0666."

I grinned again. "Lamiel. I'm trying to tell you I want something."

He raised an eyebrow. "Oh?"

"Y'know, I'm a pretty chill guy. Very Zen. Very forgive and forget, Lamiel. I want to fulfill my end of our bargain. But maybe it could get altered. Let the Hell Wardens do their job, instead of an idiot like me. Let's add a clause— 'people under my command' count as 'me'—"

"I can't."

"*What?*"

He shook his head. "Impossible to alter a bargain like that. Adding or subtracting items. Interpretation of existing material is a different matter."

"So," Mallory said, voice strained. "I was supposed to get pregnant? Be a baby incubator?"

"What does it matter now?" Lamiel asked.

Her jaw worked. She said nothing. *Fuck this guy.* I opened my mouth. She shook her head.

"I need to throw Lorraine back into Hell. Let us go."

"Us? Miss Worner is dead, Project 0666."

Existing material. I'd resuscitated Mallory. Broken that. Wait.

"Roy's living it up, huh?"

"Yes, child."

"Great. Return my magic gun, please. Didn't our bargain say something about an *assistant*?"

Lamiel pursed his lips. "Your assistant perished."

"Funny—I don't remember hearing anything about a one assistant limit. You know what I do remember? A time frame. Roy Pike's assistance until the Worner issue got solved. Is it solved?"

He heaved a sigh and rolled his eyes.

"Don't exhume Roy. I'd like Mallory Worner as my alternate assistant. Please and thank you."

"Wouldn't you rather touch her? Love her?"

"We love each other just fine," Mallory said.

"I asked *him*."

"I'm not letting Lorraine go free," I said. "Not for anything."

"Miss Worner is dead," Lamiel said. "She doesn't have an anchor to Earth. She'll be tortured and processed like any other soul."

Unless she possessed me. But there wouldn't be enough time to find and kill Lorraine. Too risky. Either my body would disintegrate, throwing us both into Hell, or she'd leave—and go directly to Hell.

Orange energy flickered at the edge of my vision. The Hands weakly responded. *pulse. pulse.*

"What if I put her back? Into her body?"

He crossed his arms. "She couldn't go to Earth to enter it."

"Believe me, I tried," Mallory said.

"But her body's still alive. Why isn't it her anchor point?"

"Because Lorraine coordinated it that way," Lamiel said, sighing. "Death severed the connection between Miss Worner's body and soul. Lorraine inserted her soul into the drowned corpse...and you revived it."

"So?"

"Lorraine's soul rooted itself into the living body. Do you understand how hard it would be to tear her out...even if we hadn't made our bargain? This isn't possession anymore, child. The body and soul have claimed each other. There's nothing you can do."

I ground my teeth together. "Can you make Mallory Worner an anchor point?"

"Why would I do that? I certainly wouldn't do it for free," Lamiel said, and turned towards the door.

Shit.

We had to get out of here. The Hands—they were gone again. Normal hands sat uselessly at the ends of my wrists.

Oh, come on!

He opened his hand, and the heart balloons zoomed to it as if summoned. "You'll forget the Worner situation in due time. Try to be happy."

There's nothing you can do.

Screw that.

Okay. What did I have? *Blood. Sweat. Cum.* Could I barter with fluids? Offer to let an actual demon possess me? How many STDs was it physically possible to contract in a week? And still survive? Maybe I could find a clinic with punch cards. Get a free Flesh Light every five syphilis cures. A nervous giggle burst out.

"Possess me," I said.

He stopped. Mid-step. Turned back.

"Full possession?" Lamiel said. "Entire control?"

He grinned, nose and eyes scrunching up. He looked at me as if I'd turned into the last Rocket Pop in a heatwave.

"Triple-Six," Mallory said. "What the fuck are you doing?"

This was a great idea. Totally. I could feel it in the anxious knot at the pit of my stomach.

"In exchange for making Mallory Worner an anchor point. One that allows her to touch physical items."

"It won't be permanent."

"Doesn't have to be," I said, walking into the kitchen.

"I want five hundred days. Not necessarily consecutive, dear."

"Five hundred days?"

Mallory stormed after me. "Triple-Six. Are you fucking kidding me right now? He's a demon—you want more of his bullshit on Earth?"

"I shouldn't check on my children, Miss Worner? Or give them intellectual stimulation?"

Or dolls to experiment with.

"Roy Pike hated you," I said. "And we're not doing five hundred days. Thirty, max. After I solve the Worner situation. I'd like my magic gun back, too."

"I thought it was a phase," Lamiel said wistfully. "I only…I wanted him to develop. He wasted his life, you know. He grew a little spike on the heel of his hand when he turned fifteen. He tried to pray it off. He poured muriatic acid on it…so many other things. Dear Roy turned away every human who wanted to love him. He was so ashamed. He saw a lot of himself in you, child."

So trauma means it's okay to hurt people?

I ripped open a drawer and fished out a sharp filleting knife. "Is thirty days fine or not?"

"Two days for the anchor point, then."

"Three," I said. "Take it or leave it."

I slapped the knife into Lamiel's hand. "You don't get to possess me until I throw Lorraine back in Hell. So no Faustian bullshit. It's in your best interest for me to succeed."

"Hm," he said.

A heart-shaped vial appeared on the table. I picked it up. Surprisingly heavy. Made of some opaque, poppy-red glass. It even had a chain attached.

"Let me guess—if it breaks, the anchor point fails?"

"Yes. You say it's in my best interest for you to succeed? Do you understand what that means for you?" Lamiel cooed, tilting his head. "If Mallory Worner returns to Hell, *I'll still send you after Lorraine.* If you die...*I'll still send you after Lorraine.* You won't sleep, eat, or function until the Worner situation is solved..."

Heartbeats hammered my eardrums.

"Do we have a bargain, Project 0666?"

There weren't any other options left. I ignored my fears. There wasn't room for them now.

"I accept your terms," I said.

Quick slash of pain across my cheek. Hot liquid dribbled down. Lamiel patted the cut. He drew his blood-dotted fingers back and licked my fluids off. Mallory hissed. She latched onto my arm.

"Then I certainly can't keep you."

Everything—fake house, red desert outside, battered jizz-stained couch, the faint weed smell soaked into the drapes—flickered.

He was gone.

Fake desert-hell flickered again.

It vanished.

Ozone.

Cold, dark void.

Oh God, where are we? Is this Hell?

The Hands pulsed. Earth. I tried to slash out—nothing. They ached.

We were trapped in Hell, naked, and I couldn't get us out. The only real things? The reek of ozone, black chill creeping into my bones. Mallory's hot stranglehold on my arm.

Her panicked breathing.

FORTY-EIGHT

HELL WAS COLD.

A void without warmth in the forgotten corners, a rich, bone deep blackness. I breathed in clammy air. Kept staring into the emptiness. There was no wind. The air hung dead. The air hung hellishly alive. Electricity zinged through my hair follicles. Mallory pressed against me.

"Triple-Six? Something's happening…"

"Babe?"

Nothing. Her breathing slowed. A pleasurable pulse started in my eye sockets, and I shut them without thinking. Veins rasped inside my eyelids. They meshed.

I opened my Fun Eyes.

I suddenly got answers I'd never wanted.

A leviathan neon sign loomed over a vast waste. It burned turquoise. The color of a cholera-contaminated swimming pool. Weak, dirty light. *Welcome to the Loop!* it read. Around me, dark figures stumbled through the neon-lit wasteland. Whispers buzzed through the air. Sobs.

Mallory sniffled.

"Please," she breathed, "tell me I'm good. Good."

Her arm laced through mine. She scrubbed her hands.

"If I'm good she won't hurt me. Good. If I behave she won't hurt me if I lie back and let them they won't hurt me more—"

"Mallory? What are you doing?"

Scrubbing hands. "If I'm good she won't hurt him she won't hurt him more, if I'm good I live if I pretend I'm lost and need to find her I'll live and she won't use Big Needle, be good, be good, behave…"

Mallory's skin was raw. She kept scrubbing. Clawing. Repeating.

Her pupils were dilated, her gaze unfocused. *She can't see anything, can she?*

Of course not. This place was meant for human souls.

"Mallory!"

She didn't stop.

I ran over to the nearest shape, dragging Mallory along with me. She didn't resist.

A woman, mid-thirties. Purple bruises splotched her neck. Rasping laugh. "Daddy, quit it!"

She put her hands up to her throat.

"You don't mean to hurt me. You love me." Every time she said something she finished it off with a laugh like a death rattle.

Again. And again. I listened for two minutes, watched this lady repeat the hand-to-throat gesture, the laugh, as the names changed.

"Honey, you're hurting me!" Again, that fucking laugh.

Laugh. Fondle throat.

"You don't mean to."

Laugh. Fondle throat. "Don't mean to, don't mean to, they never mean to—"

Nothing changed. Mallory kept babbling. Blood slicked her arms.

"Be good! She'll hurt you more if you're not, be good be still she won't hurt you oh God don't run," and she scrubbed, "be good be good be clean the bodies can't hurt me if I'm Good they can't come back and she can't come back oh God she'll hurt Triple-Six…"

The lady's voice hoarsened. "Sweetie, you don't mean to, I know, but I can't breathe please," same laugh, garbled by invisible hands. "You have to stop or you're gonna kill—"

Her mouth hung slack. No breathing. Null. Void.

Then, the rasping, childish laugh.

"Daddy, quit it!"

Hands to throat.

All over again.

Now you know why they call it the Loop, champ!

Over and over, the shapes around me relived their worst traumas, repeated their mantras. It never ended. They repeated the same pointless actions. Said the same phrases. Always the same. The only thing that ever changed were the names.

I had to get us out of here. I balled my Hands. *C'mon. Do the mumbo-jumbo.* Heat rose in my arms. Pulsed down towards the skeletal outline of the Hands. Red light glowed down the veins. *Lorraine. Take me to Lorraine Worner.*

"...If I'm good it won't hurt if I behave I live if I behave he lives..."

Patches of wet muscle gleamed through Mallory's arms. She'd rubbed her skin off. She scrubbed faster, sobbing.

Get me out of here! Take me to Lorraine Worner!

Crackling noises came from out of the Hands. They blazed. Too hot. Oh, Jesus, too hot. Like a diesel engine on overdrive. They vibrated. I couldn't feel rift membrane, couldn't slice through the air—

Red-hot pain zipped through them. My Hands spasmed. Some invisible switch got flipped, something, because everything stopped dead cold. No heat, no shakes, no mumbo-jumbo.

Smoke curled out from underneath my bandages.

Holy shit.

"Lorraine, please, I'll be good I promise please don't burn them please don't I'll be good be Good please don't I swear I'll be good don't use Big Needle on me, if I'm Good I get smoky candy I need smoky candy please Lorraine it hurts if I don't have smoky candy please I'll be Good..."

Smoky candy?

Oh, sweet Jesus, was Mallory talking about meth?

Concentrate. I visualized Lorraine. Heat, building. Energy sang down my arms. *Lorraine. Lorraine. Gotta get to Lorraine Worner.*

Rift membrane squelched between my pincers.

I went to slice—

Nothing.

Like trying to cut silk with a Popsicle stick. I lashed out again. Nada. *Lorraine. Lorraine. Lorraine—*

Mallory sobbed. Scrubbed at her exposed muscle. Had to snap her out of this...but how? Love? Could that work?

I spun her around so we were face-to-face. She looked right through me. Scrubbed.

"Mallory, *I love you.*"

"...Be Good have to be Good if I be Good they'll let him have his dog back, if I'm Good they won't hurt Triple-Six, please Mr. Pike don't hurt him I'll be Good I swear what do you want I'll be Good..."

Shit.

I kissed her. She kept talking as I did.

Scrubbing. Her moist, raw arms. Hairless where skin remained.

"Stop it!"

But she didn't.

Click.

My Fun Voice shrieked, *"STOP IT!"*

I grabbed her wrists and held them. She struggled. I clutched harder.

Fluids and blood soaked into my bandages. *Click.* I felt the shift in my throat. Normal voice.

"…Have to be Good be clean…why isn't it working…why can't I…"

She trailed off. She stilled. Her breathing sped up.

"Is—is that you, man?"

"Yeah. Mallory, we're in Hell, you're trapped in some trauma loop, and I can't get us out. The Hands aren't healed."

"I—I can feel it trying to hurt me. I can't…be good. Be—"

She let out a harsh breath. "Oh my God. I—I'm trying to stop the flashbacks and they keep coming."

Maybe I couldn't stop the flashbacks, but could I keep her from rubbing her skin off? Give us time while the Hands healed? Keep her safe?

I pressed my bloody cheek to her face. "Mallory. Possess me."

"You trust me enough for that?"

"Believe it or not, I do," I said.

Her tongue lapped off my blood. Lapped the sweat on my chest.

"I can't see anything…be Good she's going to hurt him if I'm not…shit! I did this before. I used to possess you in my sleep. I think I can do it."

She kissed me. Swallowed my saliva.

Blood, sweat, tears? Spit? Cum?

"I love you," she breathed. "You. Taste—"

She entered me.

Far less invasive than Lorraine. Oh, it still felt foreign. Feeling of *something in me*. But this felt less like G-rated anal with barbed wire and more like a pube caught in my throat, tickling constantly.

Not as bad in here, Mallory thought.

She didn't control my body. She peered through my eyes.

You can see in the dark?

Yeah, I thought. I visualized the red blanks of my Fun Eyes. *Clawed my old eyes out. Long story.*

Hey, try to open a rift. If we work together…

A pulse. Latent heat. Energy.

Take us to Lorraine, Mallory thought.

The Hands heated. I jammed my wrist in my mouth and bit down, drawing blood. Magic blood. Lorraine the Immane. Killer of innocents. Take me to Lorraine Worner. I curled and opened the Hands, *pulse-pulse-pulse,* and new, low heat surged through me. Mallory. Anger.

Lorraine the Immane. Predator. Her hand, groping me like I was fucking property. *You'll be a fun toy when the killin' runs low.* Her brand stung on my chest. Honeydoll…her smirk, lording over the burned remains of her victims.

She hurt me and she's going to keep hurting others and killing unless we stop her. Take us to the killer of innocents! TAKE US TO LORRAINE!

Mallory's thought or mine? Hazy. Some nebulous wall was dissolving between us, less self—

Rage.

Pulse. Pulse. Pulse. Protect. Tear. Kill. Yes.

Glowing red veins arced to life, heat in a molten line from my guts to the Hands…arousal. *Use it.* Forced the energy into the Hands. *Lorraine. Take us to Lorraine.*

Rift membrane.

Slashed out.

Tore.

The rift blossomed open.

Thanks, demon puberty.

Let's go kill Lorraine.

But the Hands kept vibrating. Too warm. Like they wouldn't cool down. Stabbing pain shot up the veins…

I? We? Entered the rift.

Welcome to the Loop!

The sign blinked behind us, and trapped souls shuffled onwards to nowhere.

FORTY-NINE

LORRAINE HUNCHED OVER a display case.

Night. Streetlamps trickled light through the windows. Glass gleamed on rows of display cases. Broken shards littered the floor. A naked woman lay on the industrial carpet, half-sobbing. Her ankles and wrists were zip-tied. Duct tape over her mouth. Dry eyes. Choking sobs. Blood and mucus slicked the wide end of a glass soda bottle. Blood. Weeping from a wet triangle of flayed-off skin between her breasts.

Congealing stream between her thighs. Blood. Mucus.

Torn chunk of flesh stuck on the soda bottle. Pink wet flesh—

Oh God she raped her with it.

I dry-heaved.

Pulse. Pulse. Pulse.

Mallory slipped out of me and stood by my side. The Hands shook, half-formed, steaming. A noise bubbled up. I gritted my teeth. Held it in. Mallory's hand slipped into my waistband, pulled out something metallic. Roy Pike's revolver. She aimed it at Lorraine's back.

Veins withered. Blackened.

Lorraine turned, arms sparkling. Her bangles. Her rhinestone-adorned death trophies. The display case placard read, *Lorraine Worner, "Barbecue Butcher," circa 1970-2008. Jewelry.*

She smiled.

"Honeydoll. You came back."

The Hands crumbled apart. Bits of bone hit the carpet. Neo-flesh melted into nothing. Shit. All I had? Stumps. Couldn't get the woman or us out of here.

"Lorraine," Mallory said, raising the gun.

"You git an anchor point? You git Hell to agree to it if you killed me? Go on then, shoot. I got ten other fucks I can possess, and enough time to find myself a fuckin' swimming pool to drown in."

"You—"

"Honeydoll. Remember your mama?"

She imitated Mallory's voice, "Triple-Six. Help me! Please—Lorraine's aiming a gun at me. She hurt this woman—"

"*Shut up*," I snarled.

No grayout. No traumatic flashbacks. *She's got other bodies?* Then I'd claw her out and take her to Hell. Somehow.

Lorraine stepped towards us, holding a foot-long metal needle. She raised a gun at me with her other hand.

"Gonna behave, honey?"

I lunged for her. She curled her finger around the trigger.

Bang!

White-hot pain exploded through my thigh—*Jesus God!*—and I buckled to the carpet, blood spurting out. Tried moving. Couldn't. *Shit.* Tried dragging but how was I supposed to drag myself across the carpet *without fucking hands*? Dry dead taste burned my mouth. Lorraine approached. Loomed over me.

Mallory inhaled. "Big Needle?"

"The one and only, kid."

"No. You can't."

"Take a gander at Big Needle, Honeydoll."

She knelt. She held Big Needle out on her palm.

It was a thin knitting needle. Pink metal. Probably aluminum. Something you could get from any Walmart or Kmart…something easily sterilized. Stowed away.

My mouth went dry. I froze.

"Never used it on Mallory. Cause that'd be a one and done. But you?"

Her voice softened to a murmur. She kissed my forehead. "Your brain will grow back however it needs to."

"You're not saying—"

She tickled the sharp end of Big Needle against my tear duct. Lobotomy. Oh God. This was a trailer park lobotomy, and she didn't want Project 0666 anymore, no, she wanted Honeydoll, her lobotomized guard, her slave, raping and killing as she ordered, and I'd never ever escape, never travel away from her.

She'd never die.

"I'll kill myself," I said.

"Don't matter, Honeydoll. Hell's gonna send you after me. If you die? They'll keep givin' you anchor points. Neither of us is ever gonna die. You escape? What the fuck do I care? We can do this dance for centuries, kid."

She fondled the red vial around my neck.

"But it'll always end here."

Everything grayed. Woozy. Mallory was tying a tourniquet around my thigh, tears streaming down her face. Lorraine didn't stop her.

"Y-you want me dumb?"

"I'll break you. At some point, I'll manage it. Over and over. My Honeydoll. You really thought I'd kill you? You got beautiful flesh. Malleable. Gonna run some fun experiments. You'll do what I say, when I say it. You will rape and burn and kill with me, Honeydoll. For-fuckin'-ever. I'll fuck you whenever I feel like it. You. Are. My. Toy. My bodyguard. And you'll repair yourself…however suits *me*. Whatever you need to be to protect *me*. You'll mold yourself around *me*, kid. That's how it works. I seen this shit. You ain't gonna be that dumb."

She laughed. "You're gonna be like me. A sociopath. Enough rounds with Big Needle will do it. But chin up, Honeydoll. You be a good boy and sit through this, I'll fry up some crispy skin. Better'n pork rinds."

Lorraine jerked her head at the flayed woman. The woman uttered a muffled scream. Tears appeared in her eyes.

I gagged. Fried skin. My snack. The needle, grinding into my tear duct.

"Get off him," Mallory said. "*Now*."

"You break a person enough," Lori said, a hint of sadness tainting her voice, "they always end up like me. Big Needle or no."

I struggled, tried to flinch away. She leaned closer.

"*She* dances in light and shadow and *she* is a great favorite," Lorraine said.

Gentle pressure. Big Needle slipped an eighth of an inch in. Tear duct. Mallory's gaze bored into me. She mouthed, *do you trust me?*

Yes, I mouthed.

One wrong move would scoop my eye out—*THAT'S BETTER THAN THIS!*—oh God, oh God, anything but being a lobotomized slave, a soulless sociopath, a toy for a serial killer for all eternity—

"*She* never sleeps, the judge. *She* is dancing, dancing. *She* says that *she* will never die."

Angled Big Needle up. Eau de Lori filled my nose. Pressure. Quarter-inch in.

Lorraine stroked the heart-shaped vial around my neck. "This her anchor point?"

Mallory placed the gun down on the carpet, inhaled.

"I—"

"You want her to see this?"

Lorraine the Immane. Her fingers closed around the anchor. Squeezed. Tears streamed around Big Needle, down my face, and I swallowed. Tasted vomit. *Is this all you've got?*

No.

I had free will. I still had a non-lobotomized brain. Resources. Bargains. Fun Teeth.

I tensed my stomach. *Jerk back. Rip her fucking throat out!*

"Mallory...you be good, and I won't hurt him as much," Lorraine muttered. "Honeydoll, let her go."

Be good. Be Good, Mallory.

Mallory Worner possessed me. Hot bolt of rage, a scream—

"You're a FUCKING LIAR!"

Lorraine pressed in.

My body jerked back. Big Needle slid out of my eye. Clean. No gore. *Thank God.* Lorraine snatched at the vial. Mallory grabbed her by the throat and *clicked* into my Fun Voice. Words tangled into nothing. Rage.

She *growled* instead.

You lying fucking cunt, you ALWAYS hurt them no matter what I did! You ALWAYS HURT ME NO MATTER WHAT I DID!

We were together, in my body, and I fucking loved it. Bubble of power. Our united rage, hot and roiling like sexual arousal.

Tear her throat out with me! The TEETH! They feel GOOD!

My Stumps pulsed. Pleasant rush through my gums. Pulsing.

Oh my God they DO!

Lorraine's face reddened. Her weak breaths rasped. She struggled for the glass vial. Her hands batted at my chest. Tough shit, Lori. No lobotomized bodyguard for you. How sad.

We sank my teeth into her shoulder. Salty, sugar-sweet metallic taste. Blood. Meat.

Oh it tastes good! I want to RIP and TEAR and EAT her! YES! Triple-Six! MEAT I want MEAT is this why you eat it raw?

Fuck YEAH, babe!

Sank deeper. Give her a taste. Let us experience—

Oh shit! This is your body! Mallory!

I don't care I hate my body.

Rush of fear. Shit. How could I forget? I let Lori's shoulder—*Mallory's* shoulder—go. Concentric rings of dots bled. My freakazoid teeth marks. *Do you trust me, Triple-Six?*

Wow, Mallory! I let you possess my body? You think?

She thought, *When I say, "fuck you," head-butt her. Or knock her away. You're bleeding out. Let Lorraine go. Her victim's going into shock. I have a plan.*

I released Lorraine. She gasped for breath. My bullet wound trickled blood, no longer spurting. Great. The flayed woman's skin grayed. Her chest barely moved.

Mallory materialized by her gun. She picked it up.

"Honeydoll," Lorraine wheezed, "Better fuckin' behave. It's only gonna git worse."

She fished for Big Needle. Seized it. Held it up.

White noise.

My left ear went deaf. Lorraine now held a broken metal rod. Only half of Big Needle. The other end flew across the room, landing somewhere out of sight. Smoke oozed out of Roy Pike's revolver.

"That was a cheap fuckin' shot."

Mallory's voice hardened. "You taught me."

Lorraine slapped a hand to her bleeding shoulder. Bangles clinked. A tooth on one. Watches. Mixed, woven bracelets and human hair, spangled into sparklies.

"I'll let you wear 'em. C'mere, Honeydoll."

Blood coated the rhinestones as she forced them onto my arms. They jingled.

"I hate you, Triple-Six," Mallory said. "You're a monster. A demonic freak."

She's acting. Wait for it.

Lorraine got a leg over my chest. She dug in her pocket, pulling out a burner phone. She dialed, panting. Okay? Sweat pooled between my collarbones. I felt weird. Wanted those bangles off. Nausea wriggled through me—

—*Aw hell no, IT WAS HER? HER!* The frizzy-haired hooker dumps the gasoline over him, cool fluid but the chemical fumes stab into his brain, and he can't move, he struggles but he can't move, *No! Bess, she's ten years old. Who's going to raise her?* Eyes burn. Snick of a match being lit. Lonely night sky overhead. He tries to scream. She laughs. Flame burns. Nobody will hear him, honey. Nobody will ever find him—

—*Oh no I can't be fixed*, and here it is, the sheer cold terror and knowing, blood slithering out of her throat, the white-hot raw pain in her cunt, *why did she have to use the baseball bat?* The truck seat smothers her nose. Sleepy. *I never got to graduate. I forgot to tell Mom I loved her.* Again, the thought. Sad. Too injured. Going to die. *If an EMT found me now, I'd still die.* The knowing of being too broken. Sleep. Bleeding. The woman's nasally, hick-laugh—

—*I wanted to HELP YOU! You and your fucking weird kid!* Something snaps in his wrists when he hurls them against the tape. *No no no, not the fire not fire anything but fucking FIRE*—

—*God, please forgive this woman. Please help Fred to heal*, a sort of numbness now, wasn't it peaceful? The saints suffered. Perhaps she should find goodness in this. She inhales the chemical fumes. Polly—*no, Lori, her name was Lori*—has been singeing the match along her face. Ain't you scared, you fuckin' bitch? Dumb bitch? But eventually, Lori ignites the fire. Sinking into layers of gray. Vague pain. *God, please forgive this woman. God in heaven—*

IMAGINE THE TERROR and rage of thirty dead souls' last memories. Embedded into Lorraine's bangles. She took an item from each victim right before she killed them. A piece of jewelry. Teeth. Hair. Dried skin.

Imagine every last one of those memories.

Imagine them slamming into your brain. All at once.

Screaming.

My throat hurt. Screaming. Who was screaming? It sounded like a man.

"911? Help—there's a fuckin' psycho at the Murder Museum! He's naked! There's a girl, real injured—"

"Fuck you!" Mallory yelled.

Wasn't I supposed to do something?

Oh.

Memories played. I was frozen.

Oh, shit. Was I screaming? Yeah. That was me. Huh.

"Triple-Six, c'mon!"

Get Lori away from you. Mallory stared at me. I stopped screaming. It stopped. One of the two. Memories. Fire. Gasoline.

I bucked. Lorraine fell off me like a glutted flea. Mallory sprinted, reached into the space, and tore the glass vial off my neck. She retreated. Lorraine clawed for it. Mallory dodged.

Trust me, she mouthed.

Then Mallory vanished, along with her anchor point.

Lorraine spat, turned back to me. She tried to wrench her bangles off. Nothing happened. They wouldn't budge. They'd tightened around my arms. Merged into my skin, veins included—*are they growing* over *them?*

Red veins branched *over* Lorraine's death-bangles. More veins covered the rhinestones with each passing second. Like tree roots, growing. I forced the flood of memories back.

God, if this is a joke, it's a really shitty one.

The flayed woman sucked in an audible breath. Her gaze sharpened. Our eyes met.

"Well, fuck," Lorraine said.

She stood, tucking a scrap of paper into my waistband. She stared at the windows. Faint red lights flickered.

"You got two fuckin' days to bring 'em back, Honeydoll. Heal your Hands. I'm gonna need 'em."

"What?"

"You're goin' to a party. Gonna learn how to light some fires."

"Lorraine," I said, holding up my arms. "I think a few people might object to that."

"I killed 'em. I won. So fuckin' what?"

Police sirens droned in the distance. Lorraine chuckled, and ran off into the building, footsteps growing fainter. I forced myself onto my elbows. The woman. Was she okay? Had to keep her talking. I could do that much.

"Hey," I rasped, "can you hear me?"

She sniffled. Shook. Nodded.

"People are coming. You're going to be okay."

She stared at the used soda bottle. Teared up. Exposed meat shone on her chest. I dragged myself a few feet closer, using my elbows.

"Can I try to get the duct tape off? Is that okay? I might have to touch you."

Shaky nod.

I worked my elbow over the seam of the tape, loosening it.

"Can you reach up? Peel that off?"

Nod. She rubbed her bound hands against the tape, pinched, and ripped it off.

"You're going to be okay—"

"N-no I'm n-not."

But she sat up, curled her arms around her knees. I bled. Red and blue lights streaked through the windows. I didn't know what to say. I didn't know her. She didn't know me.

All I could do was suck in one breath at a time. The cops came, then the paramedics, then the nice stretcher they cuffed my ankle to, as Lorraine's bangles melded into my skin. Memories babbled at the back of my skull. Everything spun. Breathe. One at a time.

A party.

Two days.

Mallory, where are you?

The pain meds kicked in. I drifted.

FIFTY

I'D BEEN IN the cell for nine hours.

I was a medical marvel. Two larynxes. Fun Teeth. Rapidly growing Hands. They couldn't fingerprint me. I told the cops I hadn't hurt the woman, I'd gone into the building after hearing glass break…but nobody believed me. Bullet wound? Mostly healed. I'd gotten a nice white prison outfit to flaunt. Nobody could cut Lori's bangles off. No food. No water. Business as usual.

Until the Hands healed, I couldn't do much. How was I going to solve the Worner issue? How could I do anything? Honeydoll. Ugh. A party? And the memories thrummed. I refused to focus on them. Too much. They remained a vague blur of pain. Fear.

I curled up on my cot. I tried to sleep.

Eventually, I succeeded.

SOMETHING SHOOK ME. Something squeezed my shoulder. *Mallory?* I groaned awake, eyes crusted with gunk.

"Kid?"

A massive guy leaned over me, voice booming. Buzz-cut black hair. He had a stance like a grizzly. Sharp eyes. Plain face.

He wrapped his meaty paw around my shoulder again and shook. "Wake up. We need to talk."

"Do I know you?"

He huffed. His hand crept up to his forehead, stopped, and jerked back down. The cell door hung open, and some other voice warbled outside.

"Mallory Worner sends her regards," he said.

"Lorraine's going to lobotomize me. She's going to live forever. She's going to jump from body to body—"

"Tell it to Pretty Boy."

Warm tingles kissed the back of my neck like sunlight. I sat up. Something good was coming. I should see it.

The voice outside lilted closer.

"…Half these people want to call the fucking Enquirer. You'd better torch those medical records."

Someone entered my cell.

This can't be a person.

The beautiful creature—*a man?*—strode over to me, body like a Greek statue. Gold hair waved to his shoulders. It set off the pearly radiance of his skin. An angel. This had to be an angel…right? He smiled at me. Perfect teeth. I wanted to cry. I had to tell him my bank account number, *right now*. Wait. Did I have a bank account? Heat flooded my face. Jesus, was that *pus* on my healing arm burn? I looked so gross. And scrawny.

His irises faded away. Pupils vanished. A pair of eyes, white as parchment, blinked at me. Gold veins filigreed through them. I leaned in. My breath caught. I absorbed the details of his face. High-bridged, proud nose. Angular bones. Pink tinged his cheekbones. Too-symmetrical face. Full lips. Overhead light gilded his long eyelashes.

"Hello, Project 0666," he said.

A scent of myrrh and cinnamon, a comforting warm smell.

"Is it okay if I call you Triple-Six? You can call me… Morgenstern. Fuck it, why not? I haven't used that name in a decade or two."

I nodded. *Anything. Call me anything.*

Tears filled my eyes. How could I improve his life? How could I please this being? I wanted to beg for the privilege of sucking him off. Or whatever else this angel wanted. Not because it aroused me—*Oh, it better not, champ*—but so that I could bring even one extra ounce of happiness to this magnificent being.

So I asked.

The beautiful creature *touched my shoulder.* "Is that your usual inclination, Triple-Six?"

"I can make it my usual inclination."

"Oh, dear."

The plain guy clutched at the air near his head again. "Is this a hostage situation, *Morgenstern*?"

"I'm *barely touching him!* Ugh. Go handle the records. Sweet-talk the humans. I've opened them up enough. Let me handle the interrogation," he said, sighing. "Dunkirk, if I get my sixteenth stalker out of this, you're giving me a pay raise."

I straightened. I could help. I wanted to help. "I know a Dunkirk! He's a terrifying, demonic monster!"

Morgenstern laughed. It made me feel good.

"Is he now?"

Plain guy made a pleased grunt. He left my cell, throwing a tape recorder over his shoulder. Morgenstern caught it. Clicked the record button.

"So Dunkirk's a terrifying monster. What do you think about the Hell Wardens, Triple-Six? What do you think about him?"

"He's got to be Lucifer's kid, right?"

Morgenstern snorted. "One of *Lucifer's* children? What makes you think that?"

"He looks like Satan," I said.

"He's not one of Lucifer's children."

He beamed at me. "But *I* am."

He cupped his hand to my face. Warm skin. Cinnamon.

I made a sound. Dimly, I noticed I was hard.

"I'm going to ask you some questions. You wouldn't lie to me. Would you?"

"No," I breathed.

"I didn't think so, Triple-Six. You have a very open mind. Very…accommodating. Mallory Worner was tougher."

Mallory?

"She's safe. She showed up at headquarters, demanding to speak to someone. She'll be by in a bit. But enough about her. Tell me about you. Tell me about the Worner situation."

The full lips parted. *Me? He wants to know about ME?*

The gold-streaked blanks of his eyes glinted. "Tell me *everything*."

I did.

SHAME BECAME AN abstract concept.

I spilled everything, even the stuff about Lamiel. I talked about killing Blueing. I talked about my childhood. Morgenstern nodded and sighed appropriately. I talked about Lorraine Worner.

Sometime during all this, the plain guy came back into my cell. He listened.

We finished. I told him I didn't know what to do.

"Triple-Six?" Morgenstern said, handing me a plastic bag. "Will you put these clothes on? I need to speak to Dunkirk."

"Is that who the other guy is?" I asked. "I thought Dunkirk was a devil dude. Is he like a werewolf or something?"

Plain guy opened his mouth, but Morgenstern cut him off. "Yes, Triple-Six. He's Head Warden Dunkirk. When we have to interact with humans, we look like them. Now put your clothes on."

The *good* feeling ebbed. I stripped my prison jumpsuit.

"...Report?" Dunkirk asked.

Morgenstern's voice lowered. "Stories match up. Neither of them are lying. This entire situation is *fucked*, sir. Worner wasn't kidding. If anything, she *understated it*. We have a Lord of Hell involved. Project 0666 has severe PTSD—at a fucking minimum—and no mental defenses."

Dunkirk clawed irritably at his arm, tsking.

"Itchy?"

"I hate costumes. You're telling me he had no concept—"

"Didn't even know about Hell. He was raised as an experiment."

I threw on the clothes. Jeans, a pair of hiking boots, and a T-shirt. Actual underwear. Thank God. My brain made a comeback. I was still semi-hard. *Let's not think about that.*

"Triple-Six? Are you hungry?" Morgenstern asked.

"Do you want me to be hungry?"

"Oh, for fuck's sake. Let's go."

We walked right out of the jail. Two guards were sitting on the floor, eyes glazed over. They waved. Dunkirk muttered something under his breath. Morgenstern breathed hard. Beads of liquid gold formed on his forehead and upper lip and trickled down.

Outside. Early morning, still dark. Humid air steamed us. We got into a black sedan, its headlights fogged with age. Dunkirk drove us away. Was this a dream? It had the hazy, drowsy quality of a dream. Maybe it was Happy Golden Boy sitting up front. Was he a Hell Warden? I leaned my head against the car window.

Mallory.

Party?

"Need me to check on Mallory Worner?"

"If you would," Dunkirk said. "I'd like to speak to them alone."

"Pleasure to meet you, Project 0666," Morgenstern said.

He disappeared. He took the myrrh and cinnamon with him.

Cue thirty second silence.

"Um," I said. "Head Warden Dunkirk? Nice to see you again. Is this what you really look like?"

"No. The other way around," he snapped.

We continued on the freeway. He took the next exit, asked if I wanted breakfast. I was pretty sure I was getting breakfast whether I wanted it or not, but hey, I was hungry. I said yes.

We'd just parked.

Mallory Worner appeared in the backseat.

Oh thank God, she's okay.

She wore clean clothes. The heart-shaped anchor point hung around her neck. She gave me a quick smile.

"You take care of it?" Dunkirk asked.

"Yes," she said.

"What are you talking about? Babe, what's going on?"

"I made a bargain, Triple-Six. Let's eat."

No.

FIFTY-ONE

"CAN YOU RIP a soul out of a body without harming it?" I asked.

Dunkirk sipped his coffee. He eyed me over the rim of the mug.

"Why do you need to know?"

I didn't have time for this shit.

A massive stack of syrup-covered plates clogged our sticky table. We'd gotten the All-U-Can Eat Pancakes, add bacon, add eggs. Mallory fed me. I'd gobbled down a ham steak the size of a hubcap, too. We'd gotten our money's worth. The plastic booth and plastic table smelled like bleach and syrup. Two old ladies chattered in a corner booth. Yellowed rose-patterned wallpaper peeled off in strips.

"I don't care if I die. I'm happier dead," Mallory said.

Really, babe?

"Mallory. You're twenty-two. Weren't you the one saying that we needed to start actual lives? Enough with the martyr shit. We both know that killing your body won't stop her. I love you. I don't want you to die. Please don't make *my job* harder."

Mallory shot me a Worner glare.

I cleared my throat. "Dunkirk. I fucked up pretty badly. I'll say it. I am now *the only person* who can end the Worner situation. One of your men tried to rip her out—"

"Oh, you're the only person who can stop her," Mallory said, deadpan. "You. I don't have anything to do with this at all. Clearly, Triple-Six, you know the most intimate core of Lorraine's being, despite the fact that she's my—my *mother*—and I killed her the first time. When I was seven."

"You know what I'm talking about," I said.

"You're putting on some hard-ass persona," Mallory said. "That's not you. You're Triple-Six. Use your heart."

Dunkirk had turned red. He opened his mouth.

I cut him off.

"Lorraine Worner wants to lobotomize me. She wants me to be her dumb, rift-opening, paralyzing-goddamn-pincered bodyguard. For eternity. While she jumps from body to body. Lord Lamiel will keep sending me after her until this whole thing gets solved—again, because I fucked up—so we *can't* ignore the issue. And I don't want to."

I brandished my bedazzled arms. "Now this. So, Dunkirk. *Can you rip a soul out of a body without harming it?*"

He put his coffee mug down.

"Yes," he said.

"Great. How do I do it?"

He drummed his fingers on the table. "It's an ability that's only gifted to Hell Wardens. For a good reason."

"I'm pretty sure this is an extenuating circumstance."

"You're mentally unstable, impulsive, have no experience with Hell, and you've never held down a single job, Project 0666."

"No shit, really?" I said. "I grew up in a psychotic demon-hybrid's *dollhouse* half the time, and in solitary confinement cells the other half. He ran experiments on me. My Ma was crazy. I had Lorraine Worner spying on me for over a decade. C'mon, man. Give me a chance."

Dunkirk smiled. It didn't reach his eyes.

"You got to grow up?"

My mouth went dry. "What?"

He threw back the rest of his coffee and stared at me for a long, silent moment.

"I was born in the early eighteenth century, Project 0666. You understand how second puberty normally works?"

"It's supposed to be sooner?"

"You think a family from eighteenth-century France reacted well when their twelve-year-old son grew a pair of horns?"

"They—you mean they—"

"They only did what they knew how, kid," Dunkirk said.

"They *killed you?*"

"Drowned me in a creek," he said, and shrugged. "They thought if they killed 'the demon' inside me, they'd get their son back. Save his soul from damnation."

"That's—that's terrible," I said.

"That's life."

He reached up for his horns again, met nothing. He huffed.

"At one time, Lorraine Worner was a traumatized child," he said.

Mallory shifted. "Can I go to the car? Start on the questions?"

Dunkirk handed her the keys. She scooted by me and left.

"When do you decide to make the world a better place? When do you take the trauma and pain and *use it,* Project 0666?"

I fiddled with my fork. Flies buzzed in the diner windows.

"I want to be a Hell Warden," I said.

"You're not getting the ability. I got it after my first century on the job."

"I'm still interested, Dunkirk."

He placed a slip of glossy paper on the table. Lorraine's party invitation.

Interviews! Questions with Mallory Worner! Tour the prison! 8:00pm-12:00am!

The date was today.

"What would you do with this?" Dunkirk asked.

"Assuming the information's accurate? She wants me there. She's expecting me, so I can't ambush Lorraine. I'd want to know how quickly she can possess another body. Would it take her longer, now that she's rooted in Mallory's? My goal? Get Lorraine Worner's soul back in Hell. I can't defeat her otherwise. I'm going to assume that she's luring people to the prison to kill them. Trap them, then set the whole thing ablaze. Is the prison abandoned?"

He nodded, narrowing his eyes.

"So she'll be there early. She'll rig it to burn before the people show up. Maybe I'll show up early. Minimize the possible casualties…"

Can he possess me? As a last-ditch effort?

"So. About the soul-ripping power."

"Yes?"

"If you possess me, could you still do it? If you or someone else is in my body…does that count as 'me'? Our abilities aren't tied to our bodies, are they?"

I'd traveled to Naamah's, sans body, and had to bandage the Hands. Ergo, I could still use the Hands, sans body. Even though Mallory was dead, I couldn't touch her soul without paralyzing it. Lamiel had tempted me with normal hands.

Made sense.

"You trust me that much, kid?"

"Dunkirk," I said softly. "If she succeeds, I want you to take over my body and jump into a goddamn meat grinder."

Lorraine had to bargain for immunity from the Hands.

Even as a dead soul.

Did that immunity include imprisonment? To being grabbed?

Dunkirk scratched his arm. Skin peeled off in flesh-colored strips like linoleum. Red peeked out from underneath. Not blood. What was the proper response to this? Write Miss Manners?

"Costume's wearing off," he said.

"Oh."

Help! I was meeting a demon-hybrid dressed in his best human costume, and it started to come off. What should I have done? Sincerely, Busy Sad Man.

"I'll, uh, give you my fluids in the car," I said. "Can we give the soul-ripping a test run?"

"Let me get the check."

He went up to pay. Could I jerk myself off in front of pseudo-Satan? Sure, but not in a public restroom. Had to have some class. Right? Shit, now I actually felt like hurling.

For a split second, Dunkirk's horns blinked into existence.

Would it start with a growth spurt? I'd wake up one day, two inches taller. There'd be a big mole embossed on my old skin, probably some unnatural color, and I'd see it, know it wouldn't be a mole for long, watch it grow over my old skin like a spreading melanoma. Until it *was* my skin. Someday I'd wake up and realize that the pictures lining the walls of my old house were of a stranger. A scrawny kid.

The Lorraines and the Blueings would always exist, wouldn't they? Someone needed to stop them. *I* had to. Worse, I *wanted* to.

Warmth flared through my upper back. New muscle, forming.

We headed out to the car. I held up my arms. Morning sunlight hit the embedded bangles. "I want to find the remains, too. There's gotta be a reason for this. The memories—they're steeped into these, or something. Wait."

Blueing's ritual. He'd used Lorraine's hair. Blood. My blood—wait a second. A hot feathery feeling fluttered through my gut.

"Kid?"

"You wrangle souls, Dunkirk?"

"Among other things."

"Let's wrangle thirty."

"*Thirty souls?*"

"Thirty souls," I said.

FIFTY-TWO

EVERY SERMON I'D ever heard on the evils of premarital sex—*thanks, ChristNet DVD set*—always warned that the Devil was watching you bang. And that he liked it.

Devil-Dunkirk sat in the car while Mallory tried to give me a handjob. He did not like it. He stared out the windshield and occasionally glanced back, with the tender sentiment of a military nurse inserting a catheter.

Clearly, my life was on a great path.

"You made a bargain?" I asked.

"Cum now, talk later."

Eventually I did. Cue blood, cue sweat, cue Head Warden—in full demon-hybrid mode—consuming said fluids.

I held up my Stumps. "Can I get these healed? They're growing, but not fast enough."

"You want those Hands to heal in time for tonight?"

"Yeah."

He grunted. "Don't complain to me later."

A fizzy rush—

HELLO, KID.

I silently screamed, stuffed into a corner of my brain. Peered through my eyes. Someone *in me*, only there was barely enough *me* to even feel it. Not like Lorraine's show-and-tell, or Mallory's synergy—this was being grabbed, hurled into a closet, and getting a tiny pinhole to squint out of.

I tried visualizing mind membrane. Couldn't. I came up with a gray cinder block wall.

This isn't the way it's supposed to go—

He cut me off. *What would you know?*

The gaggle of old ladies strolled out of the diner, neon pleather purses in hand, gossiping.

Oh God. You aren't going to rip out one of their souls?

He didn't respond. A haze like smog drifted over my sight. Grayed the diner. Grayed the sky. Fuzzed the shapes of the ladies. They muted into the murk. *Pulse. Pulse. Pulse.* Warmth ran down my arms.

A focusing.

The bodies dulled into gray shades.

In the end, kid, all bodies are costumes. Make-believe that rots.

Bits of light came into view atop the shades.

That's the real deal, Dunkirk thought. *You understand?*

I'm starting to.

Red veins glowed across my arms. The Stumps. Scarlet light extended past them, forming into ghostly versions of Dunkirk's hands. He clenched one. Heat built.

Oh yes, I could.

So we're not actually ripping a soul out?

Not now. Later.

Silence.

They may not want to get involved. They've earned that right. They've suffered enough.

I thought, *Please. Ask them. Mallory and I can find the remains. You gave her the markers?*

Yes, he thought.

Great. You'll get me the thing that can heal my Hands?

He left my body.

Dunkirk narrowed his slit-pupiled eyes at me. Cold sweat drenched my skin. I heaved.

"Jesus—that was awful," I said.

"You're not entitled to my thoughts or memories, Project 0666," he said. "You want something that'll regrow your Hands before tonight?"

Was another bargain coming up?

I gritted my teeth. "Look, I'm not bargaining with the burial site locations. Period. I'm finding them today. This isn't a quid pro quo thing. I'm doing it whether or not her victims decide to help tonight. There are real families hurting, Dunkirk. Some things you don't bargain with."

"You feel that strongly about the sanctity of human life?"

"It's not a feeling. It's just the right thing to do."

He looked at me with something like pity. "Have any dead family you'd want to visit?"

"What?"

"I can give you...a little extra something. Are you aware of what it'll do to you? Do you have any dead relatives or friends you'd want to see, any reason to go to the nicer parts of Hell?"

"No. Why?"

"After a certain amount of...change, you aren't allowed," he said.

He vanished, leaving Mallory and I alone in the car. She started it. Her hand crept down to her thigh, fingers already pinched for a cigarette that wasn't there. The A/C hissed out chemical-scented air.

"What did you bargain for, babe?"

She didn't answer. She drove onto the freeway. Her voice was too high. "We need to find the first site. I'll wait in the car."

"Mallory?"

"I can't face them," she whispered.

WE HAD AN hour's drive. A Ziploc bag full of plastic stakes.

"I bargained for therapy," Mallory said. "Some of the residential places are nice. If I live, I go to one. If I die—"

"You're not dying, Mallory."

"I answer questions in exchange. Stuff about my childhood. About her. I'm fucked up. I have information about it. I'm Mallory Worner. I hid the bodies. I drugged the victims."

"Babe—"

"Don't."

She said she wanted to talk while she drove. She had a tape recorder.

"...Twice it happened. She torched a joint because they'd canned her...

"...The first time, the gas station boss told her she was a fucking psycho. I think she might've chased some asshole, or maybe punched him. Whatever. I was two or three, just old enough to know...

"...We lived in a trailer. Moved a lot. Stole cars...

"...I know my biological father was one of her victims. She wanted a kid to use. She just started raping the men before she threw the match, and got pregnant off that..."

Pregnant.

Bleak, flat land whizzed by. The sky burned synthetic blue.

"...She'd have me hold her cigarette before she killed them. I'm sorry. I did it. I was a kid. I held the cigarette while she poured gasoline over some chained-up, gagged victim and then she lit the match and threw it. Like always..."

"...On the hooking: She liked it, because she could do it anywhere, anytime. It was work. Not punishment. God—I wish she would've... thought of it like that. But she didn't. So if I got pimped out, it happened no matter what..."

A bitter laugh.

"...Working girls. She called us that. Sums it up good. She didn't love me, didn't hate me—not until I got her fried in the chair—I was just a useful *thing*. Like her cigarette lighter. Good to have around when I worked, a pain in the ass when I didn't..."

"...I tried to kill myself when I was seven years old. Shattered one of her empty beer bottles. I cut my arm open. You should've seen Lorraine scream at me for that. She didn't want me dead. But she didn't want to have to take me to a doctor. So she dumped me at some ER—don't remember which city, just the trees everywhere—and I escaped after they'd stitched my arm up..."

"Okay," she said after a while. "That's it for this round of questions. I can do next week's early if you want to send those my way. Thanks again."

Mallory clicked the tape recorder off, popped out the tape. Squeezed it in her hand. The color drained from her face. I asked if she was okay. No answer. I directed her down a gravel turnoff. *What could I even say? Or do?*

Crunch of gravel. A canted tree.

I forced the memories back. Six people. Screaming. We drove under a canopy of trees.

"Stop. It's here."

"She—she liked to collect the stuff that wouldn't burn," Mallory said. "Dumped it."

We got out of the car. Grass rasped underfoot. Faint smell of ash. Charred wood. *Walk a few more steps.*

"Mallory, you're going to have to put the marker in. I can't."

"Okay."

Her hand shook a little. I scuffed up some of the grass, turning up ashy dirt. Something white. My guts clenched. Bone fragment. Something metallic, small. Someone's crowned tooth.

"Not everything burns," she said.

She stabbed the marker into the mound.

—*Oh God MAKE IT STOP!*—

—*Help it BURNS it HURTS fuck*—

—*That laugh I have to hear it as I die?*—

—HELP ME! SOMEONE HELP me help me help...—

Shaking in my chest. Deep in my chest. Grayout. Someone led me back to the car. Someone stroked my cheek. Someone told me we had three more caches to mark. C'mon, Triple-Six. Dunkirk left you something. Looks like a rock.

Honeydoll.

You'll be Lorraine's Honeydoll if you don't pull it together!

The bangles burned around my arms. Current time? Noon. Eight hours.

"The next one's close. Start driving."

She did.

A walnut-sized rock rested in the cup holder, along with a note. *Hold this.* It looked about as mystical and magical as a crushed beer can off a highway. It radiated energy. *Touch it,* part of me screamed, *hold it. Absorb absorb absorb—*

I cradled the rock with my Stumps. Warm. As if it'd spent the last hour laying in the sun. Not quite vibrating. But close. Energy blossomed through my arms. Red veins glowed, light pulsing at regular intervals, dimming, brightening, over and over. *God, it feels nice.*

I drifted.

Cache two. An abandoned corral. The skeletal Hands were back, nerves half-twisted. 2:00 p.m.

Cache three. More remote desert. Some muscle. I felt my T-shirt shred apart, touched the new bony spikes on my shoulders. *Hold this.* 4:34 p.m.

Cache four. Field full of wildflowers. The Hands were back. I balled them. *Pulse. Pulse. Pulse.* Rift ready. 6:30 p.m. Almost go time. Crickets sang. The air thickened into pre-dusk cool.

At each cache, we interred a scoop of the ash and bone in a baggie.

I flexed my Hands. Still pincers. Silvery, fishy sheen contaminated the new skin. Dark olive from one angle. Metallic from another. I fingered my Fun shoulder spikes. About an inch or so, bony spars. Like the claw tips on the Hands. Spikes, Fun Teeth, and bone. And red veins. Some of my hair was singed off.

I laughed. Oh Jesus. I threw the Hell rock back. Mallory, not saying a word, leaned over and kissed each spike. Her arms wrapped around my chest. I slumped, closing my eyes, and just let her hold me, her breasts pressing into my chest, the heat from our bodies mingling.

"Babe. You really want to see me kill her?"

"I killed her the first time. And I know more about her than you. You need me."

She slipped the anchor point around my neck.

"If she brainwashes me—"

"I'll kill you. Won't do much for long, but…you'd have to find an anchor point to return. I can talk to Lamiel. Do something." She held up Roy Pike's revolver.

I forced a laugh. "You love me that much?"

"Yes. I do."

"Thank you," I murmured.

We got out of the car. A sea of California poppies waved around us like candle flames.

"Have to do the right thing at some point," she said.

Travel to Lorraine, cue Dunkirk possessing me, cue him ripping her soul out, cue her, frying in Hell. Hopefully I wouldn't need thirty of Lorraine's victims to help. Hopefully. I rubbed my bedazzled arms.

"Ready?" I asked.

Mallory nodded, eyes grim. "Ready."

Lorraine. Take me to Lorraine Worner.

I'd never opened an easier rift.

FIFTY-THREE

LORRAINE HAD BEEN busy.

Strung cozy bulbs lined the walls of the execution chamber. They lit the flaking cinder block in fireside glow. More lights lay piled on the floor. Exposed copper glittered at intervals along the cords.

She lounged in front of the electric chair. Old Sparky. Someone had maintained it. Supple leather straps wound around the arms and legs. A metal bowl for the head winked in the light. A faded sign loomed over the chair, words illegible.

It smelled like wet concrete and meat charred into oblivion.

Lorraine Worner was having a great time.

She was nose-deep in a book—*Blood Meridian*—and jerking off. Her naked legs splayed open. Her sex glistened, its frilled pink lips engorged with blood, clit peeking out from under its hood like a mini boner as she rubbed, stopped, rubbed. She nabbed a pork rind off a paper plate. *Crunch.*

A portable turkey fryer bubbled and spat. A gallon plastic baggie labeled *Edward Sal Blueing* sat by it, along with Lawry's Seasoned Salt. Gotta have that for snacks. All we needed was the air fryer. I held back nervous laughter. Mallory froze beside me. In the bag? Squares of dried jerky-like matter.

Dried skin.

Lorraine liked her "pork" rinds fresh. Yum-yum. Was Honeydoll getting some, too?

Dunkirk, where the fuck are you?

He was supposed to meet us here. Possess me. But I couldn't see him. *Shit.* Okay, I could still tie Lorraine up or something. Mallory was here. *Shoot her?* Mallory mouthed. *Leg,* I mouthed back. Immobilize her.

Mallory drew Roy Pike's revolver and ghosted over towards the wall. I took a step towards Lori.

"Honeydoll?"

She put her book down. She smiled. "You came back. Are you gonna be a good Honeydoll?"

"I can't get your bangles off. Ma'am."

She tugged her shorts back on. She stood. A new Big Needle shone in her hand.

"Why don't you c'mere a minute? Ain't gonna hurt none," and her smile never changed. "We can git your arms off later. You wanna rind, honey? I saved the lucky one for you."

I swallowed. Tasted vomit. "Lucky one?"

She knelt, removed a piece of skin from the bag. Still tattooed at the center? One distorted blue padlock. She threw the skin into the fryer.

"Eat your snack, Honeydoll."

She stepped closer. The Hands pulsed to life.

Mallory aimed the gun at Lorraine's knee. She stood on the opposite end of the chamber.

"You use them Hands on me, I'll possess *you*," Lorraine said.

She waltzed right up to me and kept coming as I backed up. My back slammed into the wall. Oil seeped through my shirt. *Why is it greasy?*

Mallory curled her finger around the trigger. Didn't squeeze. Her gaze met mine. *Too close,* she mouthed. Ever-so-slightly, I shook my head. *Do it. I heal. Shoot her.*

"Is Mallory here, Honeydoll?" Lorraine cooed. "She behind me with a gun? You kids gonna shoot her body?"

"I saw your execution video, Lorraine." I said, balling my Hand.

"Oh?"

"The switch guy got so bored he started eating a sandwich. While you fried like bacon. You ever wonder about that, Lori? Like, did the charred flakes of your skin flavor it a little? As they floated in the air? I can kind of taste it now."

"Shut the fuck up!"

CRACK!

Lorraine's foot—Mallory's foot—exploded in a bloody pulp. Red viscera painted the floor. Scraps of pink foam flip-flop hit the wall and bounced off. She screamed, a raw pained shriek. Collapsed onto the floor. Clawed for a roll of duct tape.

Her eyes deadened. She wrapped her foot.

I lunged. She squirmed back, jumped up. Blood dribbled out from layers of tape. Lorraine launched herself at my knees, Big Needle in hand. Flare of pain. My knees buckled. I hit the concrete, elbow first, and almost screamed. Pain. Tears fuzzed my sight. Big Needle dangled out of my thigh like a meat thermometer. Lorraine reached. Slapped it. Drove it in—

Jesus fuck!

I punched. Hit her gut. Tingling in my thigh. Needle almost sticking out the back—

I dry-heaved. My leg was a planet away. Head spun. Not right. Ew.

Lorraine dug her knee into my balls. White-hot pain. I threw up. Half-digested ham steak.

CRACK!

Another shot ricocheted off the wall.

Lorraine tore Big Needle out, wrapped her hand around my throat. She slammed my head down onto the concrete.

Buzzing.

Warmth. Wet warmth.

Haze.

A far away voice, "Triple-Six!"

Slight pressure needled my tear duct. Two faces over me. Wait. Or one? So fuzzy. Head hurt.

Some girl—*Mallory, that's Mallory I love her*—aimed a gun at me. Barely saw her. Glint of gun. Her freckled face shone with tears.

"Don't—don't make me," she said.

More pressure. Eighth of an inch in. Cigarette smell and gasoline smell. Stale hair dirtying my neck. Haze.

Girl disappeared.

Someone was *in me*. Mallory.

Oh fuck, you took a hard knock, she thought. *Fight! Triple-Six, fight!*

Fight. Yeah.

She'll lobotomize you!

Fear, cold through me. *Oh shit oh God Honeydoll she's got Big Needle in and you're going to live forever like this if you don't—*

I jerked my head to the side. Pain cut across my tear duct. Into the bridge of my nose. Lorraine grabbed my chin. Spat.

RIP and TEAR and KILL with me, Triple-Six!

Sweet pulses ran up the Hands, *pulse-pulse-pulse* and her anger made me bare my Fun Teeth, oh they ached. Wanted meat. Meat.

Meat's holding your chin and I'm HUNGRY! Eat with me! HER THROAT!

I surged up, teeth snapping on nothing. Threw Lorraine off. Ravenous. Head spinning. Starving. *Eat bad thing to protect good thing.* Meat. *Need meat to heal.* Slick tasty blood smeared on the ground, I licked, cement taste marring the good. Lorraine staggered up.

"You're gonna be my fucktoy, Honeydoll."

Lunged again, Big Needle in hand.

Her hand swooped towards me in slo-mo, yes, good, so we angled my head for best tasting—

She's a killer of innocents!

Lorraine the Immane!

Opened my? Our? Lovely mouth, lovely Fun Teeth waiting for meat, haze in our skull clearing up, and the honey-sweet taste of blood still there, oh yeah, her hand and that goddamn Big Needle.

We bit.

Hard.

Fuck yeah, tastes GREAT!

Bone crunched. Cold metal chilled our mouth. We snapped back. Ripped. Her thumb and two fingers tore off. Delicious. Meat. Big Needle clattered to the concrete. She crawled away, bleeding. We chewed. *Pulse. Pulse. Pulse.*

Wait. Are these—

Shit.

These are Mallory's fucking fingers!

I spat them out.

Might as well eat them now, Mallory thought.

I don't want to eat your fingers! What the FUCK, Mallory?

You wanted me to watch her lobotomize you? Forgot it wasn't...her. Sorry.

I felt for the anchor point around my neck. Felt nothing.

Lorraine held the red vial in her uninjured hand, hissing, black eyes locked onto me.

"Got somethin' of yours, Honeydoll," she snarled.

Oh shit.

She smashed it against the ground.

Mallory tried to leave. She couldn't.

I'm trapped.

You can go to Hell, I thought.

Like I'd leave you to rot, man.

Okay. We still had a few hours until my body disintegrated. We could chill in my body for a few hours. Right?

Lorraine limped to the turkey fryer. Shoved. It crashed to the floor. Boiling oil puddled onto the concrete, flowing towards me. She stood on the other shore of the oil. One human rind bubbled in cooling grease. She had her lighter out. Flicked. A flame sparked to life.

Dunkirk, where the fuck are you?

"What about your guests?" I asked. "You want them to miss out on Old Sparky?"

Her lip curled.

I sprinted across the oil in three steps. She jumped back. Tucked her lighter away. Clutched her bleeding hand. She stared at it, face paling ghost white. Staggered. Stuffed her hand into a pocket. Blood seeped through denim and spread across her cutoffs. Probably trying to stop the blood flow. She couldn't reach the duct tape.

"You crazy fuckin' kids," she said.

"You're eating human rinds, bitch."

Why was the room spinning?

Dizzy rush.

Head Warden Dunkirk possessed me.

I got smashed into a tiny space in my brain. Mallory too. Everything grayed, Lorraine's borrowed body fading. Her soul—the light felt cancerous, malignant somehow—brightened.

What took you so long? I thought.

Why is Miss Worner here, Project 0666?

He piloted my body closer to Lorraine. She backed up. *Pulse. Pulse. Pulse.*

Anchor point got smashed. Seriously, you don't strike me as the sort of guy to be late. Is something wrong?

It's nothing. We don't need them.

Light emerged around my pincers. Vague fingers. Lorraine hissed.

"Who the fuck else is in there?"

"Lorraine Worner, you've violated—"

"Mister Beelzebub," she said, and grinned. "Reckon I'd be here if it weren't for you runnin' your mouth?"

He didn't respond. He lashed out.

My Hand struck solid flesh. The light-fingers vanished as they touched her skin.

She giggled like a kid burning ants with a magnifying glass.

Dunkirk calmly removed my Hand. He tried again. Same result. *Souls. It's tied to our souls. Dunkirk, buddy—you don't count as "me."*

We'll simply take the body down to Hell, Project 0666.

Did he understand?

She'll possess ME! Or someone else.

Her hand darted up. Prick of pain stung my neck. She drew back, tossing a hypodermic needle away.

Shit.

Numbness fingered up my neck. Face. Lips numbed.

What the hell could I do now? I couldn't rip her out. Dunkirk couldn't rip her out. What could I do except try not to let her lobotomize me? Maybe she'd kill me. Maybe she already had. Some overdose on injected painkillers.

She won't kill you, Triple-Six, Mallory thought grimly. *This is Sleepy Shot. Knocks out people for a few hours. Saves them for later.*

Later?

She'll probably wait to use Big Needle. She wants you conscious for that...

Dunkirk, can you pilot me if my body's doped to shit?

No.

What a great help everyone was. I wobbled in place. Sat on the concrete. Lorraine loomed over me, cradling her half-eaten hand. Blood drenched her tank top.

Her victims. What did they say?

Nothing. They're trapped.

Faint agitation. *Too long. They've been trapped for too long—*

I caught a brief look into his thoughts. A slip. Dunkirk was mentally reciting torture methods to calm down. Someone had done something horribly wrong. Traumatized souls. Someone had to have done it deliberately. Worner? Oversight?

Stay out, kid!

Her victims? I could barely remember.

Trapped? Like the Loop? I thought.

Traumatized. They created their own pocket of Hell. They can't leave, and they're unaware...

Get them out, then!

Solve that issue later, he thought. *I'll bring reinforcements. Stay put.*

Because I had so many other options. Thanks for the useful instructions, buddy. Great help.

Dunkirk left.

Lorraine bent down. Her hot breath tickled against my earlobe.

"Honeydoll."

Such a lovely place, such a lovely place...

Dragging. Blasts of pain as my head clonked onto the concrete.

Get me a room at the Hotel California...

Comfy chair. Leather straps tightened around my wrists. Ankles. My head drooped into my chest. Everything rapidly grayed into softness...

You can check out anytime you like but you can NEVER LEAVE.

FIFTY-FOUR

IN THE MINUTES before my body passed out, I realized two things.

One, we absolutely could leave. Staying trapped here? Not the best option. Even talking to Lamiel might be better. Being his meat vehicle for all eternity sounded better than being Lorraine's Honeydoll.

Two, Lorraine's victims were trapped in their own Hell. If the collective trauma, pain, and rage of thirty dead souls could create and sustain a pocket of Hell…could that collective energy cry out for help?

Her bangles.

The second I'd acknowledged the pain of those memories, they'd bit into my flesh. Literally.

Maybe I didn't need to get the soul-ripping ability from anyone else.

What would happen if I channeled that energy into my Hands? The synergy-rage I'd felt with Mallory—times thirty. Rip Lorraine's soul out? I'd probably disintegrate it the second I grabbed.

Unless I disintegrated first.

Mallory, we have to help them.

She thought, *I can't—*

You were a kid, Mallory! Want to fix the past? Come help me free them.

I thought about Hell. Naamah's. The disconnected, spacey feeling crept over me. Mallory. Had to take her with me.

Can I hold you? I thought.

A growing blackness spread across my sight.

Please, she thought.

Her. Warm against me. I visualized my arms. Rhinestones glittered beneath a mesh of red veins. Of course they'd bit into me. Now I knew where to go. Felt a tug.

We blinked outside of my body. It slumped in Old Sparky, bound by the wrists and ankles. *Southern Fried Honeydoll, anyone?*

Don't even joke about that, man.

If I don't joke, where's the insanity going?

We sank into the concrete.

Take me to her victims. Take me there.

Blood. Sweat. Cum.

But this wasn't my body. I couldn't make an anchor point into. At least I was pretty sure I couldn't. Goddamn it. If I'd torn open a rift with my body and gone to her victims, this would be easy.

We fell. Dense air all around. Smell of ozone. Void.

It looks like this in its natural state. This is what the Lords of Hell got imprisoned in…Stuck in a black, timeless void. Bereft of hope. And they created an entire world inside it. Matter. Existence. Let there be light, champ.

Was all of Hell just one endless scream from a group of abandoned cosmic abominations?

We exist! Come back!

Maybe I wouldn't have done better.

Maybe none of this metaphysical shit mattered at all. How could I get possessed by thirty vengeful souls? How had this become a real life question? *Easy, champ! Write an ad. Single Arab dude, (very sad) seeking to be possessed by multiple souls. Send nudes.*

Okay. Calling up the dead. What had Blueing and I really done when we summoned Lorraine Worner? Drawn a circle. Drawn the symbols of her life. Thrown in remains. Charged with blood. Cried a song for the dead. It'd created a doorway. What did a doorway have?

There were always two openings.

The air chilled. Woodsmoke tainted the reek of ozone. Stars blinked on overhead. Imagine a suburban park, surrounded by cut-and-paste houses. The houses, painted in regulatory grays, whites, and maybe a butter-yellow one—for the daring sort—crowd around a scrap of grass studded with big-ass trees and decorative sprouts pretending to be trees. Swing set, rusted chain. A pit with wood chips, either dank or splintery. A frying pan shaped like a slide, scorching from May through October.

Imagine all of that, redesigned by a serial killer pyromaniac. Or by her victims' perceptions of what they'd gone through.

Her victims ran, never stopping. Screamed.

Fires lit the night park. Half the trees burned. Heat slammed out from the fires. Pipe bombs lay scattered over grass. Craters pocked the ground. A young woman bled, shrapnel lodged in her stomach.

Mallory and I landed on the grass. I ran over to the woman, a blonde pixie in yoga pants and sunflower earrings. My arms glowed—blinding white light like a flash bomb.

"Hey, are you—"

"She's coming!"

Lorraine Worner materialized right behind us.

This Lorraine sported a pair of devil horns. Rhinestone-jeweled talons. Spiked bangles, coated in blood. Flames surged out of empty eye sockets. She sneered, chain in hand and cigarette between her teeth. The chain flamed. It seared Lorraine's flesh, but she didn't seem to care. She stalked towards Blondie, gas can in her other hand. Demonic monster Lorraine didn't notice me.

Six-year-old Mallory Worner materialized.

As a faceless demon.

Mallory Worner, demon-child. Frizzy hair. A freckled blank instead of a face…no eyes, no nose, no mouth, just blank nothing. She had horns like Lorraine. She held matches. She shadowed Lorraine. Guns jutted from her pockets.

Mallory hissed. "I fucking knew it. That's how they see me."

I kissed her cheek. A shaky sob burst out of her.

"Babe, they're barely conscious."

Blondie shrieked. Tried to crawl away. Lorraine threw the gas can. It hit, drenching Blondie in gasoline. Fake-Mallory took Lorraine's cigarette. Lorraine snapped her fingers. A flame appeared. She cackled.

She threw. The flame landed on Blondie's hair. Caught. Burning hair soured the night. She slapped the fire. Tried to extinguish it.

Lorraine whistled.

Zip ties appeared around Blondie's wrists.

It was quick. Thank God. I grabbed Blondie, trying to smother the fire against my shirt. Nothing. I couldn't feel any heat. I couldn't do anything to stop it.

Her face was the first to go. Blisters bubbled over her features. The sunflower earrings melted.

Blondie disappeared.

She reappeared about ten seconds later, fresh and ready for Fake Lorraine to destroy all over again.

Holy shit.

Fake Lorraine hunted her running victims, burning as "she" pleased. They'd reanimate after a few seconds, keep running. None of them seemed aware of each other. Sometimes Fake-Mallory shifted. She ranged from an actual mini-Lorraine, complete with demonic face…to a sobbing, decayed zombie. A ruined little girl.

But this wasn't actually Lorraine. This was a construct. A boogeyman forged by pure trauma.

Time to break this fucking Loop.

I journeyed over to Fake Lorraine, with real Mallory following. Lorraine stomped on a male victim's throat. He gurgled. She laughed. She raised her gas can.

"Hey, Lorraine!"

I stood a foot behind her. Could she not hear me?

She dumped gasoline over the man. A panicked, raw sound came out of him. She struck a match. She dangled it over his face, leaned down. I circled.

I punched her in the throat.

Now she startled. Fire surged out of her eye sockets. She stepped back and circled her red-hot chain over her head. A goddamn chain lasso.

Something bit my ankle. *Ow, Jesus!* Fake-Mallory, complete with a set of shark's teeth. Peachy. I kicked her off. She bit again, sharp pain digging into my ankle.

"Mallory, I'm really sorry—"

"Kill it."

She ripped Fake-Mallory off me and hurled her away like a zombie Frisbee.

Lorraine's lasso snapped towards me. I dodged. *Pulse. Pulse. Pulse.* No running. This construct had seen enough running. I dove for her.

She fell. I sat on her. I readied the Hands. Background screams faded out, leaving silence. Fake-Mallory sniffled as Mallory ruthlessly stomped on her chest. *Crack. Crunch-crunch-crunch!*

"I'm NOT this fucking THING!"

I looked up. Victims surrounded us. A circle of souls, blinking at Mallory and me. Light occasionally blinked from them, obscuring their features. *Smoothed out.* Sense of ego beginning to fade like autumn warmth. But they weren't running.

They were watching.

Good.

"She's not real. She's not God," I said. *"Put your hands on her and see!"*

Hands touched "Lorraine."

Someone said, *Where am I?*

I clawed "Lorraine" open, sternum to belly, a nice smooth rip, and the construct tore apart like a rag doll. Ash poured out. The fire left its eye sockets. It slackened. It gave a final, rattled breath.

"Rip it apart!" I screamed.

And they did. Mallory helped, her palms coated in ash. Fake-Mallory laid in tatters.

A circle. I slit my wrist. I dribbled a circle of blood onto the grass. The Hands heated. Symbols. Her bangles. I dipped into the memories, not going into flashback mode, finding some symbol of each victim to finger paint in blood.

Doorway.

I raised my voice. "Can everyone hear me?"

Nods, calls. Sixty eyes on me.

"Lorraine brought herself back to life. I'm dragging her to Hell. But I can't do it without all of you. Please. Help me."

Unanimous *YES!*

I didn't understand what they saw until later. They didn't see Triple-Six, dumb pincer dude with a giant floof of black curls and perpetual stoner eyes. They weren't seeing a brown guy that looked more like a human pipe-cleaner hybrid than a demon-hybrid.

They saw an avenging angel.

My arms and Hands shone with harsh light. I towered over everyone. I radiated energy. Veins stood out on my wiry arms. Black stubble carpeted my sharp jaw. Sharp features. Hard eyes. I'd killed their persecutor and come bearing Mallory Worner.

"Is—is that you? Her kid? Are you—"

"Yeah. It's me," Mallory said.

She glanced over to me, dark eyes panicked. *Help,* she mouthed.

Wait, I mouthed.

"Did she kill you, too?"

Mallory's voice softened. "I'm sorry. I'm sorry for all of it. I—I didn't want to."

I finished painting. Faint red glow. We needed to go and open the other circle. I beckoned Mallory over, but she shook her head.

"Have to do this. I need to."

"You don't need to apologize."

"Yes, I do."

"Babe—"

"Go. I'll come by later, probably with them. Triple-Six?"

She stood on her tiptoes, head angled up. I kissed her, tongue slicking briefly against hers.

"Thanks for letting me play Whac-A-Kid," Mallory said.

"We get to play Whac-A-Lori next."

We hugged, released. Mallory turned back to the crowd.

I concentrated on my body—*do I feel…hot?*—and slipped back in. I was still strapped to Old Sparky. My skin burned. A smell of smoke…maybe some psychic backlash from Hell?

Some of the drugs had left.

Clanging. Thuds. Flesh slapping concrete, mixed with sobs…

I opened my crusty eyes. Limbs? Little heavy, but nothing unbearable. I felt like I'd chugged an old-fashioned on an empty stomach. A thick taste soured my mouth. I pined for a nice glass of ice water.

Fire jetted from the hallway door. Bodies crushed against another exit, jamming it shut. Lorraine's party guests. Screams. Shoving. Heat.

Smoke. I coughed.

Had to get these people out.

I thrashed against my bonds. The leather held.

FIFTY-FIVE

YOU KNOW WHAT Fun Teeth are great for?

Chewing.

I struggled for five more seconds, then remembered I had a mouth full of Fun Teeth and could teleport. Necrotic patches dotted my Hands and arms.

I leaned over and gnawed at the leather strap around my right Hand. I tore it open. I yanked my Hand free. Smoke hurt my head, but I ignored it. I undid the other straps. Fire crept along the cord lights, fingering into the chamber. *Fingering. Ha-ha.*

One exit? Blocked by fire.

Other exit? Jammed by bodies.

Okay, then. I stumbled towards the center of the chamber. Avoided the oil puddle. *Pulse. Pulse. Pulse.* I focused on the Hands. *Outside. Gotta find a way outside this building. Outside.* Cool summer night, grass riffled by a wind, cherries decaying on the ground, the drone of flies around spilled melting ice cream *Outside. Take me outside.*

Rift membrane slicked my Hands. I'd already sliced a cut on my arm. Blood trickled down my Hand.

I tore the rift. It hung, ready to receive.

I raised my voice a little bit. "Hey! Everyone! Try to get—"

Some asshole shoved me. People clawed at the walls.

I clicked into my Fun Voice.

"EVERYONE GET INTO THE GODDAMN PORTAL!"

They froze.

I grabbed a random dude by his shirt, tugged him over, and half threw him in. The others followed suit. I hacked. Light bulbs exploded. Oh. Shit, was it dark? Was it dark to these people? I could see. They couldn't.

I ran over to the cluster of bodies. *Get them out before the oil catches. Get them out before—*

Adrenaline. Sweet cold adrenaline rushed through me. I lifted bodies, half-dead from smoke inhalation, and threw them to the side, not touching their skin. Arms ached. Lift. Throw. Some of them revived. Some of them didn't.

I pointed at a massive musclebound guy, some meathead scrambling for the rift.

"*YOU!*" I said, still using my Fun Voice.

He jumped. He ripped off his necklace. He spun towards me, brandishing something metallic. I squinted.

"Begone, demon!"

God help me, I cracked up. I tore the microscopic cross out of his hand, flung it on the ground. His mouth dropped open. *Really sorry about the crisis of faith you're gonna have over this one, pal, but dipshit! Save the people!*

"Take the injured out of here!" I said.

"But—"

I clicked back into my normal voice. "Dude, I don't have fucking time for this. *Go!*"

He nodded. He lugged the injured into the rift.

I kept unjamming the exit. Most of the party guests had left. I'd almost finished when someone tapped my shoulder. Great. I whipped around.

"I can handle it from here, kid," Dunkirk said.

"Good," I panted. "Listen, I found a way to get Lorraine out."

He nodded, hauling unconscious bodies.

"Where is she?"

"Coming."

"Cover me until she gets here. I need to work," I said.

"Got it."

The baggie of charred remains sat in my pocket. I pulled it out. *Blood. Sweat. Cum. Tears? Spit?* Was there a container to hold my fluids? Yeah… an empty turkey fryer. Well, when in Rome. I nabbed the pot. Lawry's Seasoned Salt, for the circle. My blood, full of mumbo-jumbo. The symbols I'd remembered from her bangles.

I knelt on the concrete. Fire baked across the walls.

I drew the circle with Lawry's. Drew another inside, using blood. Finger-painted the symbols—a bird, a set of dog tags, hearts, so many others—outside the circle. Electricity split the air. Hairs stood along my legs and chest. *Come.*

Pulse. Pulse. Pulse.

Sing a song for the dead.

There were no songs for this. No magic language, no arcane spell. I opened my mouth. Let my thoughts drift into the white-hot bangles around my arms—

—*It burns IT BURNS OH GOD MAKE IT STOP!*—

—*Please God in Heaven God in Heaven I pray it stops PLEASE GOD*—

—*AHHHHHHHH!*—

I screamed.

I screamed everything they'd wanted to say but could not. Lonely eternity under cold stars—

—*Why haven't they found me?*—

—*Please, let them find me. Please. I want Bess to know*—

—*That white trash bitch buried me this well?*—

The Hands sizzled. Light blinded off the bangles. Veins glowed red, dwarfed by the white light from Lorraine's bangles. Sweat. Sweat dripped off me, so I kept singing and shrieking, but caught the sweat in the turkey fryer pot. Droplets plinked in.

The circle glowed. Symbols burned. I bled into the center, bled into pot of fluids. *Spit.*

I threw the baggie into the circle.

Fire ate along the greased walls but didn't turn the chamber into an oven. The air around me chilled. *Pulse-pulse-pulse-pulse*—

Half in a trance, I started spitting into the pot.

I threw my head back. The shriek gestated in my chest. Wordless. Pain.

My eyes are burning.

—*I'm sorry she killed me. I'm sorry I didn't try harder*—

—*I love you*—

Tears filled my eyes.

—*I love you. Don't worry about me, I'm going home to Jesus*—

—*Sh'ma Yisrael Adonai Eloheinu, Adonai Echad, did You mean for it to end this way?*—

Her bangles exploded. Shards of metal clinked onto the floor, hit the cinder block, steaming. Some got sucked into the center of the circle.

Now the light raged there.

"Come here and *help me!*"

Tears fell into the pot, the fluids, *plink-plink,* and I sobbed, let the misery claw out in hiccups.

Building. Pulsing.

"Help me!"

The shriek clawed out—

"AAAAHHHHHH!!"

I exorcised it from some place deep in my ribs, snot running down my face—

(!!!!)
Flash of light.
And there they stood, circling Lorraine's execution chamber, solemn-eyed… her thirty dead victims.

Mallory Worner, too. She locked eyes with me. She slipped into my body. "Drink," I said. "Possess me."

Yes, they responded.

Hands, fingers, flesh, reaching in, coming out daubed in blood-tinted fluids. Fluid Communion. They drank. Some slurped.

All of them entered *me*.

FIFTY-SIX

TOO MUCH.
Fullness.
Haze.
Babbling, babbling, thirty-two different voices—
Oh shit if I don't do something they'll kill me!
We?I? dry-heaved.
Hold in. Hold.
Gagging, on Hands and knees. Necrotic flesh speckled across our neck. Chest. Splitting pain.
Lorraine Worner!
We?I? panted, something congealing low down in our innards, liquid lightning, heat. Power. *Pulse. Pulse. Pulse.*
Rip her soul out. We need to find her.
Clarity.
Me—I'm Project 0666!
You're Triple-Six, thought Mallory.
We need to FIND HER!
We?I? Scrambled to our feet.
Find Lorraine. Find her. We need to stop her. Rip her soul out.
"This a fuckin' orgy, Honeydoll?"
We turned.
Lorraine Worner stood right behind my body. Eau de Lorraine tainted the oven-hot air. Fire surrounded us. Every breath burned. Her face held no expression. Her gaze, twin voids. She wasn't holding Big Needle. Or a gun. Bandages swathed her foot and hand. She dripped sweat. Her burn scar glistened.

"This all you got, kid?" Lorraine said, stepping closer. "A bunch of dead fuckin' losers possessin' you?"

Dead fucking losers?

SHE MURDERED US!

Rage.

Heat.

Heartbeats thudded in my ears.

You murdered Mallory, you raping fucking CUNT!

Blood bloomed across our chest and face. Lorraine grazed her fingers over *Lori*.

"It don't gotta be like this, honey," she said. "You'd like being mine. Eventually. We're both too fuckin' broken to be anythin' else. So be a good boy and open a rift outta here, Honeydoll."

I'm not a FUCKING DOLL!

"I'll open something for you," I said.

Her body grayed into a shade. Everything fuzzed. *How'd Dunkirk do this?* Focus. Bright spark of light appeared. Spit filled my?our? mouth. *Pulse-pulse-pulse.* Swollen Hands ached to rip. Touch her. Rip. Tear. Drag her soul out.

Lashed out—

My Hands phased through her, plunging into her guts, *good,* grab and twist and *tear—You fucking bitch—*her, smirking as the families begged for their loved ones' remains—*OUR FAMILIES?—Yes, SHE DID THAT! Scream with me! Pour it into my Hands!*—sharp bolt of pain as I squeezed, rupturing nothing but aching to go deeper, and they raged, pulsing white-hot pain but *take it,* so I took and *dug.*

Brushed something.

Something here does not belong, foreign feeling like a tumor glutting itself on flesh—*Jesus fucking Christ, is that her soul?*—burned taste tanged the back of our mouth, disgust, something slimed, a gagging—*don't throw them up!*—hitching in our chest.

I clutched her soul.

RIP IT OUT!

Started to uproot it out of Mallory Worner's body.

Sweat ran down my face, *pulsepulsepulsepulse*—teeth gritted, something squelching as I leaned back, shifting—*loosening*—and everyone inside screamed wordlessly—

Mallory? Why aren't you—

I don't belong, I wasn't Good I hurt people, I wasn't a—

YOU WERE A VICTIM TOO! I thought.

Mallory, everyone thought, and gentle warmth tingled through my?our? body, *Mallory, we forgive you.*

But I—I don't deserve it. I helped kill you—
Mallory, JOIN US!

And another bolt of energy flowed into my Hands. *I am the conduit.* Lorraine hissed. Spit. I tugged her soul again, felt it shifting, loosening, so okay, keep tugging, keep going—*we only do what we know how*—and all I could do was keep going, going, ripping, breathing between gritted teeth, mind blanking—

I tore the soul out of Mallory's body.

Body sagged. I caught it before it hit the concrete.

Pulse. Pulse. Pulse.

I collapsed to my knees, retching. *Get them out.* Too full, too much, *get them out,* and they wanted to go, they'd done what they needed, so I let them go. I vomited thirty souls. They sank back to Hell.

Nothing left but dry heaves. And Mallory Worner.

Lorraine's soul slipped out of my Hands. She formed. Her cut arm still bled. Her torso was a gashed-open ruin. Viscera glistened. Rhinestone bangles glinted in the fire.

"You didn't do nothin', Honeydoll. Think I can't possess another fuckin' body?"

She pointed at the walls. Hell Wardens surrounded us, watching. These ones were more human-shaped but still demonic; bones jutting in a scaffold formation from the shoulders of one; three rows of horns crowning the skull of another, terminating in eye sockets full of bony spurs; skinned glistening…shapes, skinless humanoid Wardens; a female-shaped one with skewers for legs, exposed breasts, and a vertical maw splitting her open from sternum to pubis, tongues snaking out from her stomach-maw, and gills fluttered on her neck; another one had pearlescent skin and was covered in eyes; someone scuttled on the cement floor behind me, rib cage growing out from its torso, spines exploding out from its femurs, shredding its thigh muscles in the process, still the spines pulsed in and out, and it licked its lips, it had a human face still. I caught glimpses of the Wardens, but let them meld into a vague red haze around me, for the sake of my sanity.

"They can't do nothin'. This all you got, kid?"

I ignored her.

Mallory's body breathed. I scooped it up, supporting its neck like a newborn baby's. Limp. Comatose.

"Honeydoll—"

"Shut up."

I leaned over her face.

Do you still want to die, Mallory?

She snorted. *I have a choice now?*

I'll never take away your ability to choose. We're grown-ass adults. I love you, and I want you to live, whether we see each other or not. No matter how much therapy we both need...but if you want to go to whatever's next, I understand.

Heat gathered on my lips.

I love you, Triple-Six.

I kissed Mallory Worner's body, and her soul slipped out of mine.

I lowered it gently.

I faced Lorraine Worner.

"You wanna bargain, you pincered fuckin' freak?"

Jesus, she sounds like a broken record.

"No."

She tilted her head to the side. "I gotta possess another body. Maybe I leave Mallory's alone. She alive or dead? Let's say she lives. Honeydoll, I'll let her alone for the rest of her life. Reckon she can be normal?"

"Awfully tempting, Lori," I said, and the Hands pulsed.

"You ain't got another shot. What you say we bargain?"

"Another bargain?"

She licked her lips. "Anythin' for you, Honeydoll."

I was within a foot of her. Fire raged.

"You'll leave Mallory alone? You won't lobotomize me?"

Reaching closer. *Pulse. Pulse. Pulse.* Her eyes fixed on mine.

"We'll live forever," she breathed. "You'll git a purpose. Meat...and I can fuck you nicely, too. You can lick me real good, if I train you right. Think 'bout it."

Yeah, no. I've seen how much you smoke. Eat your cigarette-tasting pussy? If I wanted to eat an ashtray, I'd go to a bowling alley and at least get some beer to wash it down with.

"I only do what I know how," she said quietly.

"Yeah. That's true. But you know what else is true?"

I snapped my Hand around her neck.

"You forgot to bargain for something, Lorraine."

She wriggled. Gasped. She couldn't phase out of my grip. Her face went first, spasming until it stilled. Her arms twitched. Her torso.

Another jerk. She almost got loose. *Shit.*

Mallory grabbed her from behind. Dark circles sagged below her eyes. She'd come back.

Alive.

I blinked away tears. "Babe?"

"Told you. I have shit to do, man."

Her knuckles paled as she held Lorraine, jaw working.

Lori's legs jerked and relaxed, finally collapsing underneath her weight. Red-pink veins sprouted on her throat. *Pulse. Pulse. Pulse.*

"Help me. Please. I ain't bad," she wheezed.

I said nothing.

"Monster," she said. "Fuckin' freak. Who the hell's ever gonna love you?"

"I do," Mallory said.

"Please. She's just pretendin' so you'll protect her. Mallory ain't got a scrap of love in her. There's too much of me in there. You're already turning into demonspawn, kid. You wanna destroy me too?"

Her eyes glazed.

"Mallory. You can't—I should've expected this. Remember when I gave you your matchin' scar?"

"Yes."

"Worthless fuckin' freak. You liked hidin' bodies. Didn't you?"

Mallory's voice held no emotion. "No, Lorraine."

Red as arterial blood, the imprint of my Hand shone.

"You—ain't like me at all, kid," she wheezed. "That what you wanted to hear? After all these years? Huh?"

Rattling breath.

Then, nothing.

Neither of us responded. Mallory pressed into my side. I released Lorraine's soul. It didn't fall.

It floated a foot off the ground.

The human features blurred. Her illusion-body shifted and vanished like a shadow suddenly thrown into sunlight. The soul—a ball of dim light—began to disintegrate, bits of light sparking off, orbiting around the nexus.

Did I kill it?

Holy shit, did I destroy a human soul?

My Hands shook. I lowered them. Everything shook.

"Take us to Hell," Dunkirk said. "You'll have to hold her."

The Hell Wardens shifted in the chamber, their presence palpable.

"She's not—"

"Damaged. Not annihilated."

I opened a rift to Hell.

The jail burned around us. I held Lorraine's soul. Barely-there warmth tickled my Hands.

I ain't dead I ain't dead YET—

It was the thought of a half-asleep dreamer.

Dream deep, Lorraine.

"That's her? That's all?" Mallory asked.

"Do you want to touch her?"

She reached out, but her hand went through.

"Let's go, man."

We all entered Hell, carrying the decaying soul of Lorraine Worner.

Fire reflected in the oil puddle and on the varnish of the electric chair that'd killed her long ago.

FIFTY-SEVEN

THE ROOM GLEAMED like an industrial kitchen.

Stark white walls. Glossy paint. Easy to clean off. Drains set into the floor. Sealed concrete. Fluorescent lighting loomed far overhead. A smell of ozone and bleach. Magnetic wall strips bore metal contraptions. Familiar…but kind of wrong. Then I realized. I'd seen pictures of most of these things. In history textbooks. Usually ancient torture devices looked like rusted garbage—not these. Oiled, clean metal. Ready for use.

They told me to put Lorraine's soul on the steel table.

I did.

Flakes of light floated off it.

An excited hiss went around the room. All of the Hell Wardens looked like me, or worse…except the interrogator dude. Morgenstern. I caught his eye. He beamed, angelic as ever. Blood coated his forearms up to the elbow. Dripped on the floor. Splatters freckled his face.

Dunkirk reached under the table and unearthed a long case.

Mallory leaned against me, rubbing her half-eaten hand. Her eyes glistened. I was tired, hungry, and I needed to get her to a hospital. I'd taken Lorraine to Hell. I was pretty sure I had a job now. I'd solved the Worner situation—could I get a goddamn bed? A hot meal?

He unlatched the case.

"Do you want to watch?"

Lorraine's soul bobbed.

Lorraine the Immane—no. She wasn't a force of nature. Or entertainment. Just a broken human being that actively chose to break others for her own amusement. This was a human soul, no matter how vile.

I tried to generate a single iota of excitement. I couldn't.

"Will I be able to unsee what you do to it?" I asked.

"Never," Dunkirk said.

I swallowed. "I'll pass. I've seen enough shit to last me a millennium."

"Miss Worner?"

She stared at Lorraine's soul for a long moment. She shook her head.

"I wanted to burn her alive," Mallory said softly. "Like her victims. But now, I just…"

"Yeah. I know the feeling," I said.

A chattering, clicking noise. Talons drummed against walls. Throaty laughs.

"I need to get Mallory to a hospital. Do I have to do paperwork? Do we get money? I'm drained."

He blinked, seeming to finally notice how injured Mallory was. "Car's still on Earth. Identification's in the glovebox. Money. Don't waste it, kid."

I opened a rift. Someone wolf whistled. Good for them.

"Do I have a job now?" I asked.

"Welcome aboard, Project 0666," Dunkirk said, rummaging in the case. "I'll call tomorrow."

They started tearing.

IT WAS WELL past midnight before either of us got to sleep.

I'd driven us to the nearest hospital. Mallory rifled through the glovebox and coordinated the fake IDs. We functioned until we could find sleep.

We talked enough to coordinate our story.

Now she was hooked up to a few medical monitors. She shivered from the IV of cold electrolyte solution. They'd bandaged her hand. And the gunshot wound on her foot. Possibly surgery later. No, we didn't have the digits. No, we didn't have the gun. No, we didn't have the guy's address, and we didn't know where he'd gotten bath salts. Lots of crazy, hand-eating tweakers out there. With guns.

The doctors made her pee in a cup.

I curled up on a vinyl couch, thinner than a porn star's G-string and probably less clean.

"Mallory?"

"Yeah?"

"I don't think we're moving in together after all," I said.

She gave a weak laugh. "Yeah…Lorraine didn't let me get Plan B."

I got up. Went over to the bed. And I wanted to say a million things, things like *I love you,* and *You don't have to have my baby* and *It's going to be okay*, because those were the true things. We'd survived too much to believe the false ones.

But neither of us really needed to say anything.

So we just held each other instead.

FIFTY-EIGHT

SOMEONE SENT ME a new black suit on the day of the funeral, which would've been great—*Who finally got a suit that fits? Baby Warden, folks!*—but I was pretty sure the same someone had left me the year's calendar with thirty circled days. Both items materialized on the hotel bed.

Written on it, in gold glitter pen—*You will groom the body and present an attractive vessel, Project 0666. I may wish to impregnate women.*

The first day was exactly one week away.

We'd been slumming at a Sleep Inn for the last three weeks. I got into a million random conversations with strangers. People. I learned about grandkids and fishing trips and graduate degrees. I liked making people happy. Even strangers. I'd never realized how starved I was for human contact.

"You're dead to me," Mallory finally said.

I'd just spent twenty minutes encouraging some dude to go back to night school.

"You were dead like three weeks ago babe," I said. "Lighten up! People are fun."

She groaned. "Fuck me, you're an *extrovert*."

Mallory and I swam in the gross pool. We had sex. We ate ice cream, and I made her laugh when I tried to gag down McDonald's. We shoved thoughts about Yellow Glen—or whatever the hell the name was, some fruity psych place—away, and her intake date got closer. Now, Mallory's intake was in a few hours.

Her period hadn't come yet. It was a week late.

We couldn't miss the funeral at 3:00 p.m.

Current time? 2:00 p.m. I lifted up Lamiel's note. Mallory was slapping on makeup.

I cleared my throat. "Did you read this? Apparently my downstairs still functions."

"They said you're sterile."

"We had sex before the freakazoid veins started, Mallory."

Demon puberty had the fun side effect of frying your sperm. Or eggs. Demon-hybrids couldn't reproduce under normal circumstances, but I'd been a late bloomer.

"You only came in me one time—"

"It only takes *one time*," I said.

And it wasn't the night at the motel, because it'd started then. It was the night we'd killed Blueing. Imagine conceiving a *baby* under those circumstances. What the hell did you say to your kid? *When a mommy and a daddy love each other VERY MUCH, Mommy drugs Daddy, they get drunk, kill their abuser, and then do the birds and bees in the same room as the guy they killed. While still covered in his blood. That's how we made you, Triple-Six Junior.*

A heavy feeling settled over my shoulders. What did Mallory and I know about being parents? Or even functional adults? *Easy fix for trauma. Pretend it's not there! Love fixes everything! La-la-la!*

Our baby. Maybe the baby would look like me. Or her. The baby would love us. The baby wouldn't even have freakshow pincers like me; there was no such thing as demonic blood or family lines or any of that bullshit. If a Lord of Hell fractured part of itself and melded it with you, you were demonspawn. If it hadn't, you were human. Our baby would be a perfectly normal, healthy human baby.

I blinked away the sudden wetness in my eyes.

Love.

But was having a baby that neither of us could care for "love"? Was forcing some fantasy-baby or fantasy-family or fantasy-marriage that could magically fix our issues and patch over the flashbacks, skip over all that icky mental illness—was that actually love?

I knew the answer.

"Mallory. Do you want to go to a clinic?"

She blinked hard. Wiped her eyes on her hand, smearing black makeup.

"Yes," she finally said. "Unless…unless you want to give the baby up for adoption?"

"You'd do that?"

"If you wanna. I could go through a pregnancy. I just can't raise a kid, Triple-Six."

"We don't even know if you're pregnant. Let's just…go to a clinic, have them run tests, and find out for sure, before we make any decisions, y'know?"

She nodded, biting her lip.

I asked, "Do you want me to go with you?"

"Yes. Please," she whispered.

"Then we'll go after the funeral."

"One chance to have a kid. And you blew it on me."

I went to say something, but she shook her head.

Mallory zipped herself into a black dress. I tied my hair back. It wasn't a mess anymore. When I stopped pretending I had white person hair and actually bought the right products, I had happy curls instead of frizz and mayhem. Miracles never ceased.

"I need to pee before we go."

She went into the dinky bathroom. I shoved my Hands into the suit pockets. Something soft brushed them. I pulled it out.

Black leather gloves, elbow length. Custom-tailored. Not just to anyone's hands, either.

They were made for my Hands.

I unraveled my usual crusty bandages. I slipped on the gloves. Perfect fit. Way more comfortable than scratchy bandages, or Saran Wrap. I could take them off or on.

Why didn't I think of this before?

"Triple-Six!"

I bolted to the bathroom in three strides. Ripped open the door.

Mallory laughed. She sat on the toilet, lace undies around her ankles.

Blood soaked her underwear. Dyed lace in a red blotch. Smell of period blood tinged with rotting fish.

A strangled sound.

"Thank God," I said. "Thank fucking God. We must've gotten lucky."

"Or I miscarried. From the stress."

"Does it really matter now?"

"No," she said, voice tiny. "It doesn't."

MALLORY WORNER'S FUNERAL started at 3:00 p.m.

I stood under a black canopy with Mallory and two "costumed" Hell Wardens. Oh, everything was decent enough. The baby salmon canapés tasted okay, the decor didn't veer too goth, and the weather even behaved. Sunny and cool, good suit weather. Closed coffin, of course. There hadn't been much left to bury.

Also, people might realize "Mallory Worner" was a little too blonde.

Hell could only bargain for so many corpses. Give them some credit.

So.

Everything got pinned on Mallory Worner, the tragic demon-daughter of Lorraine. She'd snapped, and gone for broke on a killing spree, burning everything in her path. She'd even immolated herself. She'd attempted to trap fifty people in an abandoned prison and burn them alive. But thanks to the help of several brave souls, nobody was dead.

The smoke made me see weird shit, one male said. *Thought I was in Hell.*

A movie was in the works.

The real Mallory Worner watched her own funeral, twirling her hair around her finger. She scrubbed her hands.

"Who's taking me?" Mallory asked.

I pointed out the two Hell Wardens. One surly white, and a surlier Asian.

"I swear to God they're in a good mood. Really. They're on overtime right now. No rush, babe."

She suddenly looked down at the grass. I handed her a canapé.

"What if they can't fix me?" she said, very quietly.

"Look. As long as you give a tenth of a shit, you'll improve. When have either of us lived in a safe environment? I think it'll be great."

"I'll try to call. Okay?"

My voice got thick for some reason. "Yeah. Okay."

She stared into the distance.

I looked at the nice normal people milling around, people who'd never accidentally paralyzed a person—or *intentionally* paralyzed a person—or grown flesh they couldn't understand. People without the expectation of radically changing at an atomic level.

Eventually they left. The day drawled into afternoon, and dust filled the air. Summer wouldn't last forever.

The two Hell Wardens approached us. *Kid, you have training tomorrow at 0600. Sharp. We can take Worner.*

I did. I had to set up Baby's First Apartment, too.

"Visit. When you can."

Mallory squeezed my Hand. Let go.

I tore open the rift to Hell.

The last glimpse I had of Earth was Mallory, her face wreathed in sunlight, golden sunlight across her eyelids and lips, almost radiant. She waved at me.

I caught it, waved back. But I had work to do. I had a life to create from scratch and that was probably a harder job than being a Hell Warden. So I entered the rift.

Time to get cracking.

AUTHOR'S NOTE: WHAT THEY DON'T TELL YOU

THEY DON'T TELL you how personal it gets, doing this whole writing thing.

I wrote my first manuscript in late 2020. It was garbage, as all first manuscripts are, which is also something they don't tell you, but it was enjoyable garbage. I had a hell of a time writing it. I figured I'd write another. I figured I'd give this whole writing thing a shot.

I wrote the first draft of *Free Burn* in spring 2021, finishing on October 6, 2021. It was fairly lighthearted, quirky, and was just pure, fun gore and camp. I thought it was great (it wasn't). I remember this day very clearly because of what happened after.

My dad overdosed on October 12, 2021.

They found his body the next day. He'd laid down in bed, used drugs, and it killed him. It killed him instantly. He was fifty-one years old. I was twenty-two. He had no will, had been unmarried, and had no other children. I was the legal next-of-kin. I handled things. I functioned.

What I didn't say at the funeral: he loved me, but he was sometimes abusive. He was unstable, and I limited my time around him as his addictions grew worse. The final few times I saw him, he barely knew what was going on because he was high as a kite. I loved him. I hated him. He'd grown up poor, and he worked his ass off so I wouldn't be. He taught me to be proud of a job well done. He loved me as much as he could love anything.

I vividly remember entering the house and seeing the mattress he died on, seeing the vibrant purple puddle on the mattress top, soaked into the foam—the urine he'd released when he died turned purple from the positive drug indicator spray the police used. I remember everything from those first two days in technicolor snapshots: the five mini-waffles my mom made me that night, arranged on a plate, topped with little pats of butter; the lime-green-and-brown chair at the airport; the beige interior of my grandmother's car where they told me, Mom twisting back from the front seat, hair drooping in front of her face; the plastic cauldron resting on Dad's black square dining table, full of candy wrappers and candy; the giant fake spiders rotting in the flower beds, ready to be stapled to the house for Halloween, but he hadn't because he was struggling, so he left them around the perimeter of the house to be hung up later.

They tell you about the sadness, but they don't tell you about the rage.

For a long, long time, I was angry.

Angry at everything and everyone. I walked around with a massive chip on my shoulder, sweating, pacing, ready to punch something, because all of this was bullshit. I'd done everything to escape that past. I'd gone to trade school when my life hadn't worked out, lived a stable life, saved my money, didn't drink (normally), didn't screw around, didn't party. I thought I'd finally broken the codependent dynamic we'd had, and now here he was, dead, and I couldn't escape the consequences of his life. But I felt terrible for being angry. My Dad was dead, it was a tragedy for him to have died so young, and I still loved him... *What the hell was wrong with me?*

They don't tell you about angry grief.

I coordinated. I smiled. I emptied out my savings on the probate attorney. I wore the black dress. After the funeral, I went right to the bar, ordered as much hard liquor as they would give me, and got so wasted I couldn't walk.

People had a lot of opinions. A few people in particluar were of the opinion that it was partly my fault my dad had died. I hadn't talked to him as much in that last year. My fault. Selfish, terrible daughter, Drew—*and God, what a weirdo she is. Doesn't even cry at the funeral, probably isn't even sad.*

Said to me, "I tried to save him. You didn't."

I discreetly told those particular people to go fuck themselves.

I continued cleaning out the burned balls of aluminum foil, dime baggies, and other assorted drug paraphernalia that I kept finding in his house, the house filled with twenty years of bad memories. Interestingly enough, none of those particular people were around to help, not even when I was cleaning the dog shit that had crusted into the matted, filthy carpet. They didn't have to sell their possessions like I did because their bank accounts weren't wiped out like mine was from cremation expenses and attorney fees.

The anorexia I'd struggled with for over a decade came roaring back. I stopped eating. I had no appetite. I lived on coffee. I exercised like crazy to numb my rage.

It didn't help.

My anger festered. I felt like I was turning into a demon—bitter, shriveled, and full of hate. Women were supposed to get sad and depressed. I wasn't. I had shit to do. I did it. I made life happen. Seething, yes, but I still made the right choices.

I felt like a bad person for being functional. I felt awful that I was angry, not sad.

I felt like a monster.

In December 2021, I rewrote all of *Free Burn*.

This was a whole new book. I channeled my rage, horror, and shame into that draft. I poured out the trauma. I made it real, and I made it ugly. I put so much of myself into Triple-Six, especially with his shame about his anger and the repressed rage. I don't think I'll ever write another protagonist as close to me as he is.

Most of all, I wanted someone, somewhere, to read it and feel seen, and to know that they weren't an anomaly for experiencing angry-grief or mixed feelings about a parent's death.

Because that's what *Free Burn* is really about: your parent coming back from the dead to haunt you.

Something else they don't tell you: periodically, in the writing industry, something will happen and you'll think, *What's the point?*

They don't tell you that. Periodically, you'll have to choose whether or not to continue. I had one of those moments in December 2021. I decided to rewrite *Free Burn*. I said *yes*. It seemed hopeless. Who was I? What chance did I have of being published? Who the hell was I to think that me, a snot-nosed twenty-three-year-old trades worker (I'm in the IBEW), who lived in the ass crack of eastern Washington—a place known for being a sad, barren desert full of tumbleweeds—would ever get published?

July 2022 was my second moment.

Nighttime. I had decided to sell the house and to release my dad's ashes in the morning.

I sat there by the river and thought, *What's the point? Nobody's ever going to want to read this stupid book. I don't have an MFA. I don't even have a bachelor's degree. I'm not funny or witty on social media. I'm not like these other writers.*

I figured I'd gone this far, so I might as well keep writing. I wrote more short stories. I queried *Free Burn*, received some rejections, kept querying.

My anorexia got worse. I'd left my job by this point. I'd lost everything I had ever worked to earn. I kept writing. I just kept going.

I entered a partial hospitalization program for my eating disorder in December 2022. They had to put me on a meal plan for a child when I first arrived, and I still struggled to finish my food. Every time I thought about stuff, my throat would just close up.

My brain would whisper, *Maybe someone would love you if you weren't plowing through those Ritz crackers like a fucking fat-ass, Drew.*

My throat would just close up, and I'd stop eating.

Throughout everything, the consistent, good things in my life were writing and my family, especially the ones that were there for me when my father died. In many respects, I was incredibly lucky. There weren't any squabbles over his estate. Dad's workplace coordinated and paid for a wonderful wake. It was a tragedy that Dad died so young, but he was terrified of getting old. He always used to tell me, *Drew, if I ever get cancer or any of that shit, I'm heading up to the mountains to die. I don't want to get so old I can't do anything, or I'm pissing myself. Fuck that.* If he was gonna go, at least he died quickly in his own bed, in the house he loved. There are worse deaths.

You know those conversations you have with your friends and family at three a.m., when someone's drunk and the TV's blasting some weird animated show nobody can remember, and the conversation slithers around until someone starts talking about their hypothetical funeral? Everyone's throwing around stuff like, *Man, I want to be scattered in the ocean,* and *I want my ashes to go the moon,* or *Make sure you get that nice casket at the chapel.* Those late-night ramblings? I used to have those with my dad.

Pay attention, because there may come a day when you're scrambling to remember exactly what they said.

They don't tell you these things. They also don't tell you that writing is one of the best sources of stability when everything else crumbles.

I kept writing. I wrote the first draft of *The Divine Flesh*. I wrote the short story that would later become *The Exodontists*.

My third moment came in January 2023.

I'd woken up at six a.m. or so and seen some magazines open for short story submissions.

The periodical writer's question: *What's the fucking point?*

I ignored that thought. I submitted a short story to *Dark Matter Magazine*, not expecting anything. I did it to say *yes*. Yes, I was still going to do this whole writing thing. It had me for life, whether or not I published anything. I understood that now. They don't tell you how much writing becomes a part of you, but eventually, you find out.

I got ready for the day, got into my car, and drove to the eating disorder clinic to begin my eight hours of intensive therapy and meals. Your phone is in a cubby for those eight hours. You have to ask to pee, and they check the toilet after you use it to make sure you haven't thrown up. You go home at night, but otherwise, it's basically a psych ward with an emphasis on mealtimes.

Before I walked in that day, I checked my email one last time.

I had a new one.

Paraphrased from the editor of Dark Matter INK: *Hey, Drew! I really liked your short story, so I checked out your website. "Free Burn" sounds awesome! I'd love to check it out.*

I sat there and stared for a solid thirty seconds at my phone.

Of course I responded. I was thrilled. I just needed some minor tweaks. It'd take me two weeks, max. Then I went into the clinic, checked in, put my phone into the cubby, and smiled through my Ritz crackers.

What I didn't say: I had to rewrite about twenty percent of the 100,000-word manuscript, and I had no clue how I'd pull that off in two weeks when I was stuck at this clinic for eight hours a day, forty hours a week. I needed to rewrite the entire beginning segment of *Free Burn*, and I'd known that since the last full-rejection.

I did it.

During the day, I'd go to the eating disorder clinic. When I got home at night, I'd write. Then I'd sleep. Get up. Repeat. Two weeks. In that time, I wrote about 20,000 words of new material, and then I sent *Free Burn* off, and the rest is history.

It's early 2024. Life has finally settled down. I got my job back. I got most of my sanity back. I don't constantly feel like an angry, spiteful demon. I stayed on my meal plan and got a lot of my brainpower back, too. I keep writing. I keep improving.

I write, but I don't think I'll ever write something quite as raw and unhinged as I did with *Free Burn*. Maybe that's a good thing. Call it maturing. Call it discernment.

If you're reading this, I hope you like what's coming next.

—Drew Huff
January 31, 2024

ACKNOWLEDGMENTS

I'LL START BY thanking my Mom. Mom, thanks for being there through everything. You've been my biggest supporter, and *Free Burn* probably wouldn't exist if you hadn't encouraged me to keep going. You're the person who taught me perseverance.

Thanks to my stepdad, Todd. Todd, I don't think I would've made it very far in life without you supporting me and giving me a solid foundation. I can't thank you enough for that.

Thanks to the rest of my family, but especially to Mimi, Papa, and Stan. Thanks for helping to raise me, Mimi and Papa, and thank you for encouraging me to follow my dreams. Thank you, Stan, for your support, and especially your support during the aftermath of my father's death.

Thank you Dad for supporting me as best you could. Thanks for all the afternoons we spent watching cheesy horror movies from Dollar Tree. I wish you could see this book. I know you would've liked it.

To my friends outside of the writing community, thank you.

Special thanks to Pat McDonough for being a true friend throughout all of this, and also to Candace Nola.

Thanks to Rob Carroll. Thanks for taking a chance on me, Rob. I appreciate it.

Thanks to the rest of the team at Dark Matter INK, especially Maddy Leary and Jonothan Pickering. I can't tell you how much I appreciate the opportunity to publish *Free Burn*.

Thanks for those that have supported me by blurbing and promoting this book: Steph Nelson, Brennan LeFaro, Duncan Ralston, Angela Sylvaine, and Candace Nola.

Thank you to my readers—I hope you find some comfort and laughs in this weird, gory book I wrote.

ABOUT THE AUTHOR

DREW HUFF is the author of *Free Burn, Landlocked in Foreign Skin, The Divine Flesh, The Exodontists,* and *Run to Beat the Devil.* Born and raised in eastern Washington, Drew enjoys writing stories that explore the intricacies of trauma, body horror, and fear. Her short fiction has appeared in numerous anthologies, including *The Sacrament, It Was All A Dream,* and *Hot Iron and Cold Blood.*

ALSO AVAILABLE OR COMING SOON FROM DARK MATTER INK

Human Monsters: A Horror Anthology
Edited by Sadie Hartmann & Ashley Saywers
ISBN 978-1-958598-00-9

Zero Dark Thirty: The 30 Darkest Stories from Dark Matter Magazine, 2021–'22
Edited by Rob Carroll
ISBN 978-1-958598-16-0

Linghun by Ai Jiang
ISBN 978-1-958598-02-3

Monstrous Futures: A Sci-Fi Horror Anthology
Edited by Alex Woodroe
ISBN 978-1-958598-07-8

Our Love Will Devour Us by R. L. Meza
ISBN 978-1-958598-17-7

Haunted Reels: Stories from the Minds of Professional Filmmakers Curated by David Lawson
ISBN 978-1-958598-13-9

The Vein by Steph Nelson
ISBN 978-1-958598-15-3

Other Minds by Eliane Boey
ISBN 978-1-958598-19-1

Monster Lairs: A Dark Fantasy Horror Anthology
Edited by Anna Madden
ISBN 978-1-958598-08-5

Frost Bite by Angela Sylvaine
ISBN 978-1-958598-03-0

The House at the End of Lacelean Street by Catherine McCarthy
ISBN 978-1-958598-23-8

When the Gods Are Away by Robert E. Harpold
ISBN 978-1-958598-47-4

The Dead Spot: Stories of Lost Girls
by Angela Sylvaine
ISBN 978-1-958598-27-6

Grim Root by Bonnie Jo Stufflebeam
ISBN 978-1-958598-36-8

Voracious by Belicia Rhea
ISBN 978-1-958598-25-2

The Bleed by Stephen S. Schreffler
ISBN 978-1-958598-11-5

Chopping Spree by Angela Sylvaine
ISBN 978-1-958598-31-3

Saturday Fright at the Movies: 13 Tales from the Multiplex
by Amanda Cecelia Lang
ISBN 978-1-958598-75-7

The Off-Season: An Anthology of Coastal New Weird
Edited by Marissa van Uden
ISBN 978-1-958598-24-5

The Threshing Floor by Steph Nelson
ISBN 978-1-958598-49-8

Club Contango by Eliane Boey
ISBN 978-1-958598-57-3

The Divine Flesh by Drew Huff
ISBN 978-1-958598-59-7

Psychopomp by Maria Dong
ISBN 978-1-958598-52-8

Disgraced Return of the Kap's Needle
by Renan Bernardo
ISBN 978-1-958598-74-0

Haunted Reels 2: More Stories from the Minds of Professional Filmmakers
Curated by David Lawson
ISBN 978-1-958598-53-5

Dark Circuitry by Kirk Bueckert
ISBN 978-1-958598-48-1

Soul Couriers by Caleb Stephens
ISBN 978-1-958598-76-4

Abducted by Patrick Barb
ISBN 978-1-958598-37-5

Cyanide Constellations and Other Stories by Sara Tantlinger
ISBN 978-1-958598-81-8

Little Red Flags: Stories of Cults, Cons, and Control
Edited by Noelle W. Ihli & Steph Nelson
ISBN 978-1-958598-54-2

Cold Snap by Angela Sylvaine
ISBN 978-1-958598-55-9

The Starship, from a Distance by Robert E. Harpold
ISBN 978-1-958598-82-5

Dark Matter Presents: Fear City
ISBN 978-1-958598-90-0

Shiva by Emily Ruth Verona
ISBN 978-1-958598-93-1

PART OF THE DARK HART COLLECTION

Rootwork by Tracy Cross
ISBN 978-1-958598-85-6

Mosaic by Catherine McCarthy
ISBN 978-1-958598-06-1

Apparitions by Adam Pottle
ISBN 978-1-958598-18-4

I Can See Your Lies by Izzy Lee
ISBN 978-1-958598-28-3

A Gathering of Weapons by Tracy Cross
ISBN 978-1-958598-38-2